"WHO SUMMONS ME NOW?
WHO HAS FREED ME?"

Morlac stared in horror as the stone demon became real and turned its malevolent gaze on him.

"I do not know you," the demon said. "But I sense in you something quite remarkable. Yes, you have a man's body, but your true nature belongs more to my realm, does it not? I like that. You could be of use to me. Much use."

"I have no desire to serve you, demon," Morlac spat out. "Nor will I worship you."

"You owe the humans nothing. And with my aid, you could become a king among them, and the land will run red with the blood of the weakling prey."

"Only if I serve you,"

"You will," said the demon. "In one manner or another. . . ."

MORLAC

THE QUEST OF THE GREEN MAGICIAN

by
Gary Alan Ruse

A SIGNET BOOK
NEW AMERICAN LIBRARY

NAL BOOKS ARE AVAILABLE AT QUANTITY DISCOUNTS
WHEN USED TO PROMOTE PRODUCTS OR SERVICES.
FOR INFORMATION PLEASE WRITE TO PREMIUM MARKETING DIVISION,
NEW AMERICAN LIBRARY. 1633 BROADWAY.
NEW YORK. NEW YORK 10019.

SIGNET, SIGNET CLASSIC, MENTOR, ONYX, PLUME, MERIDIAN AND NAL BOOKS
are published by New American Library,
1633 Broadway, New York, New York 10019

First Printing, August, 1986

1   2   3   4   5   6   7   8   9

PRINTED IN THE UNITED STATES OF AMERICA

Dedicated to the memory of
Fred W. Markland, 1923–1985,
gentleman, raconteur, bibliophile,
writer, family man, and friend.
His conversations and encouragement
were always much appreciated,
and he left us all too soon. . . .

Acknowledgments

Thanks are owed a number of people, for a variety of reasons, and I wish to take this opportunity to convey them. . . .

To Sheila Gilbert, who got this epic project rolling in the right direction; to Karen Haas, who saw it through to completion; and to Jessica Kovar and John Silbersack, who made sure it was all properly wrapped up, my profound gratitude. And to Ken W. Kelly, three cheers for his magnificent cover painting.

To my parents, Layton and Virginia Mae Ruse, for putting up with me and all the various inconveniences over the past year; to my grandmother, Virginia Hensley, who left me her own magic legacy of dreams and persistence, my love and thanks.

To special friends like Keith and Nina Leonard; Jeff Bost and Vicki Townsend; and Judy Winber (who suggested Broct really *should* have a girlfriend), special thanks for their steadfast friendship.

To Mel, Rita, and Aaron Morris at Rex Art Supplies, for not yelling too loudly when I said I needed time off to finish this book; to Lois, for holding down the fort in the book section; to Chris, Scotty, Hope, Gary M., Jesse, Gladys, Steve, Granville, Joe, Karen, and my other friends and co-workers, for their support, my thanks.

To my friends at Xero Copy center of Miami (who copied the manuscript), and at Bennett's Typesetting (who reduced the map and logo), for their quality work and extra effort, my deep appreciation.

To Robert E. Howard, who paved the way for us all; to L. Sprague De Camp, a favorite writer I'm pleased to have met; and to John Morressy, a writer friend whose wit and humor I admire as much as his elegant prose, my thanks for providing countless hours of entertainment and for setting examples I can only hope to approach.

And to Errol Flynn, Ronald Colman, Douglas Fairbanks Sr. & Jr., four of the best swashbucklers of all; to Erich Wolfgang Korngold and to John Williams, whose rousing musical scores were further inspiration, I extend the thanks of a diehard fan.

—Gary Alan Ruse

THE FABLED LANDS OF

NORDA

TRAVELED BY

MORLAC

LEGEND:

1 Sordros' Village
2 Kem, North Kingdom
3 Castle Chalthax
4 Krellos
5 Qua K'Nar
6 Ortal Du Bodne
7 Kamuria, South Kingdom
8 Kadmudar
9 K'Dral
10 Phendurem
11 Neuphendurem
12 N'Bikcumboro

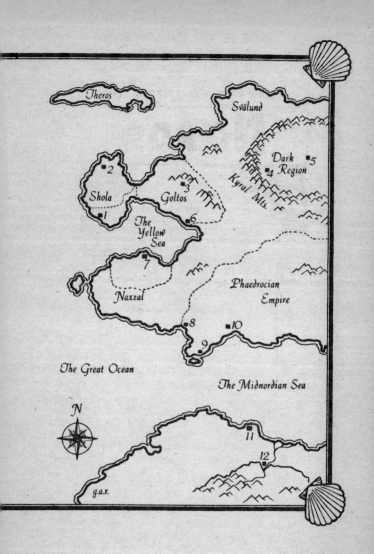

BOOK ONE

The
Stranger's Tale

BOOK ONE: THE STRANGER'S TALE
CONTENTS

Prologue

"Aye, 'tis a fine night for ghost stories and tall tales," said the old wayfarer. He pulled his cloak closer about him against the chill and stretched his other hand toward the fire to feel its warmth.

Thirteen men circled that fire, sitting on the sand or upon their packs or the smooth-surfaced rocks that dotted the beach. Their pack animals were tethered nearby, and the small caravan of merchants and their guards had made camp for the evening. The flames sent shadows dancing around the circle of men, enlivening their tired faces.

"You, there—stranger—" said the old wayfarer "—'tis a long trip we've made, and we've grown weary of each others' stories. We're sharing our fire and our company with you, not to mention our ale! Give us a tale in return. Something we've not heard before."

The stranger seemed not to hear at first. His features hidden by his hooded cloak, he stared at the jutting rocks set like monstrous teeth along the southwest coast of Shola. The wind-lashed surf broke angrily over those rocks, sending salt spray flying. The stranger listened to the roar of the surf and breathed in the tang of the spray, immersed in thought.

"Stranger—?" repeated the wayfarer, a bit louder.

"I hear you," he said at last, turning toward the man but still keeping his face in shadow, "and I acknowledge my debt. If it is a tale you wish, a tale you shall have. I do not know many, but I know one that is new, and you may judge for yourselves if it is worth the hearing."

The circle of men settled in a bit more, making themselves as comfortable as they could upon that night-drenched, mist-shrouded beach. Though tired they were, they were still eager to be entertained, and there was something in this stranger's manner that suggested he might be good at spinning tales.

"The story I have to tell is a tale of magic," said the stranger, "of vile sorcery and unnatural spells. It is also a tale of greed and treachery. But I must start at the beginning, and this tale begins in the sea, at a time and place not far from here and now.

"It was a morning like many mornings, and the sunlight was glimmering coolly upon the ocean. A creature, a great green sea turtle, was swimming in that ocean, just off the coast. He was young and strong, and full of the force of life. He was approaching a boat full of fishermen, but he did not see it. He was enjoying his freedom too much, cleaving the water as he swam in pursuit of an elusive gray fish. He was reaching out for it, almost tasting it, when their net caught and entangled him, and the fishermen pulled him struggling from the sea.

"They were too strong for him to overcome and he sank heavily into the hollow of their boat. They secured him with more netting and ropes, and made for shore as swiftly as their oars would take them.

"A man was waiting at the dock, a man the creature would come to know as Sordros—tall, thin, cloaked in robes dark green in hue, a matching length of cloth wrapped thrice about his neck, then brought up over the top of his head in a kind of hood. He seemed a statue at first, no sound or movement betraying his stillness.

"He studied the creature, brought struggling before him by the fishermen. Discerning eyes missed nothing of the captive's form—eyes that narrowed slightly as the hint of a smile touched the corners of his wrinkled mouth. Sordros nodded his approval, then beckoned for the men to follow.

"They carried him, still fighting for his freedom, along timber walkways worn and weathered, flanked on both sides by moored fishing craft. Then on through the village of merchants and farmers and plain fisherfolk, until at last they reached their destination—a castle whose crude walls reared high into the awakening sky, and which stood perched upon a rocky pinnacle overlooking the sea. The castle's form was bizarre and twisted. It seemed made of dripped sand, congealed into rock walls. All of it was strange to the creature. Understanding would come later.''

''Wait,'' interrupted one of the men in the circle, a guard by his appearance. ''You speak as if this turtle could think, and we all know they are but dumb beasts, fit only for the stewpot!'' The last few words came out with the gusto of a hearty laugh.

The stranger was silent, and though his face was still in shadow, his eyes seemed to glimmer with something more intense than mere annoyance at being interrupted . . . something more dangerous.

''Please—'' interceded the old wayfarer ''—allow our guest to tell his story.''

The stranger paused a moment more, then continued. ''Hours passed, while the creature could only lay bound and helpless within the castle's lower dungeon. Sordros moved about him purposefully, assembling an assortment of odd liquids in crystalline vessels and arranging them with care upon the surface of an ornately decorated table. The magician, for a magician he was, never let his attention waver from his task, not even for a brief glimpse of his captive.

''The creature watched Sordros closely as he moved next to the center of the large subterranean room. A great domed cover of bronze glistened dully in the torches' fiery glow—a cover bigger yet than the span of Sordros's arms.

''Twisting away latches that held the cover in place, the magician strode back to the edge of the room to take up a long, stout staff that was propped against the wall. Sordros returned and slipped the staff through a handle in the center of the bulging lid, rested one end against the floor, and used the other to lever up the cover. He swiveled it around to one side, away from that which it had hidden.

''A gaping pit loomed beneath,'' the stranger said, emphasizing the words, ''boring down through the odd stone to unimaginable depths. Darkness seemed to well up within that pit. An evil darkness, with substance and form, that threatened to blot out the torches' meager light.

"The creature struggled again. And again he could not free himself.

"Sordros took one last look at everything to satisfy himself. He unwound the length of rich-green cloth that wrapped his throat and the top of his head, laying it aside upon a stand carved like many serpents twining. His outer robe followed, leaving him bare-armed.

"His head was smooth-shaven save for a tuft of hair at the crown, jet-black instead of the gray one would expect from his wizened look. A gold ornament bound the tuft, and both the markings etched upon its surface and those tattooed upon his arms were symbols of occult power.

"At the magician's command, his menials came forward to man a winch on the far side of the pit. Straining with the effort, they began to turn the great pegged wheel, one notch at a time, and each click of its progress was answered with a grating moan from the depths of the pit.

"A rushing roar of sound followed, cascading, spilling, rumbling within the darkness. Spray rose up to the level of the opening, then fell back, biting the air with its salt.

"When the pit was almost filled with seawater, Sordros ordered the floodgate lowered back into place. It settled with a dull clang, muffled by the great volume of water, and then all was deadly still.

"Standing by his table of implements, the magician took up the first vessel of fluid and slowly poured its greenish contents into the pit. The second liquid was amber in hue, the third a blood-red; the fourth was an inky-black substance that oozed forth from its container and stretched down into the pit ever so slowly. With the addition of the fifth vial's deep-blue liquid, the pit's water began to churn and froth, as if tormented by the presence of the evil potions. Last to be emptied into the waiting pit was an urn of chalk-colored ashes, settling like snow upon the water.

"His eyes closed, Sordros stood at the edge of the pit, a steady droning sound issuing from his lips. The sound changed, modulated, became an incantation—a beseechment to allied spirits, a beckoning to forces dark and menacing.

"Instantly, the torches along the walls began to flicker, each flame leaning in the same direction, as if stirred by the touch of a circular wind coursing around the room. From the pit itself came a muffled roar, as of a thousand kettles boiling. And indeed, the water *was* boiling, though with an eerie green glow that dispelled the darkness of the pit and cast new illumination about the interior of the dungeon.

"Sordros was in his glory now, arms outstretched over the tumultuous water, reveling in the raw power he held within his grasp. A power feared by his castle slaves, for they pressed low against the walls for shelter, and were slow in answering Sordros's call for assistance in the next stage of his occult operation.

"Reluctantly, they obeyed him, bringing down the end of a rope suspended from an overhead swing-arm. Fastening its hook into the open weave of the capture net, they hoisted the turtle up into the air.

"The inner storm of occult energy still raged within the dungeon as the net was swung around to a point just over the gaping hole. With Sordros's nod, the slaves began to feed out the rope, slowly lowering their captive into the pit.

"Down, down . . . first into contact with the stinging mist that swirled just within the opening, and then plunging into the roiling liquid itself. Confined within the net, the turtle strained every muscle in an effort for freedom as the awful liquid closed in around him.

"As he sank into its depths, futilely biting at the heavy strands of netting, he felt the full torment of the green fire that Sordros had called into being. It seemed to burn through him, reaching to his core with its fury. A wrenching pain seized him . . . a feeling that he was being torn asunder, limb from limb, flesh from bone, body from soul.

"The pain persisted for an eternity of seconds, then was dulled by a blackness that settled over him. A blackness that he almost hoped was death. . . ."

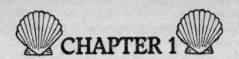

CHAPTER 1

The Magician's Daughter

Morlac awoke, remembering nothing at first, then slowly remembering everything. The pain was gone now—a blessing in itself—but in its place was another feeling, one that was perhaps even more disquieting in its strangeness. Every nerve, every fiber of his body, seemed newly awakened . . . newly formed. He felt oddly naked, as if the green fire had burned away his skin and left only raw flesh unprotected from the elements.

He opened his eyes, and was surprised to find he was no longer in the dungeon. This was another room, aboveground, with a window that opened out onto darkness. Window? Room? Dungeon? He did not know how he understood these words, yet somehow he did. They sprang into his mind unbidden, cold and alien things that had no place in the world he had known. And yet . . . somehow . . . these strange words and the meanings behind them now seemed vaguely familiar. How? Why?

His memories of life in the sea were still fresh and warm in his mind, his blood and bones, his very soul. The feel of the ocean flowing around him, caressing him, buoying him up. The tang of the salt within his beaklike mouth, the soft flesh of the fish that were his sustenance. The sun's harsh glare at water's surface, the cool, murky tints of greens and grays far below. The feeling of strength in his muscles, overcoming the water's resistance as his flippers made their strong, rhythmic swimming strokes.

But now, in addition to all these familiar things, new

feelings and memories impinged, frightening in their complexity. Their very presence in his mind was an unwanted intrusion, an affront. And worse, this new part of his mind seemed to be growing stronger, and trying to gain control.

The darkness beyond the window told him that it was night, so he knew he must have been unconscious for hours at least. Perhaps days. He could not guess, nor even comprehend the confusion of thoughts within his own mind.

Awakening more fully, he tried to orient himself. He saw he was at the far end of the room. He was upright, his eyes staring straight ahead, yet his back was flat against the stone wall. That seemed strange and awkward, and impossibly wrong. How could it be? Morlac did not know, and attempting to think about it only brought the wrenching pain of the pit flooding back into his mind.

His arms were bound somehow, each held out to the side. Morlac twisted his head around to see, carefully at first, then with more assurance. Not only his arms, but also his legs were bound, wrists and ankles held in place against the stone by crystal shackles of pale translucent green.

He felt detached, as if looking at some creature other than himself. For he had changed, even though the manner of the change was not yet clear to him.

His gaze went suddenly to the other side of the room, where a slight movement had caught his attention. Beyond the long table where candles burned in gilt holders, curtains hung along the wall. Those curtains had stirred, and there was no breeze sufficient to move them. What a strange place this was, with unnatural textures and shapes. Part of his mind recognized and accepted them, even though they were like nothing he'd ever seen before.

His vision focused sharply on a narrow gap between two of the heavy draperies. He thought he glimpsed an eye peering back. An eye that disappeared into darkness in an instant.

Morlac tensed and waited, expecting some new threat . . . some new torture. But as he continued to watch the draperies, what emerged from the darkness behind them seemed less threatening than he expected.

The young woman, barely an adult from the look of her, entered the chamber with caution. Her eyes studied Morlac appraisingly, coldly, taking in everything about him. As Sordros had been, she also was clothed in green. Slender and pretty, her hair was a cascade of black ringlets that reached down to her young, firm breasts. Sea-green eyes peered out from beneath long and shadowy lashes, burning through him like the green fire of the magician's pit.

She stopped, less than an arm's reach away from him. Her mouth opened, a mouth with lips that were full and sweet-looking, but with a cruel twist to them. She began to utter sounds that were strange and yet not strange. They were words and phrases, and Morlac understood them, even though they buzzed in his ears like bothersome insects.

"A fine specimen," she was saying. "The best one yet! Sordros has his captain now, I am sure."

Morlac tested his own voice, sensing he could speak. His throat tightened with the effort, and the words came out thick and raspy.

"Sss—*Sor-dros* . . . ?"

"Your new lord and master," she said smoothly, in a way that irritated Morlac. His memory was still clouded, but of one thing he was certain—there had never been a "master" in his old life, and he did not relish having one now. Still, the name "Sordros" echoed oddly in his mind. From where did he know it? Why did it seem to tug at him? The young woman stepped to his right, studying his profile. "I am Kadrana, daughter of Sordros. You will find him to be a most beneficent master, as long as you please him . . . and me."

"Please him?" Morlac said, the words coming with less difficulty now. "What . . . does he want of me?"

"Your strength. To kill an enemy."

"Enemy? Whose enemy?"

"Sordros's enemy, of course," Kadrana said. "And your enemy, too, now."

"Why?"

"There are reasons, Morlac . . . you *are* Morlac, you know, henceforth, and for as long as we desire it. Your destiny is your name, and your name is your destiny."

"What have you done to me?"

"Sordros has worked a wondrous spell," Kadrana said, going to the table and returning with a hand mirror. She held it up for him to see. "You should be pleased with the results."

Morlac studied the image reflected there. A stranger stared back at him, a young man strong and healthy, perhaps even handsome, but a stranger all the same. His skin was coolly pale, the color of milky jade. His hair was light blond, like sea froth, and cut straight around as if by the aid of an inverted wide bowl tilted from forehead to nape of neck. His proud eyes stared beneath arched devil-brows; intense green eyes, probing and distrustful of all he saw. This was not a face he knew from either his old memories or his new ones.

The girl continued to look approvingly at him, studying the rock-hard muscles of his arms and upper torso. "Indeed, the finest specimen. With a sword in your hand you will be Death himself!" Her own small hand reached out suddenly, impulsively, and gripped the muscles of his upper arm.

Her touch was unexpectedly warm, and alien to him. He recoiled, inadvertently.

Kadrana released her grip in a flash, frowning at his swift reaction. But then that frown changed to a look of wicked humor.

"You shall grow used to my touch—that I promise." She laughed lightly, enjoying her own self-confidence. "You amuse me, Morlac. After you have slain Drygo, I think I shall have Sordros give you to me as a pet."

He watched her dispassionately as she put the mirror down and started to walk toward his left. "You are so sure I will win?"

She continued to slink in an arc around him, her cruel eyes always on his bound form. She tilted her head slightly, smiling.

"Sordros's powers are great. He is a clever and cunning man. If he has placed his trust in you and your sword, then you will win. He does not like uncertainties."

"And I," Morlac replied, "do not like being held captive."

Kadrana shrugged, sending soft ripples through her black hair. "A necessary measure. The specimens do not always react perfectly to the enchantment. Some awake as raging beasts, and could wreak much damage before they are destroyed. I am glad to see that in your case the spell is flawless. Very glad, indeed." She stepped closer. "So, since such precautions are no longer needed, I think it is time you met the others."

With a graceful movement she reached out and touched the crystal shackle at Morlac's wrist with the jeweled finger ring on her right hand. Instantly, the device that had held him split open, releasing his arm.

She moved to his right and repeated the action with the second shackle, then stooped to undo the lower ones about his ankles. Watching her, it occurred to Morlac that she was placing undue trust in him, since in her bent position she could not watch his hands . . . could not see a blow directed at the exposed and vulnerable back of her delicate neck. He waited, massaging the tender marks left on his wrists.

Kadrana straightened, and as her eyes again burned through him she seemed to read his very thoughts. "You are wise to save your violence, Morlac. If you harmed me, you would not get ten paces from this chamber. The Watch-Devil would see to that. . . ."

Her sea-green eyes blinked upward for a second, and Morlac followed the direction of her glance. Up there, near the rafters of the high ceiling, something small and dark swam through air currents with a soft, slow, rippling motion. Morlac had not noticed it before, and even now as he looked it seemed almost ghostlike . . . without substance. It was a manta, no bigger than an outstretched hand, and on its gray, fleshy underbelly was a single, protruding eye, blood-red and glistening. As the thing circled the room in its steady progress, that eye was always directed upon Morlac, neither wavering nor blinking. And, watching it, Morlac could suddenly smell the poison at the end of its sharply barbed tail.

"And one other thing. . . ."

Kadrana's words called his attention back. The woman reached into a fold of her gown, bringing forth a sparkling oval amulet suspended from a loop of heavy golden chain. She did not give him a chance to study it, quickly reaching up to place it over his head. Carefully settling it about his neck, she allowed her warm hands to linger there.

She was very close to him now. Ringlets of her black hair brushed his chest, and her breath was a warm, sweet-scented breeze against his skin. As strange and dangerous as she seemed, she was also undeniably seductive, and Morlac felt strange stirrings he was reluctant to acknowledge. He also felt that, like Sordros, he knew this creature from somewhere. Her image, her manner, even her touch seemed to echo through his newly acquired memories.

She smiled, again seeming to know his thoughts, but merely indicated the amulet with a cautionary gesture. "Guard this well, Morlac . . . as well as you can. For if you lose the amulet, you also lose any hope of freedom from Sordros's spell." She paused a moment longer, then turned abruptly and started for the door. "Now come, for it is time you join your compatriots. . . ."

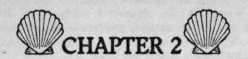

CHAPTER 2

The Sea-Warriors

Despite her imperious command, Kadrana did not force Morlac to hurry as they walked. Though he doubted it was an act of kindness, she did at least seem to sense the difficulty he was having. Initially, there was the stiffness from having been bound to the wall for many hours, not to mention the lingering aftereffects of muscles and tendons and bones having been radically altered and reformed.

Some of that was fading now, diminishing with each new step. But there was the additional problem of a creature that had never been physically adept on land now having to walk erect on two legs. All of the needed equipment was there, but there was an aching lack of coordination and experience. A sea turtle's rear limbs are weak compared to its foreflippers, and used for little more than steering. Now Morlac had long, supple legs that were forced not only to take striding steps to propel him forward, but also to help keep the rest of his body balanced above them.

It was impossibly awkward. Or should have been. But somehow, amazingly, Morlac found that he *was* able to walk, and as the minutes passed, to do it with increasingly more skill. The new pathways in his mind, the new feelings, the new voices, were taking over. Showing him how, guiding him, making the muscles work in their proper way. And gradually, as he relaxed and quit fighting against these new feelings, Morlac found that the steps were coming without effort. There was even a growing sense of exhilaration as he felt the old burdens of moving on land slipping away. But what a price he had paid for that freedom. There was a deep twinge of pain in the very thought.

The Watch-Devil followed them every step of the way through the twisting torchlit corridors of Sordros's strange castle, staying always just above and behind them. Morlac had almost become accustomed to its eerie presence when he spied a second one, slowly circling ahead.

They had reached the far side of the castle, the corridor ending in a larger one running crossways to it. Facing them in the far wall was a massive oaken door, and although it bore no locks or bars, one look at the Watch-Devil patrolling above it convinced Morlac that the room beyond was as much a cell as any in Sordros's deepest dungeons. *Odd*, Morlac thought, bringing a hand to his head abruptly as an image flashed through his mind. He had never seen this place before, but he seemed to recall it from some time earlier. An image of the door standing open, yielding entrance to a place that was comfortable and familiar. That was the way it was then. *Then? When? Who? I . . . am of the sea. Not this place. Not . . . human.*

Kadrana crossed to the door and released the latch. Morlac followed, hesitantly, wondering whether to risk an escape attempt. With the ever-watchful demons floating overhead, any attempt seemed doomed to failure . . . and death. Besides, Morlac knew his fate was bound to the green magician, for now at least. Even if he could escape the castle, he could not escape the prison his new form represented. And he was even mildly curious to learn more about this new world he had unwillingly entered. For now, he would play along, and watch for a more favorable opportunity.

The door opened into a lofty chamber, ill-lighted by a few scattered torches and a small fire at the hearth. Crude wooden cots were arranged along one side, and above each hung a sword and shield. A separate rack held a variety of other weapons, and by the opposite wall a table with benches still bore traces of the evening meal. *There*. That flash . . . that thought . . . dare he call it a memory? . . . returned again. A sense of having been here before. A sense of homecoming. But the feeling was part of that alien new mind, intruding, unreal . . . not born of his own natural memories.

There were at least two dozen men in the chamber, and they all eyed Morlac with curiosity as he entered. Why the girl had called them his compatriots Morlac could not even guess, for they all were strange to him.

"Ho! A *new* one," one of the men exclaimed. He approached Morlac, and the others followed his lead, forming a half-circle around him. "Shall this be the one we take orders from?"

Morlac studied their faces in the faint golden light of the torches. Their looks were mildly threatening, openly contemptuous.

The door closed behind him and, turning, Morlac saw that Kadrana had gone. But he did not have time to ponder on that matter long, for as he again faced the others, he discovered that they had closed the half-circle still smaller.

One of them, a giant of a man a full head taller than Morlac, stepped before him. Luminous yellow eyes were wide-set in his broad hairless head, and his form was well-cloaked in dark fabric. He looked down at Morlac with grim amusement.

"Orders from this one? I see nothing special in him!"

With that, the stranger reached out suddenly with both hands, pushing Morlac off balance. Stumbling back, Morlac regained his footing just before he would have smashed into the oaken panel behind him. He straightened, hesitated, then stepped back to the spot where he had stood.

"Ho! He has spirit at least, even if he has not brains." The giant shoved his hands out again, seeking to knock Morlac off his feet.

But this time Morlac anticipated the move. With greater speed than his antagonist, he caught the man's wrists and held them in his steely grip, stopping the blow before it reached him. He was pleased to find that the natural strength of his old forelimbs was still just as great in his new form.

The giant smiled oddly, and did not resist. But then to Morlac's horror, *two more* hands reached out from under the cloak, seizing his own wrists.

"*Now* who is the captive!"

Morlac struggled in the giant's grasp, but could not break loose. His own hold on the giant's wrists hampered his movements, but he knew if he released that hold, he would only find four hands gripping him instead of two. Finally, tensing, he tried the only thing that seemed left.

Quickly shifting his weight onto his left foot, he kicked out with his right, aiming at the giant's cloaked midsection with all the strength he could muster.

His opponent let out a surprised grunt, doubling with the force of the blow, but still keeping his hold. And to make matters worse, yet a third set of hands appeared from under the cloak and seized hold of Morlac's ankle.

Holding him thus off balance, the giant laughed with a wicked mirth. "You are running out of limbs, little man! I think I would need two of you for an even match."

The giant seemed only to be toying with him, and enjoying it, which made Morlac all the angrier. Sordros and the others all seemed intent on making him bend to their will. This was one time he would not bend. He would not!

Despite the considerable strength in his own two arms, he realized those limbs were well outnumbered. But however many more hands might lurk beneath the giant's cloak, one thing was certain. There were but two legs reaching down to the floor . . . two feet on which to stand.

Anger and frustration welled up within him, escaping in a bellow of outrage that surprised even him. With his free foot—his last remaining free limb—he stamped down hard on the man's toes and instep.

Bellowing in pain and surprise, the giant lifted the foot in reflex action. But he could not stand on one foot and hold Morlac's sudden weight as well, and when he began to tip forward, losing his balance, he had to release his hold. The action came too late to prevent his falling, and the two of them pitched over into a frantic tangle of arms.

Morlac scrambled out from under the giant and, putting a knee well into his back, twisted one of the man's arms around behind him. His opponent struggled briefly, but ceased all efforts the moment Morlac forced his arm up another few painful inches. It was a tactic that came automatically to him, and one that he felt he had used before, though obviously never as a creature of the sea.

"So," Morlac said, "even with all those arms, it still takes but one to defeat you."

"Enough!" the other called out. "You have made your point."

Morlac hesitated a moment, waiting to see what the others would do. A brief glance told him, for they all remained where they stood, only watching, and with amused looks at that.

Releasing his hold, Morlac got to his feet. He watched alertly as the giant also rose, half-expecting a renewed attack. But the fight was obviously over for all concerned. The giant beamed with a respectful smile, slapping Morlac's shoulders in a friendly gesture.

"You are a wily one, you are," he said, dusting himself off. "But don't expect that trick to work the next time!"

"There'd best be no next time," Morlac told him, anger still simmering beneath his calm.

The giant quickly sobered. "Aye . . . you're right, but not for the reason you mean. We'll have enough to do just fighting Sordros's enemies." He pulled his cloak from his shoulders and tossed it across a bench. It could now be seen that there was indeed a limit to the number of arms he could call forth to do battle. There were three pairs in all, growing out of multiple shoulder joints like the spokes of a wheel. The giant faced Morlac again, folding the top set of arms. "I am Broct. I was Sordros's first capture, so I have been in this prison they call a castle the longest of all."

"If names matter, they call me Morlac. They brought me here in the morning, but whether it be this day or another I cannot say."

"Well, whatever your past may have been," Broct said with grim comradeship, "if you've come from the pit of green fire, then you be a brother to us all."

"Aye!" said another of the men, and the rest echoed the sentiment.

Morlac relaxed somewhat, sensing among them a friendship forged of mutual frustration and anger. They had tested him, as they might any stranger thrust into their midst, but clearly they did not consider him an enemy. And, knowing this, he wanted to question them. There were so many things he did not yet understand . . . so very many things. But before the words could even form, there came a sound at the great oaken door behind them.

All turned their attention to the portal as it opened, but the looks of alertness on the others' faces eased at the sight of the one who entered. A small man, square-shouldered yet slightly stooped, pushed his way into the room. He carried a large bulky object, loosely wrapped in some coarse material, along with a sword in its scabbard. Morlac took him to be one of Sordros's menials, and yet there was about the man an air of wisdom and strength lacking in the others who so fearfully did their evil master's bidding.

"Ha—it is only Ardo!" Broct said with mock humor.

"Only Ardo—*indeed,*" the small man replied, as if insulted. "If your swordsmanship falters in battle, then curse your own poor learning! If it were up to me, I would not be wasting my skills on the likes of you." He lowered his burden to the table, still muttering. "Only Ardo. . . ."

"But it is not up to you," Broct said. "And so you teach us . . . and teach us well." He turned. "Do not mind the small one's sour look, Morlac. Of all Sordros's foul servants, this one is the only decent and trustworthy man. It would pain him to admit it, but I think he worries about our wretched souls."

Ardo snorted his disapproval, but did not correct the statement. "Since I see you are all acquainted now, you may as well meet your other friends. Friends your life will no doubt depend upon."

He took up the sword from the table and handed it to Morlac with a certain reverence. Morlac held it awkwardly in both hands for a long moment, reluctant to fully accept the deadly responsibility it suggested.

At last, grasping the hilt, which was bound in some tough gray hide, he loosed it from the scabbard and pulled the blade free. He frowned at the sight of it, for the sword glistened oddly in the torchlight. He had expected, after seeing the others' weapons, to find another blade of cold iron. He found instead a thing of blanched whiteness, like shiny bone or cartilage. Its edge was razor-sharp, and the base of the blade, just before the hilt, was serrated, with sharp prongs sticking out.

"Take care, Morlac," Ardo cautioned, his voice softer and deadly serious. "When once the sword belt is fastened about you, do not unsheath the blade casually. It is one of Sordros's magicked implements, and it is said that it has a ravenous appetite for the blood of men."

Morlac looked upon it a moment more, then quickly slipped it back into its hidebound scabbard. It made him feel uncomfortable, in more ways than one. "This man Sordros wishes dead—this *Drygo*—who is he? Why does the magician fear him?"

"He be a dark mercenary from the Eastern Lands. A dog of a man, really, but thanks to Sordros's own magic, an unbeatable warrior."

"Thanks to Sordros—?"

Ardo's voice grew softer still, as if fearful his words might be overheard by his wicked master. "Yes, Morlac, due to a chance encounter seven years ago. Drygo was a mere cutthroat and robber then, and his band of thieves happened upon Sordros as he journeyed back here after a mystic pilgrimage south. They captured Sordros at a moment when his guard was down, and he would have died had he not granted Drygo an enchantment—a spell making him invincible."

"And the wizard cannot change this spell?"

"Not without the sword of Drygo in his possession. And the only way he's likely to have it is through his heart, by Drygo's own hand!"

"If Drygo is invincible, then how can I hope to beat him?"

"Sordros says there is a way. I suspect it is part of the spell which changed you."

"Enchantments," Morlac said, shaking his head in disgust. "But why should Drygo wish to harm his benefactor, if it is by Sordros's spell that he conquers?"

"He would do it for the golden coins of L'Dron Kerr, Master of the North Kingdom and Sordros's sworn enemy. The rumors have it that Drygo and his raiders are in Kerr's hire, to lead the army of the North Kingdom in an invasion of this domain. Sordros is an ally of the wizards who rule the South Kingdom, across the Yellow Sea, and it is no secret that L'Dron Kerr wishes to purge Shola of their influence."

"I wonder . . . which ruler is the greater villain?"

Ardo shrugged. "There is little good in either. But there is no doubt that if Drygo should prevail here, there will not be enough of a village left to rule."

"Besides," Broct added sullenly, "if we are ever to be free of Sordros, then we must do his bidding and fight for him."

Ardo nodded grimly, then turned to the wrapped object on the table. He began to unwrap it slowly, reluctantly. "There is this other thing you must have, Morlac. A shield—also of Sordros's magic. . . ." He left it there, uncovered, and watched Morlac with troubled eyes.

The shield was oval and slightly domed, its length a little less than half of Morlac's height. A broad leather strap had been fastened diagonally from top to bottom and ran out of sight beneath the shield.

The very sight of the object filled Morlac with dread, and when he touched it, a chill seized his spine. His hand was nearly trembling as he ran it over the patterned, green-brown shell that had once been a part of him. He had never seen it from this angle before, but still he recognized it with a certainty that made his flesh crawl. As he studied the bony carapace of which the shield was formed, he felt his head swimming, and fatigue creeping over him.

Broct steadied him. "Easy, now, my sea-brother. You need more time to adjust. And you had better get some food in your belly and some rest tonight. There is much yet ahead of you. . . ."

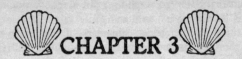

CHAPTER 3

Iron and Leather

The dawn of a later morning brought the clangor of swords and the crash of shields to Sordros's village, shattering the calm and displacing the gentle cry of seabirds and the slow whisper of rolling surf. Awakening shopkeepers peered from the windows above their shops, and fishermen looked up from the nets they mended, fearful that invading troups from the North Kingdom might have reached their village under cover of darkness. But their fears were premature. It was not invaders but defenders whose swords rang out in the early-morning stillness.

Morlac and the other sea-warriors were practicing their swordsmanship in the rocky, uneven plaza that fronted Sordros's castle and formed a sort of stage fanning out into the sprawling clutter of village streets and buildings. Ardo moved among them with a sharp eye and an even sharper tongue, cursing their mistakes and frequently shoving one of a pair of mock combatants aside to demonstrate himself just how a sword should be wielded.

Morlac held a plain iron sword in his right hand. His left forearm was slipped through the straps of a conventional shield constructed of wood and hardened, layered leather. He went through the motions of battle with one of the other transmutants, but his heart was clearly not in it. He had been training for days, learning the techniques of sword-battle . . . or perhaps relearning it. For he felt alternately ill at ease and oddly comfortable with a sword in his hand. For the most part, this business of warfare made no sense to him. While it was true that creatures of the sea killed for survival, and even fought over food or territory, they never relied upon artificial weapons to do battle. And with only rare exceptions, they never murdered or maimed members of their own species. Puzzling. Humans seemed to be unreasonably aggressive beasts.

Morlac saw Ardo approaching out of the corner of his eye and automatically tensed in anticipation. In the past several days of practice, Ardo had singled him out for "special attention." This meant Morlac was on the receiving end of more advice, more criticism, and more cursing than any of the others. It was an honor he would gladly have foregone. He did not hate or fear Ardo, but the small human was still a force to be reckoned with.

"Well, well," said Ardo in a booming voice that belied his short stature and normally subdued manner, "it seems some of us are still asleep! For surely no fighting man full awake and in clear possession of his wits could put on so pitiful a display. Do you think your enemies will be so sluggish? Do you wish to die?"

"No," said Morlac. "Neither do I wish to fight."

"Would that we always had a choice," Ardo said softly. "Now! Perhaps you are not sluggish, but merely bored. Perhaps you need more of a challenge!"

The point of Ardo's sword twirled enthusiastically, and the sea-warrior who sparred with Morlac started to step aside. "No—wait!" Ardo said. "You remain. The captain of the guard must be a valiant leader and a master swordsman. And as befits such a warrior, he must have a proper challenge."

Morlac frowned at the thought of his fledgling skills being tested against two swordsmen at once. Especially when one of them was Ardo. But there was no time to protest or even draw a deep breath in preparation. For in the next instant Ardo's blade came flashing toward him. He barely had time to halt the blow with his shield, and before he had fully recovered from that jolt he saw his brother sea-warrior launch his own attack.

Morlac parried the second blade with his sword. Ardo struck again, harder this time. Again, Morlac caught the brunt of the blow squarely on his shield. The second strike from the other warrior came quickly now, and Morlac barely stopped it. He felt off balance and staggered back a step.

"I fear you expect too much of me," he said.

"You had better fear—" said Ardo with a lunge "—that I do not expect—"and yet another thrust "—enough!"

The blows were coming faster now. He could barely watch both attackers, let alone defend against them. He knew they did not truly mean him harm, and he knew that Ardo was skillful enough to avoid inflicting serious injury. Or he *thought* he knew. Could he really be sure of anything in this strange new existence? Morlac felt his heart pounding, and a tangible chill of fear coursing through him.

"Weakling!" Ardo shouted. "If you cannot defend yourself, how can you defend our village—?"

Morlac was being beaten back by the blows, barely protecting himself, with no time for a single offensive strike. Stepping back blindly on the uneven ground, he suddenly stumbled on a rock and went down on one knee. Ardo's attack was unrelenting, though the other warrior seemed to hesitate a bit. Ardo's blade abruptly nipped the flesh of Morlac's sword arm expertly, making little more than a scratch but stinging nearly as much as a deeper wound.

The pain seemed to awaken him, and to awaken something in him. Morlac suddenly realized he had been responding with turtlelike instincts, barely using his training, hiding behind his shield and his sword, trying to escape instead of fighting back. The pain provoked more than fear now. It, and the knowledge of his own weak response, provoked anger. An anger that cut through the barrier between his old mind and his new mind. Something slipped into place. Something meshed. And suddenly, the sword in his hand became a weapon with a will behind it.

Gaining his feet again, he leaped slightly forward and to the side, placing the other warrior almost behind Ardo. His sword flashed upward, forcing Ardo to bend back away from him. He thought he caught a glimpse of a smile on the little man's face, but in the next instant Ardo directed a hacking blow at Morlac's knees. Without even thinking, Morlac gave a flick of his wrist, bringing his sword down and around to parry the blow, then slashed up to force Ardo back still further.

The other warrior was coming around Ardo's side, trying

to get back into a fighting position. Morlac had given himself a momentary advantage by placing himself on a line with the other two, and now with Ardo on the defensive for the first time, he seized the opportunity. As the other warrior swung his blade around to strike, Morlac gave a backhand slash with the full force of his arm and shoulder muscles behind it. His own sword caught the flat side of the other blade just above the hilt and snapped it cleanly. As the severed blade clattered to the plaza's stones, the sea-warrior wielding it looked amazed, then backed away from the battle.

Only Ardo remained now, and with but one opponent to concentrate on, Morlac forced his teacher back farther still. Their swords rang out a melody that was intense and commanding. The others on the plaza gave up their practice, standing and watching, and staying clear of the flashing blades.

Morlac was breathing hard now, his temples throbbing with the effort and the intensity of his emotion. He was thinking about nothing, just letting his reflexes and instincts work.

At last he saw an opening. Morlac had backed Ardo against a large outcropping of stone and brushed aside a parrying thrust. Ardo's sword was in a poor position to strike. In an instant, Morlac held the tip of his blade poised before Ardo's throat, scant inches away from a mortal injury. The others on the plaza gasped.

Morlac waited, his sword still poised. Ardo studied him for a long moment, a questioning look in his eyes, then he smiled broadly and dropped his sword.

Still breathing hard, Morlac lowered his own weapon and sheathed it. Relaxing more, he put a hand on his teacher's shoulder and said, "I am sorry, friend Ardo. I came close . . . very close . . . to the edge, then. That was quite a risk you took, not knowing how I would respond to your prodding."

"I was fairly sure I knew the man within you," said Ardo, breathing hard himself. "Besides, one must sometimes take chances, when one's goal is important."

"I do not blame you for that," said Morlac, looking away from Ardo as his thoughts turned inward. "I only wish I knew the man within me as well as you seem to. . . ."

Ardo made no reply to that. But he paused to grip Morlac's

shoulder strongly before turning away to pick up his sword and walk back toward the center of the plaza.

"Ho! Getting lazy, are we?" Ardo called out sharply to the other sea-warriors. "Resume your practice. Quickly now! The North Kingdom plans to test your skills soon, and to fail their test is to die. . . ."

Watching the plaza from a high balcony of the strangely formed castle, Sordros squinted as the glare of the rising sun steadily increased. He continued to study the scene below, expressionless, vulturelike, deep in thought.

At his side, Kadrana beamed with enthusiasm. "Did you see that? The way he fought back and bested Ardo. He's magnificent! There is much of Calrom in him."

"Yes," said Sordros at last in an odd, high-pitched voice that was like the whispering of rats in the dark of night. "It is as I planned. But he will need all that and more, if he is to best Drygo and the others."

"He will. I am sure," Kadrana said. "And I intend to see that he is as much like Calrom as possible."

Sordros turned slowly, his withering gaze falling full upon the exquisitely formed young woman. "*I* shall make the plans, Kadrana. Never forget for a moment who you are, and what you are, and from whence your power comes. Morlac is *my* creation . . . my weapon . . . my toy. I do not want him distracted even for a moment from his true purpose—to destroy my enemy. He exists for nothing more, and nothing less."

"Yes . . . of course," Kadrana said uneasily. "But you need a strong fighter for that. I only want to remind him that he has something to fight for."

Sordros's clawlike hand closed around Kadrana's delicate arm. "I know full well what you want, and I really do not care. But nothing must jeopardize my plan. Nothing. Besides," he said, releasing her arm and looking back toward the plaza, "it is better that you not get too attached to Morlac. You did so with his predecessor, and I'm sure you recall *his* fate. . . ."

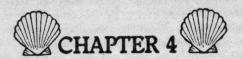

CHAPTER 4

The Past Rekindled

"We grow better each day," said Broct tiredly. "And you, Morlac, put us all to shame today. But still I wonder if we are up to the challenge of the North Kingdom."

Morlac nodded in somber agreement as he and the other sea-warriors stood in their castle chamber after practice, stripped to the waist, putting away their weapons and washing the sweat from their fatigued bodies. "Yes, I wonder that, too. There seem too few of us, even with the rest of the guard and the village men behind us. There have always been too few of us."

Morlac looked up from oiling his sword, his eyes troubled. "How do I know that? I cannot explain how, yet I do know it. Just as surely as I know that I, in this life or some other, have already fought against soldiers of the North Kingdom. That my sword has tasted their blood, and that their swords have. . . ." He halted as a chill seized him.

Broct placed several hands upon his shoulder. "You are not alone in that, my brother. I have felt the touch of thoughts and memories I should not have." He gestured around the room. "All of us have. And I do not think it is any of Sordros's trickery. It all seems too real. Aye—a true mystery, it is."

"A mystery I intend to solve, if I live through this," said Morlac.

"If any of us do," said one of the other sea-warriors, a brooding man called Xaja. "Sordros does not care if we live or die. And if we fight the North Kingdom we shall surely die."

39

"What choice have we?" said Broct.

Xaja frowned but said nothing in reply. He turned away from them and stalked over to the far corner of the chamber, where his bed and weapons chest stood apart from the others.

"Something else that troubles me," said Morlac. "Cannot Sordros merely conjure up a vast army to do his fighting? Why does he need us?"

Broct stepped closer to Morlac and lowered his voice. "Ardo tells me that even magic has its limits. Some wizards be stronger than others. Not all have the same powers. It depends upon which gods or devils they worship, and how much of their souls they've bargained away. I'm sure if Sordros could create an army out of thin air, he would have long ago."

Abruptly, the massive door to their chamber began to creak open, and all conversation stopped. Everyone looked to see who would enter.

Kadrana pushed the door open partway, but did not enter. She stood there, straight as a sword and imperious as royalty.

"Morlac—" she said "—come with me."

Morlac waited a moment, then glanced at the others and sighed inwardly. He wiped his hands on a rag, tossed it down, and joined her in the corridor.

Kadrana tugged the door closed behind him. She smiled. "There is something I wish to show you."

She led the way down the corridor and turned right, taking him along another corridor he had not previously traveled since his new life began. A short distance down this new pathway yielded another wooden door, less massive than that which gave access to the sea-warriors' chamber. She halted here, standing to one side of the door and gesturing toward it with a slow sweep of her hand.

"Enter—" Kadrana told him.

Morlac hesitated. He was suspicious of her, wondering if what lay behind the door was some new trickery . . . some new torture to be endured. He would not be surprised if that were the case. And yet he had to admit that once the initial agony of his transformation had passed, he had not been badly treated thus far. If he was needed for Sordros's plan, what purpose could be served by tormenting him more?

Besides, whatever this room was, at least it was not the dungeon.

Morlac reached out and pushed the door open cautiously, looking inside before venturing to enter. Kadrana waited a moment more, then gave an impatient shrug and stepped inside ahead of him.

"You have nothing to fear here, Morlac," she said. "And no reason to fear. You did very well today. We are pleased with you."

"We?" said Morlac, looking around as he entered after her.

"Sordros and I."

"I did not think anything pleased Sordros."

"You do not know him as well as I do."

Morlac continued to inspect the room. His initial mistrust seemed unfounded. There was nothing dangerous or threatening here. Still, he found the place disturbing. Light from a high, narrow window cast an even glow upon the room's interior, and the place had a faint musty smell, as if it had been unused for some months. It appeared to be someone's private chamber, but it was too spartan and simply furnished to belong to Sordros or even the girl. There was only a bed, a chair, several chests, and a weapons rack, similar to the furniture that was in the sea-warriors' chamber. A mirror of brightly polished metal hung on one wall, and a scattering of personal belongings stood atop one of the chests.

Kadrana stepped closer to him, her posture no longer that of the arrogant master. She stood casually, one foot extended, her hips and shoulders at a mildly provocative tilt.

"Well, what do you think of it?" she said smoothly. "Do you like this room?"

"It is a room. Nothing more," said Morlac. But he found himself wondering why it seemed so familiar. Part of him felt at ease here. But even that thought was disconcerting.

"It is not just any room, Morlac. This chamber belongs to the captain of the guard. And you are captain of the guard."

"So I have been told."

Kadrana said smoothly, "Therefore, this room is your room."

"Is it?"

"*Isn't* it . . . ?" Kadrana's eyes studied him closely, probingly. She was still standing within reach of the door, and she now pushed it quietly closed behind her.

Morlac seemed not to notice. He walked slowly to one of the chests and picked up a broad, ornamented band of metal, heavy and masculine in appearance. The touch of it in his hands, the glints of light from its engraved surface, brought an odd thrill of recognition.

"These things—" he asked "—whose are they?"

Kadrana approached him with catlike grace. "They belong to no one now. Consider them yours."

Morlac studied the man's bracelet a moment longer, then slowly slipped it around his wrist. It seemed to belong there. But the action of placing it aggravated muscles that ached from hours of sword practice. Without thinking, he rubbed his arm and shoulder.

Kadrana reached round him and picked up an earthen vessel filled with unguent. She dipped her fingers into it and began to rub the soothing salve across Morlac's broad, pale shoulder. Deep in thought was he, and only dimly aware of her ministrations. But the balm felt good, and eased the pain. His eyes were still fixed upon the metal band that seemed to have been his from before this moment.

"Why did you show me this room?" he said absently.

Kadrana began applying unguent to his arm now, her delicate hand moving in slow, gentle circles across the sore muscles. "Because it is yours. A gift from Sordros. The captain of the guard should have a room of his own. It is fitting."

"But I enjoy the company of my friends. And if I am to lead them, why should I stay apart from them?"

"Because that is as it should be. A true leader does not make friends of his followers. He is above them, stronger than they, better than they." Kadrana's hand dipped into the unguent once more, and this time came to rest upon the tight muscles of Morlac's chest. "Besides . . . there are advantages to privacy. . . ."

The warmth of her hand intruded on his thoughts. Morlac took hold of her wrist and moved her hand away, but he kept it in his grasp. Looking up into the mirror on the wall, he could see her standing so close at his shoulder that she seemed molded to his side. Her breasts pressed so tightly against him that he was sure he could feel her heart beating. Her eyes met his in the mirror, unwaveringly, knowingly, burning into his mind as intensely as her physical warmth insinuated itself upon his flesh. To that aspect of him that was still sea turtle, she seemed alien and vaguely repulsive. But to that new part of his mind that seemed older, more knowledgeable and oddly human, she was anything but repulsive. Her mass of ringleted hair, black as a moonless night, framed a face that was smooth and perfect and nearly childlike, yet lacking childlike innocence.

Seeing her beside him, here, in this room, brought an odd sense of history repeated. He . . . they . . . had been here before. As he thought this, her mouth twisted up into a smile, making him uncomfortable and forcing him to look away from her reflected image.

"Sordros rules this village as king," Morlac said. "And you are his daughter, his princess."

"I am your princess, too, Morlac," Kadrana whispered close to his ear. "I am not one of your followers . . . I *can* be a friend. That, and more. Much more."

Morlac pulled away from her, and found himself fighting not so much against her grasp as against his own strange feelings. His heart was racing, nearly as much as it had during sword practice. He took the unguent vessel from her hand and put it back upon the chest top.

A frown of irritation flickered across Kadrana's lovely face. "Why do you resist me? I sense you do remember, though not yet well enough, it seems."

"I remember," Morlac said softly. "Perhaps too well. I thank you, and Sordros, for the gift of this room. But for now, I choose to remain with my sea-brothers."

Kadrana's exquisite, slender form trembled with anger and thwarted purpose. The last trace of softness and desire vanished as her face became the cruel mask he had so often seen. Her body straightened, becoming rigid and haughty once more.

"All right, Morlac. You may have your way . . . for now. But you are not yet through with me, it seems. For Sordros desires that I accompany you and the others, once you've put away your weapons.''

"Accompany us? Where?"

"Into the village," she replied. "Sordros wishes to reward your hard work, and to give you an opportunity to walk among those you will protect. You are all to be dressed and ready to go within the hour."

Morlac arched a devil-brow in thought. "As you wish. I'm sure the others will be pleased to have a taste of freedom."

With that, he strode to the door and swung it open, gesturing for the girl to pass through. "Princess—"

Kadrana's eyes narrowed as she walked from the room and into the corridor, to wait for him there. As he closed the door behind him, she gestured down the hall.

"After you," she said, in a tone that was formal, mocking and cruel. "My captain. . . ."

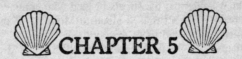

CHAPTER 5

Reward and Punishment

The cobblestone streets of the village were still busy in late afternoon as Kadrana led Sordros's band of sea-warriors into town and away from the imposing castle on the cliff. All along the way, villagers stopped what they were doing to stare at these strange men, who were garbed in the uniforms and cloaks of castle guards, yet carried no weapons. Kadrana marched straight and proud at their lead, her slender and delicate form armored by her own arrogance. Villagers silently moved clear of their path, like the sea diverting around a ship's bow.

Morlac walked quietly alongside Broct, and just behind the girl. His eyes peered out, somber and brooding, from beneath brows set low in a quizzical frown. He was as curious about these villagers as they seemed to be about him. His eyes sailed a sea of faces that were strange to him, and yet not strange. Not strange at all. A voice inside his mind called out to him, teasingly, irritatingly, whispering of things past. *This is my village. These are my people. I grew up on these streets. There . . . over there . . . that spot! Yes . . . it is still the same.*

After the starkness of Sordros's castle and their day-to-day existence, the village was a heady experience. It was full of new sights and sounds, a rich tapestry of textures and smells and color and form. There was nothing luxurious about any of it—far from it—but still the place teemed with life, vibrant and real. Merchants hawked their wares, fishwives cleaned their husbands' catches, laundry hung from windows and across alleyways, and the streets bustled with commerce.

"I wonder," Broct mused aloud to Morlac, "if this little trip is really to reward us or merely to show us off."

"Perhaps both," said Morlac thoughtfully. "And perhaps also to give us more to fight for."

A few minutes later, on the village's main street, they reached their destination. Kadrana came to a halt before a large tavern and directed them to enter. The tavern keeper, apparently prepared for them, led the group back to a pair of long tables and benches that stood empty in a corner of the establishment. Kadrana followed them in and quietly put a pouch of coins in the tavern keeper's eager grasp.

The boisterous conversation around them faded to whispers as the sea-warriors strode in and took seats upon the benches. All eyes were upon them, and while the faces that turned their way were not hostile, they also were not friendly. One voice, from a man braver or drunker than the rest, rose enough above the other whispers and mutterings to be heard.

"Look—" said he "—'Tis the wizard's demons."

Morlac frowned in the direction of the voice, and heard the shushings of those who would quiet the man. He turned to Broct with a sour look.

"Demons, they call us."

"Aye," said Broct with a grim nod. "They fear us, as they do all magic. And perhaps rightly so. But still I think they know we be the only hope they have against the North Kingdom's soldiers."

"Know it, they may. And if the truth be known, I *will* defend this place, with my life if need be. For whether I understand it or not, this village is somehow a part of me, and I of it, and I will not stand idly by and see it destroyed." He sighed deeply. "I just wish they would not stare at us so. I don't know, Broct—perhaps they're right. Perhaps we *are* demons."

"Well," said Broct jovially, "if we be demons, then let us eat and drink like demons, for we may not get the chance again!"

Serving wenches were already placing tankards of ale before each of the sea-warriors, and more were on the way with bowls of stew. The steaming, fragrant broth was filled with chunks of meat and vegetables, and if it was not greatly different from the fare in Sordros's castle, it was at least seasoned by a different hand and served in less grim surroundings.

Soon, Broct was enjoying himself with such fervor that Morlac could not help but smile at the sight. The party atmosphere quickly spread to the rest of the sea-warriors, and before long they had become such a cheerful, rowdy group that the villagers themselves seemed to forget their fears and resumed their own merriment.

Kadrana, seated near Morlac, kept an eye on this all, saying nothing but smiling a catlike smile of satisfaction. She ate no food, but sipped at a vessel of wine brought by the tavern keeper himself.

Of them all, only Xaja seemed not to be enjoying himself. He ate his food quickly, furtively, as a caged animal might, his eyes constantly shifting from one part of the tavern interior to another.

By the time the meal was done, no one seemed to care anymore who was villager and who was sea-warrior. Most of Sordros's special guard had joined in singing bawdy tavern songs, with perhaps more gusto than the villagers themselves. And loudest of them all was Broct, who, though he was managing to keep his surplus of arms hidden from view, was boisterously keeping time to the music with a tankard of ale raised high in the air. As the song ended, he roared his delight, then decided to further express his high spirits by grabbing a passing serving wench, pulling her to him, and planting a passionate and ale-moist kiss squarely on her pretty mouth.

The girl, well experienced with such bravado, merely pushed him away with a wry smile, then went on about her duties. Nevertheless, this brought a roar of approval from everyone in sight.

Morlac smiled broadly at his friend, truly enjoying himself for the first time in this new life. "It feels good to laugh, my brother. There has been little enough of that in the castle."

"Aye," said Broct, "it does feel good!" The yellow-eyed giant emptied his tankard in a few large gulps and cast his mischievous gaze in the direction of the next serving wench who appeared to be heading their way.

Morlac laughed out loud again, then turned to Kadrana, curious about her reaction to all this. At first he thought she was frowning in disapproval at their merriment, but then he noticed that she was not really looking at either himself or Broct. Nor was she displaying the haughty smugness so often seen on her otherwise lovely face. Instead, she seemed to be quickly surveying the tables at which the sea-warriors sat, her eyes darting down each row and becoming more and more troubled.

"What's wrong—?" said Morlac.

It took her a moment to answer. She was still lost in thought. "Someone's missing!"

Morlac quickly scanned the faces present and saw that she was right. And he knew almost without having to think just who was gone.

"Xaja. . . ."

Kadrana was already on her feet and heading for the door. Morlac quickly followed, and Broct and several of the others looked up in puzzled alarm.

As he moved, Morlac did not see any sign of Xaja anywhere in the tavern. Not that he expected to. He had his own idea about where the brooding sea-warrior might be found.

Morlac reached the door and quickly joined Kadrana in the street. Behind them, the tavern songs continued, but Broct and others of the sea-warrior band were now following, their merriment fading.

Kadrana's sharp eyes peered down the street in the fading light of dusk, then she whirled and stared in the street's opposite direction. An accusing finger thrust out suddenly.

"There—!" she shrieked.

A fair distance down the street, Xaja halted in his tracks at the sound of her voice, looking back fearfully over his shoulder. Then he bolted, continuing away from them.

"He's escaping!" Kadrana drew herself up, inhaling deeply and clutching at an amulet she wore about her neck. "Sordros—!" she called out sharply.

"Wait—" said Morlac "—I can bring him back! Don't—"

Kadrana did not wait. "Sordros! Hear me!" Her scream

cut through the night. She closed her eyes and tilted her head back, sucking in air through her teeth and holding her amulet raised in a tightly clenched fist.

Morlac started to run after Xaja, but had not gotten far when he again saw the fleeing sea-warrior halt and look back. But if Xaja thought that danger would come from that direction he was wrong, as he quickly found out when he once more turned to run.

Xaja had not taken two full steps when he suddenly jerked back at the sight of a strange light directly in front of him. Green in hue, the ball of light abruptly elongated into a glowing pillar, then that pillar took on the outline of a man. In a flash, Sordros stood revealed, his hands raised, clawlike and threatening.

"Go back, dog!" Sordros's voice commanded, and Morlac thought he felt it in his mind as much as heard it. "Obey me, or die!"

Xaja stood frozen for a long moment, cowering before the magical image of Sordros. Then his head jerked around as he sought a new direction, and he started running down another street.

He had not gone more than thirty feet when the image of Sordros suddenly materialized directly in front of him once more. Xaja staggered back, out of breath, and went down on his knees. Sordros's glowing, spectral hand reached out and grabbed hold of Xaja's conjure amulet. Then the hand jerked it free, breaking the chain. Sordros held the amulet aloft, then hurled it onto the cobblestone street, smashing it into tiny fragments.

"No one defies me," said Sordros's ghostly form, "and lives!"

Still on his knees, Xaja let out an unearthly scream of agony and terror, his head bending back at an impossible angle. Then he toppled forward, flat upon the cobblestone roadway, twitching and jerking, his body contorting horribly. Until at last it became utterly, utterly still.

As Xaja ceased to move, Sordros's image vanished. It was as if it had never even been there in the first place, and the street seemed normal once more.

Morlac started forward again, hurrying to the spot where

Xaja lay. He reached the sea-warrior's fallen form and halted, staring down in horror.

Kadrana came running up behind him and halted a few steps away. Broct and the others reached the spot a moment later. All now stood and gazed, awestruck by what lay before them.

Xaja was not merely dead. His body had, in a matter of moments, become a corpse that now steamed and smoldered and rotted before their very eyes. It was as if the magic force which had bound it together had suddenly been released, and it was now deteriorating into whatever substances had formed it.

Morlac tore his disbelieving eyes away from the sight of it, and his gaze fell upon Kadrana. She stood there, breathing hard, her face radiant with a self-satisfied smile. Her eyes met his then, and narrowed slightly. It was a spiteful, challenging look.

"So may you all learn of the power of Sordros," said she to the group. She folded her arms. "It is time we go back. I hope you all enjoyed your little celebration. And the rest of you are to be commended for not following the bad example of one coward. Assemble your men, my captain!"

Morlac stared long and hard at her, hating her for her cruelty. Then he gestured for his men to do as she ordered. "As you wish . . . daughter of Sordros. . . ."

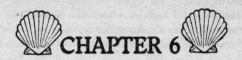

CHAPTER 6

Aboard the *Flying Fish*

A chilling rain was falling through the darkness on the night of the new moon. At the rear of Sordros's castle, a procession of people made its way down winding stone steps cut into the cliff above the sea . . . steps that reached all the way to the water's surface. Torches lighted their narrow path, flickering and smoking in the sea breeze, and casting treacherous shadows.

Sordros, six of his spell-gripped warriors, and a handful of attendants reached the level platform at sea's edge and stopped before a small sailing craft moored to a great bronze ring set in stone. The ship had a wide, shallow hull, with high, straight cutwaters at stem and stern. It was more like the warships that occasionally ventured down from the snow-bound kingdom of Theros, to the north of Shola, than the simple fishing craft of Sordros's village. Its jet-black form rested like a shadow on the sea, a slash of green above where the furled sail waited.

Morlac studied it. It was a thing of the sea, and yet, like so many things here, touched by Sordros's magic.

He pulled his russet cloak about him in the chill, moist air. His amulet now was hidden beneath the coarse fabric of a brown jerkin, and about his middle was belted his scabbarded sword. His special sword. During the past weeks of sword practice, Morlac had continued to learn well under Ardo's tutelage, working always with a plain iron weapon of equal weight and balance, never daring to draw the wizard's magicked blade in mock battle. His shell-shield hung on his left arm, also ready to be used for the first time.

Broct, also cloaked, studied the ship. "So this be the craft that takes us there." He shook his head, frowning. "I still think a fast horse for each man would be better!"

Sordros was aloof, a calm about which dark forces coiled and eddied in the night. "You would not get past L'Dron Kerr's patrols if you took the land route north. And do not worry about speed—you'll find no swifter vessel than the *Flying Fish*."

Morlac viewed the magician with cold hatred. His hand rested upon sword hilt, and he was half tempted to learn if the blade's power could be used against Sordros himself. But Sordros's death would endanger the village, and also destroy the sea-warriors' only hope for freedom from the evil spell that kept them in limbo, halfway between sea creatures and humankind. And the fearful awareness of this was stronger than his hatred . . . for the moment.

He turned suddenly as another figure came down the stone stairway from the castle above. Kadrana, her slender form cloaked against the rain and chill, descended the last step and joined them. She carried a round bundle of silk, cradling it carefully as if it were a babe in arms.

"Kill the warrior Drygo, if you can, Morlac—" Sordros continued in that dreaded voice of his, pitched higher than a man's, yet unlike any woman's. "If not, there may be a later chance to deal with the ungrateful dog. But you must not fail in one thing at least—you must learn the invasion plans of the North Kingdom, so that I may prepare our defenses. The first snows of winter are near, and their attack will come soon."

Morlac's look would have chilled the marrow of any normal man. "I . . . will do what I *must,* Sordros."

"Then leave at once—you need all of the night for what lies ahead."

As Kadrana started up the gangplank of the ship, Morlac looked around in surprise. "*She* goes, as well?"

Sordros's shrouded head nodded slowly. "She has the power to command the *Flying Fish* . . . she and none other but I. You will obey her as you do me."

Morlac glared his disapproval, but said nothing more. He turned and started into the ship, the others following him. In a moment, the lines were cast off and the warriors manned the oars, taking the odd vessel out beyond the rocky coast.

The tall, gaunt figure of Sordros standing at water's edge faded from view in the darkness, and soon even the coastline was indistinguishable from the sea and the moonless sky. There was only the inky blackness, and the rhythmic sound of the oars dipping into the water, pushing against its yielding resistance.

"It is peculiar logic," Morlac said under his breath to Broct as they pulled their oars in a downward stroke. "Sordros feared we might be seen by L'Dron Kerr's patrols if we went by land, yet he has no fears of our being encountered by ships of the North Kingdom."

"There be less chance of that than you think," Broct replied. "There are not so many North Kingdom ships now as there once were, thanks to Sordros's sea powers. I have heard Ardo speak of whole crews lost to the depths."

"Even so," Morlac said, "I do not see how Sordros expects us to reach the North Kingdom tonight."

Broct shrugged. "Nor do I. But then, I am only a warrior, not a wizard."

As they rowed, Morlac noticed that Broct paused briefly to reposition a large finger ring that the oar had caused to twist. It was something new, a round chunk of obsidian in a heavy silver setting, and he had not seen it before.

Gesturing toward it, he said, "What is that thing?"

Broct held it closer to him, a faint glint reflecting off its incredibly dark gem. "This? A toy of Sordros's making. A coward's weapon, really, but it may have use some day."

"How does it work?"

"Enough—!" Kadrana called out suddenly. "We are in open water now. Raise your oars—bring them in and make them fast to the deck!"

"What deviltry now?" Morlac breathed, for there seemed not enough wind for sailing. But he and the others did as she instructed, so that only the dripping blades of the long oars protruded from the ship's sides.

Kadrana walked between them, stepping up to a slightly raised platform at ship's center, just behind the mast. There, a decorated tripod of metal stood, its upper ends curving out like clawing fingers. Slowly unwrapping the silken bundle she had been clutching, she removed the object concealed within and lowered it into the tripod's grasp.

The black pearl rested heavily within its support, wondrously dark and lustrous, and large as a man's head. It had no doubt come from the depths of some distant ocean and traversed many lands before falling into the hands of Sordros.

Morlac wondered to what use the evil magician had twisted this bit of treasure from the sea. It did not take long to find out.

"Raise the sail . . . *quickly,*" Kadrana commanded them. She stood at her place behind the great pearl, proud and daring, and easily as wicked as Sordros himself. She watched with supreme confidence as two of the warriors manned the winch at the helm, hoisting the sail skyward.

Even in the feeble light of the one small lantern brought aboard ship, Morlac could see the embroidered ensign, deep black against the green of the sail—the horned staff of Tritus, chief of the sea-gods worshiped by the fisherfolk of Shola and beyond. And Morlac saw something else as well.

There above the masthead, almost invisible in the darkness, circled two of Sordros's Watch-Devils—grim, silent reminders of the magician's authority and power. No wonder, Morlac thought, that Kadrana stood so confident and poised before Sordros's small army. Apparently, the wizard was taking no chances after Xaja's attempted escape.

And now Kadrana began an enchantment of her own. She slipped off her sandals so that her bare feet, well-braced and wide apart, made contact with the deck. Then she extended her open hands along the immense black pearl, her fingers near but not touching its smooth, round form. A frown of concentration set her features and her lips moved strangely, whispering spells unheard by Morlac and the others.

A moment later there came an answering whisper, from the wind, or perhaps from the sea itself. It was followed by a creaking sound—a moaning of wooden timbers and planking suddenly under new stress.

Or was it rather . . . stress *removed?*

Morlac sensed a shifting of the deck beneath his feet, and braced himself. There was a brief lurch as a cold and unworldly wind began to fill the sail, almost unbalancing them. But then the sea turned calm beneath them, or seemed to, for they no longer rocked upon its surface.

Abruptly, its keel breaking free of the sea's grip, the *Flying Fish* rose dripping from the water. It floated skyward, blown north by the conjure wind.

"By the Gods—!" one warrior exclaimed, and others drew in their breath in sudden fear of the unknown.

Morlac watched in wonder as the surface of the sea disappeared beneath them. Faint lights of the tiny coastal village on their starboard side became visible as they ascended, shifting and spreading into a wide cluster. Morlac turned and made his way toward Kadrana, with Broct close at his heels.

The girl stiffened slightly at their approach, but she maintained her look of mastery. "It will take little more than an hour to reach our destination," she told them. "There is a spot on the northern coast where we can safely moor . . . only a mile from Kem, capital of the North Kingdom."

"We could get there faster," Morlac replied, unmoved by this new demonstration of Sordros's skills, "if we went in a straight line instead of going so far out to sea. With a ship such as this—"

Kadrana shook her head quickly. "The *Flying Fish* may not pass over land, Morlac. It draws its power from the sea. If we tried to cross Shola with it, we would surely die on the rocks of the coast."

"So . . . Sordros is not quite all-powerful after all."

Anger flashed in her exquisite face, but she did not let it consume her. "He is powerful *enough*, my warrior-slave. And I am an extension of that power. Never doubt that. *Never!*"

Turning away from her, Morlac settled on a thwart near the prow of the craft. He stared sullenly into the blackness that was sky and sea, his back to the conjure wind and the chilling rain, keeping his thoughts silent, and biding his time. . . .

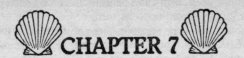# CHAPTER 7

Kadrana's Secret

"*There* . . . down there!" a warrior called, excited, yet mindful of the distance his voice might carry. "Guard fires."

They gathered near the prow, looking out into the gloom. Below, at a point perhaps only a mile ahead, a string of lights glowed, yellow and flickering, along the northern coast of Shola.

"L'Dron Kerr's posts," Kadrana said softly. "But more for defense against the ships of Theros than any plot of ours."

Morlac frowned. "That will make them no less difficult to pass."

"We will pass them," she replied, with a confident toss of her head that sent new ripples through the black ringlets of her hair. "Now make ready to land. We are near the spot where we may moor the ship."

With swift precision, Kadrana brought her enchantment to an end, letting the *Flying Fish* float softly back to the water's surface. The sail was lowered, and as silently as they could they rowed into the shelter of a tiny cove.

"We must leave four of the men here," Kadrana said quickly. "The ship must be guarded."

Morlac considered, then nodded in agreement. "The fewer that go, the better. We don't want to attract attention in the city. Broct and I will go."

"And so will I," Kadrana said, adding before he could protest, "You have no choice! It is Sordros's wish."

Morlac looked at her for a long moment, but knew it was

useless to argue the point. And somehow, he felt better about keeping her in sight than in leaving her behind. Finally, he said, "Very well."

In a moment the gangplank was extended and they set foot upon the shore. There, Morlac removed his cloak momentarily and swung his shield upon his back, letting the broad leather strap hang diagonally across his chest. The shield felt good there. It was where it belonged. He readjusted his cloak to cover the shield, and its folds concealed the sword at his side as well. Broct followed suit, and Kadrana pulled the hood of her dark-blue cloak up over her head.

Morlac peered cautiously above an outcropping of rock. "Now if we can but pass the sentinels—"

"There is a way," Kadrana said curtly, "but it lies in the other direction. Come—follow me!"

At a point no more than forty paces from where they came ashore, the young woman suddenly headed back toward the edge of the water. Abruptly, she disappeared around a large rock at the base of the low cliff, soundlessly beckoning just before leaving their view.

Morlac splashed into the ankle-deep water and followed, though he still wondered if he could trust the magician's spawn. Or her sanity.

Suddenly, he faced nothing but solid rock. The girl had totally vanished, nowhere to be seen. Morlac probed the sheer rock surface with his hands as well as his eyes, but he could find not even the hint of a crevice through which the girl might have gone. He knew she was capable of enchantments, but did she also possess the power to pass through solid stone? He was about to give up—to retrace his steps—when the sound of her voice came from just ahead, muffled and seemingly out of the rock itself.

"*Morlac*—the opening is down here," she whispered. "You must bend low."

He reached down and searched the rock again, lower this time, and discovered a small tunnel entrance whose top edge was nearly level with his knees. In the darkness it had been indistinguishable from the water-blackened base of the stone.

He squatted low and forced his way through the opening. His shield grated against the top of the narrow passage, dragging his cloak back taut against his neck and shoulders, but he kept on, struggling his way forward, mindful of the fact that Broct was entering the tunnel just behind him.

Morlac emerged within a larger cavity of stone, now faintly illumined by Kadrana's match, newly lighted and filling the humid air with sulfur stench. He looked about the tunnel, brushing himself.

"Only a swimmer would know of this place."

Kadrana ignored the question in his words. "The sea carved it out, eons ago, when there were great mountains of ice upon the land."

Morlac frowned. "How do you know this?"

'Sordros told me. He knows many things of the past and the future."

"Then perhaps he knows also if we will win for him . . . or if he will die at the hands of Drygo?"

She turned her eyes away. "A wizard may not see his own future. It is forbidden by the gods."

Morlac watched with interest as she began to light another match, the first just sputtering out. "Where does this place lead?"

"To the other side of these hills . . . well past the guard posts. If we are careful, we may come and go without a challenge. But we can not talk any longer. We must reach the city of Kem within the hour, and there is no time to waste. . . ."

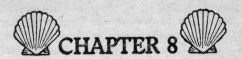 **CHAPTER 8**

The City of Kem

The great octagonal outer wall that surrounded Kem had four
gates, one in the center of every other side. These outer gates
were not guarded now, although Morlac could easily picture
them well-defended in the event of raids from the north. He,
Broct, and Kadrana stood by the side of the road, well within
the enclosure. Entering the city had been easy. Almost unbe-
lievably so.

"It seems they fear no local invaders," Morlac said softly.

Kadrana nodded, pulling her cloak closer about her. "L'Dron
Kerr's power in this region is unquestioned. None dare challenge his army, or tempt the blade of his executioner."

Broct added grimly, "Aye—none but us!"

Even at the late hour, hundreds of people were walking the
narrow cobblestone streets of Kem. Many of the shops were
open, their torches lighting the streets and their banners and
signboards adding both color and clutter overhead. From the
taverns came a rowdy din that mingled and competed with the
other sounds of the city. The stench of Kem galled Morlac's
innocent nose, so that not even the pleasanter smells of wine
and hot food could compensate. This place had a far different
smell than the homey scents of Sordros's village . . . Morlac's
village.

A group of soldiers straggled past Morlac and the others,
but the men seemed more interested in their off-duty pursuits
than in the presence of cloaked strangers walking casually
along the street. Still, it would not do to linger too long in

any one spot, Morlac realized. A passing mystery would be more quickly forgotten.

They stayed with the main streets, flowing with the movement of crowds as much as possible. And they did not have to search for their objective. It towered above the rest of the city, like an island in a sea of buildings.

L'Dron Kerr's palace, the stronghold of the North Kingdom, rose mightily above the close clutter of merchants' shops with their upper-floor living quarters. A thick wall of stone surrounded the palace, and it was obvious that the entire structure had been built upon a high point of land. It looked as if the surrounding city had developed later, with the outer enclosing wall perhaps the latest structure of all.

As they neared the base of the wall, Morlac's sharp eyes searched for some other way into the palace grounds. But for all his skillful looking, there seemed only one way—through the great armored gate in the wall's western face. And staunchly guarding that gate were half a score of Kerr's men-at-arms, resplendent in their furry jerkins and polished iron breastplates. There was no hope of entry here.

They made their way around the great fortress, until at last they were almost three-fourths of the way back to their starting point. The entire length of the wall was rimmed with a parapet, behind which patrolling men-at-arms could be glimpsed. An attempt to scale the wall would surely be doomed to failure. Morlac paused in the shadows of a darkened shop and the others drew close.

"I can see no way for us to gain entrance," he said.

"But we must!" Kadrana's tone was anxious, yet still commanding. "We dare not go back without at least gaining the information we seek!"

Morlac gestured angrily toward the wall. "Then you had best use your magic to take us through that stone!"

She glared angrily back at him. "I cannot—it is not within my power to do such an enchantment."

"Bah! I am beginning to think you have no powers, save for a few tricks Sordros has reluctantly given you."

Her eyes narrowed still more, an odd amusement flickering within them. And as her gaze focused fully on him, it carried more than mere anger.

Morlac stiffened under that gaze. Within his mind and body there echoed a feeling straight from the sorcerer's pit. A dread, consuming chill, a sense of confinement, and a pain that crept along his spine with wicked energy. It was a feeling he had almost succeeded in forgetting, and he resented having that memory reawakened now. He fought against it, not wanting to let the feeling overwhelm him—not wanting to submit to the will of this spoiled young woman. He fought, and the fire awakened within him was fueled by weeks of pent-up anger. How dare she!

Even as the pain coursed through his very limbs, a stronger force ebbed out as well, seeking and regaining control of his body. The paralysis weakened as he bent his own will against the evil energy, and although it took all his considerable strength to do it, he raised his hand and made his ironlike fingers close around the delicate neck of the young woman who aroused such conflicting emotions within him.

Kadrana gasped, as much at the realization of her waning control as at the sudden deadly pressure against her throat. Her pretty eyes opened wide and darted up as she realized that her guardian Watch-Devils were both back at the ship. There was to be no help from that quarter. Her perfect lips moved silently in a vain effort to reinforce her power with an incantation to Tritus and other sea-gods.

Morlac forced a grim smile to his straining, sweat-soaked features. "I *might* not be able to kill you before you bring down the wrath of Sordros's magic to smite me, Kadrana. I might not. Do you wish to find out—?"

She tried but a moment longer to regain control, then wavered and knew she was lost. Blinking suddenly in fresh terror, she managed to gasp out, "No—no! Release me! I will not use my power against you again."

Morlac relaxed his grip, letting his hand move up to gently cup her chin. "Not that I truly believe you, dark princess . . . but I think we would both be wise to save our talents for our true enemies."

At that moment, Broct brought finger to lips and hissed a warning. The others fell silent, looking to see what the yellow-eyed giant had spotted.

He pointed to an area half a block away, opposite the

palace wall, on the same side of the street on which they now stood. In the shadows before one of the buildings, something moved. A bent figure, carrying a basket of some sort, strode silently to the edge of the street. Pausing briefly to glance about, the figure turned the basket over, dumping its contents into the steaming gutter. Then the figure turned and headed back into the building.

Her hand still gingerly rubbing her tender throat, Kadrana shook her head impatiently. "Only a fat merchant, throwing out his garbage. You need not be concerned."

"Perhaps . . ." Broct ignored the girl and started toward the spot, his nostrils sniffing the air.

Morlac and the girl followed. They reached the spot in seconds, gazing down into the gutter.

Rats were already feasting on the bones and scraps. The frantic movements of their small, loathsome bodies made Kadrana shudder. But Broct studied the pile of scraps, its quality and its size. He looked to Morlac and Kadrana.

"Costly table-leavings, even for a fat merchant," he said at last. "More the fare of some high official. Perhaps even a king . . . ?"

Kadrana glanced over toward the lofty wall, then back to the building behind them. She frowned. "But . . . here?"

Morlac started for the door of the drab building. "Let us find out."

They gathered in the darkness as Morlac tested the door. It resisted his efforts at first, but when he brought his full weight to bear against it, the bolt on the opposite side snapped quickly, yielding entrance.

Morlac sprang in with its momentum, catching the shop's inhabitant by surprise. Facing away from him, the stooped figure made a hurried movement, then whirled.

"What . . . what are you doing?" the man blustered. "My shop is closed—get out!"

He studied them more closely, and seeing that they were not merely drunken rowdies he fell silent, easing toward the wall to his right. His hand reached out for the tassel of a thick cord that entered the wall and disappeared.

Broct, nearest him, let his sword flash out. The blade's

iron tip sliced neatly through the cord at a point above the man's reach. The dangling end fell limply to the floor.

"Who were you going to warn—?" Morlac demanded.

The shopkeeper stepped away from the wall, smiling nervously. "Warn? Why, no one . . . no one at all." He continued to back away. "Tell me, what is it you want? Gold? Wares? Food? I have very little, but you're welcome to it all, only. . . ."

His voice trailed off as he watched Morlac pace about the room, studying everything. The hood of Morlac's cloak had fallen back, and even in the dim candlelight, the shopkeeper could tell that the tall intruder was different from the usual cutthroats and mercenaries of the North Kingdom. His features were too exotic . . . his complexion an almost emerald pallor.

"What manner of man are you?" the shopkeeper said softly. "Be you a sailor from far-off Corsenthos?"

"A seaman," Kadrana said with wicked amusement, "but not a sailor."

Morlac ignored her taunting remark and continued to probe the room. He moved slowly to the spot where the shopkeeper had been standing when they had first burst into the room. What had the man been doing then . . . ?

Looking down, his attention was caught by a wrinkle in the dusty rug beneath his feet. One corner of the coarsely woven fabric was pulled back slightly. It might only have been kicked up in the shopkeeper's hasty turn, and yet, in the corner of his eye, Morlac thought he saw the man tense as he inspected the rug.

"Let us see what dirt has been swept under here—" Morlac said suddenly, reaching for the rug's corner.

Instantly, the shopkeeper lost his timidity. Lunging for Morlac, the glint of a small blade flashed suddenly in his hand.

Morlac was ready, but even before the dirk could be brought down toward his heart, Broct had acted, striking the man's head with the rounded pommel of his sword. The man fell senseless into a crumpled heap. Kadrana stood regally above him, glaring down at the fallen form.

"Kill him!"

"We need only bind and gag him," Morlac said flatly. He let Broct attend to that matter while he himself began to pull away the rug that covered nearly a third of the floor. When he had finished, the thin outline of a rectangular panel was revealed in the wooden surface.

"This may be what we seek." Morlac tried to pry up the panel. "*Someone* has been here this night. There are four cups on the table, some with traces of wine still in them. And I do not think whoever was here left by means of the front door."

"Drygo and his generals?" Kadrana wondered aloud, her eyes gauging the distance from the shop's trapdoor to the palace wall across the road. "Perhaps, if they were to dine here, and then enter the palace secretly. I have heard L'Dron Kerr fears the spies of the South Kingdom. Spies who might well watch the gate's comings and goings. But can this be a way into the palace?"

"There's but one way we can know."

Broct moved quickly to the panel to assist, squatting down opposite Morlac. First one pair of strong hands, then another, reached out to aid in prying up the solid-oak trapdoor. It resisted for a long moment, then abruptly wrenched free with a metallic snap.

Morlac examined the underside of the panel as he set it aside. The remnants of iron rods still clung to it.

"No wonder," Morlac said, sweating after the effort. "It had latches on the other side."

"Aye." Broct smiled. "It *had*."

Morlac grabbed a lamp from the table and held it over the opening in the floor. The flickering light spilled down, revealing a shaft walled with more heavy oak, opening into a tunnel. A wooden ladder gave access, and appeared to be unguarded.

He started cautiously down the ladder, glancing over his shoulder as he descended to beckon the others after him. He stopped abruptly as he caught sight of the bound form of the shopkeeper. The man's throat was turning crimson. And Kadrana was silently returning her small and evil dagger to its hidden sheath.

The sorcerer's daughter saw the disgust in Morlac's withering gaze. Eyes narrowing contemptuously, she said, "He saw you too well to live. L'Dron Kerr, and especially his mercenary, Drygo, must not learn of your existence. Not yet."

Not even acknowledging her explanation, Morlac continued on down into the shaft. Broct and the girl followed, and the three made their way along the tunnel that had no other direction but toward the palace.

The air in the tunnel was chill and stale, and the only light was the meager amount the small lamp provided. Morlac could only guess at the tunnel's ultimate point of exit, but there was little doubt that they should emerge somewhere within the palace grounds. What bothered Morlac most about this assumption was the fact that the passage seemed unguarded.

After continuing straight for a considerable distance, the oak-paneled tunnel now took a sharp turn and began to incline upward, through the very rock that underlay the rise upon which L'Dron Kerr's palace had been built. Morlac slowed his pace, motioning for absolute silence from the others.

Another bend in the passage came swiftly. And still there was no sign of danger ahead. So why the strange tingling along his spine, Morlac wondered. Was it a warning voice from his old animal instincts, or his newly acquired human ones?

Suddenly the lamp's yellow flame wavered and ebbed, leaning away from them as if stirred by a dark breeze. Even before Kadrana's gasp, Morlac and Broct were whirling to face the threat behind them. Yet still a moment too late!

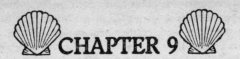

CHAPTER 9

Capture!

Sharp sword points wavered before their eyes, then lowered to menace their vulnerable throats. Four palace guards stood a mere sword's length away, their sudden appearance behind them explained by an open panel in the passage wall. The "empty" corridor was not as simple as it had looked.

Morlac was prepared to fight it out. His hand rested on his magicked sword. Its hilt throbbed in his fingers, aching to be free of its scabbard and eager to do its bloody work. Yet both he and Broct delayed, for the cold iron which pricked at their necks spoke more eloquently than any verbal warnings.

Morlac reluctantly released his grip, bringing his hands away from his sides. From the corner of his eye he could see that Broct was following suit—the yellow-eyed giant was also yielding to the guards, for the time being at least. Kadrana hovered near them, her lips parted in surprise and her imperious look tempered by a trace of fear. Morlac wondered why Sordros's daughter did not apply her wondrous talents to combat the guards, or for that matter, why Broct had not used the special ring the wizard had given him. Perhaps the quarters were too close for magical tactics.

"South Kingdom spies, I'll wager," said one of the guards.

"A safe bet," said another. "And if they are, you can bet the king will have their heads on pikes by the morrow. On the city's *South* gate, of course."

The guard laughed coarsely at his own joke, and Morlac found himself annoyed by the man's overconfidence. Morlac's lamp was still in his hand, and he held it low and slightly behind him, so that its light illuminated the guards without revealing his own features. These men in the passage were garbed the same as those posted at the front gate. And they, like the others, looked more than fit enough to back up their threats.

"If these be spies," the third guard said, "the king will want to see them right away."

The first man fumbled at his belt with his free hand and brought forth a set of chains with thick wristlets dangling. "Yes, but not without these."

They were shackles of hammered iron, roughly made, but no less effective in their function. With the three other guards still ready to mete out instant death should resistance be met, there was no other choice but to accept them.

The bonds chafed at Morlac's wrists, and more still at his dignity. First Sordros, and now these new strangers, had held him captive. Raw outrage welled up within him, barely contained by the logic which told him to bide his time and play along.

The guard went to Broct next. "Extend your hands!"

Broct hesitated for a moment, then stoically submitted as a set of hands came out from under his curiously cut and bulky cloak. As the manacles were put in place, he glanced toward Morlac. A brief and wicked smile flashed across his features, but he said nothing.

Morlac saw that look and knew what the giant was thinking. He looked toward Kadrana, to see if she too knew what to expect. But the girl was totally consumed with barely repressed anger at being bound. Imperial self-righteousness and scorn flashed from her eyes like the gods' own lightning.

As the guard snapped the shackles around Kadrana's wrists he studied her more closely in the lamplight. "The king will want to question *this* one at length, I'll wager."

"So might we all," said the first guard, with an admiring look. Then he sighed, and gave Morlac a rough shove along the passage to get him started. "But, if we fail to bring these vermin to the quick attention of the king, 'twill be *our* heads decorating the South gate."

The passage continued to incline as they made their way forward, then turned sharply back upon itself as it rose toward the palace of L'Dron Kerr. Lamps now burned at regular intervals, and a second guard post was passed, from which men were dispatched to replace those who had quit the first post.

Morlac viewed it all with an appraising eye, storing the knowledge away should he need it. He did not relish the prospect of fighting his way free of L'Dron Kerr's well-guarded fortress, but if that was their only way out, then he was determined to be prepared. Learning what he could of the guard's procedures and the castle layout might help.

At last, they were brought to a heavy oaken door which gave them entrance to the palace itself. A long corridor framed in stone loomed before them, musty and deserted. Ill-lighted and lonely for guards, it seemed the perfect place to make use of their secret advantage.

Morlac caught Broct's questioning gaze and winked a signal. The yellow-eyed giant nodded slightly in acknowledgment, agreeing that the time was right.

One of the guards was leading the way, while the remaining three each followed closely behind their respective prisoners. Broct could feel the nearness of his own guard's blade at his back. Working carefully, he brought his second set of hands up behind him until they rested immediately below the spot where the guard's sword occasionally pricked his cloak. Picking a moment when the other guards' attention was not on him, he half-halted, allowing the guard's momentum to force the sword point within his grasp. Instantly, his strong fingers seized the cloth-wrapped blade and held it immobile.

"Argh!" Broct bellowed in mock pain. "I am stabbed!"

The guard behind him looked incredulous for a moment, then tried to free his sword. To the man attending Kadrana, it appeared that he was merely tormenting Broct further.

"What are you doing?" he shouted. "Their fates are not ours to decide!"

"I've done nothing," the man said defensively. "It is a trick! See—he holds my blade beneath his cloak."

"Are you crazy? His hands are still before him, and still shackled!"

Broct chose that moment to turn loose the sword tip and

sag, moaning as if mortally wounded. He staggered a few steps to the wall, leaning back against it for support.

"Let me see those chains!" His guard approached, surprise turning to anger. "If this be not trickery, then I—"

His words ceased abruptly as he tugged at the shackles, for one of Broct's free hands darted from beneath his cloak and closed about the guard's throat, constricting his windpipe. Another hand relieved him of his sword while yet another was picking the ring of keys from his belt.

"What's wrong?" Kadrana's guard pushed her roughly aside and started toward them, as did the leader of the group. He stumbled back in the next instant as Broct tossed the unconscious man into him.

Seeing his own guard's attention diverted, Morlac kicked powerfully at the man's midsection, sending him slamming into the wall. Morlac leaped toward him, knowing full well he would have to subdue the man before he regained his feet and made use of his sword.

Broct had his own battle. The leader of the guard patrol was nearly upon him, and the second man would join him as soon as he freed himself from the weight of the unconscious guard.

The leader held his sword raised high in both hands, ready to split the skull of the yellow-eyed giant. "This time the wound shall be real!"

As the sword crashed down, Broct thrust out his shackled hands, letting the chain stop the downward chop of the blade. The iron links nearly yielded to the impact, but held, with the sword's sharp edge being checked mere inches from his bald head. At the next moment, Broct's other hands were grabbing the man, raising him above his head and throwing him directly at his second attacker, where he died on the blade of his own countryman.

As the last man struggled to free his sword, Broct knocked him senseless with the back of a clenched fist. He looked to Morlac, ready to aid his friend if aid be needed. But he saw that Morlac's guard too was now unconscious upon the floor.

Hurrying over, Broct worked the borrowed keys on Morlac's shackles until he found the one that freed him. He freed his own wrists next, applying the bonds in turn to two of the unconscious men. The third was tied with a length of sash taken from the man's own uniform.

"We'll leave them in that alcove," Morlac said, dragging two of the men to a niche they had passed in one of the darker sections of wall. He stood aside as Broct shoved the other two out of view.

Kadrana strode haughtily toward them, finding her voice now that the danger was momentarily past. She held out her wrists, the chain taut between them.

"Remove these at once!" she demanded. "There is little time left."

For the moment, Morlac ignored her. To Broct he said, "We must find Kerr and his war council, and learn his plans. But it will not be easy. The place must be crawling with guards."

"There's no time for trial and error," Broct replied. "We must take a hostage . . . force him to tell us where Kerr may be found."

"No!" protested Kadrana. "Such a clumsy method would be doomed to failure."

"Have you a better idea?" Broct said.

The girl produced a small vial of amber fluid from a hidden pocket and held it out. "Here—use this. The last man you bound is near enough consciousness to be of use. Pour the contents of the vial in his mouth, beneath his tongue. In a moment, he will be under our control."

Morlac took the potion offered him, examining it skeptically. "I dislike the tools of sorcery. Besides, your magic seems to work only on those things already under the spell of Sordros."

"Don't be a fool, Morlac. It's not magic, it's mere chemistry. Use the drug now, quickly! And remove my shackles!"

Morlac considered but a moment longer, then uncapped the tiny vial and let its amber contents flow into the guard's mouth as the girl had directed. For many seconds there was no visible reaction, and Morlac began to wonder if he had been right about Kadrana's limited powers. But then gradually the man's eyes opened, staring up dully, expressionless and void.

"There—you see?" Kadrana said softly, defiance tinging

each word. "It is as I said. He will tell us what we need to know now. Unshackle me at once!"

Morlac got the man to his feet, still watching for some sign of returning awareness—awareness that could result in a shouted warning to others. But the man seemed totally passive. Glancing back at Kadrana's bound wrists, Morlac's eyes narrowed slightly, one devil-brow arching up in thought.

"Telling us the information will still not get us past the other guards," he said. "No—I have a better plan. And if you will forgive me, my princess, your captivity is part of it. Let's go!"

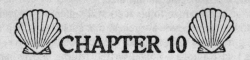

CHAPTER 10

The King's Chamber

The drugged guard's hands were unbound for the sake of appearances, and the man was directed to escort them to a place where they could observe L'Dron Kerr's meeting with his military leaders. Morlac and Broct straightened their cloaks about them as they marched behind him, flanking the girl they now appeared to hold prisoner. It took no acting on Kadrana's part to appear the hostile captive.

As they made their way boldly through the interior corridors of the palace, Morlac's plan seemed to be working. The presence of their escort and the sight of Kadrana in bonds gained them passage into the very heart of Kerr's stronghold. The posted guardsmen passed them with no more than a brief nod to their escort, and even the palace servants showed only the mildest curiosity.

Morlac kept the hood of his cloak over his head, with his features in shadow. Without appearing to, his ever-alert eyes sought out every detail of the palace that came within his view. He found the differences between Kerr's palace and the castle of Sordros striking. Besides the more conventional construction of stone and timber, Kerr's domain displayed far more evidence of wealth—wealth taxed from the local citizenry, and plundered from now-defeated neighbors.

Rich tapestries decorated the cold stone walls, with statuary fashioned by Kem's finest artisans filling the gaps between them. And as they neared the center of the palace the gaps between the objects became fewer and fewer, until at last the place lost all semblance of tasteful design and resembled nothing more than a rich thief's warehouse.

Morlac had never before seen anything like it, even in that part of his memory that was so strangely human. Fascination mingled with disgust in his mind. For all of Sordros's evil, at least the sea magician had not surrounded himself with treasure and stolen baubles. And now Kerr planned a new conquest. There would not be much in a humble fishing village to add to the king's collection.

Their ease of passage ended abruptly as they reached their destination—one of the king's several private chambers. A burly guard stood posted there, as much for effect as for security. But the sword at his belt and the pike standing upright in his grip were more than mere decorations.

Blocking the chamber door, the guard said, "What business have you here?"

The drugged man escorting them did not speak, and Morlac was quick to fill the silence. "We are emissaries from a distant land menaced by the treachery of the South Kingdom. We bring news for the great L'Dron Kerr's ears alone." Morlac tugged an unwilling Kadrana into view. "And we bring a gift."

His eyes coolly appraising the girl, the guard said, "The King attends to other matters now, and cannot receive you. Perhaps if you return a few hours hence—"

"Return? Return from where?" Morlac said quickly. "We have journeyed here in greatest secrecy. Would you have us while away our time in the taverns of Kem, where the loose tongues of wine-sotted soldiers can spread word of our presence? Or perhaps in the streets, where even the beggars may be South Kingdom spies? And with a treasure we have already defended more than once with our lives." He felt Kadrana squirming within his strong grip, but kept his intent gaze upon the guard. "Or do you place such little value upon your king's possessions—?"

The guard listened to Morlac's words . . . knowing words, ringing with arrogance and authority. He paused, uncertain and hesitant, seeking a solution that would appease his conflicting senses of duty.

"Shall we stand out here in the hall like palace servants?"

Morlac prodded further. sensing the guard's failing resistance. "Surely we may w_ut in this outer chamber. If you fear we'll steal something," he added contemptuously, "then let our escort remain to watch us."

The guard's eyes went to the man with a questioning look. Unobserved, Morlac applied pressure to their drugged escort's arm.

"I will watch them," the man said, a certain flatness to his voice that Morlac hoped would go unnoticed.

Hesitating a moment longer, the guard studied the other man's face, then finally nodded. He opened the chamber's door and stepped out of their way. As they entered, he said, "I will let you know when—and *if*—the king will see you." And then he closed the heavy door behind them.

Once well inside the chamber, Broct rolled his eyes, breathing out a heavy sigh of relief. He sheathed the dirk he had held ready in one of his hidden hands all the while they conversed with the guard.

Morlac, with some reluctance, unshackled Kadrana's wrists. He looked up, to find her eyes smiling with wicked amusement.

"A very good story, my Captain," the girl said softly as she straightened the collar of his jerkin. "It seems that in addition to your other skills, you have also learned the arts of deceit and cunning."

Morlac replaced the shackles on the drugged man. "Not so well as you, dark princess." Ignoring the flash of anger in her sea-green eyes, he now hurried to the wall which separated them from the adjacent chamber.

Placing an ear to the oaken panel, he strained to make out sounds in the next room. After several long moments, he turned away.

"I can hear nothing," he said, keeping his voice low. He turned to the drugged man with growing impatience. "I said you were to lead us to a place where we might observe L'Dron Kerr and his war council. Did you not understand?"

The man remained silent but walked to the wall opposite the door. He paused before the drawn curtains, then thrust a hand into the draperies and pulled them aside.

Morlac joined him, peering cautiously through the opening. Beyond the chamber in which they now stood was another, vastly larger, the floor of which was a good twenty feet below them. As he gazed down into the chamber, Morlac saw that the place was fit for all manner of royal ceremonies. A gilded throne stood at the far end on a lavishly decorated dais. Huge tapestries depicting the glories of the North Kingdom were hung along the side wall, and long heavy curtains were draped along the end walls, parted in graceful arcs over doorways.

All these cloaked the stone and timber of the palace, making it resemble a rough man attempting to hide his coarseness with fine garments, and not quite succeeding.

The great hall was deserted and only a few lamps were burning to light it. Not even servants remained now.

Still wary, Morlac eased out onto the balcony which looked down over the great hall. More curtains were draped in long arcs along the low balustrade, fastened with heavy cord. Looking to his left, Morlac saw that the balcony extended nearly the length of the hall, and that two other chambers opened onto it. The curtains of both were drawn, but light shone around the edges of the second doorway.

Motioning for Broct and Kadrana to follow, Morlac crept silently along the balcony until he reached the doorway where light emanated. Staying low, he peered through the narrow gap between the curtains.

The chamber beyond was not unlike the first, through which they had gained access to the balcony. It too seemed to be a secondary room, with the king's private quarters apparently between the two. Easily a dozen men were gathered in this far chamber, ranging around a low table, the upper surface of which bore a painted map delineating all of Shola. Iron markers representing companies of soldiers were scattered around the boundaries of the North Kingdom, with an especially heavy concentration at the southernmost edge, nearest Sordros's domain. All eyes in the room were on the map as the man at the head of the table pointed a regal finger toward the southwest coast of Shola.

"Whatever the cost," L'Dron Kerr was saying, "you must purge Shola of the taint of wizardry once and for all. I can no longer tolerate that South Kingdom collaborator, Sordros. His presence is an encroachment upon the Realm."

Kerr was a great bear of a man, a warrior once removed, with little more than his throne's authority to distinguish him from the soldiers to whom he spoke. His beard and curly mass of hair were striking red, his head virtually aflame with the color. A black leather band circled his head above his brow, a bright golden disc at its center. Covering his torso was a fur jerkin similar to those of his guards, but beneath it a lustrous garment of finely woven fabric. His dark eyes displayed the directness and confidence of a man long accustomed to unquestioned authority.

"The cost thus far has been great, sire," the officer nearest him reminded. "Seven of our galleys and their crews, one company of foot soldiers, and farm land poisoned beyond use."

Kerr regarded him severely. "In the past—but no more! Our men know now to take his powers seriously. Besides, this time we have the aid of a man who has already bested Sordros once."

The officer let his gaze drift across the table, to the hulking man standing at the king's left side. He remained silent, but viewed Drygo with a loyal soldier's contempt for mercenaries.

"What say you, Drygo—" Kerr asked "—are you certain of your plan? Can you destroy this enemy?"

"It is as good as done," the one called Drygo boasted, in a raspy and guttural tone. "The wizard has before used the sea to his advantage. He taps it, draws his power from it. That is why your ships had no chance against Sordros. Even your foot soldiers strayed too close to the sea in their assault."

Morlac studied the man whom Sordros had sworn him to kill, should the chance present itself. Drygo was a big man, as tall and broad-shouldered as the king himself. But there the resemblance ended. Ardo had described Drygo as a dog of a man, but Morlac had not yet seen a dog so ugly. His small eyes were set flatly in a face that was knotted and oily. The muscular build was becoming blubbery from overindulgence and easy victories. He looked less like a warrior than a vile grave robber.

Morlac considered an attack only briefly. They were hopelessly outnumbered. A chance at Drygo might come later, but for now the best course was merely to remain quiet and observe.

"Our past plans may not have worked," L'Dron Kerr said somewhat defensively, "but they were chosen because they were direct and offered the best chance of victory."

"Aye, Your Majesty," Drygo replied. "That they would. Against anyone but a sea wizard. That is why I intend to lead your forces through the valley to the northeast of Sordros's castle."

"A long distance of open fields and little cover," Kerr said. "That route may cost you dearly."

"Against a true army, it would. But all Sordros can call to arms are fisherfolk and farmers. And when they see that their wizard cannot aid them, even they shall flee before us."

Kerr considered. Then after a long moment he said, "When may you begin?"

"I can be back at the forward outpost in two days. Give me a day more to launch the invasion."

"Three days it is, then. And if you succeed, you shall have all the gold you've been promised—"

Kerr's words ended abruptly as a sudden outcry came from beyond the chamber. He and the others leaped to their feet even before they could know the nature of the warning shout.

On the balcony, Morlac's eye left the narrow gap in the curtains. He whirled and faced the source of the outcry. At the far end of the balcony, emerging from the first chamber, came the guard who had admitted them only moments before. The man was followed by a handful of other palace guards, their swords drawn as they advanced.

At that moment, one of Kerr's officers appeared within the doorway of the king's council chamber, thrusting a sword out as he threw the curtain open. "Spies!" the man shouted. "Take them!"

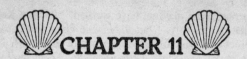# CHAPTER 11

Escape!

Morlac fell back as he dodged the officer's probing blade, then regained his balance. He pushed Broct and Kadrana toward the door of the middle chamber, hoping escape might lie in that direction, but with even their first few steps they could see that the advancing guards had shut off their last avenue of flight.

Broct already had his sword and dirk out, ready for the fight. But even the yellow-eyed giant knew it would be a brief fight at best against the number they now were facing.

Morlac knew it as well, and had other plans. "Broct! Your ring! If ever there was a time for it—"

The giant hesitated only a split second, then the free hand which bore the magicked ring thrust out from beneath his cloak. There was a momentary glint of reflection upon its obsidian stone, then even that dull gleam was lost as a wave of darkness flooded out to engulf the balcony in inky blackness.

Even as the guards encountered the stygian cloud, Broct had whirled and unleashed a second dark wave at the chamber where Kerr and his officers prepared for battle. They too were enveloped in the murk, momentarily shut off from all vision.

"Quickly!" Morlac commanded, his hands on the balcony rail. "This way!"

Broct swung over the side immediately, lowering himself the full reach of his arms before releasing his hold. Kadrana watched him land heavily on the floor of the hall below, then seeing the distance with fear-widened eyes, she balked at Morlac's order.

"No—I cannot!" she wailed.

From the corner of his eye Morlac saw one of the palace guards emerging from the black cloud. "We've no time to argue!"

Grabbing Kadrana roughly around the waist, Morlac pulled her over the railing. Seizing one end of the heavy drapery that looped along the balustrade, he tore it free and twisted it about his hand. Then in the next instant he leaped free of the balcony with his squirming burden.

Kadrana screamed as they dropped, then the heavy drapery gave resistance and swung them in a descending arc that slowed their fall. A moment later Morlac released his hold on the fabric and they landed lightly on the floor a short distance ahead of Broct.

The three ran for the doors of the great hall, literally racing for their lives. Behind them, shouts from Kerr's officers were rising in intensity. It could not be long before the guards reached the floor and gave pursuit.

Morlac wondered if there were guards posted outside the hall's twin doors. He would have to assume there were.

With a signal to Broct, Morlac ran straight at the door on the left, throwing his full weight against it. Broct did likewise with the door on the right. With a shuddering crack both portals broke free of their decorative hinges and came crashing forward.

Startled cries came forth as the flattened doors rocked unevenly on the guards pinned beneath them. Morlac gained his feet, then reached back for Kadrana and tugged her past the obstacle.

"Hurry!" Morlac urged. "There will be more guards soon enough."

"Aye!" Broct confirmed. "Let us hope it be easier to break *out* of this place than to break in!"

On they ran through the main corridor, the echoes of their footfalls mingling with the sound of guards converging from other parts of the palace. Cloaks fluttering behind them, they searched for the main entry hall and a way out.

Bursting through yet another set of doors, they at last reached the antichamber. Two surprised guards snapped to attention, but before they could fully recognize the intruders for what they were and reach for weapons, they were promptly flattened by Morlac and Broct, who straight-armed them without ever slowing down.

Morlac moved directly for the heavy double doors that led outside. Straining as he hefted the thick beam bolting the doors, he freed the bar and tossed it aside.

"Stay behind us," he cautioned Kadrana. "But not too far behind!"

Opening the door slowly, Morlac peered outside into the open courtyard. The light of wall-mounted torches revealed a wide flight of stone steps, at the bottom of which were posted two more guardsmen. Far beyond them was the gate and between it and the palace a number of guards on walking posts could be seen. A short distance from the open gate a trader's wagon was parked, its enclosed sides covered with dust from its journey. But what interested Morlac most about this was the fact that two horse soldiers had dismounted to speak to the trader. Their steeds were carelessly accessible, if only they could be reached in time.

All this Morlac saw in a moment, and they had little more than moments now as the sound of approaching guards from within the palace became more audible. Swinging one of the doors open wide, Morlac motioned the others out, turned and saluted a nonexistent officer. He then led Broct and Kadrana boldly down the steps at a pace slow enough to quell suspicion.

They passed the guards at the bottom of the steps and continued on into the shadows. Water gurgled in drains at the base of the huge palace, sending plumes of steam rising into the chill night air of Kem. Torchlight illuminated parts of the great courtyard, including the area where the trader's wagon stood waiting. But much of the open area lay in shadow, and Morlac made full use of the darkness.

Suddenly from behind them guards burst from the palace, shouting commands, bellowing their rage. They did not yet see the intruders and for a moment there was naught but confusion in their actions.

Morlac and the others now hurried for the trader's wagon. Broct reached the illuminated area first, exploding into the light. He held his sword ready, but concealed beneath his cloak.

"Madmen in the palace!" he yelled wide-eyed at the startled guards by the wagon. "Bloody corpses everywhere! The king's very life is in danger!"

The guards exchanged alarmed looks, then, trained soldiers that they were, they started toward the palace, wresting their swords from their sheaths as they ran. Ahead of them, the confused milling of guards seemed to confirm Broct's statement.

As they faded into distant shadow, Morlac and Broct mounted the abandoned horses. Pulling Kadrana up behind him, Morlac glanced back at the wagon, expecting trouble. Perched upon the bench seat, half-obscured in shadow, the trader regarded them with unexpected calm. Beneath the man's turbaned brow were features somber and contemplative. His keen eyes seemed to bore through Morlac, but he made no attempt to alert the guards to their thievery. Puzzling, but a puzzle not to be dwelled upon for long.

Wheeling the horses around, Morlac and Broct started for the gate. The massive armored panels were just beginning to swing closed as the men stationed at them became aware of the commotion at the palace. In seconds, escape would be barred.

Bringing their horses to a gallop, they rode directly for the opening. Already, the soldiers at the gate heard their approach and looked around. But with the light behind them Morlac, Broct, and Kadrana were mere silhouettes on horseback, apparently coming from the palace. The guards hesitated, and that fraction of a second made the difference.

Broct thrust out his obsidian ring, casting a wave of darkness before them, enveloping the gate and the men who stood by it. The cloud blackened the area so totally that even Morlac and Broct could not see as they rode into it at full speed. Yet they kept their stolen mounts plunging headlong for the opening where last they had seen it.

Providence and their own good aim prevented a collision with the gates, and in a moment they exploded from the light-hungry cloud on the other side of the palace's high walls. Frightened townspeople scattered before them as they drove their horses on. And from behind came the blare of trumpets . . . the sharp reverberations of war gongs . . .

alerting all within hearing distance. It sounded like a full-scale invasion. The citizens of Kem would get little sleep tonight.

Something about the strident notes of the war gongs sent a chill along Morlac's spine. And yet that sound was not quite so chilling as the next that issued from the fortress they were leaving behind—the dull thunder of a full company of mounted soldiers.

Morlac turned down a side street crowded with merchants' stalls, then found another parallel avenue leading out of the city of Kem. He did not think the pursuers had them in sight yet, and the tactic might gain them a few moments more.

As they reached the outer wall, all of Kem seemed to be stirring, aroused to near panic by the strident peal of the gongs. They made the gate in the next moment and started down the road to the sea. The sound of horsemen still came from somewhere behind them, and it was a sound that seemed to grow louder.

Morlac and Broct drove their horses on at a killing speed, heedless of the dangers of a rough road in darkness. Kadrana clung behind Morlac with a desperate strength, whispering curses, her cheek close against his back as her eyes cast a fearful glance behind them. And she knew that ahead, separating them from the beach where they had come ashore, would be the coastal sentinels.

There was no time now for the circuitous route they had used before to avoid the patrol's attention. They must drive straight for the sea . . . straight into an armed camp.

Long minutes passed before the first torches of the sentinel post came into view. They flickered and guttered in the coastal sea breeze, a breeze that bore the familiar tang of salt spray, and beckoned to Morlac with an old, instinctive call. Danger lay ahead, and behind. Morlac looked over his shoulder. He could not see the pursuing horsemen in the moonless landscape, but he could hear the now less distant rumble of hooves as they steadfastly closed the gap. And if *he* could hear them. . . .

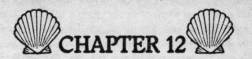 CHAPTER 12

The Sword Unsheathed

Startled shouts and a flurry of activity greeted them as they crashed headlong into the camp's midst. Sentinels long used to uneventful nights now deserted the warmth of their fires to take up weapons. The momentary confusion was all that allowed the intruders to penetrate as far as they did.

Morlac was out in front, becoming the first target for a soldier running toward them with a pike. At the last moment, Morlac turned his mount a fraction of a degree to the right, letting the iron-tipped pike slide past his arm. He kicked out with his left foot and caught the man's head with bone-crunching impact.

The beach was in sight now, and just beyond the high rocks to the south the *Flying Fish* was waiting in its hidden cove. If only they could reach it in time! Morlac looked quickly to be sure Broct was keeping pace, then he drove his horse onward.

Suddenly, disaster struck. Morlac's exhausted steed had reached the limit of the shore's hard ground and started out across the beach. Its hooves bogging down in loose sand, the animal stumbled, crashing heavily to the ground. Morlac and Kadrana tumbled from its back and rolled over and over with the momentum of the horse's full gallop. They stopped in a heap upon the sand, some of the impact softened by the ground's yielding surface.

Morlac quickly freed himself from the weight of the girl sprawled across his legs and regained his feet. His cloak entangled him, twisted around as it now was, and he ripped the bulky garment from his shoulders. A glance told him that Broct had dismounted. They could now make better time on foot. But rushing at them were the camp's soldiers, over three dozen men. There were too many, too far apart, for even the magic of Broct's ring to ensure escape.

Swinging his odd oval shield off his shoulders, Morlac pulled Kadrana to her feet and got her well behind him. This time there was no choice—the fight was upon them.

Almost reluctantly, Morlac pulled his sword free of its hidebound scabbard. It was the first time he had done so with the swordbelt fastened about him . . . the first time in battle. He had a dread feeling it would not be the last. The blade seemed to breathe a welcome, awakening sigh. Its hilt throbbed in his grip like a repulsive living thing. The blanched whiteness of the blade revealed in the torches' glow was hideous and unreal. Without any effort the blade tip circled slowly in front of him, swimming through empty air, waiting for its prey.

That prey was not long in coming. Two of the sentinels at the head of the group came for him, brandishing the hard steel weapons of Kerr's North Kingdom, faces alight with the confidence of an easy kill. It was a mistake they would not live to repeat.

The first man, stocky and well-muscled, came at Morlac swiftly, his blade flashing down with impudence. Morlac ducked low, raising his shield above his head to deflect the blow. At the corner of his vision he saw the second man approaching from his left, sword ready for a strike at his unprotected back.

Anger seethed within him. Morlac had not desired a fight with these men, any more than he had desired to become a magicked tool of Sordros. In either case, though, the choice was not his.

Raw anger exploding through him, he thrust mightily upward from his crouched position, swinging his shield up and around in a powerful arc that knocked the first attacker backward and then came around in time to block the second man's slash. For a moment, the spell of the conjured sword consumed him, its will becoming his. The ivory blade thrust out with demonic swiftness, darting past the sentinel's oblong shield and polished breastplate to taste unguarded flesh.

The man staggered back, blood gushing from the wound, his only sound a dying gasp. But even as he fell, the other sentinel was renewing his own attack. And close behind him were yet more of the camp's soldiers.

Not far from him, Broct had his own battle joined. Working with shield and sword he kept three attackers at bay. A third hand lurking at the edge of his cloak held a dirk, waiting for the first man unwary enough to press in too close.

Morlac and Broct slowly worked their way toward water's edge, leaving a bloody path behind them. Kadrana followed close at their heels, dodging the fray about her with an agility born of sheer terror.

In mere minutes, more than half the camp's soldiers were dead or injured beyond the ability to fight, yet the rest still fought. Even Morlac's powerful arms, inhumanly strong, were beginning to tire from defending himself against the onslaught of Kerr's men. Broct had already changed his sword to an untired arm, yet he too was wearying.

The remaining soldiers were massing now for a direct attack. And on the road, their horses at full gallop, fresh troops from the capital were drawing near.

Morlac gathered Kadrana in his arms and yelled at the yellow-eyed giant. "*Broct*—if we don't reach the ship now—!"

His friend understood. The remaining guards were a close group now, and within easy range of his conjured device. A black ray flashed out from his obsidian ring, enveloping the soldiers in a murky cloud that grew out of nowhere, darkening, thickening, completely obscuring them from sight. In the next instant, Broct turned and ran, close at the heels of his ally.

They did not look back. From the sound of their horses, the approaching troops slowed somewhat, apparently confused by the stygian darkness that had momentarily fallen upon the camp. Excited shouts broke forth from the cloud as the coastal sentinels frantically identified themselves, lest in the murk they might be mistaken for the enemy.

Morlac was grateful for the pandemonium . . . grateful that it continued even as they reached the *Flying Fish* and hastily boarded it. As had been ordered, the other sea-warriors had not quit their posts or given away the ship's position, even as the battle raged. Now they swiftly cut the lines that held them in the cove. "Man the oars—get us into clear water," Morlac commanded in low tones.

Watching at the ship's stern for movement on the beach, Morlac stood grimly waiting as the men rowed the ship out from shore. The cloud of darkness would surely have dispersed by now, and the sentinels would be searching for them. He prepared to sheath his sword, picking up a rag from the deck to wipe the gore from his blade. Then in astonishment he saw that the end of his sword was no longer red. The ivory blade was now clean, the only vestige of battle a faint pinkish tinge that faded even as he watched, drawing into the very substance of the sword.

He barely repressed a shudder, remembering the unnatural ferocity which had ebbed up from the sword hilt to engulf him. He glanced up into Broct's own serious gaze.

"There can only be one name for such a beast as this," Morlac said. "I know it from the sea. . . ."

"Aye," Broct said grimly. "*Shark*."

On shore, a torch was thrust around the extending rock of the cove they had just left. The soldier who held it peered into the darkness, eyes searching. Then his head abruptly stopped turning, and Morlac could tell from his torchlit features that the man had seen the dull glimmer of the ship's wake.

"Kadrana—" Morlac called out, turning to the center of the craft. But the girl had already removed the cover from the huge black pearl which stood poised in its clawed support.

She stood behind the mystic gem, fingers so close to it they seemed to caress its glistening surface. Her eyes squeezed tight in concentration, her lips moved quickly in urgent whispering.

Morlac saw that in her haste she had neglected to have the sail raised into position. Hurrying back to the winch, he began to hoist the sail even as the others continued their rowing. The green fabric had barely reached its topmost limit when Kadrana's conjure wind breathed life into its folds.

With a slight lurch the craft broke free of the sea's cold grip and began to rise, dripping, into the ebon sky. Morlac ordered the oars secured and strode toward the prow as the *Flying Fish* turned and nosed southward. Once on their way, it would not take long to reach home.

Home? The word burned in Morlac's mind. The village ruled by Sordros *was* clearly home to that part of his mind that was human, and the very thought brought more memories flooding back. Yet the sea was also home to him, the single constant source of life, the rhythm and flow of his existence since that first hatchling moment upon a sun-warmed beach. Would he always feel this split, this tug in both directions? He wondered. And wondered too at the complexity of this new mind that could ponder such things.

On the shore, shouted orders were now being issued by the coastal sentinels that remained, and the palace troops that had joined them. Whatever their other weaknesses might have been, they did at least know how to deal with enemy ships. Their officer commanded several of his men to take up bows. Long arrows were kept ready by the fire, and now their straw-wrapped tips were ignited. To fight an enemy, that enemy must first be seen.

Fitting shafts to bows, the soldiers launched their missiles into the air on a high arc. The purpose of the flares was to reveal the intruding ship's position in the water, and although the first three of the flaming shafts were fired too far south of the *Flying Fish,* the fourth fulfilled its purpose in an unexpected way.

Arcing high in the air, the arrow struck a corner of the mystic craft's broad green sail. Before it could be reached, the burning shaft spread its flame up along the sail's entire vertical edge. In a moment, the whole of the flying ship was revealed in the bright yellow glow.

On the shore, L'Dron Kerr's men stared wide-eyed, shouting oaths, momentarily awed by the sight of the ship suspended above the sea's dark waters. The sentinels' officer overcame his superstitious fears first, hurrying to the arbalest that was positioned at the edge of the camp.

Struggling to aim the large, wheeled weapon, he shouted for assistance. "Here! Quickly! That blasted ship may be foul magic, but by Tritus if it can *burn,* then it can be destroyed!"

Breaking free from the fear that gripped them, first one, and then more of the soldiers came to the arbalest to aid in its operation. They turned it to face a point ahead of the airborne ship's path, cranking back the massive bow that powered it.

Two men raised a large stone into place, then waited for the command to fire.

The arbalest was placed to be effective against ships sailing at a greater distance than the *Flying Fish*, but its high trajectory fit in well with the officer's plan. Carefully gauging the flying ship's speed, the man hesitated a second longer, then shouted his command—

"Now!"

Morlac had been struggling to cut free the burning sail before the flames spread to the ship's wooden structure. Now the sounds from the shore caught his attention, and he looked round at the moment the arbalest was fired. He watched helplessly as the heavy stone hurtled upward, directly at them.

In the next instant the missile struck the bow of the ship. With a shuddering crunch the wood planking gave way as the stone lodged there. The impact sent a tremor coursing down the length of the *Flying Fish*, as a mortal wound might affect a living thing.

The ship tilted abruptly. Several men fell overboard. Kadrana shrieked as the clawed support that held the great black pearl unbalanced and lurched sideways. The girl stumbled forward, grasping futilely after the mystic gem in an effort to recover it and the power it represented. But the pearl was out of her reach. It struck twice on the tilted deck, then careened over the edge to tumble down to the element that had spawned it.

All at once, the wind that had held the promise of freedom and a safe return ceased with a dying moan. The mournful sound reverberated a long, lingering moment after the pearl splashed into the waiting sea below.

Deprived of its source of power, the *Flying Fish* plummeted into the water, its deck now catching fire from the sail's burning fragments. There would be no saving the vessel now. There was only survival to consider, and a hope for escape.

Morlac shouted to the others through curtains of flame. "Swim for your lives! Hold your breath—swim underwater if you can, or their archers may find you."

Broct and the others quickly obeyed, leaping into the sea on the far side of the boat so that they would not be seen. But Kadrana remained on her hands and knees, sobbing and cursing on the sinking deck. Morlac grabbed her by the shoulders and pulled her over the side. He was prepared to have to tow her along through the water as well, leaving both of them dangerously exposed, but the cold touch of the sea seemed to bring her to her senses. She immediately pulled free of his grasp and dove cleanly beneath the surface, swimming with a fierce and fluid dolphinlike movement. He followed her below the waves, his own strength renewed by the bracing water that enveloped him.

On shore, the soldiers looked away from the burning ship as yet more riders came into their midst. Drygo and the king's own officer, Hadron, rode to a halt beside the arbalest, followed by a handful of palace guards. They had seen the fall of the mystic ship as they approached.

Watching the dying flames, the two men's faces bore differing looks. Drygo viewed the destruction with an almost ghoulish satisfaction. The expression of the king's officer was solemn and unsettled.

"Such wizardry as this, so close to Kem!" Hadron said. "I do not like this. The scheme is awry . . . we must change our plans."

"No!" Drygo said quickly. "There is no need to do that, you fool. Their ship is finished. If any of its spies survive to reach shore, they would still have to travel many miles of North Kingdom land on foot. Your patrols would catch them long before they could reach Sordros to alert him of our plans."

The officer struggled to contain the deep-burning anger he felt for the mercenary in whom the king had so casually placed his faith. "And if you are wrong, our soldiers will be going to face an enemy that is prepared for them." His eyes narrowed. "Should that happen, Drygo, I promise you that if Sordros's men do not kill you, *I* shall."

Drygo's gnarled features contorted into a sneer as he watched the last smoldering remains of the *Flying Fish* vanish from sight. "No man may challenge my sword and win. Not even you, Hadron. But it matters not. Sordros will never learn what was said in the palace tonight. . . ."

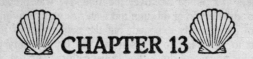

CHAPTER 13

The Trader's Wagon

In a narrow pocket of land near the coastal road, sheltered by high rocks on three sides, Morlac broke another branch from a dead tree and added it to the fire. He knew full well the risk they took by having even a hidden fire, but their clothing was soaked, and chilled by the air. Broct was standing watch along the ridge, his large yellow eyes alert to whatever danger might come their way.

There were only five of them now, including the girl, for two of the men had not been seen since their craft's fiery plunge into the sea. Morlac and the others swam as far south as they could after abandoning their vessel, to avoid contact with the coastal sentinels. Even after they had clawed their way back up the rocky shore, they had pressed on for yet more miles, until at last, near exhaustion, they found their present haven.

Morlac stood for a moment before the fire, trying to shut out the fatigue that ached within him. He could not help staring into the flickering flames licking up from the dead wood . . . could not help remembering the chill burning of those other flames he had known. Even so, these flames were different, more familiar, and their warmth felt good upon his skin.

Something tugged at his awareness, and he glanced over to see that Kadrana was staring at him. She sat huddled before the fire, her cloak and outer garments spread out on a rock to dry, her thin inner gown stuck wetly to her. As she shivered in discomfort, she was more the child than the woman.

90

Almost despite himself, Morlac felt drawn to her. He doubted she deserved any compassion, least of all from him, but he could not resist going to her.

He sat beside her, put his arm around her shivering shoulders, and brushed some of the soaked strands of hair away from her face. Her green eyes flashed up at him with some of the fire and challenge he expected to see there, but the look quickly faded. Either what they had been through this night had tempered her imperious disposition, or else she was just too tired to bother.

"What now, my Captain?" Kadrana said, but her words lacked their usual mocking tone.

"We rest," Morlac said. "Then we find a way back to Sordros."

"If we can. With the ship gone—"

"We will steal horses if we must, but we will get back."

Kadrana glanced at the other two warriors gathered at the fire. Both looked exhausted. They stared at the flames and seemed oblivious to the conversation across from them. Kadrana looked back to Morlac, her gaze troubled, her voice lower as she spoke.

"Morlac . . . you seem to hate me, yet twice this night you saved my life. Why?"

Morlac took a long moment to answer. "Perhaps I feared the wrath of Sordros had I not."

"Perhaps . . . as well you should," Kadrana told him, nestling her head against his shoulder. "But I doubt you fear anything."

"You are wrong," he said softly. "I fear many things. Perhaps most of all, myself."

Kadrana looked up into his eyes, seeming to read the thoughts behind his words, but this time without the cruel smile that so often twisted her lips. "Do not fear that, my warrior. You were magnificent tonight. Truly magnificent. You have become everything I'd hoped you would. Everything."

Morlac considered this aspect of her nature with puzzlement, wondering at his own complex emotions. It felt good to hold her, sitting there before the fire on this cold and miserable night. The sweet softness of her body next to his was pleasurable and . . . familiar. The sensation called forth memories and passions difficult to understand, and just as difficult to ignore. If only she were not so cruel and treacherous. If only she were not Sordros's daughter. . . .

Suddenly, a hissing sound came from the ridge. Morlac was instantly alert, letting go of the girl and rising to his feet.

"Morlac—" Broct called softly down. "Something comes."

Reluctant as he was to do it, Morlac hurriedly kicked sand over the fire, smothering the flames that could so easily give them away. He hoped the lingering smell of smoke would not betray them.

Climbing to the ridge alongside Broct, Morlac peered over the edge. His eyes following the direction of the giant's extended arm, he searched the distant darkness. Far to the north, on the road from Kem, something was indeed approaching. But its form was indistinct even to Morlac's sharp eyes.

"What do you think? A patrol?"

The giant's large yellow eyes continued to peer into the distance, his nostrils occasionally sniffing the breeze. "A small patrol, if it be one," he replied. "Only a few horses." He listened intently, cocking an ear toward the faint clatter that approached. "It might be a traveler. A wagon would make such a sound."

"A wagon?" Morlac said with interest. "Then come—it may do us well to greet it!"

They climbed cautiously down from their vantage point and rounded the end of the hilly barrier. Keeping behind a large rocky outgrowth, they waited as the traveler neared.

Rumbling along the rocky roadway, the wagon continued at its unhurried pace. Drawn by two powerfully built horses, the vehicle could now be seen to be tall and completely enclosed. It looked to be a trader's wagon, old and dusty, hauling wares from village to village. Morlac waited until it was almost upon them before springing out into the road.

Even as Broct moved to grab the horses' reins, Morlac was leaping for the front of the wagon. In the next moment, the driver found an unexpected passenger on the seat beside him, and the keen edge of a dirk held convincingly close to his throat.

Morlac waited until certain that Broct had settled the horses, then said to the man still obscured in darkness, "Try nothing! I could kill you in an instant if I wished it."

"No doubt you could," the man replied, so calmly that Morlac felt oddly troubled. "But you would be wise to spare me, and let me aid you."

Kadrana approached them and struck one of her stinking sulfurous matches. As it flared into life, a yellow glow washed over the features of the man Morlac held hostage.

A face that was narrow and somber stared back at them. The man wore the colorful tunic and long vest of a trader, and the top of his head was swathed in a turban. His nose was hooked and slender, his lips thin. There was no trace of beard upon his face, and though he seemed old, there were no wrinkles, either. But all other features dwindled to unimportance beside the eyes, each an abyss of darkness that threatened to swallow their very souls.

Morlac recognized him for the man he had seen within the palace grounds, and he felt certain that the trader remembered his face as well. He kept the dirk in place.

"Do you always greet highwaymen with such hospitality?"

"Had you been a highwayman," the trader said calmly, "I would have greeted you with *death*."

Morlac stared deeply within the man's eyes and felt an odd chill he could not quell. Still, he said, "Brave words for an unarmed man."

Close behind him now, Kadrana spoke in a voice lacking its usual confidence. "He may speak the truth, Morlac. I sense that he is one of the Enlightened. Do not taunt him."

As the others moved in closer, Morlac cautiously put away his dirk. "A wizard in the very midst of Kem? Then what we heard about South Kingdom spies was true."

Relaxing somewhat, the man's face underwent an actor's change, becoming less menacing. The irises of his strange eyes became visible, a deep blue that sparkled.

"A wizard? How you speak, friend! I am but a humble trader of commodities. None bar their gates from such as I."

"An observant trader, I'll wager," Morlac said. "Tell me—does your path take you beyond the border?"

"Yes. Far beyond the border."

"As far as the village where Sordros rules?"

An unnerving smile formed on the man's lips. "Sordros. I thought you might be one of his. No—I cannot take you directly there, but there is a hidden South Kingdom outpost a short journey's distance from Sordros's domain. I will take you there, and see that you are given horses. To aid Sordros will ultimately aid us as well."

Morlac considered the offer of assistance. It bothered him to have to deal with yet another of Sordros's evil kind, no matter what the circumstances. But their chances for survival, let alone a return to the village in time to bring news of Drygo's plan, seemed slim at best without aid. Dawn would be coming soon, and the king's patrols would be alert to the presence of intruders.

"All right, then—" Morlac said at last "—if you can get us past L'Dron Kerr's men."

"Get in the wagon," the trader replied. "There's room for you all. You won't be the first contraband I've smuggled out of the North Kingdom. . . ."

They gathered their clothes from the rocks and climbed up into the back of the enclosed wagon. There were several crates and chests, and loose items of merchandise, but still it was surprisingly spacious inside. Morlac closed the door behind him and they settled down within. The smooth wooden interior was comfortable, and had soaked up the scents of spices and herbs from a hundred journeys.

"There are blankets there in that large chest," the trader called back to them. "Use them, if you wish."

Morlac opened the chest and pulled out blankets for the others and himself. They were of dark, heavy wool, and their dry warmth felt good. As he leaned back tiredly against the side of the wagon, Kadrana moved beside him, snuggling against him and pulling both her blanket and his up to their shoulders. Resting her head against his chest, she fell into an exhausted sleep. The others were soon asleep also, lulled by the swaying motion of the wagon and the quiet rumble of its wheels as it rolled into the night. . . .

The first test of the trader's pledge came hours later, long after sunrise, as they left the coastal road for the inland route to the south. One of the North Kingdom checkpoints came into view ahead, a small detachment of guards manning the post.

Morlac leaned forward as the wagon halted, quickly alert. He peered through a gap in the curtain immediately behind the driver. He saw one of the soldiers approach the wagon with the plodding manner of a man bored by his job. Morlac's hand rested upon his sword hilt, ready to draw the awful weapon if the need arose.

The soldier studied the trader but for a moment before saying, "Back so soon, Jepso? Was business that good, or did the merchant's guild finally send you packing?"

"And why should they do that, when I deal in such unique commodities," the trader replied, slipping easily into his role. "No, for a change business was good. I am just now returning with my bartered items."

The soldier smiled, but scratched his chin. "Nothing you should not have, I trust."

The trader shook his head negatively. "There's no profit to be made in the king's dungeons."

Passing the side of the dusty wagon, the soldier headed for the back. "Just so, we had better have a look all the same."

Morlac tensed at the words. He saw Broct draw his dirk and flatten against the side of the wagon, and he wondered how alert the other guards would be. Listening intently, he heard the trader, Jepso, leave his seat and join the soldier at the rear of the wagon.

As he worked the latch on the door, the trader continued talking. His voice took on a droning intonation as he described to the soldier the objects he had bartered.

Bright sunlight suddenly flooded the interior of the wagon as the door was thrown open. Morlac wondered for an instant if the trader had betrayed them—if his tale of being a South Kingdom agent had been but a lie. He had almost begun to draw his sword to silence them both when an inner voice told him to wait.

There was no look of betrayal on the trader's face, only one of intense concentration. And his eyes had acquired their strangeness once more, the blue in them having fled to leave only depthless black holes.

The soldier gazed inside, with no sign of alarm despite the

presence of the four men and the girl. He viewed them dispassionately, as if seeing nothing more extraordinary than the kegs and crates the trader had described to him. As a parting gesture, the trader gave the man a bottle of wine from a crate near the door.

A moment later, the door was closed again and the soldier was waving them through the checkpoint. Morlac waited until the post was well behind them before poking his head through the wagon's curtain.

"Well done," he told the trader.

"I doubt there'll be any more such checks," he replied. "A passing patrol, perhaps, but my wagon is a familiar sight along this road."

Morlac studied him with a certain curious awe. "Tell me—back there, what if more than one of those soldiers had looked into the wagon? Could you still have maintained the illusion?"

There was no reply, and Morlac sensed the truth in the man's grim silence, a silence that continued as he whipped the horses into a gallop and followed the road south. . . .

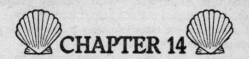

CHAPTER 14

The Spirit Flame

A peal of thunder split the night as the trader's wagon rolled swiftly on, careening along the uneven road, the horses whipped to a gallop. The threatening storm drove them on as surely as the whip, their fear-widened eyes reflecting each new lighting bolt with flinching clarity. The rumbling wheels kept up their steady dialogue with an angry sky.

It was well past midnight of the first day after leaving Kem. They had crossed the border of the North Kingdom hours ago, having successfully passed the patrols and checkpoints with the aid of the one who called himself Jepso. The wagon had stopped only briefly along the way, and had made good time.

A chilling rain was just beginning to fall as the lights of a small settlement came into view ahead. Lantern lights they were, and window glow, winking among the trees as the wind whipped their branches to and fro. Morlac peered through the curtain behind the trader as this strange new place drew near. It did not seem like much, really—a tiny inn, a merchant's shop, a horse pen and stable. A blacksmith's weatherworn sign swung in the breeze on squeaky, rusty rings.

The wagon slowed, then pulled to a halt before the main building that served as an inn. It was a crude wooden structure, waterproofed with resin, the cracks and joints sealed with pitch. Facing the roadway, it had its back against the very base of the hillside that rose above it. The place seemed dependent upon travelers and traders, for no village was near.

A small, burly man hurried out through the rain to take

care of the horses as the one called Jepso climbed down from his wagon seat. At the rear, Morlac cautiously pushed open the door, then climbed out and helped Kadrana down to the ground. Broct and the other two sea-warriors followed them out, closing the door behind them.

"This way—" said Jepso, motioning them toward the inn. He led the way up wooden steps and entered ahead of them, looking about with disguised caution.

Inside, the place was ill-lighted with the golden glow of lanterns and the fireplace. A handful of tables stood at one end of the room, most of their chairs empty, but some filled with somber men, long of face and intent of eye. They studied these new arrivals with wary interest.

Kadrana raised a disdainful eyebrow as she stared back at them, and pulled the edges of her cloak more tightly about her. Striding over to Jepso, she said in a low, imperative tone, "Are you sure you cannot take us the rest of the way to our village—? I do not relish staying here, and I have urgent news for Sordros."

Jepso looked calmly around at her. "You will be quite safe enough here. And even if I were going in that direction, which I am not, the horses are tired and the storm grows worse."

"But—" said Kadrana, respectful yet impatient "—you said you would help us."

"I did, and I shall. You will have the horses that you need, as promised, and by first light you may set out for your village. In the meantime, your message need not wait."

The proprietor of the inn now came forward from the back of the room. His hawklike face bore a wary smile of welcome.

"Ahh—Jepso! Back so soon, are you?" But despite the friendly words, his eyes darted suspiciously to Morlac and the others.

"It is all right," the trader/wizard said softly. "They are friends of the South Kingdom."

The proprietor gave a slight nod of acceptance. "Good, good. If you vouch for them, they are welcome. We are secure tonight. No strangers, and no prying eyes from the north."

"That is well."

More thunder rumbled outside now, and the rain began to

pelt harder against the walls and roof of the structure. There were little cracks around the door, and the wind moaned and whistled through them.

"Now," said the man, his manner more that of a fellow conspirator than a friendly innkeeper, "how may I serve you?"

Jepso said, "We have need of rooms for the night, and a hot meal."

"You shall have them."

"And," added Jepso, with a gesture encompassing Kadrana, "we shall need to contact our brother, Sordros, before they continue on tomorrow."

The man considered, then nodded. "All right. I shall arrange it. The flame burns pure and clear tonight. After I've made my report, you may contact Sordros." He directed them toward a table. "In the meantime, sit . . . rest . . . I will bring you food."

In a matter of minutes, they were seated around the crudely carved table, with bowls of thick, hot soup before them, and great slabs of coarse, dark bread. It was a simple meal, made delicious by their hunger and the storm. The fire and the ale also helped to warm them.

Drafts of storm-wind set the lantern light flickering, toying with the flames, threatening to quench the amber glow. Brought together by events not of their own making, the odd circle of people that were gathered around the table studied one another's faces in silence. Morlac found himself marveling at the complexity of this strange human world, and also, oddly enough, a bit in awe of his memories of life in the sea. Both existences were alternately strange and familiar . . . alien and real. It was disconcerting, being able to see both aspects of his mind from objective and radically different viewpoints.

His thoughts on the matter ended as the inn's proprietor returned, once their meal was over. The man made a hasty gesture for them to follow.

"Come—" he said. "It is time."

They rose from the table, led by Jepso, and headed toward the rear of the inn. Ahead of them, the proprietor paused by a doorway leading into another room. He gestured inside.

Once in the room, the man drew a curtain across the

doorway. The only other way out of the room was a narrow hall leading to several rooms and a flight of stairs.

But the proprietor did not go in that direction. Instead, he walked over to the rear wall and pressed the stone of an ornate finger ring into a knothole in one of the wooden panels. Something clicked within the wall. With an odd groan of sound far heavier than seemed natural, the panel slowly swung away into a darkened recess behind it. A cave stretched blackly ahead, deep into the hillside that backed the inn.

Taking up a lantern, the proprietor entered the mouth of the cave, glancing back toward the others. "This way—" he said "—there is no time to waste."

Morlac had no idea what a secret South Kingdom outpost might be like, even from his human memory, but this seemed an appropriate place for one. There was almost a tangible smell of sorcery in the air, and the thought of it sent a chill up his spine that not even the cold rain had evoked. He looked to Broct and saw an expression on the giant's face that mirrored his own thoughts. Even Kadrana seemed a bit uneasy.

The cave passage wound its irregular way into the hillside, gradually descending below ground level. The storm outside could now scarcely be heard. Small scurrying things darted about underfoot, and the flutter of leathery wings occasionally passed unnervingly close to their heads. At last, the passage turned abruptly and broadened into a fair-sized underground chamber, naturally formed. Lamps of burning oil were set in niches along the stone walls, but cast a feeble glow.

" 'Twould seem," Broct whispered, "that magic works best in the dark."

Kadrana shushed him, not only out of reflex but also out of an apparent awe for this place. That in itself was disconcerting.

In the center of the chamber, a pile of darkened stones had been erected in an orderly arrangement, stacked in seven circles, one atop the other. The stones were nearly identical in size and shape, and even the spaces between them seemed measured. But these oddities were nothing, compared to the flame that burned above them. A blue flame, hazy and indistinct, slowly writhed and coiled in empty air above the stacked stones. Nothing fed the flame—no wood, nor oil, nor wax, nor fat-soaked rags. And no smoke rose above it . . . no heat reached out from its ghostly glow. It merely hovered above the stones, ethereal and unreal.

"It is a spirit flame," Kadrana whispered to Morlac and Broct. "High magic, indeed. I have heard of them, but never before used one."

Morlac nodded without reply. He was fascinated by the flame, yet found it unpleasantly like the green fire of Sordros's magical pit. It seemed to arouse an unreasoning fear in him; a basic, instinctive, primordial fear. But the human aspect of his mind fought to control that fear, and it was succeeding.

"You must hurry," cautioned the proprietor. "The flame grows weaker."

Kadrana nodded in understanding and approached the stacked circle of rocks. Reaching into a pocket of her garment, she withdrew an oilskin pouch, tightly sealed. Drawing very near to the flame which floated just above eye level, Kadrana opened the pouch and poured a small quantity of powder into the palm of her hand. Morlac thought his sharp sense of smell could pick out the odor of dried seaweed, of herbs, and unknown chemicals. And was it only his imagination, or was there also a trace of crystallized blood? He was not sure.

The delicate young woman now took a stance before the flame, flung the powder into its very heart, and began to chant an incantation that was little more than a whisper of sound. Her right hand clutched the amulet that hung from her neck, and as she continued to chant, her breathing became more rapid and deep until her whispered words were faint gasps of sound.

Slowly, a change in the blue flame became perceptible. Less like fire now, it began to swirl and contort, eddying and flowing into a shape. And the shape it formed was that of a man's head, ghostly and translucent. The glowing blue face that came into unsteady focus belonged to Sordros, larger than life and somehow even more commanding here in this form than in his flesh-and-blood visage.

"Sordros—hear me," said Kadrana, her voice husky and weak from effort. "For I have news of our enemy's plans. . . ."

As Sordros's image responded with a nod, Kadrana began to relate what they had heard in L'Dron Kerr's private chamber. As she did so, Morlac and Broct watched from a short distance back.

Broct turned and studied his sea-brother, observing the way Morlac's eyes were riveted upon the girl. "She is a strange one," whispered Broct, "and quite powerful, in her own way."

"Yes . . ." said Morlac ". . . in her own way."

"And I wonder," the yellow-eyed giant said cautiously, "what manner of spell it is she's worked on you."

Morlac's gaze swung quickly around upon his friend, a trace of anger tinging his expression. But that look soon faded and he extended a hand to Broct's shoulder.

"I wonder, too, my friend. I wonder, too. . . ."

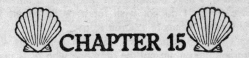# CHAPTER 15

Preparations for War

Dawn of the third morning found Morlac back within the congealed sand walls of Sordros's castle, and the village that was his home. Jepso had made good his promise and supplied horses for Morlac and the others. They had ridden most of the previous day, returning to the village by sunset. There was much to do, much to get ready, but Morlac had found time for a few hours of fitful sleep, and was as rested as he could be. Now a new day was beginning . . . a day that could well be their last. In the chamber that served as quarters for the magician's special guards, the men were making ready for battle.

Morlac stood solemnly by the long wooden table, one foot braced on the bench as he polished the shell-shield resting across his knee. He hoped he was ready for the combat that would soon be upon them.

"Our fight with Kerr's men outside Kem was but a small taste of what lies before us, my sea-brother," he said to Broct. Morlac's voice was low, and his expression grim-faced and thoughtful. "Even with the villagers behind us, it will not be easy to succeed against Drygo and Kerr's army. And if we fail. . . ."

Contrasting Morlac's mood, the yellow-eyed giant was almost jovial as he checked the sharpness of his sword. "If we do fail," he said, "you may be certain that a better than equal number of North Kingdom soldiers shall die with us!"

Anger flared within Morlac's proud eyes. "This is no game, Broct! Our lives, strange as they now are, could end this day.

Worse, this village could end this day. Though I do not understand it, I have memories of this place. I am bound to it. I care for it. I do not wish for it or its people to die, especially at the hands of L'Dron Kerr.''

Broct's eyes glistened in a way that belied his seeming good humor. "You are not the only one who feels that way, my friend. We conquer our fears differently, you and I, but fears they still be.''

"It is not only fear I feel, but anger as well. Anger at L'Dron Kerr. Anger at Sordros. Perhaps even anger at myself, for reasons not fully clear to me. And I have the uncanny sense of our having gone out before to battle Kerr's invaders beyond this village. Of our having dealt death . . . and tasted it.''

"Aye," said Broct, nodding solemnly. His mouth twitched as his own memories knifed through him.

"And," continued Morlac, "I am also angered by the knowledge that if we do win against Kerr's forces, we will help perpetuate Sordros's tyranny in this region.''

Ardo, who had been moving amongst the guardsmen to inspect their preparations, heard Morlac's words. He paused beside Morlac and Broct, adding his own grim countenance to theirs.

"I sympathize with your position," he told Morlac. "But you and your men may very well be our last line of defense against Drygo's attack. We of the village value your presence here. Forget about Sordros for now. It is *we* who need your help.''

Morlac breathed out slowly, releasing some of the pent-up emotion he felt. He placed a hand on Ardo's shoulder. "I do not forget your kindness or your friendship, Ardo. Even were I not bound by Sordros's spell or by my concern for this village, still would I fight alongside you.''

Ardo smiled weakly. "I thank you for that, Morlac. And anyway, do not dismiss too quickly the support Sordros enjoys in this realm. The people fear him, it is true, but they also have need of his enchantments. The fisherfolk have flourished under his rule, and even the farmers have benefited. Sordros is often cruel, but he has done much good here.''

"You may be right. But it is hard for me to see any value in Sordros's magics." Morlac fell silent for a moment, contemplative and somber. "Odd that L'Dron Kerr has not tried to fight fire with fire . . . use sorcery against the wizard himself."

Ardo shook his head. "Not really so odd. Even if Kerr would traffic with those who work magic, it is unlikely he could find one of the Enlightened who would go against his own kind. Besides, there are safeguards."

"Safeguards?"

"To be sure! For example, Sordros's own name—or what he calls himself, at least. *It cannot be reversed*, as names often are to invoke a spell against someone. Even as yours. . . ."

His words faded to silence, his expression becoming nervous, as if he feared he had revealed something better left a secret.

"My name. . . ." Morlac said softly. "What about it?"

"Perhaps I've said too much," Ardo replied.

Morlac would not let it pass. His steely gaze demanded an answer. "Tell me. I would know more of the wizard's spell."

Sensing that he could not avoid the matter, Ardo said at last, "All right. I pray it will do no harm." Drawing a breath, he began to explain. "There was a man, a villager and the former captain of Sordros's guard. He died in a raid about six months ago, when L'Dron Kerr first sent soldiers south to probe our defenses. His name was Calrom, and I believe that the dust of his bones was used in the spell which transformed you into what you are now."

Morlac frowned, uncertain of his own feelings about this news. But however he felt about it, it seemed to explain much. "Calrom . . . Morlac. Then that is what Kadrana meant when she told me that my name was my destiny. And if his soul is somehow tied up with mine, then . . . how much of what I am now is truly me? Am I a dead man re-formed from a turtle's flesh? Or merely a sea creature burdened with a man's memory?"

"I cannot answer that," Ardo said. "Perhaps you are both, and more. Only Sordros knows. And perhaps the girl."

Broct sought to break the mood that hung in the air like a

cloud before them. "If the wizard sought to protect himself by using a clever name, then I wonder why he did not do the same for his daughter?"

Ardo raised an eyebrow. "Kadrana . . . his daughter? Is that what she's told you?"

"Yes," Morlac replied. "Isn't she?"

"Perhaps, but I doubt it. I cannot be certain, of course, but I have never yet heard of a wizard with offspring." Ardo glanced around, then confided in a whisper, "There are stories told of the pacts they make to gain occult power . . . pacts which forever deny them a normal mortal life."

"That the girl would lie does not surprise me," Morlac mused aloud. "But if she is not his daughter, then how else can we account for the responsibilities Sordros has given her?"

Ardo shrugged, a cautious smile on his lips. "It's a mystery I've never dared explore."

Broct sheathed his sword and fastened the broad belt about his waist. "What does it matter? Once this battle is done, we'll either be dead or conquering heroes, free at last from the magician's spell."

Morlac arched a devil-brow in thought. "But *will* we be free, even if we win? Sordros has never really promised to release us from the spell he cast upon us. He has only sworn that he would not break the spell unless we served him. So even if we win, we may still be forever spellbound to him. Forever trapped in these bodies . . . halfway between beasts and men. Neither one nor the other, but merely freaks . . . 'demons' . . . fit neither for our old lives in the sea nor for human society."

For the first time, Broct's features darkened with concern. "You think then that he may hold us in his power always? Ardo—you know the wizard better than we. What say you?"

The man who had been their tutor and friend looked back with knowing sadness. "I cannot guess. But I fear Morlac may be right in what he suggests."

With that, Ardo turned away to resume his preparations, leaving Broct and Morlac to ponder their fates. A silence fell over them . . . a silence that was not broken until several long moments later.

"I will speak with the wizard," Morlac said abruptly, buckling his swordbelt with sudden determination. "And if it is within my power to do so, I will obtain his oath that he will free us from his sorcerous slavery. . . ."

The halls of the castle were nearly deserted. Morlac knew Sordros's menials must be preparing the castle's outer defenses, as limited as they were. He encountered only a few people within the interior, and none paid any attention to his presence.

On his way, he passed the door to the room Kadrana had said was his. Calrom's room, he knew now. He could not avoid stopping there, could not resist the urge to push open the door and look inside. The room was still just as it had been when Kadrana had shown it to him, and once more, memories coursed through him as his gaze traced the outlines of every object within the small chamber. *Calrom.* The word reverberated through his mind. *So that was my name before . . . before I died. Before I breathed life anew, as . . . what?* As if to shut off the thoughts that troubled him, Morlac reached inside and pulled the door quickly closed. Then he started off once more for the wizard's chamber.

Morlac was surprised at the absence of the Watch-Devils. He had seen none in the halls as he made his way through the castle, and even now, as he neared the doorway to Sordros's private chamber, he did not see even one of the small aerial demons. Perhaps the mystic energy they required was needed more urgently elsewhere. The heavy curtains of the doorway were closed, but Morlac parted them and stepped cautiously inside.

The chamber, which Morlac had never seen before, was startling in appearance. The room brimmed with artifacts and magic implements that were bizarre and unsettling in their appearance. Dark tapestries with occult symbols covered the walls and gave an ominous aspect to all they encompassed. Oddly shaped bottles and jars crowded the shelves of several tall cabinets, filled with powders, vile liquids, and unspeakable objects. Morlac did not care to contemplate their uses, remembering his own encounter with the sorcerer's magic.

A chill coursed through him as he observed Sordros's collection of sea creatures—dead beasts all, yet preserved

with subtle skill to look almost alive. Some he recognized
from the sea that had been his home, but others were strange
and unlike any he had ever seen. At last he fought off the
morbid fascination that gripped him and concentrated on the
thing which had brought him here.

Sordros was seated at his table, cloaked in a dark emerald
robe that was embroidered with golden symbols of the sea.
His bare head rested on the tips of his fingers as he braced his
arms upon the table's cluttered surface. Sweat beaded on his
head and soaked the gold-bound tuft of hair at his crown. He
was silent . . . totally unmoving. If he breathed at all, Morlac
could not discern it. His eyes were closed, yet even so they
seemed to stare into the depths of a large crystal before him.
Mist swirled within the sphere's glowing interior, casting a
shimmering light upon the wizard's frown of concentration.
Beside the sphere an enormous leatherbound book lay open
atop other volumes, its yellowing pages covered with magical
symbols and the words of a strange language. A wizard and
his tools. The eeriness of it made Morlac nervous despite his
resolve.

"Sordros—" Morlac said softly, his voice sounding to him
like an intruder's shout.

He waited a moment, then repeated the name. When there
was still no reaction, Morlac reached out a hand to touch the
wizard's shoulder.

Something stopped him like an invisible wall. He did not
know whether there was some powerful aura surrounding
Sordros at the moment or if it was merely a cold and unreasoning fear of the unknown that stayed his hand from that
dreadful contact.

At that moment, Sordros's eyes slowly opened and his
head raised to look at Morlac. He did this with great effort.
His face was drawn, his eyes red-rimmed and dangerous of
aspect. His lips parted dryly and his horrid voice rasped out
two words—"*Leave me—*" Then his eyes closed and his
profound concentration resumed. His words seemed to hang
in the air, still echoing their warning, their threat. A threat
not to be taken lightly, Morlac thought, remembering Xaja's
fate.

Morlac turned away from the wizard, his features moist

with cold sweat. Striding to the window, he sought the sunlight and relief from the chamber's disturbing aspect.

Morning air greeted his nostrils as he peered out. The view from this high point in the castle was impressive, almost enough so to make him forget the dark force which labored behind him. Morlac could even see the distant farmlands and their irrigation ditches . . . ditches which had been hastily altered during the previous day and night, at Sordros's command. He even thought his sharp eyes could detect the dull glint of weapons, far beyond the fields. L'Dron Kerr's men would be out there somewhere. They, and the mercenary, Drygo.

A whisper of sound interrupted those thoughts and brought Morlac's head quickly around. Kadrana had entered the chamber from the other side and she approached him with a look of fearful disapproval.

"You should not be here!" she said in a low but insistent tone. "He prepares for the enemy!"

"I would talk with him."

"He can speak to no one now." the girl said firmly, regaining some of her imperious manner now that she was safely back in Sordros's castle. She motioned for him to follow and headed for the doorway to a connecting chamber.

Morlac hesitated a moment, casting a lingering glance at the wizard's motionless form. then he turned and followed the girl. For the time being; Sordros was clearly unreachable, and Morlac did not much relish staying in the sorcerer's room. . . .

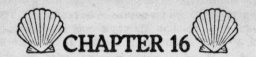# CHAPTER 16

The Mermaid's Lair

Morlac followed Kadrana along a short passageway and down a spiral stair to the next floor below Sordros's high keep. She parted a curtain of glistening beads and motioned for him to enter the room beyond. He had never been in this part of the castle before, and was curious what it might contain.

He knew as soon as he stepped inside that the room was Kadrana's own quarters. It was as different from Sordros's chamber as the sea is from the land. Morlac had never really thought of the warriors' quarters, or for that matter, any other part of the castle, as being particularly masculine in design, but this room was so totally and utterly feminine in its decoration that every other room he had ever been in now seemed brutish and plain.

Where Sordros's chamber had been dark and somber, this place was light and airy, with soft pastel colors everywhere. Amber glass mirrors were on several walls; the better to gaze at her own beauty, Morlac told himself, for the largest hung over a low table that bore an assortment of combs and other grooming implements, perfumes, and jewelry. The scent of those perfumes, and of the oils and emollients and powders as well, began to cause little echoes of memory. Pleasant memories. Lengths of gossamer drapery hung from the ceiling at irregular intervals, and the large divan at the end of the room was sheltered with great masses of the filmy material, making it resemble a garden of kelp beneath the sea.

Kadrana walked to the center of the room and turned to face him. Her normal aloofness had disappeared.

"Are your men ready for Drygo and his soldiers?" she asked.

"Yes. As ready as they can be," Morlac replied. "But it is not the coming battle I wished to discuss with Sordros."

"Well, what then?"

Morlac hesitated, reluctant to acknowledge her presumed authority by conferring with her. Besides, only Sordros could give him the pledge he needed.

Impatient at first when he did not answer, Kadrana's look soon became one of curiosity. "What is it, Morlac? You may tell me anything. We have been through too much to keep secrets now."

Morlac stood his ground as she approached, even though she had fixed her unnerving gaze upon him. The green of her eyes began to blaze, holding his unwilling attention. Or was it unwilling? He wondered. Her attitude seemed softer now, less threatening, less imperious. Was the hostility he felt toward her necessary, or was it only a defense against other feelings?

As Kadrana studied him, her head tilted slightly to one side, an odd expression settled upon her perfect features. "So," she said at last, "it is your freedom that concerns you. You plan to extort a promise of freedom from your master."

"Sordros, my master?" Morlac said dryly. "He is more my jailer."

"Jailer—?" she said, taken aback. "Have we not given you the freedom of the castle . . . of even the village when you desire it?"

"Only since the preparations for battle have begun. And you know that is not the kind of freedom I mean. Sordros has imprisoned me and the others in a way that no chains or dungeons ever could. He has imprisoned me within a form that is not truly mine. He has made halfling creatures of us. Human in shape, yet not quite human. And I fear he intends to keep us that way, and force us to serve him always."

Kadrana studied him for a long moment, absently twirling a ringlet of jet-black hair about a finger. "But it does not have to be bad for you, Morlac. Once we have repelled L'Dron Kerr's attack, we will have proven our strength and our worth to the South Kingdom. Our influence will expand.

This will become a true kingdom in its own right, and we will have need of someone like you. You will have power of your own. Our Captain, my Captain, will be no one's slave. And you will always be treated well. *Always*—I will see to that.''

"Why stop at a mere kingdom?" Morlac said coldly. "You dream of empire."

The girl opened her mouth in surprise, as if for a change he had read *her* thoughts. It had been a mere guess, but obviously a correct one.

"I wonder," Morlac continued, "did you have the same plans for Calrom before he died?"

Kadrana blinked twice. Moisture briefly welled up in her eyes, and Morlac realized his callous words had brought pain. He instantly regretted them.

"He . . . he was the captain of our soldiers," she told him, "and a brave man. He was also my sworn protector, even as you are, Morlac. And . . . and he was my lover. How did you learn of him?"

"It matters not. But it seems he has shaped my new life in more ways than I can guess. Anyway, this is what you wanted, isn't it? When you gave me his room . . . his things? You wanted me to remember him."

"I wanted you to remember *me*, and what we were together. That is all I ever really wanted. All I want now." She sighed, lowering her eyes. "I do not deny nor excuse what I've done. There is much of Calrom in you—so very much. I could see that from the start. And yet there are differences, too. Differences that make you unique, and very special."

"I am a freak, in the eyes of humans."

"Not in mine," she said. She stepped very near to him, gazing up imploringly into his hard eyes. "Why resist our will, Morlac? What you are now . . . what Sordros's spell has made you . . . is not so terrible." Her slender hands brushed his arms, her delicate fingers gently tracing the outlines of the muscles. Her eyes were large and moist and glimmering.

Morlac sought to escape the power in those eyes, to divert his attention to anything but their mystic influence. It seemed hopeless. The mass of dark hair framed her face, focusing attention once more to her eyes. Even the pale-green clinging garment she wore echoed the color of those dreaded, seductive eyes.

It was a more revealing gown than she commonly wore, sheer and lacy, and doing little to conceal her exquisite figure. The low neckline allowed her pendant to be seen clearly. Morlac had never paid attention to it before, never viewed it at such close range. The odd amulet was shaped like a large teardrop formed in crystal and suspended from her neck by a long golden chain, hanging between her perfect breasts. It had the cool glint of ice, and Morlac thought he saw within its murky interior a shape, a wisp of light, a symbol perhaps of occult power.

As his eyes more fully focused on the ornament he began to discern the nature of the tiny form. It was a figure, incredibly detailed for its small size. It was human, or nearly so, and he could almost swear that it was formed in the very image of Kadrana. Yet something was wrong with that likeness. For while the image of the girl was true from the waist up, there was something unnatural about the legs. They appeared fused, joined together into one long extremity, and the feet were flared into a wide, tail-like appendage.

Morlac's mind swam, reeling under a barrage of strange thoughts and emotions, until at last the pendant blurred in his vision. Again he found himself looking into her emerald eyes, looking deeply into their large and luminous depths. The green fire within them flickered brighter now, burning into his mind. But this time it was not the fire of the sorcerer's pit. This time it was a different flame that blossomed there, and threatened to consume him.

"We have more in common than you might think." Kadrana whispered softly, pressing closer to him until her breath caressed his shoulder. "Oh, Morlac, do not resist your fate. Share it with me. Death may yet claim you in the battle that is to be, but I would claim you now. . . ."

He hated her. She was wicked and more cruel in her own way than Sordros himself, for there was at least a straightforward purpose to the magician's evil.

He hated her, he told himself as convincingly as he could. And yet. And yet. . . .

Kadrana's scent was sweet, her warmth and softness more

alluring than he had been willing to admit. Her slender form cried out to be held, and Morlac found that he did not resist as her arms closed around him, her lips reaching up for his.

He was not as he had been. He was different. And now remote and alien forces of this new life stirred within him. The kiss she had begun, he now found himself returning, willingly, again and again, and with a passion as intense as his magicked sword's bloodlust. . . .

It was hard to know how much time had passed—mere moments or an eternity, but abruptly now a distant sound came blaring. A mellow sound, yet one whose significance lent it a chilling note, cutting through his mind like an icy blade.

Morlac tore free of Kadrana's embrace, pushing her away as he rose from the lace-shrouded divan. He strode to the chamber's north window, looking out at the farming fields beyond.

Behind him, Kadrana trembled, her eyes flashing outrage. But as she studied his alert stance at the window, the outrage became alarm.

"What is it—?"

"The horns of the field guards," Morlac replied grimly. "They are coming—Drygo and his soldiers!"

With that, he grabbed up his swordbelt and hurried for the door, pausing briefly to glance back over his shoulder. "You have the devil's own magic in you, Kadrana, and I do not deny my feelings for you," he said chillingly. "But you had better pray to whatever gods you honor that we succeed in stopping Drygo beyond the village. . . ."

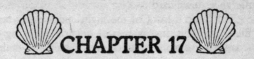

CHAPTER 17

Swords and Magic

The battle cries of two hundred men tore through the early-morning stillness. Raw sunlight gleamed upon the swords and shields of L'Dron Kerr's soldiers as they advanced upon the farmlands of Sordros's domain, led by the mercenary whose invincibility had been granted by the wizard himself.

Ahead of them stood the first line of defenders—bronze-skinned farmers armed with whatever meager weapons they could muster. Their labors in the fields had made them hard and strong, yet even so they seemed no match for trained soldiers. And the sight of Kerr's marching companies, helmeted and garbed for war, would have put fear in any man's heart.

The advance line of soldiers, their battle pikes probing sharply forward, had barely come within a dozen yards when suddenly a cry came from the ranks of the farm defenders. Almost as one the men turned and fled the advancing forces, abandoning their positions and their pride.

Drygo's gnarled features contorted in glee. From his position at the head of Kerr's men, he shouted, "See how they flee us? There is no resistance at all. They will die whimpering cowards! *Onward!*"

As the soldiers charged after them, Sordros's farmers continued to run, their shadows stretching away from them in the morning light and scurrying across the furrowed field. A long irrigation ditch loomed before them, but without the heavy weapons and breastplates of the soldiers they easily jumped the distance to the other side. As they did, each man stole a fearful glance downward.

They had worked most of the night and the day before to alter the interconnecting system of ditches, blocking off the main channels from the smaller ones which fed their fields life-giving river water. The main channels were now isolated from both the river and their crops, and newly opened to a different source of water. For impelled by Sordros's occult powers, the sea itself now flowed along the ditch's bottom. And although he was too far away to be seen clearly, Sordros's gaunt figure even now stood upon his high balcony, overlooking the fields where the battle for his small kingdom was about to rage.

All of them past the ditch, Sordros's farmers ran on. Still close at their heels, Drygo and his soldiers quickly reached the obstacle. Drygo cleared the ditch with a strong leap, but the soldiers, some of whom were carrying a long battering ram, slowed. Burdened by the weight of their North Kingdom battle gear, they trudged down the slope and splashed through the knee-deep water. Fully half their number had crossed before the first pained outcry alerted them to danger.

Drygo turned and stared in dismay at the man to his immediate right. The soldier grimaced in pain, his tall form bent as he slapped at his leg. For there, adhered leechlike to a spot just below the knee, was a slimy white mass of living tissue. The thing was featureless, limbless, nothing more than a membranous blob, slightly iridescent. It was already the size of a man's fist and rapidly growing. Needle-sharp teeth gripped the man's leg as the grotesque creature sucked his blood with rhythmic convulsions.

And it was far from the only one! Another soldier cried out, then more and more until any semblance of order among them vanished. Of the men who had waded through the ditch water, nearly all had acquired the monstrous parasites. Several of the soldiers had already fallen to the ground to lie still, pale as stone and wasted looking.

Some were successful in killing the beasts before their own lives had been claimed, but now they faced the engorged parasites that had abandoned the dead. Touched by Sordros's mystic energies, they *still* grew. Nearly as large as a man now, their formless shapes writhed and flexed, blindly seeking new victims.

"Throw your weapons over first," Drygo shouted to the men still on the far side of the ditch, "and then jump across!" Falling silent, he watched in horror as those near him slashed madly at the bloated obscenities Sordros had called up from the depths.

As the others safely crossed they joined their comrades, hacking at the writhing forms with a ferocity born of terror . . . a terror enhanced by the realization that the blood they spilled in killing the things was that drained from their fellows. The ground at their feet became red and sodden as they struggled to slay the beasts before falling victims themselves.

The grotesque battle raged on and on, until at last there was a perceivable change in its progress. The bloated leeches were struggling now, not so much against Kerr's men as against some unseen force that slowed their movements and made easier targets of them. It appeared that, for all his preparations, Sordros's ploy was failing, the limits of his power reached.

By the time the monsters had been subdued, fully a fourth of Drygo's men were dead and some that lived were weak from loss of blood. Reorganizing under the mercenary's command, they slowly resumed their advance on the village, more wary now and less confident of an easy victory.

Their newfound caution proved wise, for as they neared the edge of the village, they discovered that the farmers had re-formed rather than continuing their flight. They had been joined by burly fishermen from the coastal side of the village, and Sordros's elite guard headed the group.

Morlac stood tall and silent at their fore, his brown jerkin covered by a breastplate that gleamed with the ghostly iridescence of mother-of-pearl. A helm of identical material covered his sea-froth hair, and on his arm was the broad green oval of his shell-shield.

He watched grimly as the soldiers halted just fifteen yards away from them, then said in a loud and ringing voice, "Go back to the North Kingdom! There is nothing for you here but death."

Drygo threw back his head in a careless laugh. "Brave words for one so pale, and with such a meager army. Stand aside, weaklings, and we may spare you. It is only the wizard we seek."

Morlac knew full well what mercy the villagers could expect from Drygo and his men should they surrender. He sensed the others knew it, too. Outnumbered though they were by almost three to one, their fate seemed far more certain if left to Drygo's whim.

"No—we stand and fight," Morlac answered.

"If you value your lives, you will reconsider. You cannot stop us."

"We must do what we can. I do not wish you death, soldier, but know that I am duty-bound to defend Sordros's domain. There is no choice for me."

"Then you are duty-bound to die, defender!" Drygo shouted, ordering his men forward with a sweep of his sword. With a great roar of voices they attacked, rushing toward the lines of men.

Morlac silently cursed Sordros for acquainting him with the madness of humankind. He gripped Shark's hilt and pulled the dreaded sword free, shivering as he felt its hungry force awaken. The white blade dully gleamed in the stark brightness, eager for the kill.

They were upon them in the next moment, and although Morlac sought to reach Drygo first he found himself immediately shut off from that goal by the press of battle. All was madness as the soldiers of L'Dron Kerr's army engaged the villagers and Sordros's elite guard.

Shield clashed against shield and swords rang out in an unholy symphony. Farmers fought with lances fresh-hewn and -tipped, and with scythes meant for a less gruesome harvest. Fishermen used their broad fish knives in a valiant effort against the better equipped soldiers, and it soon became apparent that whichever way the battle ended, the only true victor would be Death himself.

Morlac pressed ever forward, cutting a crimson swath through the enemy's ranks as wide as the sweep of his magicked sword. Even so, the fighting was drifting steadily closer to the village, and Morlac's eyes continually darted to the position where last he had seen Drygo.

More minutes dragged on. It seemed that the fighting would never end—that there would not be even a moment's rest except for those who had already found eternity's peace. And something else was becoming frighteningly clear. Despite the progress of Morlac and the elite guard, *they were losing*. The defenders' ranks were dwindling, even while more North Kingdom soldiers, fresh from the rear ranks, pressed forward.

They were within the boundaries of the village itself now. Faces full of fear and horror appeared at windows, only to quickly vanish as the fighting neared them. The walls sent back sword-clanging echoes and seemed to amplify the sounds of battle.

And then another sound was heard, a sound that might almost be mistaken for a moan of despair. It came blowing through the village, swept on a wind from off the sea. Whether it was a last effort by Sordros to call forth his powers, or merely a storm of ordinary origins, it seemed too late to offer any hope of escape from the onslaught.

Yet its potential threat had not gone unnoticed. Through a chance opening in the conflict, Morlac caught a glimpse of Drygo as he broke free of the crowd and ran purposefully toward the castle, followed by a handful of men carrying the battering ram.

Morlac started to pursue him, then abruptly had to defend himself against the attack of two more of Kerr's soldiers. They came at him with a killing anger, still robust while Morlac was growing battle weary. The constant press of the fighting threatened to sap even his supernatural endurance, and worse yet, it now delayed him from following Drygo at a time when it was imperative to stop him. Time . . . there was so very little of it left now. With a growing frenzy, Morlac sought to disengage from the battle.

Suddenly, Broct was at his side, seeing what had happened, knowing what must be done. Still wearing a short cloak to conceal his multitudinous arms, he took on the men Morlac was fighting.

"Go on!" the yellow-eyed giant commanded.

"Desert you and the others—?"

"It matters not," Broct said, deflecting the blows of both attackers. "But if Drygo reaches the wizard and slays him, then we are eternally doomed! *Go!*"

His words were true enough and Morlac needed no further convincing. He ran for the castle as swiftly as he could, his mind and body aching, troubled with the knowledge that too much time had already passed. Despite his present speed, he was reminded of the past . . . of his slowness when venturing out of his element. He only hoped he was not already too late. . . .

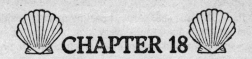

CHAPTER 18

Warrior's Doom

The castle loomed ahead, somber and silent despite the clamor of the village. As Morlac neared he could see the gate had been breached. The heavy battering ram lay halfway through the opening where Drygo's men had dropped it, amid splintered fragments of the gate itself.

Morlac reached the entranceway and passed cautiously through, his sword ready in a hand raw from gripping it. A short distance inside the hall were the bodies of four of Sordros's menials, cut down as they had attempted to block the passage of Drygo and his men. And their efforts had not been totally unsuccessful, for near them were two of the North Kingdom soldiers, glassy-eyed and still.

Morlac slowed his pace as much as he dared. There were too many confusing corridors in Sordros's mad castle, too many ways Drygo might have gone. He could not even be certain whether the wizard still remained on the high balcony, was in his private chamber, or had sought refuge elsewhere within the castle.

Entering the corridor onto which the guard chamber opened, Morlac suddenly found horrible proof of Drygo's passage. For sprawled there were the bodies of more men, North Kingdom soldiers all, the blood still pulsing from their wounds. Some lived yet, and all bore the marks of a sword whose style Morlac thought he knew too well. His suspicion was borne out in the next moment as he rounded the corner. For here was the body of yet another man, maimed but still breathing: a small man, square-shouldered and with graying hair.

"Ardo—" Morlac said softly, kneeling quickly beside him. The man who had taught him everything he knew of swordsmanship lay beaten and dying, his hand still clutching his iron weapon.

"Morlac—?" Ardo's eyes focused on him and a faint smile touched the corner of a mouth twisted with pain. "So you live yet. You are a better pupil than I am a teacher. Had I a son, I could be no more proud of him than I am of you." He hesitated, coughing weakly. "Drygo passed but a moment ago. He is . . . truly unbeatable, my friend, unless Sordros is right about you."

Morlac gently cradled the old man's head in his hand. "What of the Watch-Devils? Could not they stop him?"

"They are gone . . . Sordros could not maintain them. He needed his full concentration for his plan. And in the end . . . even that sacrifice was not enough."

"There must be some force the wizard could call to his defense."

"Perhaps. But I doubt he has the strength now." Ardo's eyes began to glaze and his coughs were gurgling sounds that tore at Morlac's heart. Squinting now, he fixed his gaze imperatively upon Morlac. "Stop Drygo if you can . . . but if it is too late to save Sordros, then flee. There is nothing left to defend. Make some good use of your life, my friend. Turn Sordros's evil into good . . . into. . . ."

Ardo's head became a burden in Morlac's hand, and silence consumed him. Morlac gently removed his hand and stood up, for there was nothing more to be done for him.

He turned away, and after a final quick glance, hurried on in search of his prey. A blind, unreasoning hatred welled up in him—a blood lust that very nearly matched the dread power of his magicked sword.

A scream came from ahead and started him running. Turning into a cross corridor, he suddenly saw Drygo. The mercenary had sighted Kadrana and was pursuing her. Fleet as a deer the girl ran, staying well ahead of Drygo. Morlac set out after them, trying to close the gap between himself and his enemy.

On they ran, through one corridor after another, until their flight brought them to a spiral stair leading down. Drygo managed to reduce some of the distance as the girl slowed her pace on the steps, and so it was that when they reached the bottom level he was almost upon her.

Bursting into a chamber that must surely be underground, they caught a glimpse of Sordros himself. Casting a fearful glance over his shoulder, the magician disappeared through a panel in the otherwise seemingly solid stone wall. The dark passageway beckoned, and the girl obviously desired to reach it and whatever safety it offered.

With a grunt of dismay, Drygo shoved the girl aside with a rough sweep of his hand and pursued the wizard. He was almost within the opening of the secret passage when a sudden rumbling shook the castle.

Dust poured out of the passage as tons of rock fell down to block the way, cutting off any further pursuit. Drygo staggered back, cursing Sordros's ingenuity.

Standing at the entrance of the chamber, Morlac gasped, not at the escape of Sordros, but at the sudden realization of where he was. The dismal chamber, torches still blazing along the walls. The wooden winch . . . the large bronze lid near the center of the floor.

And the pit.

The very sight of it sent a chill down Morlac's spine that nearly overwhelmed him, blotting out for the moment even the presence of Drygo. Memories of the green fire which had transformed him flooded his mind, awakening old torments and arousing an almost abject fear that threatened to send him fleeing from the chamber. It was finally Kadrana's sharp outcry that cut through the mind-numbing terror.

"Morlac!"

He forced his gaze away from the pit where seawater still gurgled softly, away from the demon thoughts it conjured up to taunt him. The mercenary was advancing upon the cowering girl, sword poised menacingly.

"That tunnel—where does it lead?" Drygo shouted at Kadrana, his anger making his ugly face livid. "Tell me, wench, or die!"

"Far from the castle," the girl gasped. "But Sordros never told me where."

"You're lying!"

"*No—!*"

Morlac's resolve returned as he strode quickly toward Drygo. "Leave her alone, dog! It does not matter whether she tells you or not. You are not leaving this chamber."

Slowly, with a cold and contemptuous sneer, Drygo turned to face Morlac, whom he had virtually ignored until now. The mercenary studied his bruised and nicked body, and his seemingly sickly pallor.

"I've no time for you now, fool," he said. "Do you still think you can thwart me? Do not tempt fate!"

Morlac readied his sword and shield. "It is you who have tempted fate, Drygo . . . too long. Now fate would have its due, and *I* am its willing tool."

A snarling curse was the mercenary's only answer, and he charged Morlac with raised sword. It was a crude move, born of overconfidence, and Morlac stepped easily out of the way, parrying the blade with a thrust of his own. He glanced to be sure Kadrana was clear of their fighting.

Drygo wheeled about instantly, alert and quick—unexpectedly so. He lunged at Morlac with a sudden thrust of his sword that was aimed at his legs.

Morlac jumped back, quick enough to avoid serious injury, but slow enough to feel the shallow bite of iron along his shin. His special strength was in his arms, he remembered, and he would have to take care not to give his enemy that opportunity again.

Drygo's evil smile faded in the next instant as Shark lashed out, darting past the mercenary's shield to crease his arm. He fell back a step, surprised, then he frowned with newfound appreciation for his adversary's skill.

"It seems I shall have to take you seriously!" he said, launching another attack. Lunging, hacking, probing, he found each time his blows met and countered by sword or shield as Morlac's defenses became impenetrable.

Their fighting carried them to the far side of the chamber, away from the girl, and with a sudden and surprising movement Kadrana sprang from her position and ran swiftly for the center of the chamber. Both Morlac and Drygo saw her, but neither dared give her much attention. Morlac cast a quick and worried glance in her direction, and caught a glimpse of Kadrana's haunting face, her luminous eyes meeting his for an instant, and then her lithe and lovely form diving directly into the water-filled pit, her purpose unknown.

Even as the splash of Kadrana's dive settled into stillness, Drygo pressed forward again, more viciously than before. Feinting to the left to draw Morlac off balance, he instead lunged to the right with sword raised high.

Drygo slashed down violently with an unusually heavy blow and Morlac barely deflected it with his shield. The strike should have been followed by a quick lunge to Morlac's unguarded side. It should have been—

But Drygo hesitated, staring in wonder and shocked amazement. For where his sword had raked Morlac's odd shell-shield, a rivulet of *blood* oozed from the gash.

The mercenary's gnarled face paled. "By the gods! What manner of trickery is this!"

Morlac remained silent, too intent upon his adversary, too consumed by his hatred for Ardo's killer, to even notice what had happened. Seizing the opportunity, he launched his own attack, putting Drygo on the defensive.

Raw power from some unsuspected source welled up within him, supplanting his fatigue with new strength and focusing itself in his upper limbs. In his strong hand, Shark flashed out lightning-fast, its wicked white blade a blur that slashed and gouged, a deadly ghost that tormented Drygo with every movement.

The mercenary tried every trick, every villainous assault ever learned in a life full of treachery, all to no avail. He could not gain the offensive, could not even move Morlac toward the open mouth of the pit, where he might stumble in and become an easier target. Sweat ran profusely from his face and arms, mingling with the blood of his wounds and glistening in the torchlight.

Desperate now, sensing the possibility of defeat for the first time in years, he bellowed like an enraged bull. Changing his grip on his shield, he hurled the heavy disk directly at Morlac's legs, following it with his raised sword held high in both hands.

Morlac could not jump clear in time and the shield struck his legs above the ankles, nearly knocking his feet out from under him. He staggered back, dropping to his knees in pain.

Drygo was poised over him now. His raised sword was ready to crash down upon him with enough power to crush even his magicked shield. For a moment, Ardo's words rang through Morlac's mind—*he is truly unbeatable* . . .

But while his mind balked, his body responded. Shark, almost with a will of its own, lanced forward an instant before Drygo could strike, its point seeking a narrow gap in his meager armor. Seeking, and finding. Plunging in a full third of its length.

Letting out a raspy cry, the mercenary fell back a step. Drygo stared in surprised horror at the mortal wound, confused and disbelieving. Anger and defiance flooded his ugly features, even as his color faded.

"This cannot be!" he said. "I have the wizard's oath—*on his very soul*—that this sword be proof against the skill of *any* man!"

"And the spell be true." Morlac gained his feet, raising his weapon for the final strike. His tone was grim, quavering with anger. "But though I be now in human form, *I am no man*. . . ."

Drygo died instantly as Shark slashed through him, spared a lingering end even though he deserved no such consideration. He collapsed in a heap upon the cold flooring, his evil soul consigned to whatever hellish realm awaited it.

Morlac gave him no further attention. With the pitch of battle behind him now, the fatigue and pain flooded in once more. With some effort, he walked slowly toward the pit at the chamber's center. He did not know what to expect there— Kadrana was surely either drowned, or lurking there at water's edge, in hiding.

Venturing to the gaping pit's edge required all the courage he could summon. Cautiously, he stepped nearer, leaning over slightly and staring down into the well of mystic power.

Seawater glistened dully a few feet below the edge, throwing back glints of torchlight. The water was still and untroubled now, clear through its depth.

Nowhere could the girl be seen. But far from a magical disappearance, the manner of escape was soon apparent. For near the bottom of the pit, visible to Morlac's keen eyes even in the shadows, the gate to the sea was open. Whatever purpose Sordros had in opening the pit, whatever final effort had been interrupted by Drygo's appearance, it had at least served to give Kadrana an avenue of escape.

Morlac did not doubt she had made it. If anyone could swim the treacherous channel that fed the pit and reach the sea outside, it was Kadrana—no true daughter to Sordros, but instead his familiar, his link to powerful Tritus. She was in her own element now, even as he desired to be himself.

Wasting not another moment, for he well remembered Broct's predicament, Morlac fled the chamber and climbed the stair, returning to ground level. Hearing a clamor from without as he neared the entrance of the castle, he peered through one of the narrow windows that dotted the odd structure.

Coming through the village, nearly upon the path which led up into the castle, were the remainder of Drygo's soldiers. They came almost at a run, their swords stained and waving in the air.

Their sight sent a chill through Morlac, not so much for his own danger as for the realization that the North Kingdom men could not have reached the castle unless Sordros's defenders had been vanquished.

"Broct. . . ."

Morlac lingered but a moment at the window, contemplating the fates of those he knew, then quickly turned and ran back along the corridor toward the castle's rear. For he knew there was no chance of escaping through the front. There was nothing left but the cliffs that backed the structure, and the crashing waves below.

He could hear the soldiers in the halls behind him now, their victorious voices and the clatter of their gear. Morlac turned a corner and continued until he reached a window that overlooked the sea. Sheathing his sword, he slipped into the wide strap that stretched diagonally across his shield, letting it hang upon his back, where it truly belonged. Climbing up into the window, he paused to look down at the sea that had given him up, and now waited to claim him.

It was a long drop, with the danger of hidden rocks that could crush and tear him. He might not survive a moment in the water. But did it matter? Morlac wondered.

Then the sound of Kerr's army grew louder within his ears, the first of the soldiers nearing his position. He could not beat them all, and his fate at their hands was far more certain than whatever the sea held in store. Suddenly, his torments momentarily forgotten, Morlac felt the one most powerful force that surged through the hearts of all living creatures—*survival*.

Without a backward glance, he sprang free of the window and dove for the sea, kicking out in an attempt to clear the rocks. Long seconds he fell, with the shouts of North Kingdom soldiers ringing in his ears. Then at last, he reached the water. Salt spray arched high into a shimmering crown as he cleaved the surface, to fall back as he swam strongly away. . . .

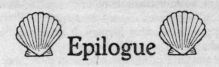

Epilogue

"And so ends my tale," said the stranger, some several hours after he had begun. "I hope that you found it pleasing, and payment enough for your kind hospitality."

"Most pleasing," said the old wayfarer. He and most of the others were still awake and alert at this late hour, though some of the travelers had drifted off into sleep. "And a tale well-told, if I am any judge. But it seems somehow unresolved. What happened next to this . . . this *fellow* known as Morlac?"

The stranger paused a moment, then replied, "This is of course only a tale, a fantasy without substance, for how could such strange events be true? But it is said that this Morlac returned to the village as soon as he could, under cover of darkness, to determine the fate of his friends. Sadly, his search came too late.

"The dead had been dealt with quickly. Those of Kerr's army had been buried in the field where they fell, with crude markers erected before the mounds. The village's defenders shared a common grave—a rude pit that had been dug and covered over after filling. Scattered weapons had long since been gathered up for trophies, and nowhere was there anything to tell for certain what had become of his friends. Even the girl, Kadrana, had vanished without a trace.

"Morlac, I'm sure, hoped that Broct and some of the others might have escaped with their lives. He hoped . . . yet he doubted that they had. It seemed certain that he was the last, the only one left to know the torment of Sordros's sorcery. Beyond that, I cannot imagine what next he did. Can you?"

"I have little imagination, I fear," said the old wayfarer. "But I thank you for entertaining us."

"It is small repayment," said the stranger. "Perhaps some other night, on some other journey, if again we meet, I will have found a proper ending for my tale."

The old wayfarer nodded slowly, with more understanding than he seemed willing to admit. "I wish you luck in finding it, wherever your journey takes you."

Something splashed in the distant waves, and the stranger's eyes focused on a herd of sea turtles as they surfaced, their strong foreflippers propelling them on tirelessly. He sensed it was the herd he had known, but the recollection seemed eons old. Once brothers, they were strangers to him now. They were separated by more than distance, and it was a chasm he could never cross, even had he wished to.

Morlac fingered the amulet he still wore about his neck, the sea crystal placed there by Kadrana. Within it a tiny form echoed the shape of the creatures now swimming in the distant waves, and the creature that he once was. Kadrana had said it was his only hope of freedom from the spell which entrapped him . . . that, and Sordros's evil skill. If he wished freedom.

He was not even sure who or what he was. Morlac . . . Calrom . . . man, beast, or demon. At least before, he had known that he was Captain of Sordros's guard, Kadrana's lover, Broct's friend. Without them, who would he be?

Kadrana's words came back to haunt him. *What you are now . . . is not so terrible.* Even Ardo seemed to accept the fact that Morlac's destiny was to go on. *Make some good use of your life, my friend,* he had said before dying. *Turn Sordros' evil into good.*

So many torments . . . so many unresolved questions. Morlac did not know what the answers might be, but whatever their shape, perhaps Sordros held them. *If* he could be found. And if Kadrana was with him . . . ?

In the morning, he would take leave of the caravan and continue his journey alone, with Shark at his side, his shield at his back, and his future before him . . . a vast mystery . . . an unknown adventure.

The quest had begun . . .

THE END—BOOK ONE

BOOK TWO

The Wanderers

BOOK TWO: THE WANDERERS

CONTENTS

DARK LEGACY

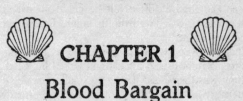

CHAPTER 1
Blood Bargain

It was night in an unknown land, weeks after the fall of Sordros's village, as the one called Morlac strode along the well-worn trade road, wearily, warily, and alone. High overhead, the full moon lit his path with cold clarity. The familiar realm of Shola was left far behind now, for Morlac had crossed the land bridge that connected that peninsula with the mainland. This was the region known as Goltos, and Morlac knew little of it, from either his animal or his human memory. He knew only that Sordros's trail led this way. For now, that was all he needed to know.

The path twisted its way through the rolling countryside, through farmlands and occasionally mountainous terrain. Innocent land. Dangerous land. The brisk night air brought the smells of freshly tilled soil and mountain flowers, and other, older, stranger scents. In the distance ahead were the lights of a village, beckoning to him with the promise of warmth and food and shelter. But was the promise a false one? How might a stranger be received here, especially a stranger as unusual as he? Morlac wondered, and as he walked on, he pulled his hood and cloak closer about his exotic features.

The food he had brought with him, scavenged from Sordros's village, was gone now. Wild fruits and berries from the fields, and small game when he found it, had sustained him since, but he craved a good hot meal. He hoped the few coins he still had left would be enough to buy that meal.

A wolf howled suddenly in the distance, sending a chill up his spine. A grim reminder that this was a different sort of realm he now traversed, with different hazards than those he had known in Shola.

And then, startlingly, a second wolf howled in answer, very near. Much too near for comfort. The sound was crisp and clear and loud. Morlac felt he could almost sense the warmth of the air escaping from its lungs, almost perceive its furry, animal scent.

His hand moved swiftly to sword hilt as a rustling in the bushes to his right teased his ear and jerked his head around. Something was there, and it was no small animal.

In the next instant, a wolf bounded into the roadway just ahead of him, pausing to turn and stare at him in the semi-darkness as if it had not seen him until now. Its breath came in quick gusts of vapor in the chill night air, its eyes aglow with the haunted blue of moonlight.

The beast was quite large, though lean and finely formed. Its coat was golden in hue, and remarkably clean and unblemished for a wild animal. Its even white teeth were sharp and glistening. The scent of its fur and its skin was unmistakably real now, filling Morlac's nostrils. It continued to stand there in the roadway, blocking his path, and studying Morlac with a look that might be curiosity . . . or hunger.

Morlac started to edge Shark free of its sheath, and immediately felt the repulsive tingling in the magicked sword's hilt—the awakening hunger and fury—the blood-frenzy. And yet, even as he prepared to defend himself, he hesitated, leaving only the barest portion of the strange white blade exposed. The wolf was a predator that could well be recognized and feared, both by his human side and by that part of him that was still turtle. And yet, he could not bring himself to slay this creature without cause. Even Shark seemed to waver now, its emanations oddly confused.

Morlac pushed the blade back within its sheath, feeling a kind of quieting sigh escape from it as his hand released the grip. The wolf stared at him a long moment more, head tilted to one side in puzzlement. Then it gave a low whine, almost a whimper, oddly melancholy, and darted across the road to disappear into the foliage beyond. There was only a rustling of the undergrowth to mark its progress up the hillside, then even that faded to silence.

Morlac waited a few moments longer, listening and watching, his entire body attuned to the night. Then he quickly pressed on, striding with renewed energy toward the village ahead.

The sign outside the inn said "Kettle and Cup," and the smells and sounds emanating from the place seemed pleasant enough. Morlac hesitated a long moment at the doorway, staying in the shadows and surveying the interior. It was a simple village inn, nearly empty. There were less than a dozen men inside, mostly tradespeople and a few farmers from the look of them. Men tired from honest work, but oddly somber for an inn. There were only two serving women, one older, one younger. Both were sturdy, decent-looking women. Probably the owner's wife and daughter.

Morlac drew a deep breath, then stepped inside, hoping travelers were a common sight here. He could hear the conversations dwindling as he entered, but he continued walking toward the counter at the far side of the room. Heads were turning in his direction—he could feel their gaze even without seeing it—but he ignored them and steadfastly approached the older of the two women at the counter.

Stopping directly before her, he said, "Good evening. How much for a bowl of stew and a place to sleep?"

The woman studied him a moment, cautious and unsettled. "Three tekahs."

Morlac produced a handful of coins from the pouch at his waist. There were not many, and he wondered how they would equate with the local currency.

The woman looked at the coins. "That's enough for food and drink only."

Morlac considered but a moment, then placed the coins upon the counter. "Then that is what I wish."

She scooped up the coins, but kept her eyes upon him as she did so. "Take a seat. I will bring it to you."

Morlac watched her pocket the coins and turn for the kitchen. Then he sought a table. It was not difficult to find an empty one, and he chose a seat away from the others in the room. Self-conscious, yet still proud, he looked defiantly back at those who stared at him. But it was hard to match the unwavering gaze of men who belonged here.

In a few minutes the woman returned, carrying a large bowl of stew, bread, and a flagon of ale. She set them before him, then remained to watch as Morlac ate. He noticed her curious gaze, and gave a questioning look.

The woman gestured toward his side, where Shark was revealed by his opening cloak. "You are a swordsman . . . ?"

Morlac studied her a moment as he continued to eat, then slowly nodded.

"Are you any good with that blade?"

"Good enough," he said without enthusiasm.

This either satisfied her curiosity or else convinced her that he did not wish to talk, for with that the woman left and went to another table where a handful of men sat. But Morlac noticed that she spoke to them in low whispers, and as she did so, the men glanced in his direction, nodding. This troubled him, but did not really surprise him.

What did surprise him was that, after he had finished his meal, the woman returned with a second flagon of ale. She set it down before him and waited.

Morlac said, "I have no more money."

"None is needed," the woman told him. "And there is a room you may sleep in this night. There is no charge for it."

Morlac glanced at the others, then back at her. "I should not question kindness, if indeed it is that, but I can't help wondering if all strangers are received here with the same hospitality."

"You are right. It is not mere kindness. We have a bargain we wish to make, for we have a need of a man who can fight, and fight well."

"Fight who—?"

"We will explain everything tomorrow, after you have rested. We ask only that you listen. Then, if you decide not to help, you may go on your way, owing us nothing. Is that fair enough?"

Morlac considered. If their intent was evil, it made little sense. He had no money to steal, nor anything else of worth to these folk. Perhaps that was not the same thing as trust, but it was close enough. Besides, he was tired and his belly was full, and he had spent enough nights with the chill wind blowing down his back to relish a roof above his head once more. He made his decision.

"Yes," he said. "It is fair."

Morlac awoke the next morning, his hand still clutching his sheathed sword to his chest in the manner he had become accustomed to sleeping these past weeks. But he found that he was sprawled comfortably upon the bed instead of being tensed up in the alert posture he assumed outdoors. He stretched and yawned, then quickly got to his feet.

The room was small and plain, but pleasant enough as morning sunlight streamed in. There was a pitcher of water on the table, and he washed his face before gathering up his things and going to the door. The latch was still secure, and as he opened the door and stepped into the narrow hall Morlac wondered what need this small village had for a warrior.

He realized the answer would be given him soon when he entered the main room of the inn, for gathered there now was a crowd of people that must surely be the entire population of the village. There were men, women, and children, farmers and merchants and craftsmen. And he realized, too, that he had slept later than he had expected.

All eyes were upon him as he approached and halted. Curious eyes. Appraising eyes. Eyes that seemed to hold hope as well as questions. The woman who had waited on him the night before came out from behind the counter, wiping her hands on a piece of cloth, and studying him with that same questioning look.

"Did you rest well?"

"Yes," Morlac told her. "Thank you."

"And you will listen to our bargain . . . ?"

"I said I would, and I shall."

"Very well. We are willing to pay for your skills, if you will aid us."

Morlac was sick of battle. He had shed enough blood fighting against L'Dron Kerr's soldiers and Drygo's men. But he was on his own now, with no other skills to earn his way—no other means to continue his journey.

Reluctantly, he said, "Who do you wish me to fight?"

"It is not a man," someone said from the front of the group. "It is a beast."

The man stepped forward, gray-haired, stout, a merchant judging from the cut of his clothes. His face had a haunted look.

"I am Josaffa, the village elder. For the past two months our village had been preyed upon by a beast. A terrible beast. It has killed many of our farm animals . . . sheep, goats, even cattle. Far worse, it has slain two men, a woman, and three of our children. Slain . . . and eaten them."

Morlac felt a chill traverse his spine, not so much from the man's words as from the tone of terror that underlay them. "What sort of beast?"

"We are not sure," said Josaffa, "but we have seen a wolf in the area, and believe it responsible."

"Surely a wolf is not unusual here."

One of the farm men, with skin darkened and wrinkled by work in the fields, said, "It be no ordinary wolf. It be a demon in the guise of a wolf!"

"Aye!" said another man, and the rest nodded their agreement.

Morlac remembered the wolf he had encountered the night before, the strange creature with the moon-bright eyes. Was it the killer of which they spoke? If so, then why had it not attacked him?

"It does not take a warrior to kill a wolf. Even a beast of a wolf. Did you not set traps? Or send out a party of armed men?"

"We did both, more than once," said Josaffa. "Our traps caught nothing. Some were rent apart, though strong iron they were. Thrice, we sent out a dozen men, well armed, to search for the beast. Even at night, with torches. They saw nothing. Heard nothing. The damnable beast is cunning. It hides from large groups. Only those who were alone have seen it."

"And died," said the woman. "As my husband did. And Josaffa's granddaughter."

"Aye," said the farmer, "and my son."

Other sad murmurings echoed through the crowd, soft and

pained and tinged with anger. Morlac could almost taste the fear and horror that permeated this room.

"And so," continued Josaffa, drawing himself up, "we need a warrior . . . a man good at fighting and killing . . . a man not afraid to venture alone where he might draw out the beast, and slay it. We know little of you, stranger, but you appear strong, and you have weapons, and you have the look of war about you. If you will do this thing we ask . . . if you succeed in killing this monster, we will give you one hundred gold pieces."

"And if I fail," Morlac added, "if this beast is all you say it is, I shall likely die in the effort."

"As may we all, one by one," said the woman as she put her arm around her daughter. "We know full well what we ask. You may refuse and go on your way, with no ill will."

Morlac considered, as they waited in silence for his answer. This was not truly his concern, and yet, these were good people, asking for his help. Not demanding, as Sordros had done, but *asking*. And the gold they offered would carry him far upon his journey.

If he lived. . . ,

"All right," Morlac said, as the silence became unbearable. "I accept your bargain. . . ."

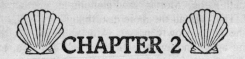

CHAPTER 2

A Glow of Magic

The day seemed to stretch on endlessly, but the food and the night's rest had renewed Morlac's strength. He had set out from the village no more than an hour after his meeting with Josaffa and the others. Marda, the woman who owned and ran the Kettle and Cup, had packed Morlac enough food for two days, with the promise he could return for more if needed. The village had also provided him with a goat to use as bait, should the presence of a lone man not be enough to lure the beast. Leading the poor dumb creature around on a tether, knowing its probable fate, troubled Morlac. But more than once during the day, he paused to consider the possibility that there was a far dumber creature on the opposite end of the tether. At least the goat did not know what lay ahead, nor did he have any choice in the matter.

Morlac had gone first to the path where he had seen the strange wolf the night before, as he had approached the village. But there was nothing there now, and he could find no tracks to follow.

Next he circled the farms that lay outside the boundary of the village, making himself an easy target for whatever might be waiting and watching. Morlac was searching. Probing. Keeping his senses constantly alert, even as he paused for a brief meal.

The deepening woods loomed beyond the farmlands, sinister and brooding, full of hidden places and ominous shadows. This was where his search took him next. If ever there was a place where a beast might attack a man, this was it. Often had he the feeling of being watched, but aside from the birds and small game, Morlac saw nothing to account for that feeling. That was all the more disturbing.

As the hours slowly passed, Morlac found his thoughts returning again and again to Sordros and Kadrana, to Broct and the other sea-warriors. And Ardo. Morlac flinched inwardly at the pain and anguish of these memories . . . the longings . . . the anger and despair. They ate at his insides as worms upon a corpse.

Human emotions . . . so complex, so deep, at once so familiar and so strange. He wondered how he could bear them. And he thought again of how Kadrana had fled from Drygo in Sordros's dungeon, escaping through the pit into the sea. She had saved herself, for which he was glad. But in so doing, she had abandoned him to his fate, with scarcely a backward glance. Not knowing if he lived or died. Not caring . . . ? How easy it would be to hate her for that. And, he realized, how easy it would be to forgive her, if again they met. What sorcery love must be, to make such fools of men.

Shadows stretched long and the woods were bathed in an amber glow as Morlac reached the mountains which partially ringed the farmlands and village. The sunlight was fading, the azure sky slipping into twilight's purple cloak. Night would be upon him soon. Night, and perhaps the beast. . . .

A clearing ahead seemed to offer the best place to make camp. A place to build a fire and tie up the goat, and to prepare for a long night's vigil, for he dare not sleep.

He had barely reached the center of the clearing when he became aware of the ruins before him, lying partway up the incline of the mountain. Bathed in the dying light of day, the moldering stones looked forlorn and grim. But there was also about them a sense of ancient and majestic power. This was no mere village building ahead of him. The immense outline of the tumbled stones hinted at the scale and grandeur of the castle that once had been, though vines and other plant growth now obscured it. Who had lived here? Who had *ruled* here?

Morlac's wonderings came to an abrupt halt as something else caught his eye. There—near the edge of the ruins—a small fire burned. Or something like a fire. But the glow had not the orange color of true flame. There was a slightly blue-green cast to it, and something unnatural about its slow flickering. It reminded Morlac of the spirit flame within the cavern at the South Kingdom outpost.

Could Sordros be here? Was it possible he could have already caught up with him, here at this place and time? Morlac quickly tied the goat's tether to a narrow tree stump, and cautiously advanced toward the mysterious glow.

Silently he moved through the tall grass, eyes always on the wavering point of light. He tried to see who tended the flame, but his view was blocked by one of the large tumbled stones at the edge of the ruins.

Morlac's nostrils flared as the scents of magical powders reached him. Whether Sordros or not, there was surely at least some sorcerer here. Also, becoming more pronounced as he drew nearer still, there was yet another scent, different, yet strangely familiar. What did it remind him of?

As he reached the tumbled stone, his hand moved to grasp Shark's hilt. Morlac edged cautiously around the stone, and as he did so, a cloaked figure came into view, kneeling before the fire, back to him.

Morlac stopped where he stood, and said, " 'Tis a poor fire that gives so little warmth. . . ."

Jerking around, catlike and quick, the one in the cloak whirled to face him, drawing an odd sword in the same motion, holding it defensively, menacingly. But it was not Sordros who faced him, nor any other wizard, nor any other man. . . .

"Who are you—?" said the girl. "What do you want?"

He paused a moment, then answered. "I am Morlac. I was about to make camp for the night when I saw your fire."

The girl still stood in a fighter's stance, wary, alert, ready to do battle in an instant. And it seemed not a bluff. There was something about the way she stood, and the steadiness of her sword hand, that convinced Morlac she knew how to handle a blade.

She was an unlikely warrior, though, so young and slender, her features so finely formed. Beneath the hood of her cloak, blond hair cascaded to her shoulders and hung in bangs across her forehead. Blue eyes as pure as a cloudless sky sparkled with reflections of the strange fire and the setting sun. Her face was delicate and pale, her cheeks ruddy from the chill air and the excitement of the moment. Morlac estimated that she was a bit older than Kadrana, in years at least, but she seemed younger.

Still she stood ready. "I do not trust strangers," said she. "Especially those that creep up behind me without a sound." She paused. "And yet, you could have drawn your sword upon me, and you did not."

"Pray that I don't," said Morlac. "For its hunger grows, and I cannot always fight its will. . . ."

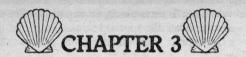 **CHAPTER 3**

Daughter of the House of Chalthax

The girl looked at Morlac for a long moment, puzzling at his words, studying the gray hide-covered sword sheath and his odd oval shield. Finally, she lowered her sword and cocked her head to one side.

"I swear . . ." she said, the words cloaked in vapor as she spoke in the crisp air, ". . . I swear I've seen you in a dream."

Morlac watched her golden hair blowing in the soft breeze that swept across them, hair that smelled clean and pleasant, and vaguely familiar. He took his hand off Shark's hilt and relaxed a bit. But not entirely.

From the clearing came the sound of the goat, bleating in discontent. The girl's lovely eyes alertly shifted toward the sound and her lips parted in an odd expression. She had to move slightly to see around the stone, then saw the goat, straining against its tether.

Looking back to Morlac, she said, "Is that yours?"

He nodded.

"An odd companion on a journey," said she, "for one who has not the look of a goatherd."

"I am merely transporting it. It is . . . for another." Morlac realized how strange he must seem to her. The girl was right to be wary. And so was he. He looked at her sword with curiosity. "I have never seen a weapon quite like that."

The blade glinted in the sunset glow as she glanced at it. It was an odd sword, thin and light in weight, with a blade that flared broader near the tip. Two daggerlike small blades stuck out above the hilt in a wide fork. It seemed awkward, but potentially lethal. She carefully replaced the sword in a sheath made to accommodate the special blades.

"It is a dirksword," explained the girl, "not uncommon to my people."

Morlac eyed the dove-gray cloak she wore, the patterned tunic of purple and blue, the gray leggings and the soft leather boots. "Your people—?"

"The Durkesh Tribes. We belong to no land. We roam as we please, fighting if we need to, but more often trading, telling fortunes, making music, practicing many crafts."

"It sounds like a good life."

"It is," she said, but her tone of pride had a cutting edge to it. "Most of the time. But many people there are who despise us. Some call us thieves. Some call us worse."

"Once," Morlac said thoughtfully, "I saw a Durkesh caravan traveling through Shola. They were handsome folk, dark of hair and eyes, sturdy of build, and none were quite as tall as you."

The girl's face flushed a bit. "You are right . . . I was not born to them. I was orphaned while still a babe. A Durkesh family took me in, raised me, taught me their ways. I will always feel a part of them, no matter what."

Morlac took a seat upon a low section of wall. "And yet you are not with them now."

"No," she said, eyes downcast. "What brought me here, I must do alone."

"I could well say the same about myself," Morlac told her. There was a note of sadness underlying his words.

The girl stepped closer, studying his exotic features, puzzling at his emerald pallor. "You are like no man I've ever seen. Are you a wizard of some kind?"

"A wizard?" Morlac gave a short grunting laugh. "No, my lady. I have oft been the *victim* of wizardry, but never its practitioner." He gestured toward the small flame she had tended. "What about you and this demon fire? Are you a sorceress?"

"I—? No. Would that I were," she said. "I might have better luck with this spell."

Her words rang true, and as Morlac looked deep within her

troubled eyes he thought he saw echoed there a pain he knew only too well himself. Her expression seemed to soften. Did she see the same in him?

"You have not told me your name yet," said Morlac.

"I . . . I am called Glendauna."

"A name as lovely as its owner," said Morlac. "But though I am pleased to meet you, I fear neither of us is safe in these woods, from what the villagers have told me."

"The villagers? I suspect we have more to fear from them than from anything here."

Morlac frowned. "Why do you say that?"

Glendauna began to pace slowly about the strange fire. "Perhaps I should let the past lay dead and unremembered. But I cannot. You see these ruins—? Once there was a castle here, centuries old, a stronghold of the kingdom of Goltos. It was also the ancestral home of a family of nobles, the House of Chalthax. Was, but no longer. Because twenty years ago the ruling family was killed in a bloody revolt, a revolt led by many of the same villagers who still live in the valley. It was the fire they set that destroyed the castle and brought the walls down."

"How do you know this?" asked Morlac. "You could have been no more than a child at the time."

"Barely a year old," she replied, and there was anger in her words. "I was told by the Durkesh family who took me as their own child . . . the family who found me crying in the smoldering ruins where now we stand. For you see, Morlac, I am the daughter of Jules, Marquis of this region, and the last surviving member of the Chalthax line."

"Then that is why you are here?"

She nodded. "This is my home. I am of the royal blood."

Morlac folded his arms in a thoughtful pose. "Blood that might be spilled if you stay here."

"That is a chance I must take. But I do not plan to confront the villagers. I care nothing for power or the trappings of royalty. What they took from me can never be given back."

"What then . . . revenge?"

Glendauna sighed heavily. "No . . . not even that. Only peace of mind. If I can find it here, and I pray I can."

Morlac got to his feet and approached her. "Let me build a larger fire. There is no need for each of us to be isolated and alone in these woods. I have food down by my campsite."

Glendauna frowned and shook her head in a troubled way. "I do not think it wise."

"I know you do not trust strangers, but—"

"It is not that," said Glendauna. "Though I cannot explain it, I do feel an odd kinship with you. And that dream . . . I cannot shake the feeling of that dream. But there are dangers you do not know. Dark secrets I dare not share."

"I have faced danger many times," said Morlac. "And I have secrets of my own. They can be a burden."

The girl seemed undecided, wavering, her emotions on the thin edge. She looked to the setting sun and the darkening sky. Then her azure gaze returned to Morlac.

"Perhaps . . . perhaps it would be all right. If my spell works, it should be safe enough. And if it does not, then it may be better if you are forewarned."

Morlac was still puzzling over the girl's strange words as they finished their dinner. He had gone back to his own campsite to get his pack and the goat, then returned to the spot where Glendauna waited. He tied the goat to the trunk of a small tree nearby where it could graze without being in their way. A large fire he had built several paces from the small occult flame the girl was tending, and it served to warm them and to heat their food. And now that they had finished eating, the girl was still oddly silent.

Darkness had fallen, and Morlac set about making ready for the long night. He kept his sword belt buckled about him but stood his odd shell-shield beside him against the stone wall. He polished it with a scrap of cloth from his pack.

Glendauna carefully emptied another vial of iridescent powder over the small flame of flickering green and blue, grimacing and waving away the acrid fumes that suddenly assailed her nose. She stared deeply into the mystic fire, with a look that was hard to fathom, then she sighed and turned her gaze upon Morlac. The sight of his shield replaced her troubled look with one of curiosity.

"Is . . . is that real?" she said, breaking her silence at last.

"Yes. As real as I."

"Would not a shield faced with metal give more protection?"

"Perhaps," said Morlac solemnly. "But this one has protected me all my life, and it has greater strength than you imagine."

"I don't understand."

"I know. Nor do I, at times. But if we survive this night, I may explain it to you."

Her eyes looked down for a moment, her mouth opening to speak, but hesitating. At last, her eyes seeking his with an urgent look, she said, "Morlac, there is something I must tell you . . . something dreadful."

"You need not say anything you do not wish me to know."

"No—this I must tell you!" She turned to face him fully. "I am here alone, now, because I had to leave my people. I dared not remain among them."

Morlac wondered what dread secret could so trouble such a beautiful young woman. He also wondered if what she told him about her own past was true. From what he had heard of the Durkesh people, they were good at lies and fanciful tales.

"It began with my coming of age . . . my twenty-first year," she continued. "That was three months ago. Just three months, but by the gods, it seems an eternity."

"What happened?"

"I don't know why I should be so cursed," she said, the words tumbling out now. "It has something to do with my past . . . something about this place, though I do not understand what or why. That is why I had to return. I *had* to. If I cannot find the answer here, I think I shall go mad. If I have not already."

Morlac felt uncomfortable. Madness was an intangible thing, difficult to fight or to deal with. Yet her torment seemed real enough. He realized his own sanity might well be questioned if he told of his true nature. And he also could not help thinking how unlike Kadrana she was. The vanity, the self-centered pride, were missing.

"I think the spell will work this time," she continued. "At least, I pray it will. I paid almost everything I had for it. But in case it fails, you should know—"

She bit off her words, twisting in sudden pain, clutching at her stomach and dropping the empty vial to the ground. Her eyes squeezed tightly shut and a faint cry escaped her lovely lips.

Morlac started, began to rise, reaching toward her. "What's wrong—? What hurts you?"

"No . . . oh, no . . ." Glendauna moaned softly. Her tear-filled eyes opened to gaze skyward with a look of heart-wrenching sadness. "It is happening . . . again."

Morlac could not help following that troubled gaze, turning to look back over his shoulder. But there was nothing in the sky except the rising moon, full and bright and coldly beckoning. He looked back to see the girl nearly doubled over, but clawing frantically through her pack for something. What? It was an unnerving sight that chilled him more than the night breeze.

"Here—" said the girl, pleading, begging "—here, take these."

Morlac quickly knelt beside her, and saw that she was holding out to him several lengths of rope. "But why—? What should I—"

"Bind me!" she nearly screamed. "My hands and my feet. Quickly! Please, just do as I say!"

It made little sense, but there was something so imperative in her tone, something so pathetically vulnerable in her look, that he could not refuse. He quickly set about binding her wrist and her ankles, tightly, but not so tight as to cut off circulation. Perhaps she *was* mad, he thought. Or perhaps she was afflicted with some sickness that made her lose control of herself, so that she must be restrained to avoid injury. He had heard of such things, though never had he seen them.

"Is there nothing else I can do?" he asked.

"No. Just . . . just guard yourself. And pray to whatever gods you worship that I—"

Her words ended in a gasp and her head wrenched back, tossing her hair and removing her hood. Her eyes stared wide and fearful at the sky, unwillingly, unavoidably.

Suddenly, those beautiful blue eyes acquired a luminance that could not be mere reflections of the rising moon. The glow spread out across the whites of her eyes as well, until their total surface was ablaze with the ghostly color. Her bound hands clawed the air, the fingers bent and contorted, their delicate beauty lost to the pain that twisted them.

Morlac staggered back from the girl, stunned by what he saw. He had witnessed things sorcerous and strange while in Sordros's employ, yet nothing quite like this.

Glendauna turned her head toward him, her lips peeling back in a snarl as animal sounds rumbled deep in her throat. She strained against the bonds which held her, writhing with a fury that was frightening to behold.

And still the transformation continued. She turned away from him now, seeming to fold inward upon herself, the very contours of her body reshaping themselves. Her lush blond hair grew and spread, covering every part of her that was visible, and her hands and wrists, even her legs . . . how narrow they were becoming! And suddenly, as the thing that had been a human girl now solidified into something else, Morlac understood. Now he knew why her scent was so familiar. Now he knew. . . .

The golden wolf shrugged out of the loose human garments, stepped free of the ropes that no longer were tight enough to hold. It turned its moon-haunted eyes upon Morlac and uttered a growl that was low and uncertain. This was the very creature he had seen on the road last night. There was no doubt in his mind about that. But was it also the beast he had been sent out to slay . . . ?

She had told the truth, as far as she had gotten with her story. She had tried to warn him . . . tried to fight against the transformation. That much was to her credit. Surely she deserved better than death at the hands of a stranger. But then, Morlac thought, so did he.

Now he understood why Shark had seemed hesitant and confused the night before. His magicked blade had somehow sensed the wolf's odd nature. Would it balk a second time? Morlac did not know, but he vowed to himself he would not use the blade against her, regardless.

The wolf stared at him a moment more, then abruptly turned and started to run away. Where would she go? Deeper into the woods, or down to the village, there perhaps to kill or be killed? Morlac ran after the wolf, uncertain of how he would stop her, but determined to do just that.

The creature ran around what remained of a thick outer wall which stood at the perimeter of the ruins, then darted past a pile of tumbled stones. Morlac followed it, running swiftly. The moonlight which created this nightmare helped illuminate the ruins, but there were still deep pockets of shadow. Shadows that concealed dangers.

As he rounded a corner, Morlac stumbled over something hard. Regaining his feet in an instant, he saw that it was a wrought-iron gate with elaborate grillwork that must once have stood at some entranceway to the castle. Then he caught sight of the wolf once more and hurried after it.

The place was a veritable maze, with many walls too high to see over. Brush and trees loomed like demons in the night, reaching out from nearly every corner. But just as pursuit began to seem hopeless, the wolf's escape route suddenly ended.

The path between the outer and inner walls now terminated. Solid stone walls closed off that corridor, with the only doorway so completely blocked by fallen rubble that not even a rat could get through.

The wolf reached the dead end and stopped, looking frantically about for some passage, some exit, some possible way out. But there simply was none.

Advancing cautiously, Morlac spied a second wrought-iron gate, identical to the first, lying on the ground near one wall. With a plan now in mind, he lifted the gate and carried it before him, moving quietly. The gate was old, encrusted with rust, but still quite strong.

Sensing his approach, the wolf whirled about and stared at him, a low growl erupting from her lips. She started to dart off to one side, attempting to get past him. Morlac moved swiftly to block her path.

The she-wolf now started to move to the other side, but again with surprising swiftness, Morlac moved to thwart her attempt. He continued to move forward, driving her back. Closer . . . closer to the end of the narrowing corridor.

There was nowhere to go now. The corner of the closed corridor was all that remained, and into this niche Morlac maneuvered the wolf until her position was exactly right. Then with a sudden lunge he forced the iron gate forward, against the ground and the walls, forming a barrier . . . a cage. If he could make it fast somehow, force something against it to hold it in place, then it would effectively imprison the girl-wolf until morning.

But as he looked about for a means to wedge the gate in place, the wolf snarled savagely, angry and fearful at being cornered. In desperation, it lunged forward, driving its head and shoulders through a narrow space within the ornamental design.

Morlac was still leaning with all his weight against the gate as the wolf wriggled through, twisting to get free, at his very feet. Even as Morlac released his hold and staggered back, the wolf was clear and springing at him.

He caught the creature in midleap, her claws raking at his neck and chest and her glistening teeth clicking together near his throat. Did she mean to kill him, or merely to frighten him into letting her escape? Morlac did not know, and for the moment had no time to ponder the matter.

His strong right hand clamped around the wolf's muzzle and as he turned it away from him his arm encircled the beast, pinning the wolf with her back to his chest. His left hand grabbed her forepaws and held them together, immobile. While her hind paws clawed empty air, they could not reach him.

He had succeeded in catching her. But what to do with her now—?

Maintaining his hold, Morlac carried her back to the campsite, noting to himself that the wolf's weight must surely equal that of the girl. He looked for the ropes on the ground, thinking he might yet bind her securely enough to keep her, him, and the countryside safe. But even as he spotted the ropes, he realized there was no way in which he could pick them up, untie the old knots and apply them to the animal's limbs without releasing her completely. And once released. . . .

For a moment he considered knocking the wolf senseless. But how could he know how great a blow a were-beast might require? Or how much damage it might do? He did not wish to risk it.

Finally, as the wolf still struggled within his arms, Morlac reluctantly sank to his haunches and sat upon the ground, his back to the low stone wall. His great supernormal strength and endurance was in his arms, after all, and as long as they lasted, he would hold the creature safely immobile, till dawn if need be.

Morlac sighed wearily. The remaining hours of the night seemed to stretch before him like eternity itself. Worse than that, he wondered just how he would manage to fulfill his bargain with the villagers now. . . .

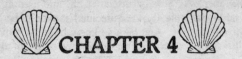

CHAPTER 4

The Castle Crypts

The pure light of early morning greeted Morlac as he opened his eyes. It cast a pleasant glow upon the castle ruins, making them look far different than they had the night before. Nevertheless, it was still a strange place to awaken.

Awaken . . . ?

Morlac gave a start as he realized he had fallen asleep. When had it happened? He remembered staying alert all night, or nearly so. Surely he could not have fallen asleep in the last hour before dawn, when his goal was so near. Or was that perhaps the reason? Just when he thought the long night's ordeal was over, he had relaxed his guard and fatigue had won out.

As he came more fully awake, he realized that he was still in the same position, leaning back against the wall, that he had held all night. His body ached from it, and was slow to respond as he attempted to move. And he quickly realized something else as well. His captive was still with him.

The golden wolf was gone, but Glendauna was not. In human form once more, she lay naked within his arms, for her garments were still on the ground where the wolf had shed them hours ago. Her head was turned toward him, pillowed against his chest, and she slept the untroubled sleep of the innocent.

Morlac felt uncomfortable seeing her thus, though he could not help marveling at her exquisite beauty. Her garments had concealed a body that was strong, yet delicate and alluring. It was a different, gentler beauty than Kadrana's, yet no less desirable.

Morlac sighed heavily, and decided it would be wise to think of other things. And he also knew he must move soon, before his stiff and aching muscles screamed in protest at further inactivity. Moving carefully, he tried to slip away from the girl without waking her. He unfastened his cloak, so that she might use it as a coverlet.

But he had barely begun when Glendauna abruptly stirred. She rolled toward him, throwing an arm across his chest and yawning. Then a frown clouded her features and her eyes fluttered open.

Those eyes, a bright and vivid blue in this early-morning light, stared up into his with a confused look, her lips parted in an unspoken question. Recognition came with a word softly uttered.

"Morlac . . . ?"

"Yes, my lady."

Glendauna seemed to relax a bit, but then as she felt the rough texture of Morlac's garments against her own bare skin she looked down in alarm. As she sat quickly upright, a blush of color spread from her face almost down to her breasts.

Morlac held out his cloak to her, diverting his eyes. If Broct were here, he thought, that great rogue of a yellow-eyed giant would probably laugh and say something funny, or wicked, or both, just to break the awkward spell that had settled upon them. If Broct were here. . . .

Glendauna took the offered cloak and wrapped it about her. She got clumsily to her feet, stumbled toward her clothes, still keeping her eyes downcast. "I . . . I had better get dressed."

Morlac rose stiffly, moving after her. "Wait," he said. As he caught up with her, he gently turned her face toward him, and into the full light.

She looked up into his gaze, and Morlac saw that there were light bruises running across the bridge of her nose and under her chin, the marks of his own fingers where they had held tightly shut the jaws of the golden wolf. There were similar marks upon her wrists, and from the corner of her mouth ran a slight trickle of blood where she had bit her lip.

"Last night—" said Morlac "—what do you remember of it?"

Her voice was soft as she replied. "I remember all that happened before the rising of the moon. I remember the pain of the transformation. That much is clear and vivid. The rest is as a dream. But I know you were part of that dream."

"I'm sorry if I hurt you. The ropes did not hold."

She reached out to touch the marks upon his neck and chest where wolf claws had raked his skin. "Did I—?"

"A cornered animal cannot be blamed for fighting back," said Morlac. "Now, go on and get dressed. I will give you your privacy. Afterwards, we have much to talk about."

Morlac left her alone to dress, going around the wall which had sheltered them. He hoped walking would loosen his cramped muscles, and hoped also that the time apart from the girl might give him a chance to sort out his thoughts about her and this strange situation.

He had gone but a short distance when he found something that only made matters more difficult. He was not squeamish, but he could not help recoiling in surprised revulsion at the sight.

For there on the ground before him was the goat he had tied up for the night. Or rather, what once had been the goat. Blood was everywhere, still red and glistening in the early sunlight. The animal's head lay twisted, its neck broken and its throat ripped out. The rest of the carcass had been torn open like a ripe fruit, with the raw bones exposed and the internal organs missing. Devoured, Morlac thought, or carried off somewhere.

Morlac realized with a sudden chill that the beast had struck, within a short distance of him, even as he slept. If the goat had cried out when attacked, he had not heard it. Even more chilling was the thought that the beast which had done this butchery may have awakened in his arms.

No . . . *No,* surely not Glendauna. Surely . . . ? How could he be sure of anything? The thought that she might have done it pained him, and he found himself rebelling against it. Why? Perhaps he was too trusting. Was he becoming too human, or not yet human enough?

True, she was there in his arms when he awoke, and back

in human form. But she was still a wolf before he had fallen asleep, and he could not be certain how much time had passed before dawn. The golden wolf was certainly strong enough to have done this thing, and perhaps savage enough. But if it had, it could have ripped out his own throat while he slept, just as easily.

A startled gasp behind him made him turn quickly about. Glendauna, still fastening her garments, had come up behind him and caught sight of the goat's remains. Her face registered a kind of sickened horror, but she could not tear her gaze from the bloody carcass.

"By the gods!" she said. Her arms dropped limply by her sides and tears began to trickle down her cheeks. Her gaze shifted uneasily to Morlac, her bright blue eyes full of pain and fear and uncertainty. "Do you think . . . that I . . . ?"

"I know not what to think," said Morlac, his tone grim and his heart steeled against feelings he was reluctant to trust. But the sight of her distress was too much to bear. Finally, he reached out and took her hands in his. He turned them and examined her nails. "I will say this—the claws which killed this goat would still have its blood upon them, and I see none here."

Glendauna looked down through her tears and studied her hands. "I pray you are right."

Morlac looked back at the slain goat, and as he forced himself to view it objectively he noticed that some of the blood was not scattered in a random pattern. Striding purposefully toward the spot, he looked more closely.

"Have a look at this—" he told the girl. As she joined him, he gestured at the ground. "There are drops of blood over here . . . and there . . . and there again. See how it leads away from here."

Glendauna wiped moisture from her eyes to better see. Her gaze drifted in the direction Morlac indicated. "Toward the far side of the castle."

Morlac nodded. "Perhaps the answers we seek may be found in that direction. If you have the courage . . . ?"

The girl straightened her tunic and the swordbelt about her hips. "Courage did not bring me here. Desperation did. And that, I find, is strong enough to risk everything. . . ."

*   *   *

Morlac had his shield now as they approached the far side of the ruins, following the trail of blood drops across the uneven ground. Glendauna walked beside him, her troubled eyes searching out each red splotch that marked the path of the goat killer. Morlac could not help wondering if she feared she would find herself at the end of that path.

The trail led along the outer wall of the ancient building, back toward the side which faced the rising slope of the mountain. They came to a break in the wall where the stones had collapsed, giving entrance to the interior.

Morlac looked through that gap, then gestured within. "This way—"

Glendauna looked desperately about the ruined walls and collapsed ceilings, but showed no signs of recognizing anything. "I wish I could remember this place. It is part of my heritage . . . my life."

"You were too young when you left," Morlac told her. "And it has changed much."

The trail twisted and turned through the maze of tumbled stones, leading deeper within the castle's structure. At last they came to the back wall of what once had been a large chamber. Fallen rubble obscured one corner, and weeds and brush further camouflaged it, but there was an opening, leading down into darkness. The branches of a bush near it had been broken, and chunks of stone appeared to have been recently pushed aside. The beast, whatever its nature might be, had come here. Did it remain?

"How long have you been in the area?" Morlac asked suddenly.

Glendauna looked at him oddly. "Six days. Why?"

"It matters not," he said. The villagers had told him the attacks had begun two months before. So the girl could not be the beast he sought. *If* she was telling the truth. "Have you seen anyone else around here?"

"No. Everyone in the region seems superstitious about this place."

"Perhaps with good cause." Morlac stepped into the dark opening, thinking he must surely be a madman to pursue the unknown beast into its den, assuming he was not in fact escorting it there. "Come, Glendauna, let us explore your heritage. . . ."

He had expected a cave, or perhaps an escape tunnel leading away from the castle, but what he found as they advanced into the shaft was something quite different. As their eyes adjusted to the feeble light that filtered in, they could see a winding flight of steps, leading down to a lower level, but staying within the confines of the castle. The dust of decades littered the stone stairway, and vines and roots had crept their way down into the dark region.

"We need torches," said the girl. "The sunlight does not reach far."

Morlac probed the walls, cautiously but thoroughly, and finally found what he sought within niches on either side. "Here—there are lamps. If the fire did not reach them and there is still oil left—"

Glendauna was already extracting a flint from her pouch. She drew her sword and began to strike the flint against the steel of her blade as Morlac held a lamp alongside. But the sparks did not catch and ignite. Finally, Morlac reached into his own pouch and got the vial of sulfurous matches Kadrana had given him after their return from Kem. Striking one against the wall, he was glad to see it blaze into life. He stuck it within the mouth of the lamp, and in a moment the flame blossomed and grew brighter. They used the first lamp to light a second, and were ready to proceed.

Morlac could see now that the steps appeared to lead down into a cellar or dungeon. And he could also see marks of recent passage in the dust of the steps. But who or what had made the marks was hard to tell. There were also tiny drops of blood periodically dotting the steps.

Glendauna stayed close behind him, her sword still drawn and ready. She held her lamp aloft, and looked behind as well as ahead of them.

The stair opened into a broad chamber with vaulted ceilings and massive support columns. Wine casks lay cradled within their racks, and furniture was stacked along one wall. The amber light of their lamp flame cast an eerie glow upon the ancient walls. There were more drops of blood, and bits of flesh, leading toward the opposite wall and another stair.

"Odd." said Morlac.

Glendauna moved beside him. "What?"

"That a place such as this," he said, "is not overrun with rats. I see nothing alive here."

"Nor do I," she said. "Perhaps this place is truly cursed."

"Perhaps." Morlac gestured toward the opposite wall. "The trail leads this way."

They crossed the storage chamber, their footsteps echoing and bothersomely loud in this silent place. Morlac ducked beneath cobwebs at the top of the doorway, and started down the stairs. Glendauna followed, her eyes alert and probing.

There seemed as much dust on these stairs as on the others, but here too there were marks of recent passage. And here too, the trail of blood drops seemed to show the path of the goat's killer.

On the next level down the air was stale and witheringly dry. And though it seemed impossible, this chamber deep below the ruined castle looked even darker than the first. The glow from their lamps seemed not to reach as far here, though the flames burned as brightly as before.

As they left the stairs and ventured into the expansive chamber, Morlac saw that it was a vaulted crypt much like the first level. But there were no wine casks here, no surplus furniture or belongings. Here there were only odd oblong cabinets, neatly placed in rows among the squat columns and arches. They were long and narrow, nearly as tall as a man, their lower halves made of dark, rich wood that was ornately carved. Their upper halves were gray as mist, with dull glints of light that mocked the movements of their lamp flames, like echoing amber ghosts.

Cobwebs were everywhere, reaching from vaulted ceiling to cabinet tops, wrapping the crypt in spectral lace. They shimmered and moved with currents of air stirred by the intruders' passing.

Glendauna looked about with cautious interest. "What . . . what is this place?"

"I think," Morlac answered solemnly, "that we have found your ancestors."

He approached one of the cabinets and discovered that the gray upper surfaces were in reality sheets of some transparent crystal, veined like marble, and coated with dust. A shadowy form lay within, difficult to see.

Glendauna came up alongside him and wiped the edge of her cloak across the dusty surface. She peered in, holding her lamp close to the crystal, then gave a gasp as the interior was revealed.

Morlac looked in as well. A man's corpse, gaunt and withered and yellowing, lay in sleep eternal. Dressed in regal garments, one arm lay straight along his side, the other was bent across his chest to hold a small decorative scepter.

"Some past marquis," said Morlac softly, as if anything above a whisper might disturb the dead. "Perhaps your grandfather or great-grandfather."

The girl suppressed a shudder. "I never expected to see him thus." She looked at the other cabinets. "All these—my relatives, my ancestors. What would they think of me, the last daughter of the House of Chalthax? A shape-shifter . . . perhaps worse."

"Do not worry about their opinion," said Morlac. "They are beyond caring. Besides, they may have had their own dark secrets."

Glendauna looked into a second ornate casket, and a third. She was about to inspect yet another when Morlac suddenly stiffened. He had heard a faint whisper of sound, a rustling, a dry and dusty scrape. Something had moved in this place of the dead. And the girl had heard it, too.

She drew in a quick breath and raised her sword, her eyes darting about the shadowy crypt. Her voice a whisper, she said, "Where—?"

Morlac had his hand on Shark's hilt. "I cannot tell. But there is something here . . . something alive . . . waiting in the darkness. . . ."

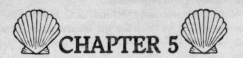

CHAPTER 5

The Beast Within

Morlac could not tell from the small scrape of sound he had heard what manner of thing shared the dark and ancient crypt with them. It could be man or beast, or perhaps something else . . . something whose shape and form he could not even guess. He was also beginning to think he had been too hasty in assuming whatever it was must necessarily be alive. For in this dreary place where darkness and death dwelled, anything might be possible. Any nightmare, reality.

Morlac moved forward cautiously, his hand ready upon his sword hilt, but still reluctant to draw the blade. The girl flanked him as he moved between the rows of royal caskets, her own sword poised before her.

Shadows cast by their lamplight's yellow glow crept steadily back as they advanced, crawling over the caskets and merging with the darkness. And always beyond the reach of that light, always deep in shadow, something else seemed to move as well, invisible, intangible, eerie, and frightening.

Morlac looked over at Glendauna, and her own eyes quickly swung to meet his. There was fear in those eyes, and yet there was also something akin to excitement and determination.

As they continued to cross the chamber, Morlac attempted to move as silently as possible. But it did not help. The other sounds not their own were too faint, barely on the threshold of hearing, echoing dimly within the dusty chamber and impossible to pinpoint.

Suddenly, unexpectedly, Glendauna gave a small gasp. She whirled around to look behind her, her lamp flame a golden streak in the darkness, her sword point a glistening threat to whatever might be there.

But Morlac saw nothing behind her. There was nothing anywhere near the girl save for the ancient crystal casket she had been passing.

"What's wrong—?" he said.

She was breathing quickly, her eyes wide. "Someone touched my shoulder."

Morlac frowned. "Impossible. No one could have got that close without—"

She stared at him with an imperative, unshakable firmness. "I *felt* it!"

Morlac stepped closer to her and put a steadying hand upon her arm. "All right. I believe you. Anything's possible in a place such as this."

But still he looked closely at the casket by which she stood, in case something could be hiding there. That proved fruitless. The surface of the crystal case was smooth and unbroken—there simply were no openings through which someone, or something, could have reached out. And there was nothing in the dusty old casket other than its long-dead occupant, a shriveled old woman wearing the same royal finery and jeweled neckpiece the other corpses wore. There was nothing threatening here. Was there?

"Stay close," Morlac told her, motioning her forward.

As they neared the end of the rows of caskets, a door came into view, set in the far wall of the chamber between two bulky columns. The door hung open wide, with murky darkness beckoning beyond. Glendauna looked at Morlac questioningly, and he nodded toward the opening.

Drawing close to the entrance, Morlac felt Shark's hilt throb in his hand. What did it sense? What tugged at its sleeping awareness, even sheathed? Morlac did not know, and dared not guess.

The ornamental frame around the door was decorated with symbols Morlac had never seen before, but they seemed to mark the place as something special even within this strange crypt. That, and perhaps serve as some sort of warning.

The glow from their lamps spread into the chamber beyond as Morlac and the girl stepped warily through the doorway.

What that glow revealed made the crypt outside seem commonplace by contrast.

Decorative friezes covered the stone walls, the arches, the squat and heavy columns. Even the floor was patterned, and inlaid with diamond-shaped tiles of colored marble. Pedestals stood at regular intervals with strange idols upon them, and rotting draperies still hung at spots along the back wall.

Glendauna looked about in awe. "It's like a temple . . . a small, private temple."

"Yes," Morlac agreed. "But what sort of god would be worshiped in a temple buried deep underground?"

Morlac glanced about, momentarily thinking of closing the massive door behind them. But he could not be certain if the thing that seemed to stalk them was truly in the crypt without, or here within the temple itself. Besides, locking themselves into a room from which there was no other means of escape made little sense. He only hoped he was not misjudging Glendauna's innocence.

"Look there," she said at that moment, indicating the frieze running across the walls above eye level. Carved into the stone surface were animals, mostly wolves and other beasts of prey. Some were walking upright on their hind legs. Others were shown in the act of killing other creatures . . . and humans. The flickering lamplight played upon the ancient carvings, making them even more ominous and strange.

"It would seem," said Morlac, "that you have more in common with your ancestors than you realized."

Tears welled up in the girl's eyes. "But if that be true, then what hope have I of freedom from this curse? What sort of monsters am I descended from? What sort of monster am I—?"

Morlac wished he had an answer for her, but he did not even have one for himself. As much to change the subject as to improve their vision, he gestured at several candle stanchions placed around the chamber.

"Help me light these. I do not like to fight what I cannot see."

Silently, the girl moved to comply, lost in her own troubled thoughts. The candles were thick stumps of waxy material, dark and strange looking, like clotted blood. They stood in ornate holders of black metal, traced in gold. Igniting the wicks proved easier than expected, and in a moment the underground temple was bathed in their combined glow. The increased light revealed things Morlac had not yet seen.

In a spot near the far wall partially sheltered by curtains of rotting cloth, some of the goat's internal organs lay in a bloody pool upon the marble floor. Presumably brought there by the beast they had tracked to this place, they lay in an untidy heap directly before a low marble altar.

But even the sight of the bloody flesh paled to insignificance before the strange object which sat upon that altar. Carved of glistening reddish stone, the sculpture was of some creature Morlac had never seen, and never wished to see. It squatted upon the altar as if ready to pounce upon whoever stood before it. It had the muscular hind legs of an animal, a narrow waist and a large rib cage, and huge forelegs not unlike a man's arms, save for the claws. The head was large, almost canine, with a snout that was wrinkled and twisted in a perpetual snarl. Long fangs filled the open mouth, and the piglike eyes were inset spheres of obsidian. It was hard to conceive of anything more frightening, or more ugly.

"By the gods!" whispered Glendauna as her gaze settled upon the bizarre idol.

"A demon, perhaps," said Morlac contemptuously. "Surely not a god."

He thought he saw a faint twinkle of light upon those obsidian eyes, but dismissed it as imagination. Still, he had the same feeling of unease that always attended his meetings with Sordros. There was something evil here. Something old and powerful, and very, very evil. It seemed to radiate from the idol as heat radiates from a flame. Only this feeling was not warmth, but intense, chilling cold.

"The goat—" Glendauna said softly "—it's like a sacrifice . . . a blood offering."

"I doubt it was the first," Morlac told her. "I suspect your ancestors were dabblers in the occult. Those words engraved upon the altar face—can you read them?"

The girl studied the letters cut into the marble. "It is in the old tongue, once used in this region. The Durkesh taught me." She frowned as she searched her memory for the words to match the symbols. "Most of it I understand. It says *By Fang and Claw Shall We Rule, By Flesh and Blood Shall We Prevail . . ."*

She hesitated, and Morlac was not sure whether it was because the words were difficult to translate, or merely difficult to accept. "Go on," he said.

Glendauna gave an uneasy sigh and continued. *"For Thy Strength We Honor Thee, For Thy Power We Summon Thee, Great Bal . . . Balboz . . ."* She was clearly having trouble with the word. "*Bal-boz-ni-bog.* Yes, Balboznibog."

Morlac felt a chill at the sound of the name, though he was not sure why. A slight breeze seemed to stir within the temple chamber, causing the candle flames to waver, and the shadows to dance.

"Morlac," said the girl, "let us leave now. Let us forget this."

"I think it may already be too late for that." Morlac looked around warily as subtle changes took place within the temple chamber. The color of the candle flames was becoming more red in hue; the shadows cast by the carved figures on the walls were elongating.

But even more disturbing were the changes in the idol itself. The very air seemed to shimmer about it, obscuring its details, blurring its form. It was like looking at an object through rippling, murky water.

A second image of the hideous man-beast was forming, superimposed upon the statue and slightly larger. But while the statue was shaped of hard, unyielding stone, this new vision taking form had the look of flesh and bone, sinew and hide. The eyes had the same evil blackness, but were alive and glistening. It was as if the gateway to some nether realm was opening, and some demon by the pronouncement of its name unleashed.

With a great hissing sigh, the thing called Balboznibog solidified. It still seemed vaguely transparent, but its presence in the chamber was too real to be a trick of the mind. The hunched form breathed and flexed its muscles, alternately opening and closing its clawed hands. The small black eyes sparkled malevolently, and the lips curled back in a snarl that revealed long and wicked fangs. Turning to take in both

Morlac and Glendauna, the apparition opened its slavering jaws.

Steam seemed to emanate from that unclean mouth, and the nightmare creature brought with it the stench of carrion and foul animal odor. Slime dripped from its claws, running down the sides of the marble altar. And as it studied the sea warrior and the wolfling girl who stood before him, his features took on the appearance of a hideous and evil smile.

With a sound that was as much an exhalation of breath as words, the temple demon said, "*At laaaaast* . . ." The voice was raspy and guttural, rising from a throat ill-made for human speech. "I have been summoned forth once more into this world, my destiny yet to claim."

As it spoke, the thing slowly swayed, changing its balance from foot to foot, always hunched and ready to spring. Morlac tightened his grip on Shark's hilt and wondered if he could even begin to fight this jackal from the pits of death and decay.

Glendauna's voice was a horror-struck whisper. "What . . . what have I done?"

Balboznibog's attention shifted down to the bloody pile of flesh near the base of the altar. Threads of saliva drooled from the corners of its snarling mouth and stretched slowly to the floor. Where the drops touched, thin trails of smoke arose, as if the marble was being eaten by acid.

The bestial demon leaned forward, and looked as if it were about to leap down upon the mutilated goat's organs. Glendauna fell back a step, and Morlac shifted his weight in preparation for a defensive strike. But the thing did not leave the top of the altar. It merely leaned out and down, its claws still rooted to the spot, and focused its attention upon the blood sacrifice.

Suddenly, its eyes flared with brightness, literally glowing like embers. Curling back its lips even more, it exhaled a column of vapor directly at the bloody flesh. The creature's fetid breath coiled about the tissue and enveloped it, obscuring it from view and seeming to dissolve it. The mist became blood-red itself, vibrant with the color, then it was abruptly sucked back up through the air and into the creature's mouth, as smoke might appear if it could reverse its path and return to the flame.

Balboznibog's rib cage swelled as he drew in the crimson mist, and when the last coils of vapor were gone, so too was the flesh that had been upon the floor. Even the pool of blood had vanished.

Can he not leave that spot? Morlac thought. *Can he feed only on the dead?*

The demon looked up at Morlac and Glendauna once more as blood dribbled from its lips. "And who summons me, now. Who has freed me?" His small dark eyes settled upon the girl. "Yes . . . yes, oh yes. The Chalthax spawn. You have returned. Dear, sweet child, do not cower so. You have nothing to fear. Nothing to fear at all, unless you do not have the strength and the will to serve me, as your family did before you. You have already discovered your special heritage, have you not?"

Glendauna hesitated, and when she could not bring herself to speak to this horrendous apparition, reluctantly nodded her head in assent.

"Yes, just as I thought," rasped Balboznibog. "Well, I can help you with that, even as I helped your ancestors. I can give you power such as you have never dreamed of. Power to rule. Power to destroy your enemies. Power to spread your influence . . . and mine."

"Your power," Morlac spoke up suddenly, "is a curse she wishes to be free of."

Balboznibog turned to take in this impudent intruder, studying him with narrowing eyes. "I do not know you. No, you are not of these folk. But I do sense in you something quite remarkable. Yes, you have a man's body, but your true nature belongs more to my realm, does it not? You are as much an outcast in the normal human world as I. I like that. You could be of use to me. Much use."

"I have no desire to serve you, demon," Morlac spat out. "Nor will I worship you."

"Do not be so quick to reject me. You owe the humans nothing. And with my aid, you could become a king among them. And this," his gesture took in Glendauna, "your queen. I once had great plans for the Chalthax line."

"More temples?" said Morlac. "More worshipers? More sacrifices?"

"Yes," came the hiss of a reply. "That, and more. The land will run red with the blood of the weakling prey."

"Only if we serve you."

"You will," said Balboznibog. "In one manner or another. . . ."

There was a scrape of sound behind them, and Morlac was reminded of the fact that they had not been alone here even before the demon's materialization. Whirling, he faced the open doorway to the crypt, even as Glendauna turned. . . .

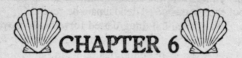# CHAPTER 6

The Bargain Kept

Something stood in the open doorway of the temple chamber, revealed in the light of the votive candles. Something that proved Glendauna's innocence in the killing of the goat. For surely this was the beast that had preyed upon the village, and provided the blood offering to Balboznibog.

Far worse than any wolf, the creature almost defied belief. It had the form and characteristics of a common rat, but there was nothing common about its size. The thing had grown obscenely large, standing almost shoulder-high even on all fours. It must easily weigh three hundred pounds or more, and reach twenty feet from its hideous snout to the tip of its lengthy tail. Its filth-encrusted hair bristled, its ears twitched, muscles flexed beneath its skin. The creature's eyes were dark and red-rimmed, and stared at them with an intensity that was frightening in and of itself. Mad eyes. Hungry eyes.

"Yes, my pet, my faithful," rasped Balboznibog in his deep and snarling voice. "You have done especially well this day. You have brought me two of great value." To Glendauna and Morlac he said, "Look at him, heiress to the House of Chalthax, and you as well, my strangely inhuman warrior. Look at my prize. Only he among all the countless petty rodents that scavenged these ruins sensed my presense and sought me out. He could not summon me with words of course, but he made contact in his own way, so that I could reach across the barriers. How he has grown under my guidance and power! And so may you also thrive in the service of mighty Balboznibog. *If* . . . you are strong enough."

172

Morlac looked in horror and revulsion at the malignant monstrosity that faced them, and sensed in the demon's words an unspoken command. "Glendauna—be ready!"

Even as he spoke, the thing darted forward. It moved with surprising speed for its bulk, heading directly for the girl, hissing through its glistening fangs.

Morlac thrust out his right arm to push Glendauna out of the way. He moved to block the path of the rushing beast and attempted to draw his sword. But the thing was upon him in an instant, lunging for his throat with teeth and claws.

There was barely time to jerk back away from those killing tools, barely time to swing up his shield. Morlac deflected the strike, but felt its tremendous impact against the carapace of his shield.

Knocked flat by the force of the giant rat's attack, Morlac found himself on his back with only his shield separating him from the snarling beast poised above him. The fall had knocked the wind out of him, and the creature's weight upon his chest made it no easier to breathe now. It snapped and chewed at the edge of his shield, frantically trying to reach his throat, its rancid breath in his face.

"By the gods, *no!*" gasped Glendauna. With a swirl of motion that was as athletic as it was graceful, she turned and leaped astride the giant rat's back. She struck at its shoulders with the sharp spikes that stuck out from the base of her blade, and when that seemed to have no effect upon the monster, she took the hilt in both hands and attempted to plunge her sword straight down into its back.

"*Die*, damn you!"

The blade penetrated partway into the beast's shoulder but halted as the tip became imbedded in the hard bone of the shoulder blade. Such a blow could not kill, it could only enrage.

Hissing and spitting, the giant rat reared back, toppling Glendauna from its back. She rolled with the fall, trying to get clear of the rat's reach, ending up on her hands and knees. The girl's head came up fast, tossing the hair out of her face as she looked to see if the creature was coming after her.

For several long moments, the rat twisted and turned, trying to reach back with its teeth to pluck out the blade that tormented it, but the sword was lodged too high on the shoulder to be reached. Finally, it gave up on that and turned to face Glendauna with a look that was utterly insane.

The Durkesh-raised daughter of royalty struggled to her feet and drew a small dagger from a sheath at her belt. But the weapon seemed meager and futile against such a monster, and the look on her delicate face showed that she knew it.

Morlac saw that look, and as air surged back into his lungs he propelled himself up off the floor and onto his feet once more. Still keeping his shield ready, he wasted no more time in grabbing his sword hilt and yanking the blade free.

Shark sprang from its sheath almost without effort, the blanched whiteness of its blade stark and menacing as it caught the glow of the votive candles. The hilt trembled within his grasp, as it had so often done before, but something about its ravenous power seemed different, more intense, as if the magicked blade was somehow feeding on the very atmosphere of this accursed place.

Morlac ran after the rat as it advanced upon the girl. Glendauna was backing steadily away, and the monster seemed on the verge of striking. There was no shield to protect her, no weapon save for the puny dagger. Morlac remembered how the goat had been torn apart, and a chill coursed through him.

"*Leave her alone!*" he yelled, and his voice reverberated in the temple chamber. Morlac swung his sword, and the blade flashed in a downward arc powered as much by anger as by the raw energy of the magic weapon.

The tip of the blade slashed through the rat's hindquarters at a depth of several inches, but missed the spine. Blood oozed from the wound almost instantly, and with equal speed the rat halted its advance, letting out a high-pitched *SCREEEEEE!*

Forgetting the girl, the creature quickly turned on Morlac. Arching its back, it raised the hackles along its spine and puffed out its body hairs, making itself seem even larger. Spittle dripped from the edges of its mouth as it hissed ferociously.

Morlac swung again, aiming his blow at the beast's head. But this time the creature saw the blade coming and with surprising agility dodged the strike. Shark barely brushed the hairs on the side of its horrible face.

Again Morlac swung, and again the creature moved quickly enough to avoid injury. It advanced, moving sideways to keep Glendauna within view as well. Its intense beady eyes bore into them with hatred and cunning and a killing hunger. Morlac stole a glance at Balboznibog, still crouching upon his altar stone with a look of grim satisfaction, and realized that no matter how this battle ended, the demon would be pleased. No matter how it ended, Balboznibog would be the winner.

Morlac lunged forward and struck a stinging wound on the end of the rat's nose before it could jerk back. The beast roared in pain, then suddenly leaped forward and with a swipe of its clawed forepaw it knocked the sword out of Morlac's grip. Shark clattered upon the temple floor, an angry sigh ebbing out from it.

Even as the rat lunged for him, Morlac jerked aside and rolled clear, the massive rodent teeth clicking together perilously close to him. He had instinctively jumped in the direction of his sword, and now as he rolled to a stop, the blade was within reach before him.

"Morlac!" screamed Glendauna.

He looked up at her warning and saw the rat stretching out in a leap toward him. It landed scant feet away, rearing up on its hind legs, its forepaws reaching for him, claws spread and ready to rip him apart.

Morlac's hand closed around Shark's hilt as the shadow of the giant rat moved over him. He saw the beady eyes glistening in that horrid face, the fangs crashing down toward him. Death was less than a second away.

Morlac did not have time to draw the sword back to strike. There was no time to think or plan. He merely reacted, guided by Shark's own ravenous skill. With a sudden surge of strength he braced his shield arm against the floor and brought his sword up in a backward slash beneath the attacking rat.

Shark sliced through the underbelly and the rib cage in one swift stroke, piercing the heart and emerging from the monster's neck in a spray of gore. It vibrated and thundered in Morlac's grip, jubilant in its triumph.

Morlac rolled to one side, barely escaping being pinned beneath the rat as it collapsed dead upon the floor. He lay still a moment, catching his breath, then slowly got to his feet. Glendauna ran to his side, put a trembling hand to his arm, but watched for any further signs of life from the creature they had battled.

"See how the power surges through you—" Balboznibog intoned solemnly. "The bloodlust—the joy. Know it. Taste it. Admit to yourselves that you like it. That serving me will only sanctify an urge that is already part of you, and always has been!"

Morlac stared down at the giant rat which lay dead before him in a spreading pool of blood and wondered if there was not some truth in the demon's words. There was indeed a dark and treacherous corner of his mind that seemed to crave such violence. And well he remembered the strength of his urge to kill Drygo after Ardo's death at the mercenary's hands. As a sea creature he had killed to eat, and as a human much of his life had been devoted to learning the skills of death and mayhem. Perhaps despite all his pious arrogance, he truly was no better than Balboznibog. Perhaps the most dangerous beast was the one that existed within himself.

And yet . . . and yet, there was a difference. There was! And Morlac knew he did not have to merely accept the demon's clever words.

"No . . ." he said softly, then turned to stare at Balboznibog with eyes that flashed defiance. "No! It is not the same. I do what I must to survive, but I do not have to enjoy it or revel in it as you do. I cannot. My conscience would not permit it."

"A conscience is a trick," sneered Balboznibog, "imposed by weaklings upon greater weaklings, to control them. The strong have no need of conscience."

"No—" Glendauna disagreed "—the strong have even more need."

"She's right," Morlac said. "It is the weak who seek what you offer. You have nothing we desire."

The demon seemed to expand slightly upon the altar, perhaps feeding upon the violent energies released by their battle with the giant rat. Its horrid face became utterly malignant.

"Do not think you can taunt me just because you have slain my pet. I can create a dozen more like him, a hundred more. A thousand! And I can bring others here like you. Yes, it will be easy, now that the gateway is fully open. And if you will not serve me with your worship, then you will serve me with your lives!"

Balboznibog drew back as he inhaled deeply, his eyes beginning to blaze fiery red. Then his mouth opened wide and he leaned forward to exhale. The flesh-destroying vapor started to emerge from that slavering, fang-studded mouth, and it was aimed directly at them.

Morlac quickly stepped in front of Glendauna and brought up his shield. Shark throbbed in his hand, but Morlac did not need its encouragement. With a loud shout of sound he reversed his grip on the hilt and hurled the magicked sword at Balboznibog, point first.

Even as the deadly vapor reached out for them, Shark flew like a ghostly spear, straight and true to its target, plunging into the mouth of the demon. Balboznibog jerked his head back as the sword lodged there, then became frozen with a look of horror that seemed out of place on his demonic features.

The column of vapor abruptly dispersed and vanished, no longer guided by its master's will. His eyes lost their red glow, and something akin to miniature lightning erupted within Balboznibog's mouth. His jowls sucked in, his throat tightened, his clawed hands contorted and trembled uncontrollably. Perhaps no ordinary sword could harm such a demon, but then, Shark was no ordinary sword. It was a sorcerer's tool, powered by unknown spells, and it seemed to have tapped Balboznibog's life-force and be drawing it out.

The candle flames in the temple chamber were flickering now, blown by an unfelt breeze that pulled them toward the altar. They wavered, now bright, now dim, and lost their livid color.

Upon the altar, the image of Balboznibog faded and sputtered, even as the flames. Then with a final wretched hiss, the demon vanished altogether. Left behind upon the altar was the stone idol, its head cracked and crumbling from the blade imbedded in its mouth.

At last, the evil atmosphere that had so charged the room before ebbed away. The ordeal was over. Morlac slowly walked up to the altar and pryed his magicked sword free.

Glendauna approached him, still looking with awe and great caution at the shattered idol. "Did . . . did you kill it? Or merely send it back to its own corner of hell?"

"I do not know. . . ."

"Well, either way, at least the cursed beast is gone."

Morlac looked down at the sword in his hands as the blood faded upon its blanched white blade. A demon-killer sword. "Is it . . . ?" he said softly.

Glendauna watched as Morlac sheathed his sword, then she reached over to where her own blade still stood lodged in the rat's shoulder. She pulled it free and wiped it clean on the rat's own hair, then purified it in the flame of one of the votive candles. Taking a last look at the monster's carcass and the shattered idol of Balboznibog, she turned to pick up one of the lamps and started for the door.

"Let us leave this place," she said solemnly. "I have found the answers I sought, if not the solution. There is much to think about before the moon rises again this evening."

Morlac retrieved the other lamp and followed after her. "We can prepare better this time. I can use different bindings, or build a cage from the iron gates which lie above in the ruins."

"For how long? Each night the moon rises full for the rest of my life?" Tears were welling up in her eyes. "Perhaps you should have let the monster kill me."

Morlac grabbed her arm and stopped her in her tracks before they'd even reached the doorway to the crypt. "Never think that way. Never. Life is too precious to throw away, no matter what you must endure."

She looked up into his severe gaze for a long moment. "How can you know what I've endured? Do you know how it feels to awaken each day, remembering all over again that you are a freak . . . a monster? To fear that you can never live a normal life?"

Morlac said nothing in reply, but the haunted look in his eyes told her that she had said the wrong thing. He released her arm and started toward the door.

Glendauna followed after, and bit her lip as her thoughts turned inward once more. But as they stepped through the open doorway and entered the crypt, she abruptly halted and grabbed at Morlac's arm to halt him as well.

"By the gods—will this madness never end?"

Morlac stopped, but saw nothing alarming ahead. "What is it—?"

"There—" she said, pointing directly before them "—can you not see it?"

Morlac was beginning to think she'd gone mad, though after what he'd seen last night and here in this place he could well doubt his own sanity. But then as his eyes strained to make out something, anything, in the darkness ahead, he began to see what she was pointing at.

Something like a thin column of smoke hung in the air not more than six paces ahead. And yet it was not smoke. Glendauna clearly was seeing it better than he, and as he touched her arm his own vision seemed to sharpen, and the image brighten. The faintly glowing cloud was coalescing. taking shape, becoming something recognizable. He quickly stole a glance back at the idol of Balboznibog, wondering if the demon lived on.

But as he looked once more at the wraith before them, Morlac saw that it was not the demon which had taken form. It was a ghostly image of an old woman. She was dressed in the regal garments of the House of Chalthax, floating inches above the stone floor and silently beckoning to them. Without actually walking, the image floated back away from them a short distance down the corridor which ran between the crypt's elaborate caskets.

Morlac and Glendauna exchanged a troubled, puzzled look. Then slowly, reluctantly, they followed. Was it some sort of trick? Some final vengeful spell of Balboznibog to destroy them? Morlac did not know, but as he touched the hilt of his magicked sword, Shark was quiet and at rest.

The wraith led them to one of the caskets and stopped. Morlac recognized it as the one they had been passing when Glendauna had become frightened and thought someone touched her. Perhaps . . . someone had.

The floating image of the old woman seemed stirred by an

unworldly breeze, slow and eddying, eerie in its soundlessness. There was a calm, a peace about her face as she stared at Glendauna. And something else showed on those wizened features, an odd mixture of emotions hard to understand. She slowly gestured at the casket, then placed her hand against her own throat. The wraith waited a moment, then repeated the gesture.

Glendauna watched in bewilderment. "What does it mean, Morlac? Is she saying we are to die, too? That our fate lies in a casket such as this?"

"If so, then why does she touch her throat that way?" Morlac stared disbelievingly at the ghost. "I swear, she looks like the woman in that very casket. I wonder. . . ."

Morlac peered into the casket and studied the corpse entombed there. Then he looked back at the ghostly image before them. Staring into those spectral eyes, he made a semicircular gesture about his own neck, then pointed at the figure in the casket, then lastly at Glendauna.

The wraith slowly nodded in affirmation. The message was clear.

Morlac quickly examined the edges of the crystal casket, searching for seams. The corners and uprights all seemed securely fastened, but the entire top of the casket appeared to be merely sitting upon the lower half like an overturned box. He moved to the head end of the casket and grasped the lower edge, digging his fingernails into the groove that separated the top half from the bottom.

"Glendauna—" he said abruptly "—I need your help."

She came to his side, but looked troubled. "What . . . what are you doing?"

"I am going to lift this."

"Lift it? Surely it's too heavy for any man. The crystal alone must weigh—"

"Just do as I say. When I raise the top up high enough, I want you to reach in and remove the jeweled neckpiece from the body."

She flinched at his words, and at the thought of coming in contact with the withered corpse. But she said, "All right."

Morlac drew a deep breath and partially exhaled it, then concentrated upon the muscles in his arms and shoulders, muscles that had once propelled him through the sea with strength and endurance unmatched by normal men. His face tightened as he strained to lift the crystal top, levering it up inch by inch, raising it higher and higher, giving access to what lay within.

"Now—" he said.

Glendauna looked at him, then reluctantly reached into the space. The odd and unpleasant smell of embalmed flesh met her nostrils, almost staying her hands, but she fought against her impulse and took the jeweled neckpiece into her grasp. The catch was unusual, and made all the more difficult to open by her haste. But at last it came free and she slipped the ornament from around the old woman's neck.

She was about to quickly withdraw her hands when, without apparent reason, a golden locket hanging on a long chain about the corpse's neck sprang open. Something was painted on the inner surfaces, and though she was not sure why, Glendauna also removed the locket and brought that out as well.

Morlac lowered the casket top, swiftly but carefully, restoring it to its original position. He flexed his hands and arms a moment, then turned his attention to the girl.

Glendauna studied the objects in her hands. "I feel like a grave robber."

"Don't," said Morlac. "I think they are meant to be a gift." He took the jeweled neckpiece from her, wiped its inner surface against his tunic and carefully fitted it about her own neck. It was an elaborately crafted collar of enameled metal, trimmed with gold. A large moonstone was set at its center, its eerie luster matched by two blood-red smaller stones set on either side.

"Why do you call it a gift," Glendauna asked, touching the neckpiece at her throat. "What is it?"

"Perhaps it is the freedom you seek. All those here wear them . . . all your ancestors. Perhaps it is a magic talisman, against the power of the moon."

"And this?" She held the open locket up so that her lamplight better illuminated it. Each side of the locket bore a small cameo portrait. One was of a young man, handsome and distinguished-looking, wearing the raiment of a high nobleman. The other was of a young woman, blond of hair, blue of eyes, beautiful and regal.

"It would seem to be a Marquis and his bride, captured by some forgotten artisan, and treasured by the woman who was buried with it."

"My parents were not much older than this when they died." Glendauna said. "If this be them, then surely . . . this woman was . . ." She looked up into the face of the wraith that loomed so near, a face that studied her with a mixture of sadness and pleasure. ". . . Grandmother . . . ?"

Tears were running down the girl's face now, and the ghost's spectral hands reached slowly out as if to touch her shoulders, then withdrew reluctantly. The image of the old woman slowly closed her fist against her chest, then extended that hand toward Glendauna and opened it in a symbolic gesture of love. Then with a final smile, the image began to fade and dissolve, and at last was gone.

Glendauna wiped at her eyes with the edge of her sleeve and stepped away from the casket. She looked up into Morlac's soft gaze and the tears began anew. Morlac took her into his arms and held her.

"Do not cry so, my lady. Do not cry so . . ."

As the tears finally subsided, she looked into his eyes again. "You hardly know me, Morlac, yet you have already shown yourself to be a truer friend than any I have known. Why did the demon call you an inhuman warrior?"

"Last night I promised you an explanation of my own dark secrets, and that is a promise I shall keep," he told her. "But first there is one more thing I must do in the temple, and then we must leave this place, and seal the entrance as best we can, to prevent others from venturing down here."

She nodded in agreement. "But you will tell me . . . ?"

"Yes," said Morlac. "You may believe or disbelieve as you wish, but all that I shall tell you is the truth. I hope that it may convince you that you are not alone. . . ."

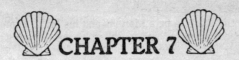

CHAPTER 7

Proof and Payment

By afternoon, clouds had drifted in from beyond the mountains to turn the sky gray and threaten the village with the first snow of winter. There was little activity in the streets, for most of the villagers were again gathered in the Kettle and Cup.

The somber men and women who filled the inn were waiting, still fearful to resume their normal activities so long as Morlac's fate remained a mystery. Some were drinking, and a pall of silence hung over the room. The silence did not last.

Heads jerked around and several drinks spilled as the front door slammed open and the wind whistled through. Morlac strode into the room and stopped to face them, his expression grim.

Almost as one, the villagers rose and formed a wide semicircle about him, their faces eager for news. Curiosity of a different kind also shone in their eyes as Glendauna entered the room behind Morlac, looking cautious and distrustful. But if anyone saw the resemblance she bore to the noble family they had once helped destroy, no one said so.

Josaffa, the village elder, was the first to speak. "You return early, after little more than a day. Do you need more provisions?" His gaze took in the girl with an unspoken question.

"She is a traveler, much as I," said Morlac. "And a friend. But it is not for provisions I return. I am here to tell you that the beast is dead. It will not trouble you again."

An excited murmur swept through the room at these words.

But Josaffa held up his hands for silence. His expression was suspicious, his tone doubtful.

"That is certainly good news," said Josaffa. "Almost too good to be true. But words come easier than deeds. After all we have been through, we must be sure. We must have proof."

Morlac nodded. "And after all *we* have been through, I would not think of disappointing you."

Morlac brought forth a bundle that had been partially hidden by his shield and tossed it on the floor before them. He did not bother to explain that the rotting cloth that wrapped the thing had been torn from the temple curtains, deep within the ruined castle's crypt. Borrowing Glendauna's dagger, for he did not wish to draw Shark here and now, he reached down and slit the knot which tied the bundle.

"Behold—" he said solemnly "—the beast of Goltos."

There was a collective gasp as the folds of cloth fell open, caked with dried blood on their inner surfaces, and revealed the severed head and forepaws of the giant rat. The head might well have belonged to a large bear, but the ratlike features were unmistakable, undeniable, too real to be anything but the truth. Most of the villagers stared in awe at the sight of the hideous trophy, while others turned away in sickened horror.

"It is a true monster," Morlac told them. "A freak of nature. There are no more like it, and I doubt there ever shall be."

Josaffa stepped closer, slowly, unsteadily, his eyes brimming with both anger and tears at the sight of the monstrous thing. "My granddaughter . . . to end this way . . ." He trembled in rage, then abruptly spat upon the rat's head.

He stood silent a long moment, then as he calmed, he said to Morlac, "Forgive me for doubting you. This must surely be the killer of our people and our animals. The tracks were never really like those of a wolf, though we thought that the only explanation."

"Then," said Morlac, "I have fulfilled my half of our bargain, and can claim my reward."

There was an uneasy silence in the room as the villagers

exchanged looks. Morlac had expected rejoicing, celebration, but found his gaze met with worried, furtive expressions.

"Is there some problem . . . ?"

Josaffa seemed reluctant to speak, but at last found his voice. "It is true . . . we promised you one hundred gold pieces for slaying the beast. And you have done so. But . . ."

"But what—?"

The village elder wrung his hands, his eyes downcast. "In our desperation, we have dishonored ourselves. We could not be sure you would succeed, and even if you did, we thought you might die of injuries while slaying the beast. In truth, we never had one hundred gold pieces to give you."

Morlac stared at him long and hard. "I do not blame you for being desperate. I could well blame you for lying, for I have little patience with deceit. What fools you are! Did you not even consider the risk of facing the wrath of a swordsman good enough to kill such a monster?"

"No," said Josaffa. "Not at the time. But if you wish to take your payment in blood, then let your blade strike only me. I accept the blame."

Morlac sighed and shook his head. "More killing I do not wish, least of all here. I pledged to slay the beast as much to help your village as for the money. But I did need the money to continue my journey."

Josaffa considered his words, then turned and spoke to several of the other villagers in hushed tones. When he turned back to Morlac once more, he said, "We are grateful—never doubt that. And if you will accept them as payment, we are prepared to offer you and the girl horses for your journey, as well as what food and coins we can spare. It is the most we have to offer, and the least that we can do."

Morlac considered it, glancing to Glendauna for her reaction. She did not seem surprised by the villagers' deception, but she gave a nod. Though still angry, Morlac knew the offer was practical and honorable, and preferable to any alternative he could imagine. Anyway, he was too tired to argue.

"All right. We accept. If you will but do one more thing."

"And that is . . . ?" Josaffa asked hesitantly.

Morlac gave a grim smile. "Bring us an ale, for we are both dry and dusty."

Josaffa sighed in relief, then laughed out loud. As the tension in the room vanished, he shouted to the inn's owner, "Ale for our heroes—for everyone! We have cause to celebrate. . . ."

On a hill three miles past the village, two riders sat astride their newly acquired mounts, their cloaks drawn against the chill night wind. The darkness about them was occasionally dispelled as gaps in the clouds allowed the moon to peer down.

Morlac stared up at that moon, which was still virtually full, then looked over to the young woman on the horse next to his. "It has been up there a good hour, now."

Glendauna stared also at the silver disk of light as clouds scudded past. "Yes, at least that." She reached to touch the jeweled ornament that hung about her throat. "You must have been right about the talisman. Since this all began, the change has always been prompt at moonrise."

"I am glad for you. Truly glad, Glendauna. You have the freedom to return to the life you left behind."

She swung around to look at him, her features exquisite in the moonlight. "Which life? I have left behind two so far. The first is forever lost to me, and though the Durkesh might accept me back among them again, I do not think I could be happy, knowing what I know now."

Morlac studied her. "Then what future do you wish?"

She sighed. "I do not know. Perhaps I never shall. But I would like to know more about you, my strange sea-warrior friend. And I am of a mood to travel, if you would not mind a companion on this star-crossed journey of yours."

"I would not mind," said Morlac. "But my own fate is uncertain. You could be asking to share in great danger."

Glendauna gave a light, musical laugh. "Worse than today—?"

"Perhaps."

She was silent a long moment, her eyes downcast. When she looked up at him again with those vivid blue eyes, her tone was more serious. "I will take the chance, Morlac. That's what living is all about, is it not—?"

He nodded approvingly. "So I've heard."

"Then let us be off! I am anxious to leave that village behind, and equally anxious to find a place of shelter from the night and this wind!"

"As you wish, my lady," he said, urging his horse forward. "As you wish. . . ."

DEATH CAST IN BRONZE

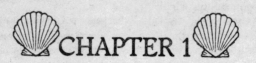 **CHAPTER 1**

The Intruder

The fire sputtered and hissed, now blossoming, now wilting, a fragile flower reluctant to take root in the frozen ground beneath it. Morlac prodded the burning wood with a long stick, sending sparks flying but doing little to encourage the blaze. It would be a long, cold night without a proper fire.

"Wait—" said Glendauna as she approached with an armload of rocks "—let me show you how the Durkesh do it."

The young woman dropped the fist-sized rocks upon the ground next to the fire and began to arrange them in a pattern so that there was air space around each one. Across the tops of these she placed thick branches, all running the same direction, then crossing those went smaller branches and twigs. Then with Morlac's aid she used forked sticks to move the already burning wood on top of her own carefully arranged pile. Within minutes, the weak flames had spread down throughout the stack and burned strongly.

"The ground has ice in it," she explained. "It melts and quenches the fire, unless you raise it upon rocks."

Morlac nodded. "I can see the Durkesh know more than I about building fires."

Glendauna was silent awhile, watching the flames. Beneath her cloak's hood, her blond hair seemed to echo the glow of that fire, and her blue eyes, the cold of the ice and snow that covered much of the ground.

"Morlac," she said at last, "what will you do once you catch up with Sordros? Over the past few weeks we've been traveling you've told me much. But you have said little about your plans.''

Morlac stared into the flames as he sat hunched before the fire ''My plans? I am not sure I know them myself.''

''Do . . . do you wish him to break the spell? Do you wish to return to your life in the sea?''

''I don't know,'' he sighed. ''Part of me does, I'm sure. I feel it within my flesh. And yet, there is much of me that is human. Much that would die again, in the process of retransformation. I do not even know if it is possible.''

''What if you could be made wholly human?''

''Even that would not be without loss. But at least then I would not be considered such a freak.''

''I do not consider you so.''

Morlac turned to face her. ''There are not many like you, my lady. We are bound together by similar fates, and ruled by forces most people cannot understand.''

''I would think our destinies are in our own hands, if we wish it to be so.''

''Perhaps. But my fate is bound up with the wizard, and until I find him I know I shall feel that things are incomplete . . . unresolved.''

Glendauna studied him with troubled eyes. ''Tell me this, though—is it truly Sordros you seek, or his daughter, Kadrana?''

Morlac found it suddenly difficult looking into her clear blue eyes. His own gaze sought the flames once more. And from the conflict in his heart, he knew he had no better answer for that question either.

A faint sound came from behind them, snapping them out of their thoughts. Both moved quickly, rising, turning, reaching for their weapons. Ready for battle, if need be. Behind them, their mounts whinnied nervously from the spot where they were tethered.

Appearing out of the darkness through a gap in the snow-burdened trees, a man was walking toward them, leading a horse. Only partially revealed by the flickering firelight, he might well have been a ghost.

The stranger paused, venturing no closer. ''May I join

you?'' he shouted hoarsely. " 'Tis a cold night, and your fire could warm three as easily as two.''

Morlac cocked an ear and frowned into the darkness. Beside him, Glendauna turned her sword to catch the fire's glow.

"He may be a highwayman,'' she said to Morlac. To the intruder she warned, ''The Durkesh welcome all. But know that we are well-armed.''

The stranger started forward slowly. ''I am not a highwayman,'' he stated, revealing surprisingly good hearing. "And know that *I* be well-armed, too. Very well-armed, indeed!'' His hoarse voice suddenly yielded to jovial laughter that threatened to shake the snow from the trees.

''By the gods!'' exclaimed Morlac, removing his hand from Shark's hilt and starting toward the tall man with unexpected swiftness.

Glendauna tensed, her blade poised. But her expression became one of bewilderment as Morlac and the stranger reached each other and embraced, like reunited family.

''Broct—!'' Morlac exclaimed as the yellow-eyed giant threw back his hood and smiled roguishly. "I thought . . . I thought certain you'd been slain by Kerr's soldiers.''

"I nearly was,'' said Broct. ''And would have been, had I not been knocked senseless in the battle and mistaken for dead. I awoke among the corpses, and barely managed to crawl away before the soldiers returned to bury us. A village woman with more compassion than good sense, bless her, hid me away and tended me until I healed. As soon as I was strong enough, I stole a North Kingdom horse and set out after you.''

Morlac arched a proud devil-brow. "How knew you which route I took?''

" 'Twas not hard. I knew you would follow Sordros, and those I asked along the way who did not remember seeing the wizard, well remembered you.''

"Do any of the other sea-warriors yet live?''

Broct's features clouded. ''I fear all the rest died in battle. If any did escape, I have not met them.''

"I hope some did survive, " said Morlac with a sigh. ''But at least it is good to know I am not the last.''

"Yes, but let us continue this conversation closer to the

fire, my sea-brother," Broct said, steering his friend toward the warmth. As they drew near the blaze, he gestured at Glendauna, who was putting away her sword and looking perturbed. "Well, I am pleased to see you have not been lonely in my absence!"

"This is Glendauna," Morlac explained. "A new friend."

Broct shot Morlac a wary look. "How close a friend?"

"A *trusted* friend. I have told her about myself."

"Ah, good, then I may relax." The yellow-eyed giant extended a hand to the girl, and as she clasped it, said, "A pleasure it be to meet Morlac's new friend. If you have not already heard, I am called Broct."

Glendauna was about to reply when the giant's friendly smile became impish. A left hand came out from beneath his cape to join his right in gripping hers, and an instant later two more hands came out to pat her shoulders. The fifth appeared, to prop against his hip in a casual pose, while the sixth reached up to scratch his ear. As she stared in wonder at his overabundance of limbs, Broct's grin became insufferable.

"Broct—!" Morlac said in exasperation. Then to Glendauna, "Forgive him. This is his idea of fun."

The girl merely shook her head and sighed. "I suppose I should not be surprised by anything, after these past few months."

"Well," said Broct, "now that we are met, let us all share a meal and some talk before we sleep. We are lucky we are three. There are indeed highwaymen about, and wolves as well."

"Wolves?" said Glendauna, with a wry look toward Morlac. "How frightening. . . ."

As they sat about the fire, finishing their food, Broct threw a well-gnawed bone into the flames and wiped his mouth on the back of one of his right hands. He looked to Morlac with a serious expression.

"I think it's close we are to finding Sordros," said Broct. "The road we follow leads up into the mountains, and I've heard it said that another wizard with South Kingdom loyalities lives somewhere in the area. Find him, and I wager we shall find Sordros as well."

"Perhaps," remarked Glendauna. "But I should warn you

that the mountains we are approaching are the Kyral Mountains. They border the Dark Region.''

"The Dark Region? What is that?"

" A vast and uncivilized realm, mysterious, dangerous . . . an evil place. Those from the west seldom dare to venture there. Those that do, seldom return.''

Morlac brushed crumbs of food from his hands and now spoke up himself. ''Nevertheless, if that is where Sordros is, then that is where I shall go. I would cross hell itself, if need be, to cross paths once more with the green magician.''

"We may have to,'' said Glendauna soberly. Silent a moment, she smiled suddenly as a new thought crossed her mind. ''But that is tomorrow's worry. For now, perhaps I should show your friend Broct the new trick I discovered.''

Morlac arched a devil-brow, then nodded with an amused smile. ''Yes—I think you should.''

"Trick?"

"Yes, my sea-brother. Something I think you should appreciate.''

The yellow-eyed giant shrugged all his shoulders and said, ''Very well. I enjoy a well-done trick. Be it juggling or cards, or something else?''

"Something else,'' Morlac told him.

Glendauna got to her feet and moved back from the fire a short distance. Settling back down on the ground once more, she pulled her cloak close about her, covering her arms and legs. With a twist of a smile at Morlac, she touched the moonstone neckpiece she wore, then pulled the hood of her cloak down so that she completely disappeared from sight within the garment. She sat there quietly, subtly moving within the folds of cloth.

Broct watched a long moment, then said softly to Morlac, ''No offense to your lovely friend, but so far, 'tis not much of a trick. What is it she's doing?''

"Perhaps you should go see.''

"It would not upset her—?''

Morlac gave him a pat of encouragement. ''Rest assured, it would not.''

"Oh, very well, then.''

Rising, Broct walked to where the girl still hunched within

the sheltering cloak. He stood there a moment looking down at the mound of cloth, then glanced at Morlac, who gestured for him to investigate. Sighing, the giant bent down and gently grasped the hood. He flipped it back.

With a startling and very aggressive growl, a large golden wolf lunged forward from the cloak, snapping at Broct's hands. Its moon-bright eyes stared fiercely at him, very close to his face, and the big sea-warrior could not help staggering back a few steps out of sheer surprise and bewilderment.

Broct was about to reach for a weapon, his warrior's reflexes and desire for self-preservation momentarily overriding all. But then in the next moment he remembered that these were friends, and he saw that the wolf was not attacking.

The wolf had in fact dropped back to a sitting position on the ground and had lost its aggressive look altogether. Its lips were raised not so much in a snarl as in a canine grin, and it was making a hoarse, coughing sound.

In another few moments, the coughing became laughter as the form of the wolf softened and changed, metamorphosing back into human shape. Glendauna was herself once more, holding her sides as she laughed.

Broct studied her for a while, then looked to Morlac, who smiled broadly. His severe look faded and the giant laughed out loud at his own surprise and embarrassment. He extended a hand to the girl to help her to her feet.

"I deserved that," he told her. Then to Morlac he added, "I like this new friend of yours. She has spunk!"

Glendauna adjusted her garments, which had magically reappeared as she regained human form. "The talisman works perfectly," she told Morlac. "With it, the transformation is painless and swift, and can come anytime I wish it, regardless of the moon. It is not such a fearful thing, now that I can control it." With an impish look toward Broct she added, "In fact, it can be quite fun!"

"I can see," said Broct, "that you two have much to tell me. It looks to be a long night."

"But not too long," cautioned Morlac. "If what Glendauna tells us is true about the road ahead, then we shall need all the rest and all the strength we can find. . . ."

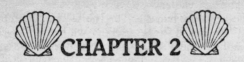

CHAPTER 2

Cavern of the Moaning Bones

A cold wind whistled through the rocks and crevices of the path winding its treacherous way up into the Kyral Mountains. It was a forlorn sound, gnawing and fearsome, an eerie melody that chilled the mind and spirit as much as the wind itself chilled the body. In a sky that was heavy and gray with clouds, no birds flew, and the scant amount of sunlight that filtered through was colorless and shadowless.

It was midday. Morlac, Broct, and Glendauna had been riding all morning, having arisen at dawn. They had driven their mounts hard at first, but then as the road began to climb into the mountains they slowed almost to a snail's pace. Their path had become a narrow trail that snaked its way alongside sheer cliffs and icy ravines, a dangerously thin line between the gray of stone below and the gray of sky above.

"Are you sure there is not some other path Sordros might have followed?" said Broct as he urged his horse onward along the difficult trail.

Glendauna gave a toss of her head to remove the wind-blown hair from her face. "I am sure of nothing. I have traveled far with the Durkesh, but never into the Kyral Mountains. They fear this place, and they are a race not known for fear."

Broct sighed fatalistically. "Then of course this must be where Sordros has gone. How could it be otherwise."

Ahead of them, Morloc rode tall and alert astride his mount, his right hand resting upon his sword hilt. With a grim tone he said, "The green magician has passed this way, all right. Shark knows it. I know it, too. Sordros's magic lingers in the air and upon the path we tread."

Morlac abruptly reined in his horse and carefully dismounted. He looked to the others. "We had better lead our horses until we find a wider path. Their footing will be more sure without our weight on their backs."

"Aye," agreed Broct as he climbed down. "And if they should slip, then at least they will not carry us with them."

They continued on foot, tugging at the reins of their mounts just enough to ensure their following. They barely covered another mile in the next hour, and the bulk of the mountain range still loomed above and around them like a great forbidding wall.

And then, just when it began to seem the path would only continue to climb toward the peaks, it leveled off at a ledge a bit wider than the trail. Sheltered by a rocky outcropping of the mountain face, the mouth of a cave loomed large and dark within the solid stone. The wind howled across the opening, mournful and ominous.

Morlac was the first to find the mark etched into the stone by the side of the entrance. His fingers traced its shape and depth, even as his mind sought to identify it.

" 'Tis an occult symbol," he said at last. "I have seen it somewhere among Sordros's things, and again in the South Kingdom outpost, where Kadrana sent her message through the spirit flame."

Broct nodded. "Then our path ends here."

"Ends . . . or perhaps begins."

Morlac motioned them on, entering the mouth of the cave first. The passage was more than tall enough and wide enough for them to ride through, but they continued to lead their mounts, walking cautiously and looking out for pits and crevices into which the unwary might fall. The sound of the wind ouside grew more distant as they advanced. Their footfalls and the steady clop-clopping of the horses echoed from the hard stone.

Though the naturally formed tunnel grew darker, enough light penetrated from without so that they did not have to use torches. Morlac wondered if the wizard that Sordros had journeyed to see lived here in this cave or merely used the place for his wizardly practices. If it *was* just a cave. Morlac began to be aware of air flowing past him, and that suggested an opening at the other end.

As they progressed steadily deeper into the tunnel that had been eroded through solid stone uncounted centuries before, the passageway gradually widened. This was no mere cave. It was clearly a cavern, and as the light from outside began to fade and weaken, it was replaced by an eerie phosphorescence that ran in glowing streaks along the rough stone walls, and painted the edges of conical formations that rose from the floor and hung from the ceiling like dragons' teeth. The vivid blues and greens burned like cold fire, casting their weird illumination over all.

Morlac paused to stare at the walls of the cavern, and saw to his amazement that some of the glowing stripes were *moving*. He reached out a hand to touch the stone surface, and instantly recoiled as he felt something yielding and slimy beneath his fingers. He realized with horror that the glowing spots of color that were moving were not trickling oils upon the stone, but were in fact creeping worms. Repulsive things, thick and sluglike, they crawled in shifting patterns across the cavern walls, creating a shimmering glow as they moved. Morlac drew away from the wall and continued to lead the others along the center of the passage.

"At times," muttered Broct, " 'Twould be nice to be a simple farmer or merchant."

"At times," agreed Morlac. "But I think you would grow bored with such simplicity, my sea-brother."

"Perhaps. . . ."

Glendauna, leading her own horse between Morlac's and Broct's, kept a wary eye on their strange surroundings. With a voice that belied her words, she said, "How could anyone not enjoy such a life as this."

"It appears that some did not," said Broct with grim humor. He pointed to an object alongside the path they followed. A human skeleton lay sprawled there, the flesh long since rotted away. "You'll find few farmers' bones in a place such as this!"

But Broct fell silent as their progress brought them within sight of another skeleton, and yet another, and *another*.

Within minutes, they encountered dozens more, all facing in the direction of the cave entrance, as if the poor creatures they had once been part of were in the act of fleeing the cavern when they died. But *how* had they died?

"We must be nearing the end," said Glendauna abruptly. "I can hear the wind once more. Listen—the howling grows louder as we go on."

Morlac was silent a long while as they walked with their horses, his ears cocked first one way, then another. "I see no sunlight ahead. And what I hear sounds somehow different from the wind."

"Aye," said Brock with an odd expression. "More like . . . *voices.*"

They began to angle around a large mound of rocks littering the cavern floor and reaching up above their heads. Then as their eyes grew more accustomed to the darkness and the eerie illumination, and as the sound grew steadily louder in their ears, they became aware of two things. The sound was indeed not the wind, but rather moaning. And the mound was not of rocks as they had at first thought. It was made up solely of human bones, piled atop each other so deeply that it was impossible to guess how many people had perished here.

Worst of all, the horrid moaning sound seemed to emanate from the very bones themselves. It was a nightmare chorus of ghostly voices, chilling and terrible.

"By the gods . . . !" Glendauna stared awestruck at the sight, her eyes wide and haunted.

Skulls protruded from the pile of bones, blanched jaws agape in frozen screams. Skeletal hands reached out, fingers twisted in pain and warning. And throughout all, the glowing sluglike creatures crept, their azure light moving through eye sockets and nostrils and mouths. That alone was enough to make one's flesh crawl. But it was to be just the beginning of the cavern's special horror.

For now, rising from the mound of bones like vapor from a steaming swamp, tendrils of phosphorescent mist left the remains, curling and swirling as they rose, growing and expanding into luminous clouds that seemed to carry the dreadful moaning sound with them. Twenty or thirty were already in view, with more yet on the way. The clouds were quickly moving to span the path ahead of Morlac and the others, and as they moved they also began to coalesce into clearly definable shapes.

Like hideous floating corpses, the glowing figures were gaunt, grim, more skeleton than flesh. But there were eyes burning brightly within their skull sockets. Staring eyes, directed at the living humans who faced them. Eyes that showed fear, and inspired it as well.

The ghosts hung there in the air, legs and feet dangling limply, shoulders hunched forward, hands reaching toward Morlac, Broct, and Glendauna in gestures of beseechment and warning. And their moaning became words, the voices clear and frightening real.

"Go back!" said one. *"Go back, before it is too late!"*

Another leaned toward them with an anguished look and wailed, *"Death awaits you! Only pain and death!"*

Yet another ghost cried out in alarm, *"Flee, Flee! You are doomed if you continue!"*

The other wretched souls now set up a cacophony of warnings and moans. It sent a chill down Morlac's spine and filled him with a compelling urge to run away and find the safety of daylight and commonplace things.

Glendauna was close beside him, her small hand gripping his arm. They stood well before their horses but clutched the reins tightly, for the animals were already spooked and might easily run off. This was no place to be stranded. "I feel such fear, Morlac. Such a cold, unreasoning fear!"

"Perhaps we are supposed to," he told her. "There is magic in this, I am certain, and it may be meant to keep us from our goal. If Sordros passed this way, then so may we."

Broct drew his sword. "I am ready to test my steel against these wraiths and whatever lies ahead. However, even if this be only a wizard's warning it could still have the power to do more than frighten, and it may be more forgiving to a fellow wizard like Sordros than to the likes of us."

"I do not doubt that." Morlac steeled himself against the mind-numbing fear he felt coursing through him. His face set in a rigid mask, he stepped forward, advancing on the ghosts that blocked their path.

Broct and Glendauna moved as well, no more than a

half-step behind him. The moanings and dire warnings increased in intensity, echoing from the cavern walls. But still they advanced.

Abruptly, several of the wraiths broke away from the wall of ghosts ahead and darted toward them with frightening speed. They were upon Morlac and the others in an instant, their horrid faces terrifyingly close, their bony hands grasping at the intruders with blood-chilling realness.

"Run, run," screamed the wraiths. *"Don't die as we did!"*

"Away with you!" shouted Broct, slashing out with his sword. The blade cut through the ghost before him, carrying swirls of glowing mist with it. But in an instant the mist had re-formed and the ghost was whole again. "By Tritus!" Broct exclaimed in consternation. "These accursed specters be real enough to touch us, but not real enough to *be* touched!"

Morlac considered drawing Shark to see if the magicked blade had any effect upon the ghosts, but despite their frightening aspect, the wraiths looked too pathetic to strike. Besides, why waste the effort with something that was not real?

"Forget them!" Morlac shouted, mounting his horse and motioning the others to do likewise. "Surely they are illusion. Pay them no heed!"

Morlac goaded his horse forward and charged the barrier of ghosts, with Broct and Glendauna close behind him. They flinched as they passed through the glowing skeletal figures, stirring them into mist, for there was a strange, unearthly feel to the things. But they continued riding in the semidarkness.

The wraiths re-formed, pursuing them, tugging at them, floating above their shoulders and whispering woeful warnings into their ears with dry and dusty breath. It took every bit of resolve within them for Morlac and the others to keep going instead of turning back.

Finally, the voices of the spirits grew weaker, their glow diminishing. It was as if their strength faded with increased distance from the bones which were their mortal remains. Or was it only that the illusion, having failed to serve its purpose of frightening the intruders away, was no longer needed? Morlac did not know, but whatever the case, he was glad to be free of their fearful presence.

Morlac slowed his mount's pace as they left the ghosts behind. He did not want to risk stumbling into some pit or trap that might lay in their path.

"I . . . I see light ahead," gasped Glendauna. "There is a way out!"

Riding close beside them, Broct sheathed his sword. "You were right, Morlac, about the specters. They could not harm us or stop us."

"Let us hope I was right, my sea-brother." he told him. "Let us hope they *were* naught but illusions. For if they were real, then what lies ahead of us may well be as deadly as they warned. . . ."

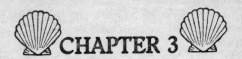

CHAPTER 3

Bronze Warriors

Morlac sat upon his steed, just beyond the opening of the cavern they had traversed. Broct and Glendauna halted their own mounts beside him. By all reckoning, they were now on the other side of the mountain range, having crossed directly through the Kyrals by means of the natural tunnel.

"So this be the Dark Region," said Broct in awe. "The name suits it well."

The three travelers looked out across a vast plateau that stretched away into the haze-dimmed distance. An open sky ranged above them, cloud-shrouded as it had been when first they entered the cavern from the other side, yet different here in this place. Though not as dark as night, the pale light that did filter through seemed tinted by the purple clouds. It was a stagnant light, murky and oppressive, hemmed in by the high peaks of the mountain range. They had entered a twilight land unstirred by breezes. A nightmare land, cold and forbidding, time-locked and lonely.

Glendauna repressed a shiver and thrust a finger toward something visible in the near distance. "Look there—something like a fortress rises above the plain. Think you that your wizard might be there?"

"Perhaps," said Morlac dryly. "He has a fondness for castles. At any rate, we may as well begin there." Morlac suddenly felt the hairs on the back of his neck bristle, an odd and unexpected sensation, and he recalled the warning of the cavern ghosts. Or the illusion. He tried to put the thought behind him, but it would not fully release him from its grip.

Urging their horses forward. they descended the short distance to the plateau and set out across the bleak landscape, pausing only long enough to rest a bit. The ground was cold here, but there was little snow upon its surface and travel was not difficult.

As they drew near the great fortress that loomed ahead, Morlac and the others could see that it stood upon a high point of land at the apex of a city that fanned out from its eastern face, an oddly quiet city with no sign of activity yet visible. The plateau itself was quiet, bleak, devoid of vegetation. There were stumps of trees, blackened and petrified, but nothing more.

Broct surveyed the city, and the plateau that framed it. "Where be the crops? I see no tilled fields, even. Surely this place has no trade that would bring food in. What do they eat?"

Morlac heard something crunch beneath his horse's hoof and looked down to see bones protruding from the thin layer of snow. More human bones, as in the cavern. They seemed to be scattered everywhere.

"Perhaps," he said, "they eat each other."

Glendauna edged her horse alongside his. Her face had the haunted look he had seen when first they met at the ruins of her ancestral home.

"Morlac," she said softly, "I do not like this. It has the look of a place long dead and moldering. Why would Sordros come here?"

"To hide from Drygo and L'Dron Kerr's men. Or from me."

They soon reached the edge of the city. More bones littered the way, as did corroding armor and weapons. It was as if some great war had played itself out here long ago. But why had no one buried the dead, or collected the trophies of battle?

The buildings were gray and white, erected of stone and marble blocks. Some of the roofs had collapsed or rotted away, revealing wooden beams withered by time. Stains marked the walls. A few of the buildings had begun to crumble. Along the avenues of the city, more weapons and

bones were scattered, mingling with tools and city implements. But nowhere was there evidence of any recent life.

With its cold stone walls and grim facades, its statues and
pedestals and great bronze urns, the place looked more like a
sprawling and neglected mausoleum than a city. And perhaps
in a way it was, for only the dead were here to occupy it.

The dead . . . and the soon to be dead, a voice seemed to
whisper in Morlac's ear. The nerves in his face twitched at
the imagined voice, and he could not help turning and looking around him, though he knew no one was near him save
Broct and Glendauna. Was this place so unnerving that he
was hearing things, he wondered? Or was it just more wizard's trickery?

To Broct he said, "Did you hear something just now?"

"Nothing but our own noise," the yellow-eyed giant told
him, then raised an eyebrow in interest. "Why—what heard
you?"

Morlac hesitated, then shrugged. "Nothing, I guess."

There came at that moment a faint glint of light from the
direction of the great fortress. It was followed a few seconds
later by a harsh grating sound, as of some huge metal door
being cranked open upon neglected metal hinges. The sound
cut through the eerie silence of the place with chilling
abruptness.

Broct straightened in his saddle, immediately alert. "Now
that be a sound I heard."

"As did we all," added Glendauna, reining in her horse.
"I think we have finally awoken a welcoming party."

Morlac listened closely as his hand went reflexively to
Shark's hilt and he pulled his shell-shield closer to him. "I
doubt we'll find much welcome here."

"Aye," said Broct. "Any friend of Sordros's will be no
friend of ours! What do you think a mountain wizard will
throw at us? Winged demons? Horned monsters?"

"Something unpleasant, I trust," Morlac said, then with a
concerned glance at Glendauna he added, "I am sorry you
must face this with me."

"I'm not," she told him, her blue-eyed gaze direct and
certain. "I could have remained behind, if I wished. But here
I be, and here I stay!"

Another sound now came from the fortress, faint at first, but rapidly growing louder. The dull thunder of many hoof-beats rumbled through the air and through the frozen ground beneath them. It echoed from the sepulchral stone in the crumbling city until it seemed to be coming from all directions.

"Horsemen," said Broct, looking only slightly relieved. "Twenty or thirty, from the sound of them. Maybe more."

Morlac arched a devil-brow in resignation. "About our usual odds."

The yellow-eyed giant flashed a grim smile. " 'Twould be no challenge with any less."

They had halted their mounts near the center of a wide plaza ringed with colonnaded buildings and dotted with huge statues. Ahead of them now came galloping into view the first of the fortress guardsmen on horseback. Yet . . . *no*, that was only the first brief impression of the things which now advanced upon them, for while the sound of their approach had been familiar, their appearance was an altogether different matter.

Glendauna let out a small gasp of alarm as realization set in. "Morlac! Those are not men on horses. They are—"

"Centaurs," Morlac finished the statement for her. "Or something like centaurs might be, if they existed."

The creatures had bodies like plow horses, large and brawny, and where the heads and necks should be, men's torsos sprouted, with well-muscled chests and arms. They wore close-fitting body armor that covered every inch of their forms from heads to hooves, its dull bronze color darkened by a greenish-gray patina, pitted and ancient looking. A variety of weapons and other items were fastened to harnesses that ran from waist to withers to lower ribs. The strange guardians fit in well with the brooding atmosphere of this accursed nightmare land.

If there was any thought of fleeing from the bronze-clad warriors, that hope faded in the next moment as a second group of the centaurlike beings appeared from the opposite end of the plaza, apparently having gone down other avenues to head off escape. The fortress guards swept in from both ends, trapping Morlac and the others between. Their armor masks, cast in identical fierce scowls, seemed to scream silent threats of doom.

Broct and Glendauna drew their swords at once, pulling their horses around to face the guards behind them. The girl's sword rang out first, clanging against the armored chest of a guardian who sought to snatch her horse's reins from her hand. She drew back to strike again, but the guardian's left hand darted out and with ironlike grip held her sword arm rigidly in place. A bronze right hand grabbed her delicate neck and lifted her squirming from her saddle.

Glendauna still gripped her sword, but her free hand frantically grasped the wrist of the bronze hand that threatened to choke the life out of her. She dangled in the air from the creature's extended arms as if she had no more weight than an empty sack.

Morlac turned from the guards that faced him and saw the girl's desperate situation. In an instant he jerked his horse around and pulled Shark free.

"Broct—cover our backs!"

The yellow-eyed giant needed no encouragement. But at the moment he had all he could handle just defending himself against the arrayed weaponry of the massed guardians attacking him. Even his extra arms seemed of little use in these close quarters against such overwhelming odds.

Morlac maneuvered beside the guardian holding Glendauna and swung his magicked blade at the arm that gripped her throat. Shark hissed through the heavy air, struck and rebounded from the armor with a sound that was bell-like and deep. It left a shiny mark upon the dull bronze surface, but did no damage. He could hear a similar melody of sword blows ringing out from Broct's position behind him.

Bronze hands were grasping for him, pulling at his cloak, grasping at his shield. Guardians were closing in from all sides, a veritable sea of bronze demons. But paramount among his concerns was the girl, whose back now arched, legs kicking as she fought for breath.

Morlac reined down more blows from his blanched blade. None did any more against the armor than the first, and time was running out. His sharp eyes sought some point of weakness, any flaw he could exploit, and he finally noticed that the seams of the armor were lined with some dark substance that did not seem to be metal. With a desperate strength he slashed at the shoulder seam of the arm which held the girl.

Shark crashed down with brutal force and accuracy, biting deep into the pitchlike substance of the shoulder seam. The result was almost instantaneous.

A massive crack spread along the whole of the seam, then ruptured even farther, up toward the neck and down along the arm. In the same instant, jets of greenish gas began to billow from the cracks, spurting out and forming vile-smelling clouds.

With a great shuddering lurch, the bronze guardian collapsed. The arm which held Glendauna broke loose from the torso, freeing her, and the helmeted head rolled off as well. With a last massive sigh of escaping green gas, the thing lay still.

Morlac and the girl stared down incredulously at the fallen guardian. For its dismembered parts revealed a startling fact. There was no creature wearing the armor. The flexible bronze shell was empty, a thick, hollow skin with nothing inside it but the strange gas that even now dispersed.

But they had no time to wonder at the mystery of this wizardry, for the remaining guardians now pressed in upon them. Morlac and the others were hopelessly outnumbered, and so burdened by the closeness of attack that there was no room to fight.

Bronze hands seized them from all sides, pulling Morlac and Broct from their mounts, recapturing Glendauna, and holding them all immobile while ropes were brought to tie their wrists and ankles. Their breath rasped in the stale and heavy air, and in a matter of moments the three found themselves cruelly bound and thrown roughly across the backs of three of the magical bronze warriors.

Other guardians gathered their weapons and horses, and without a single spoken command the group abruptly turned and galloped off toward the fortress at city's edge. Each jolting stride jarred the humans slung across their hard unyielding backs, but they did not slow their pace.

And as they neared the end of the dead city's main avenue, that grim and ancient fortress loomed large before them, its massive bronze gate standing open and waiting. . . .

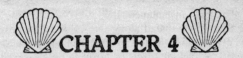 **CHAPTER 4**

Sordros Revealed

The thunder of bronze hooves reverberated through the great brooding fortress as the metal guardians entered. The gateway reached up to twice their height and the enormous entrance hall they now galloped into seemed built on a scale fit for giants. Within moments after all were inside, the huge bronze door swung slowly closed, moved by unseen hands. What little daylight there was faded with the door's progress, to be replaced by the glow of torches blazing in brackets along the walls.

As the great door closed with a solid, resounding *chung!*, the guardians carrying Morlac, Glendauna, and Broct halted and callously dumped their prisoners to the cold stone floor. Dust and musty odors that seemed ages old filled Morlac's nostrils as he struggled to rise from the floor and gain his feet. It galled him to be treated thusly. His introductions to wizards, it seemed, always found him wearing ropes.

Broct gained his feet first, using his extra arms to lever himself up. All his limbs were tied, since he had revealed them in battle, and he stood with a sour look upon his face.

Morlac was up next, and he moved to help Glendauna. Softly he said, "Are you hurt?"

She flinched as she rose. "Bruised and pride-stung, but not hurt." Her wide eyes swept their new surroundings. "At least, not yet."

They suddenly became aware of movement among the bronze guardians and moved closer together, alert to new trouble. But the guardians' attention was not on them this time. The circle of centaurlike beings that surrounded them was opening, creating a path.

The one who strode that path moved with quiet ease, making no sound other than the soft rustle of cloth. It was difficult to tell if it was a man or a woman, for the being who approached Morlac and the others was cloaked in voluminous purple robes that draped from shoulders to ground. A shadowy hood completely hid the face from view, the hands were covered in purple gloves, and even the barely glimpsed feet bore soft boots of the same deep hue. Occult symbols embroidered the robes and hood, their golden threads catching the torchlight and seeming to glow.

"Sordros—?" Glendauna whispered.

"No," said Morlac quietly. "But a wizard, nonetheless."

The cloaked figure stopped a short distance from them and seemed to study the prisoners. Then, after a long moment, a voice issued from the unseen face . . . a voice that was deep and resonant and oddly accented. A man's voice it was, yet it was somehow detached from reality.

"I . . . am Khara Rom, High Wizard of Krellos. Who are you, that disturbs the sanctity of my domain?"

"I am Morlac," he told the wizard in a straightforward and angry tone. "My friends and I are travelers."

"And warriors, it would seem," snapped Khara Rom. "You destroyed one of my guardians."

"We are warriors when we must be," said Morlac. "And I would destroy a score of your metal demons if need be, to save a friend's life."

Khara Rom paced slowly back and forth before them. The multiple shadows at his feet seemed to flicker more than the torchlight which cast them. "Bravely spoken and noble words. But I find them most impudent coming from an intruder! And most ironic as well, for who are you—" he said with a gesture that encompassed them all "—to call my creations demons? There is not one among you untouched by magic!"

Morlac was not surprised the wizard perceived their strangeness, especially with Broct's abnormalities so clearly visible. And there was more truth in Khara Rom's words than he liked to admit, even to himself.

"We are intruders," said Morlac. "There is no use denying that. But we have come seeking someone we believe to be your guest . . . the green magician, Sordros.''

"Sordros?'' Khara Rom stopped his pacing and laughed oddly. "Then he was right. He thought there might be those who would follow him. You wish to see the wizard, Sordros?''

Morlac felt his pulse quickening. If Sordros was here, then his search was over. But was Kadrana also present? Should he even care?

"Yes,'' Morlac told him. "I wish to see Sordros.''

"Very well,'' the purple wizard replied. "I see no reason not to honor your request, since you have traveled so far.'' His words were polite, but they were tinged with malevolent amusement. Turning, he gestured toward a corridor which crossed the great hall. *"Sordros*—come join us. You have visitors.''

Morlac's gaze darted to the entrance of that corridor, and his companions' attention also was riveted there. For an agonizingly long moment, nothing happened. Then at last a moving shadow heralded someone's approach. An all-too-familiar green-garbed figure appeared there, and purposefully entered the great hall.

Sordros strode toward them calmly, supremely confident, the trace of an evil smile upon his thin lips. He halted a short distance from Khara Rom and looked at Morlac, Broct, and Glendauna without speaking.

Morlac hesitated, unsure of what to say now that he was once more in the presence of the wizard who had forged his new life from the fragments of two very different lives. The wizard who was his master . . . his "king" . . . his tormentor. To have ended his search and at last stand before the green magician captive and bound—Morlac cursed his fate.

"What—nothing to say?'' teased Khara Rom. "How impolite. But no matter. This deception has worked well enough. It need not be continued.''

Morlac frowned. "Deception . . . ?''

The purple wizard flicked his gloved fingers in a gesture of dismissal at the question. "Did you really think Sordros would take no precautions? That he would allow whatever enemies might seek him to merely follow him to his destination? What a foolish mistake.''

Broct said, "What sort of game be this? Fools we may be for coming here to seek our old master, but follow him we did, and here he stands before us!"

"Does he?" countered Khara Rom knowingly. "I invite you to take a closer look at what you have followed all these many miles. . . ."

With that, the purple wizard turned toward Sordros and gestured powerfully, his left arm extended, the wrist bent and fingers crooked at varying angles. A nimbus of light glowed faintly around that hand, then shed its radiance upon Sordros.

An abrupt change came over the green magician. He stiffened strangely, and with a final look of arrogance began to shimmer and fade from view. The glowing image twisted and turned, folding in upon itself until it became a mere wisp of smoke. What little substance remained collapsed upon the floor.

Morlac stared in horror and disbelief. Of the wizard he had pursued, at such great difficulty, nothing now remained save a soggy pile of sand and seaweed. The thing they had followed was not, had never been, Sordros. They had been chasing nothing more than a ghost these past months.

"A simulacrum," said Khara Rom. "It lacked the life and substance of a true replica, but was a masterful creation nonetheless. I daresay by now the real Sordros has safely reached the South Kingdom, his true destination. 'Tis but a short journey across the Yellow Sea."

Morlac's hands became tight fists as self-directed rage boiled within him. "I have been a fool! I, of all people, should have realized that a sea wizard does not retreat far from the source of his power. In my eagerness to find Sordros, I have led us all astray."

Close at his side, Glendauna touched his arm consolingly. "Perhaps it was meant to be. Had you not passed through Goltos, many lives would be different now."

Morlac seemed not to hear her words, spoken or unspoken, so caught up in his own thoughts was he. "A fool. . . ." he muttered.

"Do not be too hard on yourself," Khara Rom said now, his tone relaxed, almost friendly, "for you have at least given me a diversion. Few are those that venture here. Few are those brave enough to even try."

The purple wizard gestured to his bronze guardians. "Unbind my guests," he commanded. "Leave their weapons and belongings here, then return to your posts."

Morlac and Broct exchanged surprised looks as several of the metal warriors came forward to untie them and the girl. With that done, they dropped the weapons and other things to the floor, then withdrew. If Khara Rom felt secure without them, then his powers must be great indeed.

"You . . . are freeing us?" Glendauna asked.

"Why not? I have no need to fear you, or to harm you. You are free to go and pursue your journey as you wish. But stay a bit, first. Rest yourselves. Your company would be pleasing, and would allow me to make amends for your treatment at the hands of my guardians. Are you hungry?"

Beware, a small voice seemed to whisper near Morlac's ear. Did he truly hear it, or only feel it in his mind? Even as he wondered, it came again, softer this time yet somehow more real . . . *Beware!* The sound of it made his flesh crawl.

Morlac turned to the others. "What say you, my friends—?"

Broct looked hesitant and suspicious, but said, "I follow your lead, my sea-brother."

"As do I," Glendauna agreed.

Morlac considered a moment longer, then faced Khara Rom. "It is true, we are weary from our journey. If we have your pledge you mean us no harm—?"

"Of course you have my pledge. I wish no harm to befall you. Now leave your things here—your horses will be tended to—and come with me."

With a beckoning gesture, the purple wizard turned and started away into the castle's interior. Morlac waited a moment, then followed.

Fools! he thought he heard the tiny voice say. If it was some inner voice of wisdom speaking, he wondered why he had not been favored with such advice before journeying to this darkling land.

They followed at some distance behind Khara Rom, and taking advantage of this privacy, Broct now leaned toward

Morlac. "I know we have his pledge, but do you really trust this spell-caster?"

Morlac kept his own voice low. "I trust no one save my friends in this human world."

"Then why not leave now? I'll not sleep sound in a place such as this."

"Would you sleep better," asked Morlac, "in the icy field of bones beyond this fortress? Or perhaps the haunted cavern? I think the journey out of this land is best left till tomorrow."

"Perhaps," whispered Glendauna, her wary gaze still sharply focused upon the wizard's back. "If we see tomorrow."

"We must be careful, I agree," Morlac told her. "But this magician intrigues me. I think there is more to this matter than he is saying. What he told us about Sordros may not be true, although it does make sense."

The girl nodded. "And why does he hide himself within those all-concealing robes? Can he be so ugly?"

"Perhaps scarred by war," Broct conjectured, "or by some dread disease. It may even be a requirement of his arcane trade. The ways of wizardfolk be strange."

"Indeed," said Morlac. "There are a great many possibilities. . . ."

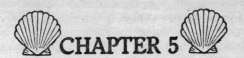# CHAPTER 5

Deadly Dream

"I have not had guests, *real* guests, to entertain in a long while," Khara Rom told them. "A very long while, indeed."

The purple-clad wizard led Morlac, Glendauna, and Broct through high-vaulted corridors of dusty gray stone. Flickering torchlight left the high ceiling in murky shadow, and cast its sallow glow upon the ancient walls of Krellos's enormous fortress-palace. It was easy to believe the place had not seen visitors recently.

"Is there no one else in the city?" Morlac asked.

"No," said Khara Rom. "Only I and my guardians."

They now came to a spacious chamber that must once have been a great banquet hall. Huge tapestries hung along the two longest walls, interspersed with fading banners. A massive wooden table ran down the center of the chamber, with a dozen candelabra arranged upon it. At a gesture from Khara Rom, the candles burst into blazing life, adding their glow to that of the wall-torches.

"I seldom use this hall," the wizard told them. "Once, it held a hundred guests with ease, when Krellos's monarch and his court ruled this land." At one end of the table he indicated chairs of finest inlaid wood, their finish darkened and dulled by time. "Please . . . be seated."

They hesitated a moment, then Morlac pulled one of the chairs out for Glendauna. "My lady—" He now took the seat to her left; Broct, the one to her right.

Khara Rom walked to the very end and pulled the chair back, but did not seat himself yet. For the golden chalices and platters which stood at each place were empty. Extending his right hand with palm flat and fingers spread, the wizard uttered words too low to hear, too strange to grasp.

Ever distrustful, Morlac wished he had brought his sword and shield with him. They might be useless against Khara Rom's powers, but he felt naked without them.

As they watched, something strange was happening with the candle flames. Ghostly spheres were forming about each one, as if they burned within many-layered bubbles. In the next instant, those spheres moved away from their candles, carrying duplicate flames at their cores.

Khara Rom twisted his hand, directing the spheres with a new gesture. They began to dart about the table with alarming speed, seeking out the chalices and platters, circling the rims again and again, until they became blurred rings of light, dazzling and hypnotic. At last they faded, but in so doing revealed a startling fact. The chalices were now brimful with wine, and the platters were heaped with food, fresh and steaming hot. Choice cuts of meat, fit for royalty and roasted to perfection, were piled next to vegetables and breads of a quality Morlac had never seen. Their aroma alone was enough to undermine whatever caution remained, and yet. . . .

Broct lifted his platter closer to his nose, the better to savor the exquisite smells. But as he lowered it once more to table top, he cast a skeptical look at the wizard.

"Be this real?" he said, still holding the platter in both hands. "It will not change to sand, or some such, once it's in our bellies?"

"The food is altogether real, I assure you," Khara Rom told them. " 'Tis no illusion. I conjured it with a simple replenishment spell, just as I once did for my monarch and his court. You may eat and drink, without fear."

Morlac took note of the wizard's own platter and chalice, which were empty. "You do not join us in this meal?"

"By my presence only. I never eat at this hour."

Morlac weighed the risk. He still did not trust the wizard, but his keen senses detected nothing unusual in the meal. Besides, if Khara Rom was as powerful as he seemed, he could surely find better ways to harm them. And if his hospitality was sincere, refusing it might anger him.

Not without reluctance, he tasted the food. Its flavor was every bit as good as its aroma, and his hunger was great. He could only hope there would be no delayed ill effects.

As the three of them ate, Khara Rom sat with arms folded, watching with interest. Or so it seemed. His face was still hidden in shadow within the hood of his robes.

"The food is excellent," Broct said suddenly between mouthfuls. Though as cautious as Morlac at first, he now consumed the delicious meal with gusto. " 'Tis the best I've ever tasted."

Khara Rom gave an acknowledging nod. "Thank you. I derive great pleasure from your enjoyment. Perhaps you would all find music pleasing—?"

Without waiting for an answer, the wizard gestured toward a dark corner of the chamber where a number of musical instruments lay upon a low table. Suddenly, without hands touching them or lips breathing air through them, the stringed instruments and flutes began to play. The music was soft and mellow, sprightly yet soothing; in short, as perfect as the meal itself. And yet, there was a haunting, almost melancholy quality to the atmosphere of this place that was vaguely disquieting.

"If I may ask," Morlac inquired, "what happened to the people of this kingdom? We saw evidence of a war as we crossed the plain to reach Krellos."

"A great and terrible war," Khara Rom confirmed somberly. "Years ago, our enemies in the eastern realm of Qua K'Nar sent an invading army to our land. Warfare between our kingdoms had been going on for centuries, but our enemies sought to destroy us or enslave us once and for all. The bloody carnage lasted for weeks, progressing closer and closer to our city, until at last the battle raged through it and to the very walls of this fortress. Neither side won, truly, for though our gallant warriors succeeded in destroying the legions of Qua K'Nar totally, they were themselves slain, to the man. It was tragic."

Liar! whispered the small voice that seemed so close to Morlac's left ear that the suddenness of it made him flinch. No one else seemed to hear it, though, and he self-consciously ran a hand along his shoulder, as if to calm a twitching nerve.

"The royal family survived, of course," continued Khara Rom, "as did many of the nobles, the court servants, and the old men, women, and children of the city, who had taken shelter in this fortress."

Broct leaned forward with a querulous frown. "Could you not use your powers against the invader?"

"I could, and I did," Khara Rom told him. "But I was not as knowledgeable or as skillful then as I am now, and my meager efforts could not turn the tide of battle. My metal guardians were a later creation."

"Yet of those that did survive," Morlac said curiously, "only you now remain?"

The purple wizard nodded. "We were a shattered people. Most of those who were left gradually drifted away to other lands to start anew. The nobles and members of the royal family eventually died, as did the few loyal servants who stayed behind. I am the last."

Glendauna pushed her platter back, too full to eat more. "Why, then . . . why do you stay?"

Khara Rom shrugged and said resignedly, "This is my land. It is all that I know, or care to know. And I have grown weary of civilized societies. Better that I spend my days here."

"What know you of the cavern that traverses the Kyral Mountains?" Morlac asked him.

"Nothing beyond the fact that it is the route to the Western Lands. I have never ventured there."

Liar! came the tiny voice once more. It did not make Morlac jump this time, but it did make him wonder. About his own sanity, and about the wizard's veracity.

"Now you know my story," Khara Rom said. "Tell me something of your own lives."

There seemed little harm in that, so Morlac and Broct described how they had come to be in Sordros's guard, of their mission to L'Dron Kerr's palace, and their own great war against invaders, with similar tragic results. Glendauna told something of her own history, and so by the time the tale-telling was done, so too was the meal.

"The hour grows late," Khara Rom told them, "and I am sure you must be weary from your journey. Come—let me show you to your rooms."

They rose from the great table and followed the wizard across the chamber and down a corridor that led to another section deep within the fortress. Doorways stood open at intervals along the hall, revealing quarters obviously intended for nobles. And surprisingly, their weapons and other belongings had been neatly placed here along the wall.

"You may choose whichever rooms you wish," Khara Rom told them. "In the morning we may speak again, before you go."

Morlac bent to pick up his sword and shield, and the small pack of belongings that had been taken from his horse. Straightening, he turned with a question for the wizard of Krellos.

"You say our horses will be—" he broke off, his gaze darting about the hall "—tended?"

Glendauna also turned, her own eyes searching and wide. "He is gone! I looked away but a moment, and he vanished."

Broct merely sighed and shook his head. "Wizards . . ." he said derisively. "How they delight in their little tricks. For all their powers, I would not give three brass coins for the lot of them."

Glendauna bent to scoop up her own belongings. "I don't know. Though I feared him at first, he truly seems different now. He seems . . . lonely."

"Yes," said Morlac. "He *seems* many things."

The yellow-eyed giant gathered up his own assortment of weapons and other items and glanced in the sleeping chamber nearest him. "Well, this room suits me as well as any, so if no one objects I shall take it. And we might all be wise to sleep with one eye open this night." He hesitated before stepping through the doorway, a wry smile upon his lips. "That is, assuming you two *will* be sleeping."

Glendauna's lovely face flushed, first in embarrassment, then in anger. But Broct was gone from view before her mouth could open in response. She looked quickly to Morlac, who arched a devil-brow in consternation and entered one of the other rooms himself.

Morlac set down his gear near the bed, then quickly surveyed the room. It was spacious and clearly once belonged to some high-ranking member of the palace retinue. The ancient gray walls were still as grim and chilly as the rest of the fortress, but the wall hangings and luxurious furnishings made the chamber quite comfortable. There was even a large marble bathing pit in the far corner, where fresh water sparkled and glistened. Candelabra and a small fireplace gave adequate illumination and warmth.

Morlac turned and found Glendauna standing close behind him. Her face had lost some of its color, but she still looked perturbed.

"Broct is . . . I mean . . ." she started.

Morlac grasped her shoulder. "He meant no harm. You'll grow used to his gibes, once you get to know him."

"Teasing does not bother me," she blurted out. "The Durkesh are full of jests and taunts—how well I know that! —but your friend, he . . . he assumes too much."

Her face colored anew and she quickly turned and left the chamber. She crossed the hall and entered a room on the opposite side.

Morlac shook his head and wondered at his own confused feelings. Though he had avoided the matter, he could not deny he felt attracted to Glendauna, or that their bond had deepened. She was right, though—Broct did assume too much, even in jest. Or did he? Despite all his free-spirited quips and bold humor, the yellow-eyed giant was, after all, the one among them who always saw straight to the heart of matters. Had he read their own thoughts before they themselves were willing to acknowledge them? Or was the remark just a passing joke after all, with no more thought given it once said? What a bottle he had uncorked!

And now came other troubling thoughts. Kadrana's image loomed in his mind, a powerfully attractive vision still, awakening memories and passions difficult to quell. How could he still feel anything for her, after she had abandoned him to seeming doom to save herself? How could he?

How could he not. . . .

A whisper of sound came from behind him, and Morlac turned to face the doorway with reflexive quickness. But it was not danger behind him. Glendauna had returned, still holding her weapons and belongings in her arms. Her face was a mask, behind which uncertain emotions lurked. As she stood there, there was something about her very awkwardness that was enormously touching.

"That room . . ." she said softly, her eyes shifting uneasily away from his steady gaze. "I . . . I thought I saw a rat in there."

"Only thought?" Morlac said, with a hint of a smile. "Anyway, 'twould make a tasty tidbit for a wolfling, would it not?"

She looked aghast. "You cannot think . . . !"

Morlac stepped closer to her. "I am teasing, and you know it."

Her blue eyes narrowing, she dropped her belongings on the floor and struck her small fist against his chest with surprising impact. "I do not need *your* taunts as well!"

She drew back, on the verge of striking him again, and Morlac grabbed her wrist. Softly he said, "Teasing. Not taunting. Taunts are meant to hurt, and I would never knowingly hurt you, my lady."

Glendauna stared at him a long moment, trembling with emotion, her face still livid as tears welled up to spill down her cheeks. Then she abruptly threw herself into his arms, her face cradled against his shoulder.

Morlac held her, gently stroking her hair. "We have been through much in a short while, you and I. And I think I know why Broct's words were so upsetting."

"They would have done no more than make me blush, had his words been true," she said softly. "But they were not true, and that made me face a hurtful knowledge. We have become more than friends, my troubled warrior, so much more. Yet despite everything, you still love Kadrana, don't you?"

Morlac drew a deep breath. "Yes. Or at least part of me does. It defies logic, but at times I am still obsessed with the thought of her."

"I think she has cast a spell upon you."

"You may be right," he told her. Touching her cheek, he gently turned her face toward his. "And an evil spell, no doubt. But you, my lady, need no spells. You have your own special magic. . . ."

Morlac kissed her, and in the moment that their lips met he

knew how vast a difference there was between Sordros's wicked "daughter" and this sweetly noble young woman. It was the difference between passion and romance . . . between desire and love. Where Kadrana's kisses had been hungry and possessive, Glendauna's was tender, innocent, vulnerable. And that endearing quality was, in its own way, highly seductive.

Morlac ended the kiss sooner than he really wished to, and as she opened her eyes questioningly, he asked, "Was there truly a rat in that room?"

"No," she admitted softly. "Must there be?"

"No."

"Morlac . . ." she said, glancing back across the hall ". . . I am not afraid of many things, as I think you will vouch. But I cannot bear the thought of being left alone in this place. And though I do not mean it in the way Broct suggested, I do not think I can sleep this night."

"I thought you were beginning to trust this wizard, Khara Rom."

"Almost," she replied. "But that is not the same as complete trust, and there is something here that unnerves me. Nothing I can express in words, but. . . ."

Morlac nodded. "I have much the same feeling. Let us do this then—we shall get what rest we can, taking turns keeping watch. Whoever is up shall wake the other at the slightest sign of trouble."

"So long as we are together," she said. She stood there a moment more, still enjoying the shelter of his arms, her eyes exploring his. Then her eyes closed as they kissed again. This time, it was a long and lingering kiss.

A kiss enjoyed indirectly by yet another, whose presence they did not suspect. Behind a gilded mirror on the wall, within a secret passage, Khara Rom stood watching, silent and motionless.

Morlac was dimly aware that he was drifting into sleep . . . that Glendauna was nearby, standing guard. He was on the threshold between true sleep and wakefulness, troubled by visions he knew were unreal, but could not control. Again, he seemed to be battling the bronze guardians, though now they were even larger and more menacing than in reality. In the next moment, a vision of Khara Rom loomed before him, a towering giant in the midst of a lightning storm, with dark clouds swirling angrily and the rumbling thunder becoming peals of laughter, evil and echoing. Then as lightning flashed, casting its stark and terrible glow upon the wizard, the purple hood fell back to reveal Sordros himself, throwing back his head in derisive laughter.

Thankfully, that dream began to fade. But something else replaced it, and though vague at first, a voice gradually became clear. It whispered and teased at Morlac's awareness. Was it part of the dream, or was it real?

Strange one . . . strange one . . . the voice seemed to say. *I will tell you the truth, if you wish to know it. I will tell you. I will show you. Let me lead the way. . . .*

Morlac felt himself drifting into deeper and stranger realms. He was torn between wanting to awaken and wanting to see where this dream might lead.

Now he felt as if he was outside the room in which he slept, walking the hall. But the gray walls seemed darker, more ominous, the corridor shrouded in mist. His movements were slow and labored, his legs leaden. And yet he seemed not quite to touch the floor. As he advanced down the hall the view before him slowly tilted from one side to the other, distorting his sense of balance.

Come with me, said the voice. *Learn the truth of Krellos. . . .*

Morlac felt himself floating through corridor after corridor, beyond the great banquet hall, beyond the royal chambers. Rising above a twisting spiral stair, he moved higher and higher within the labyrinthine fortress until at last he reached the topmost ramparts. He could almost feel the chill air that hung beneath the dusky sky, almost sense the reality of the gray and ancient stone beneath him . . . and yet, not quite . . . not quite. A nightmare in a nightmare land. Surely, he thought, this must be what death is like.

As he hovered over the ramparts, looking out over the enormous plain that surrounded the fortress, he imagined he could see the blanched bones that dotted the barren landscape. But then the voice which had been haunting him came again.

Hear me . . . hear me and learn. This is how things are now, oh foolish warrior. But I shall show you how they once were. . . .

The feeling of disorientation grew stronger, and suddenly before Morlac's startled eyes the land around him changed. The dust and grime of many years faded from the stone walls below him, and the fortress seemed almost white within this dark and dismal place. The vast plain surrounding it changed as well. Where before nothing stood as far as the distant horizon, forests now ranged far and wide. And though the sky did not brighten noticeably, Morlac felt that it was now day.

Something else had changed as well. Bare bones no longer covered the plain. Now they were clothed in flesh, alive and active. A vast army of men clad in purple-and-blue uniforms and carrying the banners and emblems of Krellos fought against an equally large army of black-and-gold-clad warriors.

The invaders of Qua K'Nar, explained the ghostly voice. *The killing has just begun.*

As Morlac watched, the battle unfolded before him, strangely unreal and silent. The events of many days seemed to take place in mere moments. And it was quickly becoming clear that the invaders were winning. The fighting was progressing slowly closer and closer to the great fortress, and Krellos's defenders were being driven back.

And now upon one of the high ramparts, a group of figures stood. The monarch and nobles of the realm watched the battle's progress with fearful eyes. Another figure stood among them. Khara Rom, high wizard of Krellos, clad in his purple robes, moved about a great framework. Suspended by ropes within that framework was an enormous crystal, deeply lavender and many-faceted.

Khara Rom was making adjustments, readying the implements of magic for some great spell. In another moment he was motioning the royal retinue back to a safe distance.

As the wizard chanted his incantation, seeming to shout above the crash of swords, blinding light erupted from within the huge crystal. Its radiance flashed out across the ramparts, searing through the city, engulfing the fighting men, and reaching over the vast plain. The incredible power of it surprised even Khara Rom, who staggered back, shaken.

As the light faded, all who crouched low along the battlements rushed forward to see what effect the spell had worked. Khara Rom moved more slowly to the edge, seeming to sense that all had not gone well. But the enormity of his miscalculation was only just now becoming visible.

The radiant light had stopped the invading soldiers in their tracks, all right. It had withered the flesh upon their bones and dropped them where they stood. But the terrible spell had also wrought the same effect upon Krellos's defenders, so that only Death stood victorious upon the great field of battle. Thousands upon thousands of corpses littered the ground.

The destruction did not end there. All who had been trapped in the city when the fighting reached it were also dead. All the fields and forests had been parched and blighted, the trees crumbling and turning to black, rotting hulks. All the animals, whether on farms or running wild, were dead, as were the birds that had once filled the sky. Beyond the fortress, the entire realm of Krellos seemed lifeless, extending as far as the eye could see. Only those within the fortress still lived.

This then, said the ghostly voice, *is how Krellos was destroyed. Not as Khara Rom told you. But that is not the limit of his lies or his treachery.*

For awhile, the voice continued, *we who survived the destruction lived on in the fortress as best we could. But some of those who had been near the great crystal when the spell was wrought were slowly dying, Khara Rom among them. He began to experiment with some of us, vile and torturous experiments, for he sought to prolong his own life . . . to cheat death, though death he richly deserved. Those hundreds of us who still lived escaped from the fortress and fled from Krellos, for we knew we could not fight him and we dared not stay any longer. We made it as far as the cavern, and might have reached the Western Lands had not Khara Rom discovered our plan. But discover it he did. That was when his madness turned to murderous rage. . . .*

Morlac found the scene around him dissolving, shifting, changing to the interior of the great cavern that cut through the Kyral Mountains. The dream vision became clear. Marching through the eerie darkness were hundreds of women, children, and old men, as well as the last of the nobles and merchants. Though haggard and near exhaustion, they seemed hopeful.

Then suddenly that hope was stolen from them. Khara Rom's twisted and malevolent form appeared behind them with startling swiftness. Morlac thought he could almost hear the wizard's curses and shouts of vengeance . . . and the fearful cries of those who sought to escape him.

Throwing his arms forward angrily, Khara Rom called forth demon powers with a sibilant spell. Flames crackled out from his clawlike hands and darted along the floor of the cavern, creating a wall of fire that quickly circled the group of people.

Amid screams and shouts of terror, Khara Rom's laughter rose as the survivors of Krellos huddled together. Some tried to escape by darting through the fire, but they died in flames as they ran, never reaching the other end of the cavern. The intense wall of fire now crept steadily inward, packing the screaming crowd closer and closer until those on the outside began to climb over the rest in their efforts to avoid the flames. Higher and higher they piled, struggling and writhing atop yet others who also sought to claw their way up.

It was a desperate and futile attempt. There was no escaping the flames, for they reached all the way to the ceiling of the cavern. And as they closed in now, the entire mass of people was engulfed by the fire. The screams and moans rose in volume as the flames spread inward to the center and the smoke of burning flesh billowed up in dark and sickening clouds.

The horror of those screams, the unspeakable agony they conveyed, rang and echoed within the great cavern . . . rang and echoed within Morlac's mind. . . .

Morlac awoke abruptly, sitting bolt upright. His sweat-drenched features glistened in the candlelight.

Glendauna was standing beside him, a frown of worry upon her lovely face. "What is it—? Are you all right?"

His breathing slowed as he began to calm down. "Just a dream," he told her. "A terrible dream."

"Your face showed such terror before you awoke, and you were moaning."

Morlac got to his feet and slowly walked to the wall where the gilded mirror hung. "How long have I slept?"

"Not long," she said. "A few hours, perhaps."

"That is long enough. I shall stand watch the rest of the night. You had better try to get some sleep yourself."

Morlac looked at his face in the mirror. Was it only his imagination that he looked somehow older and drawn? That the haunted look he had seen on the faces of his dream was now mirrored on his own? From the corner of his eye he saw a tiny glow of light, softly pulsing at his left shoulder. As he looked closer, he could see it was not a reflection. A spot of light no larger than a grain of sand, it seemed enmeshed in the coarse weave of his jerkin. It had the same ghostly color of the cavern wraiths. Could it be they were not merely an illusion to scare off intruders? Had he carried some ghostly fragment with him?

As the tiny spot of light faded from view, a haunting voice near Morlac's ear whispered, *The truth is yours now . . . remember it . . . remember. . . .*

From behind him came Glendauna's voice. "Did you hear me, Morlac?"

"What?" he asked as he turned toward her.

"I said, I don't know if I can sleep now, if this place brings nightmares so easily."

He walked back to where she stood and put his arms around her. "I think such dreams are mine alone here. They will not trouble you."

He kissed her, then hugged her gently as she clung to him. But even as he held her thus, his troubled eyes gazed back toward the mirror. Was the ghostly vision nothing more than a nightmare brought on by a bellyful of wizard's food and drink? He had a terrible feeling it *was* more than that, and that Krellos and Khara Rom and this ancient fortress were all parts of a living nightmare from which they might never awaken. . . .

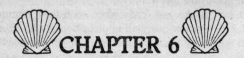

CHAPTER 6

The Secret of Khara Rom

Morlac awoke slowly, forgetting for a moment where he was. Then as details of the room became clear, he remembered the ancient fortress of Krellos and the events of the day before. He also remembered the dream whose echoing horror still haunted him. At least it had not returned to trouble this unplanned sleep.

He found himself sitting on the bed, his back against the solid wooden panel at its head. Glendauna was curled up beside him. Still asleep, her head and shoulders were nestled in the curve of his arm. The flames in the fireplace had dwindled to mere glowing embers, and the candles had long ago guttered and gone out, their once long shafts of wax now lying in congealed pools. There were no windows, but an airshaft at one side of the room seemed to admit a feeble light from outside.

Glendauna stirred, sleepily at first, then her eyes flashed open as she too recalled the nature of this nightmare place. Her gaze darted swiftly to Morlac, meeting his. She relaxed, reassured by his smile.

"Is it morning?"

"I think so," Morlac told her. "But it's hard to tell in this accursed place."

"I shall be glad to leave it."

"As shall I," he said. He gave her a kiss and then rose from the bed. He gestured toward the water-filled pit at the end of the room where soap and towels beckoned. "I suggest we bathe while we have the advantage of such a luxury. Then we must gather our belongings and bid Khara Rom and this dreadful graveyard farewell.''

Broct was awake and ready when soon they ventured into the hall. His weapons were all in place beneath his cloak, and his pack was slung over one shoulder. He looked disgustingly well-rested, but the yellow-eyed giant's normal joviality was tempered by caution.

"Where do you think we'll find the wizard?" he asked.

"I have a feeling he'll find us," Morlac said. "But we can start at the banquet hall."

Glendauna adjusted her cloak about her. "Why not just leave?"

" 'Twould be a poor way to repay our host's hospitality," Morlac said with irony. "Besides, his metal guardians may need his orders to let us pass. I do not wish to fight our way out of here if we can avoid it."

They continued down the corridor with a soft rustle of cloaks and swords, disturbing the unnatural stillness of the place. Morlac found the path even more familiar than did the others, for his dream journey still lingered in his mind.

In a matter of a few minutes they had reached the great hall where dinner had been conjured for them the night before. At first it seemed deserted. Then as they stood a moment, looking about, a voice came from the chair at the table's end. Its tall back was to them, blocking their view of its occupant.

"Ready to leave, are you?" said the voice. It seemed an innocent-enough question, and yet there was a slight edge to it. Something sinister lurked beneath those polite words.

"Yes," replied Morlac. "We thank you for your kindness."

"Oh, it was no trouble," said Khara Rom, rising from the chair and turning to face them. He was still garbed in the same enveloping purple robes he had worn the day before. Morlac wondered if he slept in them. "No trouble at all. But do not feel the need to rush off. I would be a poor host if I did not offer my guests breakfast, at least."

Morlac considered it, but said cautiously, "I think we shall decline your invitation this time. We are eager to resume our journey."

Khara Rom shrugged. "You disappoint me, but no matter.

'Twould be but a small pleasure I forgo now. There will be greater ones soon enough.''

Though puzzled by his words, Glendauna asked, ''Will you take us to our horses?''

''They are in a stable near the gate,'' the wizard told them. ''It is not far. But is there anything else you need that I may provide—?''

Morlac noticed that Khara Rom did not directly answer the girl's question, though he seemed to. He did not think the wizard's politeness rang true, and he was fast tiring of his word-sparring.

''No,'' said Morlac.

''Well, then,'' Khara Rom replied in a deeper tone as he folded his arms across his chest, ''there is something *I* need. Something that you can, and shall, provide. . . .''

Though he seemed to give no signal, hoofbeats abruptly clattered outside the huge chamber. Bronze guardians appeared at the entrance of every corridor, blocking escape. Their weapons were drawn and ready.

Broct glanced quickly about, snarling, ''What manner of treachery is this?''

Khara Rom took a step toward them. ''An unnecessary measure, I assure you. My powers alone are more than enough to keep you here.''

Morlac reached for Shark's hilt, and from the corner of his eye saw Glendauna reach for her sword as well. But as his hand closed around the weapon he was dismayed to feel the hilt dissolving in his grasp. He looked down, and indeed, the entire sword, its sheath and belt, were disintegrating into dust that settled to the floor.

A small cry of alarm from Glendauna told him that the same was true of her weapon. Glancing to Broct, Morlac saw torrents of gray dust raining from beneath his cloak. He shot Khara Rom an angry and questioning look.

''Do not worry—'' said the wizard in smug and gloating fashion ''—those were not your true weapons. Only simulacra which I created last night to put you at ease. Your true weapons never left the entrance hall.''

''One did,'' said Broct quickly. ''For your guardians never found it. Now I freely give it to you!'' A hand darted from beneath his cloak and hurled a small dirk directly at Khara Rom's chest.

The spinning blade flashed brightly in the dismal hall and struck point first just above the spot where the wizard's arms were folded. It should have pierced his heart instantly, but instead it merely pierced the robes. With a loud and ringing *clank*, the dirk rebounded from the wizard's chest and fell clattering to the floor stones. Broct and Morlac exchanged dark looks.

"You fools," said Khara Rom with grim sarcasm. "Have you not yet guessed? Must I reveal myself to you . . . ?"

He stepped yet closer to Morlac and the others, grasping the edges of his hood and throwing it back. The face that had been concealed from them now leered out with evil amusement.

Glendauna gave a small gasp at the sight before them. Morlac raised an eyebrow, intrigued by what he saw, but not truly puzzled by it. Indeed, how could he be?

Khara Rom's face glinted darkly as it stared at them. A strong and not unhandsome face, its features nonetheless bore an evil countenance. Evil and unreal, for it and the head of which it was part were all cast of bronze. The neck and what could be seen of the shoulders were also bronze. Next, the wizard removed his gloves. Metal hands glistened dully as they were exposed to view, and it became apparent that, like the magicked guardians that served to protect his lifeless domain, Khara Rom was himself formed totally of bronze.

Those who had been near the great crystal when the spell was wrought were slowly dying, Khara Rom among them— the words echoed through Morlac's mind. A chill seized him as he realized the dream vision had been true . . . the ghostly voice genuine. Now he understood. And now he knew why the wizard had not partaken of food with them the night before.

"Over eight hundred years have passed since my mortal body died," said Khara Rom. "I tried to find a way to extend my human life, but events denied me that opportunity. And so, knowing of a way to store my mind and occult knowledge within a vessel of purest bronze, I fashioned a likeness of myself in metal, with jointed limbs to enable movement. I then transferred my consciousness to it, and gained immortality. Immortality! Ah . . . but at such a price. Such a price. Never again to experience sensations. Never again to taste or smell, or feel the warmth of a human touch. You have reminded me of so much that has been lost. I learned eventually how to make my metal guardians and imbue them with a semblance of intelligence, but they are poor company.''

"If it be company you seek," snapped Broct, "then why not leave this place and journey elsewhere?"

"Because—'' said Khara Rom angrily "—because the spell that sustains me in this form also binds me here. I cannot leave this realm. I can barely journey beyond the limits of this fortress. So you see, it is not merely company I need. And thanks to Sordros, the means to my freedom now stands before me.''

"You are wrong," said Morlac, "if you think we will meekly submit to your vile tortures.''

"No—*you* are wrong. For you have no choice!"

Khara Rom shot out both hands in a magical gesture and occult energy flared from his fingertips, exploding with raw power. Morlac and the others felt themselves jerked back as if struck by a strong ocean wave. Then darkness settled into their minds, even as the wizard's words still rang in their ears.

No choice . . . no choice. . . .

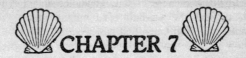

CHAPTER 7

Shackles and Bonds

Morlac felt the darkness releasing its hold on his mind, but even as it slipped away the dull ache that replaced it seemed little improvement. His senses cleared in the next moment and he became aware that he was flat on his back, strapped to some sort of wooden table. This was a chamber he had not seen before. He was not pleased to see it now.

The room was large but oddly shaped, fit into the curves and angles of the fortress as if it were the leftover space between more important chambers. Cluttered with occult implements, jars of oddly colored powders, and row upon row of ancient and moldering books, there could be little doubt this was the wizard's own chamber. As if to confirm that fact, the door creaked open and Khara Rom entered. With his hood and gloves still removed, he resembled a living statue dressed in human garb. He looked across at Morlac with a nod of approval.

"Good—you are awake now."

"What have you done with my friends?"

"Nothing more than secure them in another part of the fortress," said Khara Rom. "I see no need to harm them. In fact, they should fit in well with my plans. Especially the girl."

Morlac strained against the straps that held him. "Leave her alone! I swear, wizard, if you—"

"You swear?" Khara Rom said contemptuously. "Do not waste your threats on me. You are in no position to make them."

The wizard gestured toward the doorway and two of his bronze guardians entered. Each moved to one end of the table and together they lifted the heavy burden easily. With one of them backing toward the doorway, they moved Morlac, still bound and helpless, slowly into the hall.

Khara Rom picked up a thick book of spells from his desk and kept pace with them. "There are only a few final preparations before all is ready. It will not be long until I once more walk free in human form. . . ."

In a dungeon deep within the enormous fortress, Broct struggled against the shackles that held him to the wall. His cloak had been removed, and each of his six arms was secured in place against the cold stone, as were both ankles. All eight limbs were fanned out with space between them, so that none could reach any other. Near him, Glendauna was similarly shackled against the wall, her cloak also missing. Just now awakening from the mind-numbing effects of Khara Rom's spell, she looked about the dungeon with confusion at first, then with growing concern.

"Morlac—!" she said. "Where is Morlac?"

"With the magician, I'll wager," Broct told her.

"We must get free and help him! We must!"

"Why do you think I struggle so?" the yellow-eyed giant said with exasperation. "But these bonds be strong. I do not think I can break them."

Glendauna continued to look around the grim chamber. Her gaze abruptly riveted on the table by the door. An ornately crafted neckpiece with a moonstone at its center lay there. Though recognizing it at once, she could not refrain from twisting her head down to stare at her own throat, awkwardly out of view.

"Damn!" said she. "He has removed my amulet."

"You worry over a trifling piece of jewelry at a time like this—?"

" 'Tis no trifle!" she said in anguish. "With it, I can control my transformation. If I could but change, I might slip from these shackles and find a way to release you."

Broct relaxed for a moment, ceasing his efforts and allowing his muscles to rest. He studied the young woman as she vainly tugged against her bonds. His expression softened.

"You have a warrior's valor as well as beauty," he told her. "Tell me . . . how long have you been in love with Morlac?"

She looked at him quickly, defensively, then away again as she still struggled to get free. "There are any number of times he saved my life, or showed me kindness and understanding. Times that made my feelings more certain. But in truth, I think my heart was his the moment that we met. If I could only make him forget Kadrana."

"That witch? I'll grant she has a hold on him, but he's well rid of that one. Morlac would have to be a fool not to choose you over her."

"We are all fools when it comes to love. But thank you, Broct."

She fell silent as a shadow passed over the small window in the door to their cell. A bronze guardian crossed in front of it, the sound of its hooves ringing softly in the corridor beyond.

His voice low, Broct said, "It seems Khara Rom has posted a guard."

Glendauna gave a small gasp of anguish and sagged within her shackles. "I don't know why he bothered. I cannot begin to break free!"

"How could you!" Broct snorted. "Even I cannot."

The young woman was silent for a long time, breathing heavily from her exertions. Then as her breathing slowed, her head abruptly came up, an odd look, a wild look, blazing in her desperate eyes.

"*We* are not strong enough to break these bonds, Broct," she said. "Think you that a guardian might be—?"

"Possibly. But why would a guardian wish to?"

"Could we trick one, somehow? Khara Rom himself admitted they are not greatly intelligent."

Now it was Broct's turn to be silent in thought. At last, the yellow-eyed giant began to smile faintly. "There may be a way, at that. The wizard denied you your amulet, but he seems to have overlooked my ring. Are you willing to take a chance?"

Glendauna tensed with new hope and eagerness. "Must you ask?"

"All right, then," said Broct. "Get ready, my lady. And hope the gods are wagering against the metal magician and his minions."

Broct twisted one of his hands forward and touched his thumb to the back of the heavy ring he wore. He pressed it hard, calling forth the defense that once protected him in the sea. All at once, a glint of light sparkled upon the obsidian stone, to be instantly swallowed up in a cloud of inky darkness that billowed out from the ring. The stygian blackness quickly spread, engulfing Broct and Glendauna, totally obscuring their end of the dungeon cell.

Glendauna caught her breath in surprise. Her last glimpse of Broct was of a great wicked smile.

"See?" he said with irony. "*I* have a few tricks as well. Now, think you could manage a good scream?"

Her reply set his ears ringing and halted the hoofbeats in the corridor. The sound of bronze hooves clattered quickly now, returning to the door of their cell. A pause told them the guardian was likely looking through the small window, and Broct imagined the metal monster being confounded by seeing nothing where something should be. There came the rasp and rattle of a key within the lock, then the squawk of old hinges as the door was thrust open. Tentative footfalls grew louder as the guardian approached, entering the murk.

Broct readied himself as the sounds drew near him. He could not truly see the guardian, but he seemed to sense its position. Cold bronze hands reached forward, making contact with his chest, then the wall, then his arms. Broct remained motionless, not even breathing.

The yellow-eyed giant felt those bronze hands tracing the lines of his upper arms to the points where the shackles secured his wrists—checking to be sure the bonds still held, no doubt. Almost ready now . . . almost . . . almost. Now!

As the guardian's hands continued up past his own, Broct quickly grabbed those hard bronze wrists and locked them in his steely grip. The guardian's response was instinctive and instantaneous. It jerked back with both arms, struggling to break free of Broct's grasp. But Broct tightened his grip and with all his strength tried to move his arms with the motion of the guardian's tug.

The guardian's great unnatural strength, combined with Broct's, pulled the shackles and their mounts from the wall, with huge chunks of stone still attached to them. They scraped against Broct's arms as they fell to the end of their chains.

The yellow-eyed giant immediately released his grip on the guardian's wrists and let his arms drop straight down. At the moment when he heard their metal jailer once more stepping forward, he brought his arms up and around violently, as if to clap his hands with tremendous impact, swinging those stone chunks on the ends of their chains.

There was a great crunching clang of sound as the heavy lumps of stone came together on either side of the bronze guardian's head. Then a gush of vile vapor came spurting out, mixing with the inky cloud. Bronze hooves moved unsteadily upon the floor, then its legs buckled and the thing sank into a heap of lifeless metal.

Even as the guardian sagged to the floor, Broct was grasping across its torso with both freed hands, searching for the ring of keys he knew must be hanging upon its harness. In the next moment, his grateful fingers closed around them, yanking the ring free.

"I've got the keys," he told Glendauna. He quickly set about unlocking his remaining shackles, working his way down to his ankles. When he was free he moved to where Glendauna was bound and released her.

"What happened to the guardian?" she asked him.

"I'm sure Khara Rom would have punished him for helping to release us," Broct said wryly. "I merely saved the wizard the trouble."

They moved toward the door, emerging from the inky cloud that was just now starting to dissipate. Glendauna stopped at the table and scooped up her bejeweled ancestral neckpiece.

"Without this," she said soberly, "I would still be as much a prisoner of my heritage as when Morlac found me." She quickly slipped the ornament about her neck and fastened it. Then as the light from the corridor illuminated them better, she gasped as she noticed the wrists of Broct's upper two arms. The flesh there was purple with bruises and bleeding from many small cuts. "What happened—?"

"The shackles," explained Broct. "A small price for our freedom."

"I must bandage them!"

"Later. First we get out of here and find Morlac!"

Peering cautiously out, they found the corridor clear. Apparently, only one guardian had been deemed necessary to keep watch on their cell. Broct motioned Glendauna through, then stepped out himself, pulled the heavy door closed behind him, and locked it. He took the keys with him.

Glendauna looked both ways down the eerie, desolate corridor. "Have you any idea where Morlac might be?"

"Aye," said Broct somberly. "At least, I know the type of place wizards choose for their grandiose spells. Now let us hasten away. I fear there is not much time. . . ."

Steaming caldrons boiled and bubbled within the lofty chamber, creating a blue haze. No daylight, nor what passed for it in this nightmarish twilight land, reached in to warm this place. Torches lighted the room from sconces along the walls, but their weird glow seemed inadequate and somehow evil.

Morlac raised his head in an attempt to see more of the chamber. The table to which he was so tightly bound stood near the center of the dark and brooding hall. Beyond his feet at a distance of some few yards, a thronelike chair faced him. Just behind that seat rose an enormous sphere of hollow crystal, resting upon a heavy metal stand cast in the shape of poised dragons. It resembled a Durkesh crystal ball, but was much, much larger—easily six feet in diameter. Within its hollow interior swirled and eddied glowing clouds of vapor, now purple, now blue. He could only guess at its purpose and power.

Morlac lay his head back down and, straining his eyes upward, saw that an identical crystal globe stood poised behind his head. Even a novice in matters magical could see an ominous implication in that.

The wizard, Khara Rom, walked slowly about the chamber, marking occult symbols upon the floor with a burnt stick, forming a circular pattern around the table and throne and the two glowing spheres. He seemed intent upon his work.

"Does nothing matter to you, wizard," Morlac called out, "other than your own selfish desires?"

Without looking up from his task, Khara Rom snapped, "Be quiet, you fool! You would not even exist, save for wizardry. And you are far too young compared to one who has lived past eight centuries to even imagine what torments I have endured."

"I know what torments *I* have endured, at the hands of those who call themselves 'Enlightened.'"

"Then be silent, lest you endure yet more," snarled the wizard. "Do not worry—you shall still live, body and mind, mind and body. Though not together."

"What manner of riddle is that?" Morlac asked, as much out of anger as out of a desire to distract and delay.

"It is simple enough, my strong young friend. I shall set forces in motion which will bring about a transference . . . my mind and occult knowledge into your body . . . your mind into my special body. My immortality for your living flesh. A fair trade, I think."

"An unwilling trade!" Morlac struggled within his bonds. "You have no right—!"

Khara Rom continued with his preparations. "Right? Have you learned so little of this world, sea-changling? Those who have the power may do as they wish. Nothing else matters. . . ."

Broct and Glendauna ran softly along a shadowy corridor, trying both to hurry and to make as little noise as possible. They had left their dungeon cell far behind and traversed countless corridors here on this lower level. Now, breathless and uncertain, they paused at a corner where yet another corridor crossed the one they traveled.

"This is not working," whispered Glendauna, her back resting against the wall as she sought to catch her breath. "I swear we have covered *miles* in this accursed place, and still we've not seen anything like a wizard's chamber."

Broct nodded his head glumly. "Aye . . . you're right.

Khara Rom must be different from the other wizards I've seen. Their places of magic usually be deep within the ground.''

"We must try something different—'' She bit off her words and came quickly alert as a dark glint of metal caught her eye.

She grabbed Broct's arm and pointed down the cross corridor. Some distance away, a bronze guardian had emerged from another corridor and now stood with its back to them, apparently looking for something. Them, perhaps?

Glendauna and Broct moved soundlessly to the opposite corner and kept the guardian in sight from a safer vantage point, peering around the edge. The guardian continued to stand there at the far end of the corridor, making it difficult for them to continue in the direction they wished. Then his bronze head began to turn toward them.

Ducking out of sight past the corner's edge to avoid being seen, the young woman and the sea-warrior flattened against the wall. They remained quiet, fighting to keep their breathing shallow. No sounds came from the corridor to suggest trouble . . . still. . . . They waited as long moments dragged by, not wanting to risk being seen as they continued their search.

Finally, Broct whispered, "Has he gone yet? We dare not delay much longer.''

Glendauna was nearest the corner. She turned her head toward the long corridor and ever so slowly peeked around the edge of the wall, hoping to find that the metal creature had gone and left their path clear.

Looming virtually inches away from her face, the bronze guardian stood poised before her, its sculpted face seeming to leer malevolently. It had moved with such stealth that they had not heard so much as a scrape of sound.

Glendauna gasped so violently that she tasted dust from the wall. Her head collided with Broct, who was attempting to peer past her for his own look down the corridor. In the next instant, they were both scrambling back from the corner.

The bronze guardian started to advance upon them. Then Broct threw up his ring hand and a cloud of impenetrable darkness billowed forth, plunging the area into inky blackness.

Glendauna too was caught up in that stygian wave, but she

quickly found herself in Broct's firm grasp. He was propelling her away from the corner and down the new corridor, in the opposite direction than that from which their enemy had approached.

"This way, girl!" said Broct. "Quickly!"

They emerged from the dark cloud after a dozen steps. The details of the corridor became visible once more. Nothing blocked their way, and on they ran, the clatter of confusion behind them urging them forward.

"Broct . . ." Glendauna said in brief gasps of words as they ran ". . . think you . . . that we can find . . . the banquet hall?"

The yellow-eyed giant nodded. "Aye, if we can reach the stairs. Why?"

"That is where last we all were," she replied. "From there . . . I may yet have a way to find Morlac. . . ."

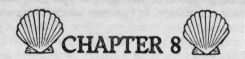

CHAPTER 8

Into the Flames

Khara Rom now sat in his thronelike seat, his back to the great crystal globe behind him. His bronze face and head caught glints of light from the torches and from the swirling gases that seemed to burn like cold fire within the twin spheres. His metal hands gripped the chair's arms with clawlike intensity, and nearby, his spellbook lay open upon a stand.

Two bronze guardians stood by, one near the wizard and one by the table upon which Morlac was bound. Morlac assumed that they were there to assist once the transference took place. For Morlac's body would have to be released, once Khara Rom's mind was safely in control of it. And the bronze body would have to be guarded as soon as it was ruled by the unwilling sea-warrior.

"Soon, now," Khara Rom said with a chilling eagerness, "I shall again know the pleasure of drawing breath, the fragrance of flowers, the taste of good food. Once again shall I feel the breeze and the flow of water against my skin. The touch of cloth against flesh. The touch of . . . so very many things!"

"Then know, wizard," Morlac cautioned, "that the body you have chosen is not like ordinary human flesh."

"I do know indeed. And my choice is perfect. For the spells that formed you make it all the easier for this transference to take place. Yours is an unusually strong and healthy body. It will serve me well."

Khara Rom tilted his head back and gave a short, self-indulgent chuckle. "You know, Morlac, I have not yet decided what to do once the transference is complete. Perhaps I will merely pretend to be you, since in your form will I be. I could pretend to escape, and journey with your friends to the South Kingdom, there to join my fellow wizards. Or perhaps I shall not bother with pretense. I can bend them to my will, regardless, and use them for whatever purpose they best suit. The opportunity of such a choice is amusing in itself, and infinitely exciting.''

Once more, Morlac struggled within his bonds. Some of them seemed to be weakening, but breaking free would take time. More time than he had left, he feared. His only hope, if he dared even entertain hope in this desperate situation, was if Broct and Glendauna might somehow reach him and stop the evil magician.

Khara Rom was sitting rigidly straight, staring over Morlac's reclining form at the great crystal globe opposite him. In a droning monotone, deep and ominous, he began chanting the words of a complex spell. His voice seemed to reverberate within the high chamber, spreading throughout it, becoming more than a mere voice.

The glowing gases in the crystal sphere behind him began to swirl ever faster, their colors changing and pulsing with the wizard's words. Morlac strained back and saw that the movement of gases in his own giant sphere was also increasing in intensity. A chill ebbed down his spine and along his limbs, a chill that was more than fear.

Something was happening. Morlac could feel it. A tingling seemed to seize his flesh, his muscles, his very bones. It reminded him of the horrible wrenching burning of Sordros's magic pit, and yet it was different from that. There was a gnawing, sickening sense of invasion, of trespass, as some other force crept into and through him.

Past his feet, he could see Khara Rom's form almost silhouetted against the glowing crystal sphere. Its light was growing brighter, and the swirling clouds were now and again emitting miniature bursts of lightning, as if a bizarre thunderstorm were brewing within the confines of the globe.

Morlac imagined Broct and Glendauna, imprisoned or worse, and wondered what torments awaited them once the purple magician had acquired a real body. But even these thoughts

were being forced from his mind. He thought he could begin
to feel the cold bronze shell that was Khara Rom's "flesh"
. . . feel it from the inside! And he realized with sudden
horror that his own lips were now moving soundlessly, forming the same words of Khara Rom's evil chant.

There now came brief flashes of vision, jolting snatches of
sight from a different viewpoint. Morlac thought he could
see, for mere seconds at a time, *himself*, strapped to the table
he still felt beneath him. He was viewing his own body from
the wizard's position in the thronelike chair. The transference
process was beginning! His time was fast running out.

For all his difficulty in adjusting to human form before, for
all his doubts about this strange existence to which the green
magician had doomed him, Morlac suddenly cared very much
indeed for this fragile mortal husk which housed his mind. He
fought against the invasion, resisting with all his will. But
though he seemed almost able to push back the consciousness
that threatened to overwhelm him, he felt weak against the
wizard's occult strength.

Tritus save me from this madman, Morlac thought. But he
seemed very far indeed from the sea god whose powers had
been invoked by the spell which reshaped him. Perhaps this
was the way it would end. The last indignity. The final
torment.

Khara Rom's droning voice seemed to fill his head, even
as the words began to come more and more from his own
lips. The coldness of that bronze prison crept closer, ever
closer. His own natural body, so warm and so real, so rich in
sensations, seemed to be slipping away. Morlac did not know
if he could endure eternity as a living statue.

Suddenly, a sound intruded upon the wizard's chant. A
disturbing sound, it was oddly remote and unreal.

Morlac looked toward the door of the chamber, and was
not sure whether it was his own head or the one sculpted in
bronze that moved. Perhaps both did. Was Khara Rom also
looking?

The end of the chamber seemed somehow farther away
now, distorted and dreamlike. Though the door appeared to
be swinging open slowly, Morlac felt certain it was moving
with great force. Someone who looked like Broct was charg-

ing into the chamber, his cloak flapping behind him. No . . . not just someone. It *was* Broct!

The bronze guardian near Khara Rom's body was running toward Broct, attempting to stop him. Bronze hooves clashed against flooring stones, throwing glints of blue and purple light. But then, just as the metal monster neared him, a small cloud of impenetrable darkness erupted from Broct's ring. The guardian completely disappeared from sight, though the clatter of its hooves still sounded.

And now the second guardian started forward, leaving Morlac's body unattended. It slowed as it reached the edge of the inky cloud, reluctant to enter.

Broct suddenly came scuttling forward, low to the floor. He emerged so swiftly from the cloud that he was under the second guardian's horselike belly before the creature could react. Rising beneath it, the yellow-eyed giant strained mightily with all six arms and lifted the bronze guardian off the floor.

Its hooves pawed empty air and its humanlike torso bent forward and around, arms flailing, trying to reach Broct. Then in the next moment it found itself being hurtled forward into the cloud. There was a great gonging crash of metal against metal as the two guardians collided, followed by the sounds of repeated blows as they mistook each other for enemies within the darkness.

"*No—!*" came a cry from Khara Rom, though the word seemed to erupt from Morlac's lips as well.

Glendauna now darted in through the open door, looking harried and out of breath. Her eyes quickly scanned the chamber, settling instantly upon the table's bound form. "Morlac!"

The swirling gases within the giant crystal spheres changed their flow, their contorted flux seeming to mirror the wizard's anger. Again came Khara Rom's anguished cry, and this time it seemed to come more from the metal figure's lips.

"*No!* The spell—it will be undone!"

Glendauna ran around the inky cloud, past Broct and to Morlac's side. She threw a glance to Khara Rom, who was struggling to rise from his elaborate chair. Picking up a decorative knife from the nearby stand, she began to saw at the straps holding Morlac to the table.

He stared at her lovely face as she worked, fighting to bring words to his lips. "How . . . did you find me?"

"We followed your scent from the banquet hall," she said, her lips twisting into a brief smile. " 'Twas not hard . . . for a wolf. There were guardians posted outside this chamber, but I led them a merry chase and doubled back. They will not be long in returning."

Morlac felt the wizard's presence seeping away, retreating to its source, even as his own awareness returned to his own body. As soon as Glendauna had released his hands, he took the knife from her and slashed through the straps binding his waist and ankles. Free now, he began to get off the table.

Khara Rom rose from his chair to stand before them, his posture erect and defiant. "Perhaps it was a mistake not destroying the others. But a mistake I can surely correct!"

As the wizard brought his hands up in a gesture, Broct quickly thrust out his ring hand and shot an inky cloud toward him. The cloud started to expand, moving quickly.

But Khara Rom moved with greater speed. Turning to face the cloud, he made a quick twirling motion with one hand, closing his clawlike fingers into a fist. The jet-black cloud abruptly halted before him, seemingly constricted by some invisible force that steadily compressed it smaller and smaller. In a matter of seconds it shrank to the size of a mere speck of dust, disappearing at last into nothingness.

"Think you that a wizard can be outdone with petty magics—?"

Khara Rom turned as the sound of many bronze hooves came from the hall. The guardians Glendauna had briefly succeeded in distracting began to appear in the doorway. Judging from the sound of them, they had been joined by others, and a score of the metal monsters would be in the chamber in a matter of seconds.

Broct hurried to where Morlac and Glendauna stood. His first magicked cloud was beginning to fade, as were the sounds of battle within it.

Khara Rom turned back to face them. "You fools! There is nowhere you can hide!"

"Then," said Morlac, motioning the others back, "I shall not try to!"

With his own unnatural power fully his to command once more, Morlac grabbed the end of the table he had just been released from and swung it in an arc around him. It knocked over several stands piled with containers of potions and other strange chemicals, then smashed into the heavy iron supports that held the crystal behind him. The table sundered and splintered against the metal. Morlac picked up the largest plank remaining and hurled it with all his strength directly at Khara Rom.

The wizard leaned back, throwing up his hands in a defensive gesture. Sparks flared along the leading edge of the plank as it neared him, then occult energy deflected it from its true and deadly path.

Before the wizard's mocking laugh could ring out, the heavy plank careened past him and struck dead center against the great crystal globe behind him. A section of the perfect sphere crunched and shattered beneath the impact, caving inward. Khara Rom jerked around, staggering back at the sound and the sight of it.

The glowing clouds of gas spilled out from the damaged globe, coiling and twisting like ghostly snakes. Angry clouds whose miniature lightning flashed and flared and lashed out at everything near. A bolt struck the thronelike chair, charring it. Others struck the stand of the ruined sphere. One touched with crackling intensity the chemicals scattered upon the floor and instantly ignited them.

Flames burst up with explosive force, spreading quickly across the floor in a line that separated Khara Rom and his arriving guardians from Morlac and the others. The fire turned into a raging barrier within seconds.

"Move back!" Morlac shouted, directing Broct and Glendauna toward the far end of the chamber, away from the widening flames.

"You have destroyed many years' work!" exclaimed Khara Rom, seeming to tremble with outrage. "But you shall not defeat me or escape my vengeance."

The wizard tore off his robes, revealing a body totally formed of dully glistening bronze. He started toward them, walking directly into the flames.

"You are flesh and blood," said Khara Rom. "But my body was forged in fire. The flames are no barrier for me."

The wizard stalked toward them through the fire, his anger so great that he seemed more interested in physical violence than in occult vengeance. His hands were raised toward them as he walked, but it was difficult to know if they were raised to cast a spell or to crush and strangle. His boots, which he had not removed, were rapidly burning away to ashes, and parts of his body were beginning to glow from the fire's heat. Yet on he marched.

"Morlac—" said Glendauna with grim urgency "—what can we do?"

"I don't know, my lady," he told her honestly. "We may yet die in this devil's domain. But had I Shark in my hands, I swear I would test its blade against all the wizard's bronze before I fell!"

Morlac looked swiftly about, but there was nothing anywhere near them that might be used as a weapon against the wizard. And there were no doors in this end of the chamber—nowhere they might escape. It seemed their only choice was direct hand-to-hand battle against a virtually invulnerable and magically empowered enemy. And Khara Rom was already three-fourths of the way through the flaming barrier, steadily advancing.

Leaning close to Broct, Morlac whispered imperatively, "I fear we may not survive this, my sea-brother. I must ask of you a favor."

"Name it," said Broct.

"I will do what I can to fight the wizard," Morlac told him. "I ask that you throw Glendauna safely over the flames to a spot away from the guardians. She may thus have a chance to escape."

Broct nodded in somber agreement.

"No—!" Glendauna cried, gripping Morlac's arm with fierce determination. Tears welled up in her intense blue eyes. "I will not leave you. I will *not*, even if death be our destiny."

"Don't argue, girl!" Morlac snapped. "There is no time. He is almost upon us!"

Khara Rom's evil laughter echoed through the great chamber. "How the rats do whimper, once they're caught in the trap!"

He reached the edge of the fire in the next moment and emerged unscathed from the flames, no more than a dozen feet away from them. His hard bronze hands clawed the air in angry anticipation.

But as he stepped toward them an abrupt change came over him, and his mocking look faded. Something was wrong.

Khara Rom halted, his attention shifting away from Morlac and the others as he looked down at his hands—hands that glowed from the flames' heat. As he continued to stare at his body, changes were wrought upon his finely sculpted chest and abdomen. Spots began to bulge, swelling out as if under great pressure from within.

Alarm crept into his voice. "What is this? What is happening. . . . ?"

The wizard now began to jerk in a series of small spasms, twitching awkwardly, uncontrollably, his body continuing to swell in places. Now small jets of greenish gas began to spurt out from his joints and seams, spraying forth with whistling intensity like many high-pitched screams. More bulges appeared. Countless tiny cracks formed and began to spread and widen across every surface of the bronze torso and limbs. The alarm now turned into fear, and in mere seconds more became terror, complete and absolute.

"*No . . . !*" shouted Khara Rom. "No! It must not end! Not like this . . . *not like thisssssSSSSSSSSSSS!*"

"Down!" yelled Morlac. He was already whirling, forcing Glendauna and Broct to the floor, attempting to shelter them with his own body.

In the next instant, Khara Rom, High Wizard of Krellos, the purple magician, the immortal one, jerked apart as his seams burst wide and the metal that formed him splayed out from the force of exploding gas. The vile green vapor shot forth in all directions, carrying bits of bronze with it and tearing limbs and head from the body. Then the shattered parts collapsed upon the stone floor with a great ringing clatter.

When at last all was still, Morlac cautiously turned to look. Nothing remained of the once artfully sculpted hollow shell that had contained Khara Rom's mind and occult knowledge for eight hundred years. Nothing except twisted pieces of steaming metal. In the silence that flooded in, Morlac thought he heard the faintest of voices, near his left ear.

A ghostly whisper of sound, almost a collective sigh. *We are avenged, citizens of Krellos. At last . . . we may rest. . . .*

Morlac rose, and as the others did also they stared in awe at the wizard's fragmented remains. Broct spoke first.

"What happened to him?"

"The fire," said Morlac. "It may not have harmed the metal of which he was cast, but it heated the vapor within him until it expanded and had to find release."

"Like a great kettle, put on to boil," observed Glendauna. She stared a moment more, then tore her gaze away as the flames once again commanded her attention. For they were still very much in danger. It was then that something caught her eye. "Look there—the fire burns low near that side. We may yet pass!"

"Then let us try!"

In a flash they moved toward that narrow avenue of escape. With careful steps and many small leaps, they safely crossed the fire's fringe and reached the other side. One danger had been dealt with. But what of the guardians?

That question was answered in the next moment as the rest of the chamber came into view. The bronze guardians that had been in the great chamber, and those that had rushed in to join them, now all stood rigid and still as the statues they so closely resembled. Each of the centaurlike metal monsters was frozen in whatever position it had held at the moment of Khara Rom's destruction.

"They move not," said Glendauna.

"I doubt they ever shall again," Morlac told her. "They lived as much by the wizard's power as by their own energies. Without him, they are useless. We need not fear them. Now let us get out of here and gather up our things. I am anxious to leave this accursed place!"

"Aye," agreed Broct. "And *this* time we shall find our *true* weapons . . . !"

The three travelers stood upon the edge of the vast plain that was a graveyard, looking back at the grim fortress they had so eagerly left behind. They held their horses' reins in hand and once more had all their weapons, cloaks, and belongings. Also were they burdened with fresh mementos of their captivity and battle—bruises and blood and aching bones. But at least they had escaped.

The clouded sky of this twilight realm looked no brighter, the bleak landscape no more hopeful, with Khara Rom's passing. Perhaps it never would.

Broct stared at the terrible vista with narrowed eyes. "Krellos will truly be a dead realm, now."

Glendauna nodded, with a trace of a shiver. "It is one place I have traveled that I shall not miss!"

"Nor shall I," agreed Morlac. "But we still have a long journey ahead of us."

"A journey that takes us once more through the cavern," said Broct meaningfully. "I do not relish that."

"There is no easier way to cross the Kyral Mountains," Morlac reminded him. He looked toward the cavern mouth, but the ghostly voice was quiet now, the eerie feeling gone. "Besides, I think we may pass now without trouble."

"What fools we be!" said Broct suddenly, with a wry shake of his bald head. He indicated the distant fortress with a broad sweep of several hands. "Untold treasures must surely wait back there, and we left without claiming any for our troubles."

Glendauna looked at the grim fortress for a long moment, a *very* long moment, then looked to Broct. "Do you want to go back?"

The yellow-eyed giant smiled sheepishly. "No . . . do you?"

"No!" said the girl. "I think I will seek my treasure elsewhere."

Morlac quickly mounted his horse, his shell-shield slung across his back and Shark once more at his side. "Then let's be off. I have seen far more than enough of the Dark Region. The South Kingdom is now my destination . . . !"

WIZARD'S GAMBIT

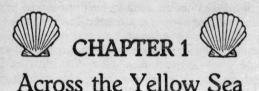

CHAPTER 1

Across the Yellow Sea

"Hurry!" cried Morlac to the others as he brought his horse to a gallop. "For the wind rises, and the ship will sail without us!"

"There will be another," said Glendauna, setting her own mount racing to keep up with him.

"Not for a week!" Morlac glanced back to be sure the young woman was not falling behind, but did not slow his pace. He saw that Broct was keeping up as well, and returned his attention fully to the ship whose red sails fluttered in the morning breeze.

The village of Ortal Du Bodne, at the southern border of Goltos, was a large one, situated as it was at the apex of several trade routes and being a port town at the edge of the Yellow Sea. But its details seemed little more than a blur as the three riders raced back through it and headed for the wide dock that reached out from the coast.

Chickens and dogs and villagers alike scattered out of their way. The clucking, barking, and cursing merged into a startled, angry chorus that spread in their wake like the dust they raised. Ahead, the ship could be seen more clearly now. Deckhands were making fast the last few crates and kegs loaded on, and the gangplank was being wrestled off. There was little time!

The drumming of hooves against wooden planking tore through what quiet remained as Morlac, Broct, and Glendauna rode onto the dock and made straight for the ship. By now, there was virtually no one whose attention they did not have,

250

and as Morlac caught the eye of the man he took for the vessel's captain, he waved his arm commandingly.

"Wait—!" he shouted. "We would sail with you to Kamuria."

The captain, a stout but tough-looking man whose years of sailing had grizzled his hair and leathered his skin, cast a hard look upon these three strangers as they reined their horses to a halt before his ship. His keen eyes missed nothing of the sea-warriors' odd features, nor of their weapons. They could well mean trouble. The girl looked fine enough, decent enough, but her Durkesh garb and the fact she rode with these other two did not speak well for her.

Reluctant, he called out, "Have you the fare?" He half hoped they did not.

"Aye," answered Broct. "We have the fare."

"Are you sure?" said the captain. "I expect sixty tekahs for the lot of you."

"Sixty?" protested Glendauna. "The fare's never more than ten tekahs for a man and his horse. Why do you double it?"

The captain frowned. "I may set what price I wish," said he with a peevish tone. "Besides, you are late arrivals and I am fully loaded."

Morlac studied the ship. "Not too fully loaded for us, I'll wager, for your vessel does not ride low in the water. We are willing to pay a fair price of thirty tekahs. Will you refuse it?"

Considering it, the captain replied, "Make it fifty."

"Forty," said Morlac. "We can spare no more. Our coins are as hard earned as yours."

The captain sighed as he saw the breeze beginning to fill the sails. The extra forty tekahs would be welcome enough, for he was barely turning a profit on this trip as it was. He decided to take the risk.

"Done. Forty it is." He gave a jerk of his hand to have the gangplank put back, then said to Morlac and the others, "Come aboard and be quick about it! We sail at once!"

They swiftly dismounted and led their horses aboard. Narrow stalls were located near the center of the deck, and in three of these they secured their horses. The captain waited until this was done, then obtained payment from Morlac. His look remained wary as he counted the coins, but he gave a nod of acknowledgement and started back for the aft deck and the tiller.

"Captain—" Morlac called after him "—how long till we reach Kamuria?"

"By sunrise tomorrow, if all goes well."

The gangplank was away once more and the lines were cast off quickly. Heeling slightly to starboard as the wind pushed it away from the dock, the vessel moved out to sea, rocking slowly with the gentle waves. The weather was good, with every promise of smooth sailing.

In the manner of most merchant ships of Goltos, the vessel was large and squat, a wide oval of pegged and well-sealed planks, with only enough keel as was needed to counter the thrust of its three short masts. Long yards hung obliquely from those masts and supported triangular sails red in hue, fading and patched. It was not an oceangoing craft, but was more than fit enough for sea crossings and coastal runs.

Morlac took a place by the rail near the bow and gazed out over the waters of the Yellow Sea. He saw now why it earned its name, for yellow indeed it appeared. Growing on the shallow bottom, beneath the clear waters, were great leafy plants golden yellow in color. They glimmered up at him, swaying with the soft swells of the sea, inviting, beckoning, sweet with the promise of hidden fish and cool shelter. It was good to return to the sea again. Good to have the tang of salt spray in his mouth and nostrils.

Morlac looked around and found Glendauna at his side. The sea breeze stirred her golden hair and rustled her Durkesh garments in a feminine and pleasing way. Her vivid blue eyes squinted into the bright sunlight, and as she observed Morlac looking at her, she arched a lovely eyebrow and twisted her mouth in wry disapproval.

"Forty tekahs, indeed," she said. "You might have bargained more."

"And we might still be on the dock," Morlac answered, "watching this ship sail away."

"Would that have been so bad? For the past month we

have been traveling, either on our own, or with the Durkesh caravan. A week's rest would not have hurt.''

He put an arm around her. ''Those weeks spent with the caravan were not all work, as I recall.''

''No,'' she said coyly. ''Not all. And we could have stayed with that caravan, and journeyed on to the South Kingdom by land.''

''We could. But that would have taken two or three weeks more to make our way around the edge of the Yellow Sea.''

''I know.'' She smiled.

''I hope you can forgive my impatience,'' Morlac told her. ''I know you do not share my eagerness to find Sordros.''

Glendauna's smile faded and her eyes shifted away from his. ''I want whatever it takes to make you happy, Morlac. But Sordros is a powerful wizard, and one who does not wish to be found, especially by you. I fear what your meeting may provoke.''

Morlac remembered Xaja, and the ease with which Sordros destroyed his sea-warrior creation. The image of his comrade, unliked though he was, reduced to rotting, oozing bits of sea life still haunted him. He knew that despite his strength he had a certain vulnerability to his conjuror-creator, and might fare no better than Xaja in a confrontation with the green magician. And Morlac knew also that it was not only a reunion with Sordros that Glendauna feared. For where Sordros was found, so might also be Kadrana.

''Do not worry, my lady. I intend to guard myself well, against *all* dangers.''

''I hope so, my warrior,'' she said, looking up into his gaze once more. Her smile returned, and she impishly poked a finger into his ribs. ''And if your guard should fall, count on me to come to your aid!''

The Goltosian cargo ship plowed on across the Yellow Sea. Its answering song to the seabirds overhead was a collection of creaks and groans and fluttering snaps as wood and ropes and sailcloth strained to keep up with the wind's relentless push. On it sailed, for the South Kingdom, for Kamuria, and for their own uncertain destiny. . . .

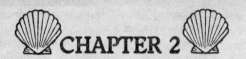

CHAPTER 2

City of Sorcery

Dawn came creeping over the Yellow Sea, spreading its gold upon the quiet waves and stirring the seabirds to flight. Cool was the breeze and salty moist, pressing the Goltosian cargo ship on across the awakening sea.

There were no passenger cabins aboard the humble vessel, but a raised portion of the deck before the rear deckhouse was walled off with railings and sheltered by a canopy. A few low benches on the sides provided seating, while the deck between offered room for sleeping. And sleep had been possible, for the night's crossing had been uneventful and calm.

The three travelers were already stirring, though, for the scurrying of the vessel's crew alerted them to the fact they were nearing their destination. The captain's estimate had been good.

"Land ho!" called one of the crew near the ship's bow.

They could all see it now, moving with the slow rise and fall of the deck. Straight ahead rose a city on the horizon, dark and strange and wonderful, with towers and minarets and odd, hulking buildings.

"The South Kingdom?" asked Morlac softly.

Glendauna nodded. "Its capital, Kamuria."

Broct studied that approaching view with a wary eye and a knowing scowl. "A whole city full of wizards and the like?" he said, shaking his head ruefully. "Crazy we must truly be!"

Within the hour their ship had docked and they led their horses unsteadily to solid ground once more. The wharf was on the northeastern edge of the city, and the road leading up from it was already busy with merchandise-laden carts and travelers from many lands. The presence of the two sea-warriors and the young Durkesh woman attracted little attention.

The road from the wharf yielded to cobblestone streets that twisted and turned through the strange city. Busy streets they were, full of hustle and bustle as citizens and visitors alike went about their day's activities.

There were the ordinary shops, taverns, and inns one might expect to find in any large city, supplying the mundane necessities of life—food, drink, clothing, tools, and weapons. But there was also a large number of shops the like of which Morlac had never seen. Strange little shops dealing in potions and ingredients for potions, books of spells copied by scribes from ancient texts, and magical implements of great and bizarre variety.

And as if the shops were not enough, there were vast numbers of street vendors hawking charms and elixirs and powders for every conceivable purpose. They jostled and competed with each other, each shrilly claiming to have the best and most effective concoctions for enchantments.

"I have traveled here twice before," Glendauna told Morlac as they walked on toward the center of town. "Kamuria is a place steeped in magic, so it attracts not only the true wizards and dabblers in the occult arts, but also the charlatans and hucksters who peddle amulets and talismans of dubious value."

"I think I begin to understand L'Dron Kerr's revulsion for this place," said Morlac, studying all about him with intense interest, "and also Sordros's fascination. Small wonder he is drawn to it."

" 'Twill make finding him no easier," Broct observed. "We may as well seek a shadow in the dark."

"If he is here, we will find him."

They began to notice that in addition to the merchants, visitors, and robed members of the "Enlightened" class, there were also others walking the streets of Kamuria. Large, well-muscled men, garbed in ghostly gray with bands of cloth hiding the lower halves of their faces from view. They wore red sashes and carried thick, short staffs a few feet in length and colored in alternate bands of yellow and black, spiraling from one end to the other. A red gemstone capped the top end of each staff, and something about the wandlike staffs and the way the men carried them suggested that they were not only symbols of the men's authority, but instruments of occult power as well.

That they were guards Morlac did not doubt. But might they also be a source of information?

As the next one approached, Morlac caught his attention. "Your pardon, sir, but I would ask a question."

"Yes?"

"We seek a particular wizard here, and wonder if you could tell us where to find him."

The guard studied the three who stood before him for a long moment before speaking. "Has the wizard a name?"

"Aye," said Broct calmly, even managing a pleasant smile. "His name be Sordros."

"Sordros?" replied the guard. "No, I do not know him, or of him. But a certainty it is that no wizard may come or go here without the knowledge of the Council of Wizards. It is they whom you should ask."

"Where may I find this council?" Morlac inquired.

The guard gestured in the direction they had been heading. "Keep going along this road and you will see it. It faces a square where many roads meet. In a few hours hence, the council will gather there for the day's business."

Morlac nodded. "We thank you for your help."

Once the guard was safely out of earshot, Glendauna said in a worried tone, "Do you think that was wise, Morlac? You may alert Sordros to our presence."

"I may," Morlac answered. "But if we do not find him in a quick and direct manner we shall have to search throughout this strange city, asking questions, poking about, attracting notice. You may be certain that word would reach Sordros of our search, and the more secret our attempt, the more convinced he would be that we were stalking him with murderous intent. In that case, finding him would be harder, *and* more dangerous!"

"Perhaps so," replied Glendauna. "But I cannot help wondering . . . what *is* your intent?"

Morlac's brooding brows hung low above his sea-green eyes. "I have not decided yet, my lady. I have not decided."

"Well, I know one thing," said Broct, looking about the marketplace in which they stood. "There be food here, and time to enjoy it. If a fight awaits us we will need all our strength. And if we must face the wrath of some hell-spawned demon and die at some wizard's whim, then I say 'twill not be on an empty stomach . . . !"

The sun was climbing steadily above Kamuria, and at midmorning activity within the great city was at its peak. The wide square that was the hub of all major roads swarmed with people, but the noisy, tumultuous crowd kept a respectful distance from the southern edge of that square. For on that side stood the large building that housed the Council of Wizards, the seat of government of the South Kingdom.

Narrow towers rose at each of the building's four corners. The top of each tower supported a large glowing sphere. They looked to be either beacons, or watchposts, or perhaps some form of occult defense. Or all those things, and more.

A moatlike band of gravel surrounded the building, and just beyond that stood a row of stone statues carved in odd and unsettling poses. Before the gateway and bridge that crossed the gravel moat and led into the building were huge cast-metal dragons, their heads upturned and angled back. Smoke had been issuing from the metal dragons' nostrils for the last half hour. Now, flames suddenly billowed forth, gushing out once, twice, three times before settling down to burn steady and low.

"It is time," said Morlac.

Others from the milling crowd had also seen the signal and were starting to move forward. The Council of Wizards was now in session, ready to receive any and all who might approach them.

Morlac, Glendauna, and Broct walked quickly toward that end of the square and joined the small line of people that was threading its way across the bridge and into the building. More of the guards dressed in gray and bearing their curious wands stood by the entrance, silent and grim, surveying all who entered with routine scrutiny.

Once inside the building, it was but a short walk to the spacious chamber where met the Council of Wizards. Incense burned in low braziers and torchlight sent shadows dancing on the smoke.

A great semicircular table stood raised upon a dais at one end of the chamber, and it was here that the nine wizards sat. They all had the same strangeness and disquieting intensity common to the Enlightened, yet each was different from the other in physical appearance and manner of dress. Most were middle-aged or older, with graying or white hair. Each man's robe was of a different color and style, though all bore occult symbols. Some men covered their heads with turbans, others with the curious steeple-crowned caps that only wizards wore. It was an odd and eerily intimidating conclave.

Speaking softly to Glendauna and Broct as they came to a halt within the gradually filling chamber, Morlac said, "What manner of kingdom is this, ruled not by a king but by a band of magicians?"

"Once there was a king, from what I've heard," replied Glendauna. "His name was Mejbabba. It is said he was a dabbler in the occult arts himself, and so surrounded himself with those who truly knew magic. Those of the Enlightened flocked here and flourished here, and when Mejbabba died with no heir to his throne, the wizards banded together to take over his rule."

"I am surprised," said Broct with a snort of disdain. "From what I've seen of wizards thus far, I would have expected the strongest among them to have simply appointed himself the new king."

"As well one might have," said Glendauna, "had he been strong enough. Make no mistake—this is an uneasy alliance at best, and here in Kamuria, political intrigue has the added danger of occult forces."

They broke off their whispered conversation as acolytes moved through the crowd, writing down each visitor's question or intended business with the Council. Morlac gave his as spokesman for the trio, then watched and waited as the acolytes finished their job and reported to the wizards. Pieces of paper were passed around the great semicircular table. Messages were compared by the wizards, with much nodding of heads and gesturing talk.

Much of the business seemed mundane for such an unusual

setting. Merchants petitioning for better locations or lower taxes, arranging for protective spells for caravan shipments and the like. Young mystics and dabblers seeking learned wizards to apprentice under or study with. These things were arranged methodically, with notes made and fees collected for services rendered or promised. There seemed an undercurrent of competitiveness and ill will between some of the wizards, but in general all was handled smoothly.

One of the wizards, a turbaned man in blue-and-white robes, now held up a slip of paper and frowned at the words written upon it. Glancing to the others upon the dais and seeing their nods of acknowledgement, he looked out across the chamber and searched the crowd with suspicious eyes.

"Who among you," said he in a clear voice, "seeks the green magician, Sordros?"

Morlac hesitated a moment out of natural caution, then raised an open hand. "I do," he told them in a strong voice.

"Step forward, please—"

Morlac moved out from the crowd and walked toward the semicircular table. He came to a halt a short distance in front of the wizards, at a point where a shaft of sunshine stabbed down from a skylight overhead. He stood before the wizards, well-visible and alone.

"Now then," said the blue-and-white wizard, "who are you, and why do you seek this Sordros?"

"I am Morlac. Sordros ruled the village of my birth, and I served for a time as captain of his guard. We were separated during the invasion by the North Kingdom, and I seek to find him once more. I am still bound by spells of his creation."

"I see," said the wizard. "And yet, we have been told that Sordros has enemies who pursue him, and mean him harm."

"His enemies were L'Dron Kerr, master of the North Kingdom, and the mercenary, Drygo," said Morlac. "I slew Drygo before he could harm Sordros, and now that L'Dron Kerr has conquered all of Shola he no longer concerns himself with the green magician."

The wizard nodded gravely. "So you say. And so it may be true. But Sordros is not here in Kamuria."

Morlac felt a chill run through him at this news, but tried not to show it. Had they traveled so far for nothing? Had

Khara Rom lied to them, or was this wizard lying now? "Can you then tell me where he has gone?"

"Enough!" called out another wizard, garbed all in red.

His robes and sash, his gloves, even his peaked cap with its strange visorlike brim, were the same scarlet hue. Held casually in his right hand was a staff that rested upon the floor and was taller than he in his present sitting position. That staff, like those shorter ones carried by Kamuria's guards, had a spiraling design in yellow and black, capped by a great and many-faceted ruby stone. A mane of white hair flowed out from beneath his cap and framed a face that was angular and hard. His jet-black eyes were cold, merciless, totally without humor. His hooked nose was tilted at an aristocratic angle with nostrils flaring disdainfully at all around him.

"Enough, I say!" repeated the wizard. "This is not a matter to be discussed with strangers before the council. Sordros's wishes must be honored, whether he is here or elsewhere. Let us move on to other business."

Another wizard at the far end of the dais, very young and clad in robes of mousy brown and gray, leaned forward and said in a voice that cracked, "Should we not put it to a vote, at least . . . ?"

"*No,*" said the Red Wizard flatly. "I am sure my fellow wizards, or at least those experienced enough to truly deserve to sit on this council, share my opinion. The matter is closed."

The wizard clad in blue and white seemed to bridle at the other's tone, but nodded in agreement. "Quite right, Zohara," he said, and to Morlac, added, "We can say no more."

The Council then went on about its business, ignoring the sea-warrior who stood before them. Morlac felt a chilling anger, a killing anger, rising within him, and Shark seemed to tremble at his side. But this was not the place for a fight, nor were these the kind of enemies he dared challenge. Any one of them, here in their seat of power and with unknown occult resources at their disposal, could easily destroy him. Him, and the friends who would surely come to his aid. Choking back the anger, he turned abruptly and stalked back through the crowd. Glendauna and Broct quickly followed him.

*   *   *

A short while later, the three stood before a shop on the edge of the square, unmindful of the travelers and shoppers who flowed past them. Morlac's solemn scowl would have been enough to silence anyone tempted to protest that they were in the way.

"Wizards!" Morlac spat the word out. "I should have expected nothing better from their kind."

"Aye," agreed Broct. "Trouble they be, and little else."

Glendauna put a comforting hand upon Morlac's shoulder. "Perhaps it is for the best. Finding Sordros again could prove your undoing."

"Perhaps," said the proud sea-warrior. "But find him I shall. The wizards were one way to do it, but there are others."

"Aye," said Broct once more. "We can question shopkeeps and potion merchants, and tavernmaids if need be. Someone must have sold him something, or seen him passing. Someone will remember."

The three became aware of a disturbance near them, then suddenly someone jostled Morlac and Glendauna as he rushed past. The fellow cast a wary eye behind him as he fled, but it was not Morlac or the girl his gaze sought.

"Thief!" shouted a short, rotund merchant who followed at some distance behind him, already red in the face and blustery. "Thief! Dog! You steal my precious goods. Stop!"

The man obviously had no intention of stopping, but in his effort to watch behind him he failed to see all that lay ahead. And so in the next moment he collided with one of the burly guardsman clad in gray. The thief jerked his head around, startled by the impact. Terror instantly replaced that look of surprise, and he abruptly turned on his heel and ran off at an angle, attempting to lose himself in the crowd. But the crowd would not cooperate, falling back out of his way and running for safety.

"Stop him!" shrieked the little merchant. "He has stolen one of my finest amulets!"

The guard nodded, but did not move to chase the thief. Instead, he rubbed the stone atop his short staff three times, then pointed the wandlike device at the fleeing man.

The thief looked back at exactly that moment, his eyes wide with fear, and exclaimed, *"NO!"*

In the next instant the ruby stone upon the guard's staff flashed brightly, dazzling even in the daylight. In the blink of an eye, the thief was frozen where he stood, his mouth still open from his last word.

Walking over to where the thief stood motionless, the gray-clad guardsman pried open his fingers and removed an amulet from his hand. He held it before the little merchant who had followed him breathlessly to the spot. "Be this yours?"

"Aye," said the merchant. "This scoundrel took it without payment."

The guard put the object in the merchant's pudgy hand. "Then you shall have it back. And the Council shall have a new ornament for their collection."

With that, the guard touched the end of his staff to the top of the man's head. A dark-gray color spread from that spot and quickly flowed down across his face and neck, his torso, his limbs, all the way to the very bottoms of his feet. His skin, his hair, his clothing—all became the same hard gray surface. Stone had replaced everything.

Morlac gazed at the transformed thief, then looked with new understanding at the row of strange statues that ringed the Council building. So that was the fate of criminals in this city of magic!

"Zohara rules the Gray Guards," said a small voice behind them, startling Morlac and the others. "Their power is merely an extension of his."

Morlac was surprised to see the youngish wizard from the Council chamber, the one garbed in brown and gray, standing very close to them. None of Morlac's usually sharp senses had detected his approach, and it was unnerving to find this youth here now, speaking casually to them as if he had been there all along.

"Did you follow us—?" asked Morlac as his hand instinctively sought Shark's hilt.

"Well, yes, of course," replied the young wizard. "I slipped away, because I had to talk with you."

"Talk? About what?"

"Zohara is a bully. I don't think he cares a whit about Sordros's wishes. He just likes ordering the rest of us around."

The young wizard was slight of build, smooth-faced and slightly awkward of stance. His hair was almost the same mouse-brown of his robes, and that part of it that protruded from beneath his short, rounded cap needed combing. As he talked quickly, his attention diverted to Glendauna. "Hi. Who are you? You're really very pretty. Are you a friend of Sordros, too?"

Broct now leaned toward him and fixed him with a dangerous look. "Tell me, small wizardling—be there a point to all this babble, or did the Council merely send you out to bedevil us?"

"Oh, no," said he, his cheeks flushing. "They do not even know I'm here. At least, I certainly hope not. Most especially Zohara. He would be greatly angered."

"I grow angry, myself," Morlac told him. "If you wish to tell us something, then do so!"

"All right, all right. I was getting to that, anyway. The point is, I think I can tell you where Sordros is. At least, I believe I can find out."

He had Morlac's full attention now. "That would please me greatly. But why would you be willing to do so?"

"If for no other reason, because Zohara has forbidden it," said the young wizard. "But in truth, I do want something in return."

Morlac arched a devil-brow. "And what could a wizard in a city of wizards possibly want from a poor traveler?"

"I shall tell you," he said softly, "but not here. Meet me at this place in one hour. The Council meeting shall be finished by then, and we shall talk. Bring your friends, too."

With that, he pressed a folded piece of paper into Morlac's palm and quickly departed. Morlac watched him go with narrowing eyes, but lost sight of him in the crowd that once more began to flow through the square.

Broct sighed mightily and shook his great shiny head. "Wizards . . . !"

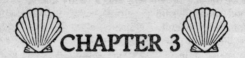

CHAPTER 3

Mekla's Mission

Morlac looked at the directions written upon the piece of paper the young wizard had thrust into his hand an hour earlier. The words were clear even though done in a hasty scrawl. His gaze now left the paper and took in the narrow two-story building that stood before him. It was an odd-looking structure with stucco walls and shuttered windows, somewhat like the shops of his own village, but with a decided foreign flavor. A storefront was on the lower floor, and a sign hung before it. The words, in High Kamurian, matched those on the crumpled scrap of paper Morlac held in his hand.

Glendauna compared those words as she stood close to Morlac's side. "The Wizard, Korthos, Master Adept," she read aloud. "This must be it."

Morlac folded the paper and tucked it into his belt. "How could one so young be a Master Adept?"

Glendauna shrugged her slender shoulders. "Perhaps he has a born talent. Or perhaps this is some other wizard's abode."

"And then again," said Broct warily, "perhaps this be a trap, set by Sordros's friends for three fools."

"I think not," said Morlac, "if I read the young one right."

He stepped up to the ornately carved door and knocked upon its wooden surface, even as Broct glanced alertly about for signs of trouble. For a long moment, only silence answered his knock. Then abruptly, scuffling footsteps came from inside and the door opened a crack. An eye peered out, framed by tousled brown hair and a ruddy cheek.

"Good, good," said the young wizard as he opened the door for them to enter. "You're right on time. Come in, quickly. Zohara's spies are everywhere!"

They stepped inside the narrow building and the young wizard closed the door behind them. The place was cool and musty, with the mingling scents of old books and strange herbs. It reminded Morlac of other places of wizardry, but somehow seemed less threatening. At his side, Shark stirred gently in his slumber, but did not emanate alarm.

"Are you Korthos?" asked Morlac.

"Me—?" the young wizard said, wide-eyed. "Oh, no no no. I am Mekla, little more than an apprentice wizard and far from being a master adept. Korthos was my master, my teacher, and the member of the Council whose seat I now hold."

"Was?"

Mekla sighed and bit his lip. "Alas, he is dead now. And I am left in charge, unprepared. It is a terrible thing!"

The corner of Broct's mouth twisted up. "Not as terrible as it is for Korthos."

"Do not jest! For though many say it was a natural death, I am convinced it was murder. And I think Zohara did it. Only, I do not know how."

"I see," Morlac said. "But I hope it is not vengeance on your mind that brings us here."

Mekla shrugged. "Vengeance would be nice, too. But I fear my motives are not that pure. You see, my master, Korthos, had a wondrous magical device, the source of much of his power. It's called a dreamstone. It disappeared at the same time he died, and all my searching has not uncovered it. I know that Zohara must have it. He has coveted it since first learning of its existence. And his power in Kamuria has increased tenfold since Korthos's death."

"Is that why the others fear him?"

"They feared him before," said Mekla. "But they have added reason to fear him now."

"So," reasoned Morlac, "in exchange for the information

we seek, you wish us to recover the magical device stolen from your master?"

"Yes," Mekla said with an enthusiastic nod. "Oh, yes. For only with that shall I ever have a chance to become anything more than I am now. True, I do hold Korthos's seat on the Council, but only temporarily, and only because tradition dictates it. Thanks to Zohara, and my own lack of experience, I have little authority or power."

"Beware of ambition, wizardling," Broct said bluntly. "Power is a double-ended sword. It often destroys he who wields it."

The young man bristled. "It is not that kind of power I seek. I merely wish to become as good a wizard as Korthos was, and to have some say in things. The dreamstone can do that for me. And if in the process of recovering it, you can also prove that Zohara killed my master, well, so much the better!"

"You are so sure that he has it?" Morlac asked.

"I'll stake my life upon it!"

"More likely," grumbled Broct, "he'll stake *our* lives upon it."

Mekla cast a pouty frown at the yellow-eyed giant. "I know what I ask involves danger. And I do not ask this lightly, or without regard for your own safety. But one of my talents that *is* developed is the ability to sense something of a person's past. I know the three of you are brave warriors. And I also know you have faced magic before, evil magic, and survived. I felt this the moment I saw you in the Council chamber."

Morlac raised an eyebrow, remembering Kadrana's disconcerting knack for reading his thoughts, and wondered just how much of his past Mekla did perceive. Wizards and their kind were an aggravating lot. Curse them! Still, this young one was mildly likable, and seemed to lack the wickedness of most.

Morlac now asked him, "Where do you think Zohara has this dreamstone he stole from your master?"

"There can be but one place," Mekla said with a sigh. "Zohara's headquarters lies deep within this city's temple honoring Shibsothla."

Glendauna gave a small gasp. Her face turned pale as the blood drained from her features.

Morlac put a steadying hand upon her arm. "You know of this Shibsothla?"

"Yes," she replied weakly. "It is a demon god of horrible aspect. I have only seen its shrines and idols, but from what I have heard, the demon we fought in Goltos pales before it."

Morlac well remembered Balboznibog. His own spine was chill-touched at the mere mention of it, and at the prospect of a greater demon.

"Let me see if I understand this . . ." said Broct with sour amusement. "The object you want us to get for you is hidden in a place of monstrous evil, and protected by guards whose touch can turn men to stone?"

"Well, yes, the Gray Guards are there, too," said Mekla uneasily. "I know it sounds difficult."

"Difficult—?" Broct said with a roar of laughter. "It sounds suicidal!"

Mekla's face fell. "Then . . . you will not help?"

"I did not say that." Broct looked to Morlac. "I do not mind a good fight, as well you know. But I like enemies I can lay hands upon, or touch with cold steel. Still, life has been boringly peaceful of late. What say you about this?"

Morlac considered. "It is not to my liking, either. But if it is the bargain we must make to find Sordros. . . ."

"It is not so much that I would withhold the information from you," Mekla quickly interjected. "Unless Zohara's power is shaken, I doubt I may even learn of Sordros's whereabouts."

Morlac looked to Glendauna with a question in his sea-green eyes. "My lady—?"

Glendauna studied those eyes a long moment, then replied, "I know how much this means to you. I cannot deny you the opportunity."

"All right, then," Morlac told them. "We will try it. But if we are to have any chance of success, we must have two things."

"What?" asked Mekla.

"For the first, we need to know as much as possible about this temple, so that we may plan well our assault upon it."

"I can help with that," Mekla said enthusiastically. "My

master, Korthos, has a sort of map of the place. He drew it after a vision-sleep, in which his mind journeyed to the temple to learn of its secrets. Here—let me get it!''

The wizardling lad quickly led them into another chamber. There were several tables and cabinets, all heaped with old books, notes and star charts. Morlac wondered how anything could be found in the midst of such untidy confusion, but after several moments of digging, Mekla came up with a rolled-up parchment. Opening it out revealed a hastily made drawing and many scribbled words.

''This is it!'' said Mekla. ''This shall be your guide. Now, what is the second thing?''

''A *living* guide,'' Morlac told him, ''familiar with Zohara's ways and magicks.''

''Oh?'' said Mekla, but his quizzical look quickly faded. ''*Oh.* . . .''

''Cheer up, wizardling,'' Broct told him with a comradely slap upon his shoulder. ''You are about to embark on an adventure. If you do not die in the attempt, you will be much the better for it . . . !''

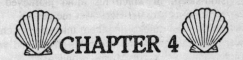

CHAPTER 4

Temple of Shibsothla

Dusk in Kamuria. Clouds on the far horizon still aflame with the glow of the vanished sun. The comfortable cloak of evening settling upon the city's shoulders. A pleasant time in Kamuria, full of exotic scents and sounds. A time for torches to be lighted and dance wicked dances in the wind from off the Yellow Sea. A time for mysteries and danger in a deliciously, wondrously magical city.

Morlac and the others walked casually along the Avenue of Diviners, heading toward the southern edge of town. The four were cloaked against the breeze, and sought to attract as little attention as possible.

Glendauna walked beside Morlac, and Broct and Mekla followed a few paces after. The young wizard had left his magician's robes behind, dressing instead as a common traveler.

As they walked, Broct leaned toward the young wizard and said, "You did not say before, but just how *did* your master, Korthos, die?"

"In his sleep," Mekla told him softly. "Or so it seemed. He had been working alone on some spell for hours, then he came down to be sure the shop was closed and to bid me good night. He retired to his chamber, and by morning he was dead."

Morlac asked, "And there was no sound of any disturbance?"

"None."

"Not even some occult disturbance?" Glendauna queried. "No demons flapping on leathery wings to strike him dead or steal his soul?"

"No," swore Mekla. "I heard nothing, saw nothing, *sensed* nothing. I even checked for obvious things like poisons, but could find nothing. Still, I know that Korthos was slain, and that Zohara's hands have his blood upon them."

"A strange city," said Broct with a shake of his head. They were passing yet another building now, but this one was obviously not set up for divination. "And yet, it be interesting in some ways."

Mekla noticed his broad grin and traced it to its point of origin. The building to their right had a torchlit patio that reeked of incense and a variety of alluring fragrances. Standing just within that patio were three young women of such exquisite and voluptuous beauty as to be heart-stopping. They cast warm, beguiling glances at the passersby, looks more beckoning than any words.

Broct's steps were slowing enough to cause the others to notice. "Remarkable," said he. "Be all Kamurian women so lovely—?"

"Women?" said Glendauna with a puzzled look. "I see no women. There are only three men. And very, *very* good-looking men, at that. What are you talking about?"

"Do you take me for a fool, girl?" chided Broct. "There may be many things beyond my ken, but I know women when I see them."

Mekla smiled knowingly. "Not in this case." His smile withered under Broct's probing look. "I mean . . . it's just that, this is the House of D'Jaris, a wizard who augments his income by conjuring up succubi and incubi."

"Which are . . . ?" asked Broct.

"Demons," Mekla explained. "Demons that appear in the guise of desirable women or men. They are all the same demons, really. They only look different depending on whether it is a man or woman looking at them. Travelers do not know this, of course. Or perhaps do not care. Or—"

"Enough," said Broct, casting a final glance at the young women—a glance that was at once disappointed, skeptical, and malevolent. As he continued on he said beneath his breath, "A very strange city, indeed."

They had not taken another twenty paces when Morlac said, "Is that the temple—?"

"Yes," replied Mekla, with a trace of a shudder. "The Temple of Shibsothla."

Ahead of them and to the right, a huge structure loomed. It looked like a set of beaded boxes, increasingly smaller, stacked one upon the other, with a rounded dome and four small minarets surmounting the top one. Torchlight gave it an eerie look, and a red glow came from the entrance.

Drawing nearer they saw that, like the building of the Council of Wizards, the Temple of Shibsothla had a wide band of gravel running all around it. From the street they now traversed, a path ran up to a low bridge that crossed the gravel and led to the temple's entrance. Members of the Gray Guard were posted there, and several were patrolling nearby along the street.

Something else became clear as they came closer to the temple. The rounded bumps that covered the walls and lent them their beaded look were not stones. They were skulls. Human skulls, blanched and yellow in the torchlight.

"Cheerful-looking place," said Broct.

"And well-defended," added Morlac. "Let us take a look around the back."

A side street enabled the four to avoid the guarded path leading to the temple's entrance and skirt the edge of the grounds. Trees and shrubbery on the property behind gave some cover as they approached the rear of the building.

"No doorways here," said Morlac, observing everything closely. "No guards, either. We could scale this wall with relative ease and search the higher levels for entrance."

"Yes, if you could reach it," agreed Mekla. "But first you would have to find a way to cross the moat."

"Moat?" Broct stepped toward the wide band of gravel. "You call this a moat?"

"Stop!" Mekla cried out softly, catching hold of the yellow-eyed giant just as he reached the edge.

The toe of Broct's boot touched lightly upon the surface of the gravel, a short way in from the edge. But instead of the expected crunch of rock against rock, there was only an odd whisper of sound, and the gravel yielded beneath his weight. Ripples fanned out from the spot as the tiny pebbles rose and fell in waves, in the manner of liquid.

Broct started to topple forward with nothing solid to support that foot, and the pebbles began to close over his boot. But Mekla's timely warning tug and Morlac's strong arm pulled him back to safety. He stared down at the gravel in amazement.

"That is sink-stone," Mekla cautioned. "A spell-cast defense against intruders. It would swallow you up in an instant. No one may cross it. A wizard might, but the spells needed could easily alert the guards. Or Zohara."

Morlac considered it. "You think Zohara is here now?"

"It is likely."

"And when is he not here?"

"For certain," Mekla said, "only when the Council meets. There are other times, but they are not predictable."

"Then perhaps that is when we should attempt this," Morlac told him. "Tomorrow, when Zohara sits in council."

Glendauna shivered, and not totally from the breeze. "I, for one, would find the daylight more pleasing."

"Yes," Mekla agreed. "That could work well, for that is also the time when travelers making their pilgrimage to this place enter the temple."

"Wait, small one—" Broct said abruptly. "Are you not also expected to appear at the Council of Wizards at that time?"

"Well, yes. . . ."

To Morlac, Broct said, "I think this one be trying to worm his way out of helping us. For in truth, he cannot be in two places at once."

"No, no—I intend to help," Mekla said hastily. "And now that you mention it, being in two places at once is not as impossible as it may sound. . . ."

"Are you ready yet—?" Broct's booming voice reverberated through the narrow building that had once been Korthos's, as the next day they readied their plan. "It is nearly time for the Council session!"

"I am coming, I am coming." Mekla's harried voice came out from a rear chamber. "These things cannot be rushed. And we still have plenty of time."

Morlac, Broct, and Glendauna all exchanged impatient glances, and then after a long moment more, the young wizard came walking out to join them, wearing a self-satisfied smile. And then he came walking out again, and stood beside himself. For now there were two of him!

"Well," said the first Mekla, "what do you think?"

Broct sighed wearily. "I think one of you was quite enough!"

They all studied the twin Meklas, searching for flaws or differences. There seemed to be none.

Glendauna walked around, inspecting them more closely. To the first one who had come out, she said, "I thought you were not a full-fledged wizard."

The first Mekla smiled. The second Mekla replied, "I am not. And I am the *real* Mekla. The truth is, my master, Korthos, created this simulacrum of me some months back, when he needed an extra assistant for a magical experiment. I usually keep it locked away and inactive, but I have just now reawakened it to aid us." The young wizard gestured at the simulacrum. "*This* Mekla shall sit in my place at the Council of Wizards, so suspicions will not be aroused. And *I* shall go with you."

"Then let us waste no more time," said Morlac. "For the hour grows near. . . ."

Once more the three travelers and the would-be wizard made their way to the ominous and hulking temple across the city of Kamuria. All wore their cloaks about them, the hoods raised to help hide their faces. Mekla had a common cloak over his own clothing, having sent off his duplicate to the Council Chamber in his magical robes.

Others joined them in the march along the Avenue of Diviners; travelers and pilgrims, the zealots and the curious. Gradually, without conscious effort, they began to fall into step, their footfalls keeping time with the gongs and rhythmic chanting emanating from the skull-encrusted building. The Temple of Shibsothla was calling the faithful.

The bizarre building loomed large before them as they reached the bridge and crossed over it. The temple entrance still seemed bathed in reddish light, though it was not as bright now with the sun overhead. Marching slowly onward step by step, Morlac and the others moved with the flow of the crowd that advanced into the temple.

Morlac glanced cautiously about him as they walked, studying those who came here and wondering what drew them.

There were weasel-faced men with evil eyes . . . slatternly
women of dissolute appearance . . . flabby-faced men who
hid their wealth between common robes, but could not conceal their looks of avarice. And then there were those who
had the unmistakable mark of occultists and fanatics. There
seemed but one common thread uniting them.

"They all seem to want something," said Morlac beneath
his breath.

"Of course," whispered Mekla. "Why else do people
worship demon gods?"

"Why else indeed . . ." Morlac frowned in disgust. "When
can we break away?"

"Shhhh—wait," Mekla told him. "We will have our
chance."

Well within the building now, temple initiates garbed in
white with red sashes guided the crowd down another corridor. Gaunt and grim-faced young men they were, with shaven
heads and tattoos upon their cheeks, and eyes that burned
with almost lunatic intensity.

But as strange as they looked, they were not out of place in
this horrific setting. Just as the stone of the outer walls of the
temple was hidden by skulls set into the mortar, so too were
these inner walls of the passageway lined with bones, both
human and animal. Every surface was covered with skeletal
remains. Only the floor was smooth and devoid of the bones,
though it did have intricate patterns etched into its surface.

The chanting droned on, echoing oddly through the torchlit
corridor. And it grew louder as they neared a great set of
doors at the corridor's end. Doors that now opened out to
admit them.

Morlac and the others saw more and more of the huge
chamber beyond those doors as they approached. The visitors
were marching into a chamber whose flooring was arranged
in tiers rising toward the back, so that those who stood behind
could see over the heads of those in front. The profusion of
bones also covered these walls and, if anything, looked even
more grotesque.

More frightening were the glimpses they had past the
moving marchers as they continued to near the great doors,
for they could begin to see details now of what faced those

tiers of spectators. Off to the side, a great altarlike platform rose upon vertical columns of bones, with rows of skulls at its base. A marble slab of ebon darkness glistened dully at its top.

Cut into the floor was a wide trench separating the altar from the rest of the chamber, and Morlac shivered as he saw what filled that trench. It appeared to be a miniature moat of blood, dark and glistening.

Glendauna almost halted as she too saw it, a shudder of fear and revulsion coursing through her. But Morlac took her hand and gripped it tight, pulling her closer and steadying her.

Burning braziers flared up with a rush of flame as the crowd drew into the chamber. A steamy mist seemed to envelope the place, and concentrated itself upon the altar stone. And now a murmur of excitement, and perhaps a bit of terror, erupted from the crowd as, seemingly from out of nowhere, something rose to climb atop the altar. The hideous thing clawed its way up there with a slow and sinewy motion, finally coming to rest in as close to a sitting position as its bizarre form could manage.

For the creature that now dominated the temple chamber was an obscene amalgam of parts, a perverse parody of a living being. Oxlike in size, its body was bloated and broad, like a great leathery sack filled and left to sag. There were no feet, no legs, only six limbs shaped like fat and ugly arms with three-fingered hands and blackened nails. And that was not the worst of it.

The toadlike head had three faces, one beside the other. Slit-eyes stared out dispassionately toward all, and the mouths stretched into one wide, grim line.

Shibsothla. The name fit the monstrosity.

Almost at once, many of those within the chamber began to toss gold coins upon the stone floor ahead of them, watching with rapt attention. Amazingly, as each coin struck and spun upon the floor, it suddenly sparkled with unnatural light and transformed into a snake. The serpents wriggled forward as if with one mind, plunging into the blood-filled pit and swimming toward the altar. A collective sigh of astonishment and approval swept through the crowd.

Slithering up the altar bones, dripping blood as they moved, the snakes now crawled directly for the demon god. Lowering its massive head toward them, Shibsothla opened each of its three mouths. . . .

Glendauna turned away from the sight, as did several others within the chamber. Morlac glanced back toward the doors and saw only one initiate standing near them.

Quietly, Morlac got the attention of Broct and Mekla. They followed as he guided Glendauna toward the doors. With the attention of all riveted upon the altar platform, it was not difficult leaving.

Once in the corridor, they gathered off to one side. Alarmingly, the initiate who had been by the door saw them and started to approach. Was he suspicious, or did he merely wish to direct them? They did not have the chance to find out, for in the next instance another roar of astonished approval rose from the crowd within the chamber and several people came rushing out, their hands clamped to their mouths, obviously on the verge of being sick.

In jostling the initiate, they diverted his attention from Morlac and the others, allowing them to duck down a narrow cross corridor near them. When again he turned, they were out of sight, and although puzzled, he was not enough so to devote further thought to it.

"This way!" said Mekla as the four hurried along this new passageway. He was studying Korthos's map as they ran, guiding them as best he could along the uncertain and ill-lighted path.

Morlac noticed with interest that this corridor lacked the bones and decorations common to the public pathways. Plain stone walls lined this route. Odd. Perhaps the deeply faithful did not need the outer trappings of Shibsothla's glory.

"Here—" Mekla said abruptly, his hand pointing to a new corridor angling off to their right even as his eyes stared at the inadequately detailed map. "Here—we go this way now!"

Morlac and the others reached the corner and started around it. They had barely taken another step when abruptly they halted.

Directly ahead of them stood a temple initiate. . . .

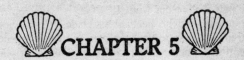

CHAPTER 5

Double, Double

For a moment, the initiate merely stood there staring at them in mild surprise. Then a frown settled upon his features and he fixed Morlac and the others with a challenging look.

"Who are you?" he said abruptly. "You should not be in this part of the temple."

Broct stepped past Morlac and glowered at the young man. "Out of our way, bug, or we may add your bones to the temple walls."

For a second or so the initiate seemed intimidated by the yellow-eyed giant's size and dangerous tone. But then his eyes blazed with self-righteous fervor and he jumped into a fighting stance.

"Ho!" said he, drawing a wicked-looking dirk from his robes and flashing it at them.

"Ho *ho!*" replied Broct as all six of his arms whipped out from beneath his outer cloak, a razor-sharp dirk in each hand.

The young initiate stared in awe, bedazzled by the many moving blades and the uncommon nature of his adversary. Then his eyes opened even wider as he read special significance into the number of Broct's arms.

"A true disciple of Shibsothla!" he gasped.

Morlac and Broct exchanged glances, quickly deciding to seize the opportunity. Morlac pulled his hood back, so that the lad might better see his own exotic features.

"Do not stand there gaping, initiate!" Morlac told him firmly. "We have journeyed far on an important pilgrimage.

277

If you wish to achieve oneness with Shibsothla, you would do well to pay heed to our words!''

The initiate quickly sheathed his blade. "Y-y-y-yes, sir."

"Go immediately to your quarters and await instructions," said Morlac. "There will be momentous news for you within the hour."

"W-w-w-wonderful! I hear and obey!"

And with that he hurried past them, still marveling at Broct's extra limbs and studying his own two puny hands. As he disappeared out of sight around the corner and his scurrying footfalls faded down the corridor, Morlac turned to Broct and arched a devil-brow in amused wonder.

"What do you think—?"

"I think we made a believer of him," replied Broct. "But just the same, let us hurry on!"

Mekla studied his map, tilting it toward the light. "Our next turn is just ahead down this passage!"

The four hastened on, nearly running as they reached the end of the passage and turned into a new corridor. This path was narrower than the last, allowing but one person to walk between its walls. Marching single file, Morlac went first, with Broct close behind.

They had reached the halfway point when suddenly there came a deep rumbling sound from the walls and the very stone beneath their feet. In the next instant a long section of the floor dropped and swung away.

Glendauna screamed. Mekla gasped.

There was a sickening moment as Morlac and Broct started to fall through the opening, then both shot out their hands to the walls and pressed with all their considerable strength to halt their descent. They succeeded in doing so just as they reached waist level. Looking down, they saw their feet dangling over a gaping pit that stretched down into darkness.

Morlac tried to look back over his shoulder. "Broct—are you all right?"

"Aye! I've still hands to spare. Do you need help?"

"I think I can manage," Morlac told him. With the great power he had in his arms he slowly pulled himself up nearly level with the flooring ahead. He swung his feet back and forth a few times, then propelled himself forward to land on the solid floor beyond the pit.

"Neatly done!" said Broct. "But I think I've an easier method, myself."

He proceeded to place two arms out slightly ahead of the four that held his weight and then shifted himself forward to suspend from those. He brought his other arms forward in successive pairs and continued to transfer his weight ahead until at last he had reached the edge of solid flooring and climbed up to it.

Morlac looked back across the gap to where Glendauna and Mekla still stood. He gauged the distance. It seemed no more than ten feet.

"You're going to have to jump. There's no other way to get past the opening."

"Jump . . . ?" said Mekla weakly.

Glendauna sighed. "Here, wizardling—let me show you how."

She backed off a score of paces down the corridor, taking Mekla with her so he would not get in her way. She paused a moment to breathe deeply, then ran swiftly toward the pit. Glendauna kicked off hard just before the edge and sailed over the gaping opening like a deer in flight.

Morlac caught her as her feet touched down on the other side, then pulled her into his arms. He could feel her heart racing, and knew it was as much from the fright of their near disaster as it was from running. Her eyes looked up into his, grateful and moist and full, and with a rush of emotion she reached up to kiss him.

Broct looked back toward Mekla. "Your turn, pipsqueak!"

"As you wish," Mekla said reluctantly. "But you do not treat me with the proper respect due even a fledgling wizard."

"If a wizard you be, then why not merely levitate across?"

"I . . . I have not yet learned that one," he said with a pout. He too now ran with all due speed, though lacking the grace of the girl.

Mekla landed on the other side, but just barely so, and Broct had to reach out and grab him to prevent him from stumbling back into the pit. The yellow-eyed giant brought him safely away from the edge, then gave him a comradely slap that nearly staggered him.

"We'll make a warrior of you yet."

Glendauna turned toward the young wizard with fire in her eyes. "I'd sooner make a ship's anchor of him!" She squeezed past Broct and took a fistful of Mekla's robe, lifting him to his toes. "Why did you not warn us of that trap?"

Startled by such unladylike behavior, Mekla whined, "I did not know! 'Tis the truth! Korthos's map mentioned nothing about it. Remember—my master did not actually walk this path. He only visited it metaphysically!"

Morlac interrupted in a stern voice. "We may argue about this later, if we survive. As for now, let us continue, and be quick about it."

"Aye," said Broct. "Quick . . . but careful."

They walked on along the corridor, searching the flooring ahead more carefully now, and watching for any signs of further traps. But there were no others and they soon found themselves at a flight of stairs leading up to the next level.

Mekla again consulted his map. "Zohara's private chamber should be up here somewhere, or else on the next floor above. Korthos's notes are not clear about that, though I know the approximate location."

The four ascended the stairs without incident and found themselves on the temple's second level. Its size was hard to gauge, for though torches lighted the place there was a kind of mist or haze hanging in the air that obscured the walls. A layer of far denser vapor, almost cloudlike in its opacity, lay over the floor, roiling and eddying, completely hiding the flooring stones.

Morlac looked about, directing a question to Mekla even as his eyes continued to search. "Is this how Korthos described this level?"

The young wizard studied the map. "I do see the word 'mists,' and some other word I cannot make out. His handwriting is—was—terrible."

"What is your guess, then?" Morlac asked. "How does this tie in with temple activities?"

Mekla lowered the map. "Oh, I doubt that it does, though it may serve some purpose in initiating new members. More likely it's part of some protective spell to discourage intruders."

"Discouraging, it be," said Broct. "But need we fear it?"

"In this place," Mekla replied, "we would be wise to fear everything."

They advanced slowly and cautiously through the mist, feeling their way with each footstep. The strange vapor lapped about their legs, nearly up to their knees. It had a musty, organic smell, as of swamps and decay.

Morlac led them, frowning at the thought of what dangers might lie hidden in the mist. More trapdoors and pits, or poisoned stakes, or serpents real or conjured. He was tempted to draw Shark and use the magicked sword to probe the floor ahead of him, but he was reluctant to awaken the hungry blade with no enemy in sight. Glendauna followed close behind him, slightly off to his right side. Her nearness felt reassuring, yet he could not help worrying for her safety.

They had crossed but a portion of the second level when Broct suddenly called out from behind Morlac and Glendauna. "Here be something—perhaps a way out of this damned fog!"

As Morlac and the girl turned they caught a glimpse of Broct and Mekla. The yellow-eyed giant and the young wizard had stopped a short distance back before a wall that had not been visible just moments before. A door stood open in that wall. A door through which Broct and Mekla now walked.

"Wait for us—" Morlac called out. But it was to no avail, for the open panel that blocked the view of his friends seemed also to block his words, and in the next instant the door closed rapidly behind the two.

Morlac and Glendauna reached it in several quick, uncautious steps. They sought to open it to follow their friends, but the panel would not budge. Though it had opened freely before, it now seemed as solid as the stone wall which framed it.

Heedless of the danger of calling attention to themselves, Morlac pounded on the door. But the wood seemed to absorb the blows and his fist only made dull thumping sounds.

"Broct—" he called through the panel. And again, "Broct!"

Silence greeted him. He looked to Glendauna, whose worried gaze offered no answers. His hand went to Shark's hilt now. The door that resisted him would surely yield to the power of his blade.

He had it partway out of its sheath and felt its awakening surge, when suddenly the door latch twisted and the panel began to open. Morlac froze the drawing of his blade and stepped back a pace, ready, but waiting to see whether it be friend or foe on the other side. He had not long to wait.

Broct stepped through, with Mekla close at his heels. He looked curiously at Morlac's partially drawn sword.

"What's wrong?" said the yellow-eyed giant.

"The door closed and locked," replied Morlac, sliding the reluctant blade back within its sheath. It seemed to resist more than usual. "You did not respond to my call. What happened?"

"Nothing. I just did not hear you."

Mekla shrugged. "I heard nothing, either."

Glendauna tried to see past them as the door closed again. "What is in there—?"

"Nothing," said Broct. "Just an empty chamber, smaller than this one. It led nowhere."

Mekla pointed ahead. "Our path seems to lie in this direction."

"All right, then," said Morlac. Though relieved to see the two again, he felt an even greater unease now than before. "Let us continue. We must find the dreamstone before the Council of Wizards completes its business and Zohara returns. . . ."

As the four walked away, a different but similar scene was playing out on the other side of the mysterious wall. In this part of the second level, red tile squares covered the floor and the walls, and even the ceiling. The wide chamber led off to a maze of corridors ahead, and here there was no mist.

Broct fumbled with the door latch, trying to turn it but having no success even with four hands gripping it. He cursed beneath his breath. "This blasted thing has locked itself!"

Mekla inspected the door closely as Broct still struggled. "There must be a spell upon it. Zohara's doing, no doubt. But why would it admit us and keep your friends out?"

"A useless question, wizardling, for I have not the answers." After more failed attempts to loosen the panel, Broct at last turned to inspect this new chamber. "Well . . . at least there be no fog here. But I do not think I like this place any better than the other.''

A sudden click behind him made him start. Broct whirled about in time to see the door which had been locked now opening. Morlac and Glendauna stepped through to join them.

"How did you get in?" Broct asked them.

Morlac shrugged as the door closed behind them. "We just twisted the latch.''

Broct rubbed his chin and scratched his head and put two hands upon his hips, simultaneously. "It must open only from the outside, then. Which means we cannot go back that way, short of breaking through it.''

"It's just as well," said Morlac. "It's too dangerous walking through that mist. I saw nothing there, anyway."

"That settles it, then," Broct replied. "we'll take our chances on this side.''

And now these four set out, heading across the red-tiled chamber with caution. Mekla consulted his map and kept pace with Broct. Morlac and Glendauna followed them a few paces back. Broct looked back and noticed the two exchanging glances. An odd time, he thought, for romantic looks. Ah, well—young lovers were seldom logical.

They reached the corridor ahead and started down it, noticing for the first time that there were no torches along the walls, despite the fact there was light to see by. They also noticed that some of the floor tiles seemed poorly placed, for they rocked slightly when tred upon.

"How much farther?" queried Broct.

Mekla pored over his map. "I am not sure. This seems the right direction, but Korthos's notes are vague about this area.''

"Did he mention those—?" asked Broct.

"Those?" Mekla looked up from his map.

All along the corridor ahead of them, every other flooring tile was raised or raising, as if hinged at one side. And protruding from the dark openings beneath were skeletal hands with clawlike fingertips, ready to grasp and tear at whomever came within reach. On impulse, the four turned, almost as one, and saw that the same thing was happening along the corridor behind them. And scattered along the walls, tile panels were beginning to open as well. . . .

Back on the other side of the wall dividing the second level, in the misty, murky chamber that smelled of swamps and fetid things, the other group of four progressed deeper into the gloom. Morlac and Glendauna led the way, with Broct and Mekla behind them.

"I think I see another wall ahead," Morlac told the others. "Hard to be certain in this haze, though."

"Morlac—" Glendauna said suddenly, her eyes upon the low, dense vapor that lapped about their boot tops.

"Yes, my lady."

"Something moves about us. Look—!"

Morlac followed the line of her gaze and saw nothing more than the low vapor at first. But then he noticed that in addition to the random eddying of vapor, there were also other disturbances decidedly not random. Something, or rather some *things*, were creating tiny swells and ripples as they moved beneath the vapor.

Even as he looked, the movements of whatever caused those ripples became faster and more noticeable. It was as if the things hidden within the vapor knew they had been discovered and no longer needed stealth.

"Keep your swords ready," Morlac said. "If anything comes toward your feet—"

Glendauna was already drawing her Durkesh blade when abruptly something reared up through the low vapor a few feet ahead of her. Another quickly rose in front of Morlac, and still more began to appear on all sides now.

The creatures were sluglike and slimey, with no visible limbs. Their bulbous eyes were gray and rheumy and without pupils, seeming to look everywhere and nowhere in particular. Multiple rows of tiny fangs lined the mouths, flexing in and out in an ugly and frightening way. They stood barely three feet high, that portion that rose up, but it seemed likely an equal length still lay upon the flooring. There was little doubt they were carnivorous.

Morlac drew Shark from its gray hide sheath, and felt it throb, alert but uncertain, within his strong grip. . . .

On the other side of the central wall, where red tile squares formed every flat surface, Broct studied the skeletal hands that reached out, stark white against the red tiles and dark openings. He apprized their chances.

"I don't suppose," said he to Mekla, "that you know any spells to counter such a menace?"

Mekla sighed. "Korthos planned to teach me that, but—"

"I thought as much," said Broct. Then to Morlac he added, "Well, my sea-brother, let us see if we can cut a path through this bone garden!"

"Yes," replied Morlac, as he and Glendauna drew their own swords simultaneously.

These four started forward with Broct in the lead, the yellow-eyed giant swinging a sword and an assortment of dirks. They chopped at the bony hands that clawed and grabbed at them, struggling forward step by step upon the uncertain footing of those tile squares that remained closed. More hands appeared behind them as they moved forward, grasping at their legs and attempting to hold them fast.

Broct threw a glance over his shoulder as he shouted, "Stay near the center—we cannot fight these things in the walls, too!"

He returned his attention to hacking away at the skeletal claws before him. But his mind was troubled by the fact that in his hasty glimpse of Morlac and the girl, the two seemed to be staring more at him than at the hands they haphazardly struck against. Had something in the misty chamber numbed their thoughts. . . . ?

And in that very chamber on the far side of the central wall, where mists and vapor obscured the dangers crawling all about them, Morlac and his party were also struggling forward. He and Glendauna slashed their way through more and more of the hideous sluglike beasts. Some of the creatures rose out of the vapor to attack them or block their path, while others sought to reach them hidden beneath the roiling cloud, revealed only by the ripples they created.

Morlac sliced through yet another of the repulsive creatures just before its pulsating fangs could reach his leg. It continued to hiss and sputter even as the severed portion sank beneath the murky layer. Shark was cutting a deadly swath before him, yet its movements seemed languid, making him work all the harder. Morlac reached to his left to fend off another slug when suddenly something whistled by his right side. He caught a glimpse of one of Broct's daggers knifing into the vapor ahead and disappearing.

Morlac jerked his head around and looked at the yellow-eyed giant questioningly. "That was close, my sea-brother."

"Sorry," said Broct. "There was a beast ahead of you I did not think you saw. My aim was off a bit."

"No matter," Morlac replied, facing forward once more as he saw Glendauna needed help on her side. But his mind still dwelled upon that dagger. His difficulty with Shark told him there might be a spell at work affecting either their weapons or their skills. That could explain it all. And yet . . . Broct's statement somehow did not ring true.

More long minutes dragged by as they fought their way forward, hacking at the monsters that besieged them. Morlac felt as if they'd covered miles within this hellish temple. Then at last the sluglike creatures began to thin and disappear. The wall he had glimpsed ahead earlier came into clear view, no more than ten feet away, with a door offering escape from this chamber set in its center. They reached it in a moment, though still wary of pits and traps that might be placed at a point where freedom seemed so near.

The heavy door stood closed before them, and Glendauna studied it anxiously. "Is it locked?"

"If it is," Morlac answered, "I will try cutting through it with Shark rather than stay trapped in here. I only hope there is not some worse terror on the other side."

He looked at the lovely young woman standing by his side and again felt a pang of regret for involving her in this. As if sensing his thoughts, Glendauna smiled reassuringly and touched his arm. Then she raised her Durkesh sword and kicked at the door with surprising vigor.

The door was unlocked. It shuddered open and banged dully against the wall's other side. Nothing dangerous charged out to face them, nor was visible through the opening. One by one, the four stepped through.

This chamber had the same stone walls they had seen throughout much of the bizarre temple, but it totally lacked the mist and swamplike vapor of the chamber they had just left. There were several doors besides the one they had entered, all closed. And a half-dozen large mirrors hung upon the walls in ornate frames. A tinkling sound came from above, where hundreds of crystal shards hung from the ceiling and stirred in subtle air currents.

Glendauna looked about with worried eyes. "I hesitate to ask, but I wonder what manner of nightmare lurks about here?"

"Hard to say." Morlac glanced toward Mekla. "What does the map tell you?"

The young wizard shrugged. "I seem to have lost it somewhere back there in the mist."

Morlac fixed him with a hard look, then turned away. "Then we shall just have to find our own path without it."

Slowly and cautiously, they began to advance within the chamber. This place seemed innocent enough. Perhaps that was what they found disturbing about it.

Broct suddenly said, "I think we should try one of those doors—"

Morlac looked at the doors a long moment, then another long moment at Broct. And then he returned his attention to something that had caught his eye as they traversed the chamber. One of the large mirrors on the far wall seemed different. It reflected the same stone walls all the other mirrors did, but the color and clarity of the reflection struck him as odd. Morlac approached it, and the others followed.

As the four of them gathered before the mirror, Morlac pointed at it boldly. "There is something crazy about this one. Look—our reflections are all wrong. We are not standing in the same positions we see in the glass. Our reflections do not move as we do."

Mekla shrugged it off. "A spell of Zohara's, I'm sure. Something to trick and confuse us. Let us ignore it and try the doors, quickly."

The reflected images of Broct, Mekla, Morlac, and Glendauna seemed to be approaching a few moments out of synch with reality. They now stopped and stared back at the other group with curious frowns.

Morlac's keen eyes stared hard at the images in the mirror . . . images supposed to be those of him and his friends. Silently, he looked over his shoulder once more at the doors which both Broct and Mekla suggested they explore. This place—it was a wizard's toy, designed to bewilder and befuddle; to delay, and very likely to kill. Each choice was important. Each choice could be his last. *Their* last.

A sound caused his ears to prick up. Overhead, the hanging crystal shards began to tinkle louder now, creating an eerie music. Perhaps a deadly music!

With surprising suddenness, Morlac let out a yell directed at no one, channeling the energy into motion. He swung Shark in a massive two-handed sweep, up over his head and back down again as he pivoted back to face the mirror. The tip of the blade struck with splintering impact near the center of the large mirror, sending enormous cracks radiating out.

Instantly the huge mirror shattered, collapsing from its frame and falling in small pieces to the floor. And yet the image remained!

"Hurry—!" Morlac quickly propelled Glendauna through the opening left by the broken mirror and jumped through after her, motioning for the others to follow.

The four barely made it through to the other side when a horrid sound filled the chamber behind them. The crystal shards were raining down from the ceiling, point first and daggerlike, and shattering into sharp splinters against the floor.

When silence came it was nearly as nerve-racking as the sound of crashing crystal. Morlac and the others looked up to face . . . themselves! For there in this chamber that was laid out like a mirror image of the one behind them were another Morlac, Broct, Glendauna, and Mekla! The two groups stared at each other for a long moment before anyone broke the silence.

"By Tritus!" said the mirror Broct. "What manner of magic be this?"

"Demons!" said the mirror Morlac, pointing at his counterpart and the others from the shattered room. "Surely they must be demons, shaped in our guise."

"Surely someone is," said the other Morlac with a hard look. "The door that divided us has supplied lookalikes, it seems. I see *your* Mekla still has his map. Mine has not."

"Which only proves what I say!" asserted the mirror Morlac. "You are all demons!"

"Ah, but I have Shark," said the other Morlac. "And I will pit its magicked blade against your phony weapon anytime. Who do you think will win?"

"This be crazy!" said the mirror Broct.

"Aye," said the other Morlac. "Crazy. Madmen in the palace. . . ."

The mirror Broct smiled. "Bloody corpses everywhere. Ho!"

The mirror Broct and mirror Mekla edged closer to this newly arrived Morlac and Glendauna, even as they moved away from the other Broct and Mekla. In a moment the two groups had re-formed, still alike, but now different in an important way.

The outcast four gathered opposite them, seemingly identical in every way. And yet in small ways they clearly were not the same. They were beginning to slouch, and their angry, self-righteous looks became evil grins, like wicked children enjoying a secret prank. And then in the next moment, their outward appearance fell away altogether, revealing something not quite human beneath. Lean and lanky, with feet like bird claws and narrow, harsh faces leering above crooked necks, the demons had flesh that was purplish-gray and oily.

"You have won so far," said one of them, with a raspy otherworldly voice. "But now you shall lose . . . your *lives!*"

Morlac, Broct, and Glendauna raised their swords, ready to do battle. Mekla scurried to one side, picking up a shard of crystal that had fallen in from the other chamber.

The demons opened their hands wide and their claws suddenly grew into razor-sharp talons easily a foot in length. Four of them against three armed warriors. Unholy fire glowed in their eyes, and they crouched to spring against the humans.

Still off to one side, Mekla held the single crystal shard before his eyes and gestured at it with his other hand, his lips quickly mouthing words no one could hear. Then he hastily threw the shard with all his strength.

The shard flew across the space between the humans and the demons and stuck in a wooden mirror frame on the opposite wall. The four demons saw it pass harmlessly before them and laughed with malevolent glee. And then they sprang.

Even as the demons came flying toward them, Mekla whispered three final words in his hasty spell. Then to his friends he yelled, *"Back!"*

The others were already moving back away from the demons that sprang toward them, even without Mekla's encouragement. And now with a great clattering roar of sound the hundreds of crystal shards, broken and whole, came hurtling from the other chamber like some silvery sidelong rain, aiming for the opposite wall where stuck the first one thrown by Mekla. Many of them reached it. Many more intercepted the demons in midspring and pierced them through and through.

In mere seconds it was over. The shards had ended their flight, and the four demons fell to the floor almost at the humans' feet, their lifeless bodies bristling with shiny crystal. A stunned silence fell over the chamber.

At last, Glendauna said, "What . . . what did you do?"

"One of the spells I *did* learn," said Mekla sheepishly. "A simple similarity spell. You ensorcell one object and bind it to those like it. Then whatever happens to one, happens to the rest."

"I knew this lad had promise!" said Broct.

"Well done, Mekla," agreed Morlac. "But let us not rest on our laurels. There are likely many demons in the Temple of Shibsothla, and we have not won this deadly game yet. . . ."

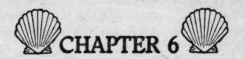

CHAPTER 6

The Red Wizard's Sanctum

"I think this must be it," said Mekla, looking from his map to the great carven door before them. "The position seems right. Korthos places Zohara's chamber here."

The four had taken the center door of the three that led out from the chamber of red tiles. A corridor beyond that had twisted and turned past ordinary doorways and brought them to a spiral stair by which they reached the third level. And now they faced the door to the chamber that should contain their goal—Korthos's stolen dreamstone.

"Be careful—" cautioned Morlac. "There are surely magical safeguards on such a place."

"I have no doubt of that," said Mekla gravely. "But I hope to undo them before we enter."

Broct watched the corridor alertly. "It be strange the other temple initiates, or the Gray Guard, have not been alerted by our passage."

"Perhaps they have," Mekla said as his hands gently traced the patterns and spell-auras of the door. "Perhaps they are only waiting to enjoy our destruction at this final obstacle." The young wizard shrugged. "Then again, it may well be that the temple safeguards function without alerting the guards, unless and until they are needed."

"How reassuring," said Broct, with mock good humor. "So the moment we enter Zohara's chamber, we shall either be destroyed by magic or attacked by the Gray Guard!"

"Ssssh! I must concentrate on these spells."

After a long while, Mekla took a step back from the door.
Morlac said, "Well—?"

The young wizard pushed back his sleeves. "I found two
protective spells, which I believe I've blocked. There only
remains the spell that locks the door."

Glendauna asked, "Can you open it?"

"That's the easy part," Mekla told her. "Zohara has an
amulet hanging from the sash about his waist. I have seen it
close enough to observe a special sign engraved upon it. That
same sign is carved here upon this door, but part of it is
missing. All I need do is trace the missing part of the design
. . . like . . . *so!*"

Mekla used his finger to draw an unusual figure upon a
blank spot in the door's carved design. The heavy portal
seemed to tremble slightly as he completed the design, then
unseen latches clicked and the door swung slowly open.
Mekla beamed with pride.

"See—?" he said, but then his smile faded in an instant
and he gasped in alarm.

Within the darkened chamber beyond a glowing image of
Zohara's face sprang suddenly to life, many times larger than
reality. His expression was fierce and malevolent, and from
his eyes lanced out burning beams of intense light.

Those beams fell fully upon Mekla, who alone among the
group stood squarely in front of the door. The young wizard
gave a shriek as the glow lighted him up brightly, then tiny
bolts of lightning crackled and crawled over his body, causing him to shake violently.

As quickly as it started, the light vanished. Mekla staggered back and collapsed on the floor. His slender body
seemed to smolder. Crimson smoke rose from it, then vanished, and the young wizard's body underwent a sudden and
startling transformation.

Morlac and the others looked in stunned amazement at
what remained. A chunk of tree trunk, several wrought-iron
fire pokers, a wad of burlap where the head should be with a
book protruding from its bundled form, and various other
odds and ends. Strange remains for a wizard. . . .

"Why, that little. . . ." Broct began, then bit off his

words. "He sent the *simulacrum* with us and stayed behind himself!"

"Well," observed Glendauna, "he may be a chicken-hearted little twerp, but it looks as if he's a wise one. At least the real Mekla still lives."

Morlac peered cautiously into the chamber. "Let us hope we do, as well!"

Zohara's ghostly face had vanished. Whatever the phony Mekla's entry had triggered, it seemed to be a one-shot spell. Broct waved his sword before the door to see if more deadly beams flashed out, but nothing happened.

Carefully, Morlac stepped inside. Broct and Glendauna followed.

Zohara's chamber was a large one, outfitted much like those of other wizards insofar as having a large collection of old and strange books and a great variety of magical implements. But unlike most such places, it seemed better organized.

"Well, he be a tidy wizard," said Broct. "Probably all the more dangerous because of it, too!"

Candles that showed no sign of having melted burned bright enough to well-illumine this windowless room. The four walked farther into the chamber, their footsteps carrying them onto a small carpet with a strangely woven design.

Suddenly they felt as if the floor had dropped out from under them. Darkness enveloped Morlac, Broct, and Glendauna as they plummeted down what seemed to be a chute spiraling to some lower level.

Glendauna's startled cry was distant and unreal, and Morlac reached out in the darkness for her. But the three of them were tumbling and sliding down the chute and any attempt to halt their descent or grasp each other for support seemed hopeless.

Skidding around another turn, an area of light now came into view. An opening in the ceiling of some lower chamber loomed before them, and in the next instant they saw enough through it to realize just which chamber that was. It was the temple worship room, and in moments they would be plunging straight into the waiting arms of the demon god, Shibsothla. Already, the hideous creature was turning to look up at them, its three mouths opening to reveal countless rows of twisted, merciless fangs.

A horrible death seemed certain for all three of them. Morlac tried, but could not even reach Shark's hilt. He fought against the looming face of stark, mindless terror, and knew the others did also. And then. . . .

And then . . . something felt wrong with this. Morlac was not sure whether it was his human or his animal senses that spoke to him, but something within him questioned the reality of their peril.

Fighting hard against the fear that threatened to overwhelm him, Morlac forced out all thoughts of the looming monster below him. Straining against muscles numbed by fear and buffeting, or so it seemed, he slowly raised his hands to each side. He was startled and overjoyed to feel Broct's and Glendauna's hands within his grasp.

He gripped their hands hard now, forcing words from the level of thought into actual spoken sounds. "Broct! Glendauna! Ignore this all. It is not real. Fight it! It is but illusion."

For long moments they still seemed poised over certain destruction. And then as he felt their own grips tightening upon his, the image of Shibsothla faded and vanished. The darkness subsided, and the three found themselves still within Zohara's chamber, and still standing exactly where they had stood upon the strange carpet.

Shaking their heads to clear them, they quickly stepped off the rug and released their hands. Broct was the first to speak.

"More trickery!"

"Be thankful that is all it was," Morlac told him.

"We could have died of fright," Glendauna said, a hand over her racing heart. "The spell . . . it was meant to frighten us to death."

Morlac nodded grimly. "Or disable us long enough for guards to reach us. We had best hurry!"

"But without Mekla," Broct said soberly, "or even his fake twin, how shall we know this dreamstone we seek?"

"I don't know," Morlac replied. "But we must—"

Glendauna held up a hand for silence, her head cocked to one side and a puzzled look upon her pretty face. "I heard a voice, I thought. A cry for help."

"Another trick, perhaps," said Broct, turning to look about for danger. But now his ears pricked up, too. He exchanged a frowning look with Morlac, who also listened intently.

A faint voice cried out pathetically, "Here . . . I am over here!"

They moved with great caution in the direction of the voice, going to the far side of the chamber where stood several neatly arranged tables and shelves. A motion caught their eyes now, and they narrowed their search to a large bottle formed of transparent blue crystal. Within that bottle, a ghostlike image stood. His tiny hands pressed against the crystal, the old man in wizard's robes looked pleadingly out at Morlac and the others.

Glendauna approached warily and bent to examine him. "What sort of demon is this small thing . . . ?"

"I am no demon!" protested the small translucent man. "I am the wizard, Korthos." His expression saddened. "Or what is left of him."

Morlac bent closer, his face very near the bottle. "You have the look of a wizard. But Mekla told us you perished."

"I'm not surprised he thought so. The outward signs would have fooled most wizards, and certainly that foolish apprentice of mine." He sighed. "I saw what happened at the door. Pity. I spent weeks fashioning that simulacrum."

The sound of running footsteps came from somewhere down the corridor. Morlac's head jerked toward the doorway, then back to the blue bottle.

"There are guards on the way. We have little time—"

"Then close the door, quickly," Korthos directed. "Once latched, none but Zohara, or a wizard who knows his secret, may enter." He saw their hesitancy. "Do as I say! There is yet another path out, if that is what concerns you."

Broct quickly crossed to the door and swung the heavy panel closed. Latches clicked around the frame.

"Korthos," said Morlac, "Mekla sent us here to find the dreamstone and to prove Zohara killed you. Can you help us find it? And can we free you from this tiny prison?"

"Yes, and yes again. The dreamstone is over there, on that shelf—that golden crystal with the small sparkles of light within it. Zohara placed it there within my view to torment me. For you see, that is how I came to be here."

Glendauna went to the shelf and gently picked up the crystal. She gazed into its mysterious depths as she brought it toward Morlac and the blue bottle. "You mean you are here because Zohara wished to steal it?"

"No," replied Korthos. "Zohara seized the opportunity, but it was I, fool that I am, who presented him that opportunity. You see, one of the special gifts of the dreamstone is astral projection—the ability to send your mind and spirit to distant places while your body remains behind. The map Mekla's simulacrum brought to guide you is one I made after just such a vision journey to this temple."

Morlac nodded. "Yes, he mentioned that."

"Well," said Korthos, "what he did not mention, because he did not know, is that I made a second vision journey here. My curiosity had been aroused by this place. I *had* to know more about it." The tiny wizard sighed. "That was my undoing. Zohara discovered the presence of my spirit self and used a spell to trap me in this bottle. Then he summoned up a demon spirit and sent it off to where my physical body lay untended. The demon spirit inhabited my body, took my dreamstone to a window and dropped it to a temple initiate who waited below. My own body, used to steal it! Then my body, still possessed by the demon, went downstairs to bid Mekla goodnight and returned to my chamber. The demon spirit departed, leaving my body in a deathlike state for Mekla to find. Zohara greatly enjoyed explaining to me how he worked his diabolical scheme!"

Sounds came from outside the door. The guards!

Morlac looked up alertly. "We had best hurry. If word reaches Zohara—"

"Yes, you are right," agreed Korthos. "If you will lift that carpet over there you will find a trapdoor. Beneath it is a secret passage leading out of the temple to the shop next door. I discovered it during my second vision journey."

"That carpet?" Morlac questioned. "When we entered, we thought at first that we had fallen through there and would provide a meal for the demon god below."

Korthos shook his wizened head. "No, my friend. It is

truly a secret escape route. And Shibsothla is nothing more than an illusion. Zohara created it and the cult which worships it merely to spread his own power and influence. It is all a sham. He is a true wizard, mind you, with more than adequate talents. But he is even more a charlatan and a scoundrel. Now you must hurry and return my dreamstone!''

Glendauna carefully wrapped the mystic gem in folds of cloth and slipped it into a pack slung round her shoulder. She joined Broct as the yellow-eyed giant pulled aside the strangely patterned carpet and revealed a heavy door built into the floor. Once that was raised, narrow steps led down into a passage, just as Korthos had told them.

Morlac placed both hands upon the blue bottle. ''Now tell us—how may we free you?''

The tiny, translucent wizard gestured over his head. ''There is a seal around the top of the bottle, with magical signs painted upon it. You have but to break that seal and remove the stopper. Then I shall be free!''

Korthos had been straightforward with him thus far. There was every reason to trust him and distrust Zohara. And so Morlac broke the seal and carefully pulled the stopper from the bottle. The tiny ghostly image shimmered and turned to smoke, rising from the bottle and fading away.

''Ahhh—at last,'' said Korthos's voice as he departed. ''Thank you, my friends. Now you must hurry away-y-y. . . .''

''Good advice,'' Morlac said to Broct and Glendauna. ''Let us follow it. . . .''

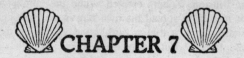

CHAPTER 7

Revenge of Korthos

Within the meeting chamber of the Council of Wizards, the daily business was drawing to a close. Mekla, the *real* Mekla, squirmed in his seat on the dais and glanced nervously toward Zohara. The Red Wizard was acting his usual self, bullying the Council members and getting his own way, and angry as always with the young wizard holding Korthos's seat. He would likely be even angrier, soon!

Mekla had been receiving impressions from his simulacrum of Morlac's progress within the temple—an ofttimes disconcerting fact since he was attempting to maintain a calm facade during the course of Council business. But that magical source of news had ended with a painful twinge when the simulacrum was blasted apart by Zohara's guardian chamber spell. No more impressions followed, and Mekla could only assume that the worst had happened to the others as well. Perhaps if he had only gone with them himself . . . perhaps if he had only studied harder and learned more from his master. . . .

The young wizard looked across the meeting chamber to the spot on the memorial wall where a long marble panel bore Korthos's name. Behind it, his master's body lay in a narrow crypt.

"I have failed you, wise teacher," Mekla said softly to himself. Then as he saw a Gray Guard approach the dais and pass a folded note to Zohara, he added nervously, "And soon I may join you . . . !"

He watched as the Red Wizard read the note with frowning interest. He cringed as Zohara looked up from that note and directed his sharp-eyed and malevolent gaze toward him. Mekla shrank back, trying to make himself as small as possible, seriously considering bolting from the chamber and running for his life, and yet knowing it would be useless. He would stand no chance against Zohara and the power of the Gray Guards.

The Red Wizard slammed his fist upon the dais top, interrupting the current speaker and making Mekla flinch severely. "Enough of this!" he said in a loud and arrogant tone, regal-looking as he grasped the tall staff that stood beside him. "Let us end this meeting at once, so that we may attend to our own private matters." He emphasized the last words, and Mekla felt their full weight fall upon his own slender shoulders.

A puzzled silence hung over the chamber as the other wizards exchanged looks. Then suddenly another voice cut through the silence with power and authority.

"Wait—! There is yet one more matter to be brought before the Council."

Zohara's eyes flashed anger. "Who speaks thusly and dares incur my wrath—?" He quickly searched the crowd for the source of the voice, and his eyes settled upon three figures, newly arrived, who stood by the memorial wall wearing hooded cloaks. "You there—is one of you so bold as to speak against my wishes?"

Morlac stepped forward slightly. "None of us spoke. We only come to return a stolen object to its rightful owner."

"It was *I* who spoke!" the voice boomed out again.

Everyone was looking about quickly now. Then with explosive suddenness and a crack like nearby thunder, a portion of the memorial wall shattered open. There was a blinding flash and swirls of blue smoke, then an angry figure garbed in blue wizards' robes stalked forth.

The wizard, Korthos, proud and full of energy despite his years, accepted the dreamstone from Morlac's hands and strode to the center of the chamber to address the Council. His eyes never wavered from the evil gaze of Zohara.

"Yes, my fellow wizards," said he, "I, Korthos, do still live. But no thanks to Zohara, this treacherous bully whom you allow to lead you. For he imprisoned my soul and left my body to be buried away as dead.''

A surprised murmur ran through the assembled wizards and the crowd as well. Those seated nearest Zohara began to draw away, isolating him further. Mekla scurried forward to stand by his master's side and hold the dreamstone for him.

"And that is not all," Korthos continued. "He stole from me this magical object, to further his own dark goals. He has violated the Council's laws . . . the Council's trust. I hereby charge him with the worst of crimes against Kamuria and the Council.''

Zohara's eyes flashed and his narrow features twisted into an ugly expression. The anger within him seemed to boil over, and the ruby gem atop his magic staff suddenly glowed. He thrust a hand forward and a bolt of light shot directly at Korthos.

A gasp came from the crowd as the beam scorched through the air, brightening the chamber. But Korthos merely gave a quick wave of his hand and the bolt of light halted before reaching him, splashing into a spray of sparks that rained down upon the flooring stones.

"Further proof of his treachery!" exclaimed Korthos. "And a new crime as well. Zohara and his guards have shown us how Kamuria deals with criminals. 'Tis a just punishment for thieves, no matter who they are!''

Korthos raised his arms high into the air so that both sleeves of his robe fell back. He slowly closed his fingers into tight fists.

On the dais, Zohara attempted to rise to his feet, but he suddenly seemed to lack the energy. Then with a look of horror that in no way diminished his arrogant scowl, he saw that the top end of his own staff was bending . . . bending . . . curving down toward him unrelentingly. In another instant, the ruby stone capping his staff touched his head. He started to give a low, desperate moan, then ceased as a gray, dull color washed down over him from head to toes.

Zohara, the Red Wizard, had turned to stone. Such was the punishment for thieves in Kamuria.

Astonished cries within the meeting chamber soon changed

to cheers and laughter. For there was no great love in anyone's heart for the red-robed tyrant.

Korthos beamed proudly, then turned to Morlac, Glendauna, and Broct. With a wicked chuckle he said, "I can put on a pretty good show, myself, when I have a mind to. . . ."

It was morning of the next day when Morlac and his friends gathered once more in the odd two-story building that bore the sign, "The Wizard, Korthos, Master Adept." The title had new meaning now.

"You did well, Mekla," Korthos said as they stood in the magician's private chamber, "your mistakes notwithstanding. I am proud of you."

The young would-be wizard smiled obsequiously at his master's grudging praise as he brought in refreshments for them all. "Thank you, most wise teacher."

"Now then," Korthos said to Morlac and the others, "Mekla has told me of his vow to help you in return for your assistance. Since you did all that he asked, and more, I can do no less than honor his pledge."

Korthos now turned to his table and took up a rolled piece of paper tied with a ribbon. He handed it to Morlac. "I have made inquiries about the wizard you seek, and have learned that Sordros is no longer in Kamuria. He has left some weeks ago and is journeying to K'Dral, a city far south of us in the Phaedrocian Empire. That map in your hands may help you."

"Thank you," Morlac told him sincerely. He was disappointed to learn that the Green Magician was still so far out of reach, but was glad to know where to continue his search.

"Also," Korthos continued, "I shall arrange for supplies for the three of you, as well as fine garments and fittings, so that you may journey in style. And this—" he added, removing a ring from his own wizened hand and giving it to Morlac "—this you may have as well. It bears the emblem of Kamuria, and my own ensign as well. The South Kingdom is well respected in the Phaedrocian Empire, and perhaps the ring may help you."

"My thanks again," Morlac told him.

"Aye," said Broct. "It be a pleasure to meet a kindly wizard. We have not always been so fortunate."

Korthos smiled. "Well, remember that you have friends here in Kamuria. We wish you well on your journey, and hope the fates will be kind to you. But for the moment, let us enjoy a small celebration here. Then I shall show you the best taverns in Kamuria!"

"Aye!" agreed Broct jovially. "Here be truly a wizard after my own heart . . . !"

THE END—BOOK TWO

BOOK THREE

Hall of the Golden Kings

BOOK THREE: HALL OF THE GOLDEN KINGS

CONTENTS

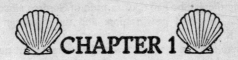# CHAPTER 1

The Trail of Sordros

K'Dral. . . .

The very name invoked images of exotic beauty and sultry splendor. An old city, near tropical in clime, sun-washed and breezy, it was a place for hedonists and lovers and decadent aristocrats . . . a port city on the southernmost coast of a peninsula jutting out into the Midnordian Sea . . . a sparkling and gaudy gem in the crown of the Phaedrocian Empire. The mere sound of its name brought a smile to the lips of he who heard it as well as he who spoke it.

K'Dral. . . .

Morlac stood with his arm around Glendauna's slender shoulders, his eyes feasting on this colorful town. Above them, palm trees swayed gently in the breeze. All about them fluttered the boldly striped awnings of shops and taverns, their vivid hues seemingly in competition with the flowers and trees, the sea and sky. Morlac and his friends had traveled south with a trade caravan and the trip had been an adventure in itself, but at last they were here.

Broct smiled as he drank in the utter sensuousness of K'Dral. "Now *this* be a city to my liking!"

Morlac smiled also, but there was a wary edge to his expression. "Like the sea anemone, it may have its dangers as well as its beauties. And it will be more to my liking when we find Sordros."

Glendauna tensed within the casual arc of Morlac's arm. "It is not yet too late to give up this dangerous search. Not too late to forget Sordros, and to just live our own lives."

Morlac gazed into her sky-blue eyes and saw old fears clouding them. She had spoken little of Sordros since leaving Kamuria, but had grown more and more solemn as they neared K'Dral.

"There are few requests I would not grant you, my lady," Morlac told her with great tenderness. "But like it or not, Sordros's fate and mine are still linked, in ways even I do not fully understand. Unless I confront the wizard once more, I may never know what my future holds for me, or even if I *have* a future."

"I understand that," she said uneasily, uncomfortable with her own thoughts and concerns. "And yet. . . ."

"Come—" said Morlac, steering them forward "—let us find a stable for our horses. We may look for Sordros in the morning. For now, we shall savor K'Dral's delights and rest from our travels. . . ."

Morning came with the gentle caress of a breeze warmed by the Midnordian Sea. At the Seven Coins Inn, Morlac, Glendauna, and Broct breakfasted on melons and fruit and fish, with strong Phaedrocian teas to wash the sleep from their minds. They gathered outside soon afterward, dressed in the fine cloaks and garments the wizard Korthos had given them.

"If we do find Sordros," said Broct as he did a half-turn to observe his new clothing, "he will not know us!"

"He will know us," Morlac said seriously. From a pocket in his jerkin he produced a folded scrap of paper. Opening it, he glanced at the words Korthos had scrawled there, even though he had long ago burned them into his memory. "The shop we seek is called 'The Dragon and the Gryphon.' It should not be far from here."

"You truly think they will help us?" Broct gave a bemused frown. "Remember the wizards' council in Kamuria."

"Korthos said it is our best chance. We can but try."

They set out down the street, threading their way through the crowd. K'Dral was a teeming city, but the hustle and bustle of activity seemed subdued, almost wantonly lazy. For in a place so pleasantly situated and so full of pleasurable pursuits there seemed no reason to rush things.

It was a rich and playful town, filled with more nobles than Morlac had seen before. Artists and musicians and mimes dotted the street corners, plying their respective trades for the coins of passersby. Even the trollops and beggars seemed a better, more prosperous class than those in most cities.

The aromas of exotic foods mingled with those of perfumes and spices, woolen carpets, oiled woods, and wicker baskets. There were many travelers here—merchants and sailors and spoiled nobles escaping the nearby Phaedrocian capital for recreation. And K'Dral was well-prepared to serve their every need. It was said that anything and everything could be had here if one knew where to look and could meet the price.

" 'Tis still a mystery," Glendauna said as they walked through the early-morning splendor of this tarnished paradise. "Why should Sordros journey here? Kamuria seems better suited to a wizard's needs."

"And better suited to his own protection," added Morlac. "But if he still feared pursuit he may have chosen to move on even so."

Broct smiled and winked at a group of young women who were passing by, and was rewarded with flirtatious smiles and giggles. "Perhaps Sordros came here to fulfill other needs. Or perhaps—"

His words ended in a grunt of expelled breath that was due as much to surprise as to the sudden impact of the person who collided with him. Looking around quickly, he was startled to see a young woman gazing up at him from the vicinity of his chest. She had apparently darted out of the shop entrance to his immediate right and turned directly into his path.

Her hair was a mass of scarlet tresses, framing a face finely sculpted and feminine. Her dark eyes mirrored his own startled look, and her full ruby lips were parted as if her breath had been knocked out of her.

"Many pardons, my fine large sir!" she said in a sweet and flustered tone. "My way I was not watching. So clumsy am I! Many pardons, many pardons. . . ."

Broct felt touched by the warmth of her apology and was taken with her simple beauty. But even as her sweet words were flying, the yellow-eyed giant also felt touched and taken in quite another way. For as she lingered there pressed against him Broct felt her hand dart beneath his upper cloak, swiftly probing with both delicacy and confident skill. Her touch was so light and sure that he might not have noticed had not she brushed against one of his hidden arms as she searched.

A puzzled frown flashed across her face at that unexpected contact, for Broct's two visible arms hung down at his sides. But in the next instant Broct felt the weight of his coin purse vanish and the young woman's hand hastily withdraw.

"Many pardons," she repeated as she stepped back away from him, brushing his cloak front as if she had somehow imparted dust to it. "Forgive me. I will trouble you no more—"

She started to turn and walk briskly away, but in a flash Broct had grabbed her arm and spun her back toward him. Both his visible hands gripped her shoulders in a firm, unbreakable hold.

"Wait!" said Broct, showing a hard smile. "Fair lady, it is *I* who apologize for my clumsiness. I hope I have not hurt you."

"Why, no! No, no. I am fine." She struggled to maintain her facade of innocence even as she struggled within his grasp. "You are too kind, sir."

"Not at all," Broct assured her, noticing that neither of her lovely hands now held his missing coin purse. "It is you who are too kind. Such kindness and loveliness must not go unrewarded."

With that, Broct pulled her to him with surprising swiftness. Locked in his iron embrace, she could say no more as he silenced her with a kiss. Broct now set his hidden hands to work searching the bodice of her Phaedrocian gown. He was amused to see her eyes widen in astonishment, then roll left and right to be sure his arms were still around her. In a moment he found his coin purse, tucked away for safekeeping between her firm, warm breasts, and returned it to his own garments.

"Forgive my boldness," Broct said as he released the breathless and beautiful thief. "I was overwhelmed by your charm." As she staggered back away from him, Broct produced a single coin from beneath his cloak and flipped it to her. "Here—keep this as a token of my deep feelings for you. Until we meet again. . . ."

The young woman caught the coin with unladylike skill, looked quickly at it, then at the yellow-eyed giant with eyes blazing. Straightening her garments, she pushed past Glendauna and strode quickly away, melting into the crowd.

"Now what was that all about?" Morlac asked with a curious frown.

"A pickpocket of less than perfect skills," said Broct. "But a pretty wench she be!"

Morlac smiled wryly. "And an angry one, too. You surprise me, Broct. You seldom leave women with anything less than a smile on their faces."

Glendauna's lovely lips twisted into a bemused smirk as she slapped something into Broct's large hand. "Well, she'll be angrier still soon enough. For she left us with less than she realized."

Broct stared at the small object in his palm. He immediately recognized it as his own ebony-stoned magic ring.

Glendauna said, "I took it from her as she passed me. 'Twas not difficult." She saw Morlac arch an eyebrow at her. "The Durkesh are not thieves," she told him with a shrug. "But we know thieves' ways."

"Let's be on with our search." Broct growled sourly.

Morlac gave a hearty laugh, joined by Glendauna's own musical chuckle, and the three were on their way once more. . . .

It was a part of town cluttered with dark and murky shops, a place where many storefronts were shuttered against the bright clear light of the region. One such shop stood before Morlac and his friends. The sign that hung above its door proclaimed its name in faded paint:

The Dragon and the Gryphon.

After a moment's pause, Morlac stepped inside. Reluctantly. Glendauna and Broct followed.

The strange shop was crowded with oddly shaped kettles and bottles, vials of bright liquids and foul-smelling powders, and unspeakable things in jars. There were only two customers inside. One was a large and brawny fellow who had the look of a bodyguard doing his master's shopping. The other was a woman who stood with her back to them, a lightweight cloak of sea-green fabric flowing from her slender shoulders. Jet-black hair cascaded in ringlets past those shoulders, and Morlac felt a shudder of recognition. *Kadrana . . . ?* Could it be?

Whether it was his intense gaze or the sound of their entering the shop that alerted her, the woman suddenly turned and studied them. The illusion vanished. Though from behind she had resembled Sordros's wicked "daughter," she was revealed to be an old crone whose lustrous hair belied her age. Her withered face was expressionless as she took in each of the three travelers in turn, and she immediately resumed her business.

Once the two had gone, Morlac approached the shop's proprietor, a Phaedrocian man of indeterminate age, who if he was not one of the Enlightened at least had the look of one long used to dealing with them. Morlac walked boldly to the counter and placed his hands flat upon it so that the ring Korthos gave him could be plainly seen.

"We have journeyed long from Kamuria," Morlac told the man. "We seek the wizard Sordros. I am told you may know where to find him."

The man behind the counter missed not a detail of the wizard's ring he wore, nor of their fine clothing. "A humble shopkeep am I," he said warily. "Many customers have I whose names are not known to me."

"This one would be a visitor to your land," Morlac said with a calm he did not feel. "A green magician, a gaunt man, bald save for a single tuft of black hair bound with gold."

"I may have seen one such as he. But I do not discuss my customers' business with strangers. . . ."

"Then think of us not as strangers," Morlac told him, lifting one hand from the counter to reveal a large gold coin. "Rather think of us as new customers."

It was a simple sleight-of-hand trick rather than true magic, but the shopkeep was nonetheless impressed by the value of the coin. He picked it up and tested its hardness in his hand, then smiled.

Glancing quickly about, the man said, "There was a wizard such as you describe. Some weeks back came he here, also from Kamuria.''

Morlac nodded. "Go on—"

"Summoned he was by high officials here, or so said he. Seems there was business for him in Neuphendurem.''

Broct frowned. "Neuphendurem?''

"Our colony, south of us across the Midnordian Sea. A rich land it is, but troubled too. The governor, Cauldos, has already sought help from Phaedrocia's generals, and known it is that wizards also does he need. There is talk of war.''

"Is there not always," Morlac said grimly. He boiled within at the news of Sordros's continued travels, but drew himself up and leaned across the counter menacingly.

"The coin is yours," he told the shopkeep. "But if the information it has bought is false—"

"True it is," the man swore. "In this trade, long ago did I learn not to lie or cheat, lest spells be cast my way."

Morlac nodded, for there was a certain logic in what the man said. "All right, then. We have the merchandise we needed.''

"Thank you for your business," said the shopkeep as they headed for the doorway. "You will see it was money wisely spent. . . .''

Outside in the street, well out of earshot of the proprietor, Broct asked, "Do you think it be the truth?''

"I fear it is." Morlac stood silently a moment, his devil-brows knit in anger. He slammed his right fist into his left palm, then sighed and let his hands drop. "Once more, Sordros has eluded us. We could journey on forever, and always be just out of reach.''

Turning to Glendauna, he said softly, "I cannot ask you to continue. 'Tis not fair to you or Broct. If you wish, I will stay with you here, or take you wherever your heart desires.''

She looked up at him, her mouth starting to open in response. But the words would not come out. She tilted her head and moisture welled up within her vivid blue eyes. Finally, she spoke.

"Oh, Morlac, as much as I have spoken against this quest for my own selfish reasons, I cannot ask you to give it up. You would never be happy, and I could not bear to be the cause of that. If you wish to go on, I shall be at your side. Always. Even if we must traverse all the world to find the green magician.''

"Aye!'' said Broct. "The same goes for me as well, my sea-brother!''

Morlac threw his arms about both their shoulders. "No truer friends could any man want. But that makes me all the more reluctant to risk your fates on my own foolhardiness.''

"We've done all right so far, have we not?'' Broct gave a lusty grin. "At the very least, we're becoming well-traveled.''

"Aye!'' said Glendauna with a wry smile and a toss of her head, mimicking Broct's own hearty manner. "The Durkesh are a vagabond race, it be true!''

Morlac gave a sad smile, knowing their enthusiasm was mostly for his benefit. But he loved them all the more for it.

"All right, then, my friends,'' said he. "Let us find a way to Neuphendurem. . . .''

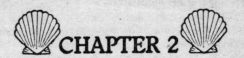

CHAPTER 2

Passage to Peril

"Surely there must be one ship on which we may buy passage," Morlac insisted.

The port master shook his head irritably. "This day there is not. Two there were yesterday that sailed for Neuphendurem, carrying supplies and men. Ten there were last week. But today? No—and again I say no! Not today. Not tomorrow, nor any day this week or next."

"I swear," Morlac said to himself, "the fates conspire against us."

Broct said, only half-seriously, "I wonder if it be too late to buy back our horses?"

Glendauna shushed him, seeing full well how distressed Morlac was at this further bad news.

"Must it be Neuphendurem?" asked the port master. "Ships have I sailing to half the Phaedrocian Empire and to many northern kingdoms. Will none of them do?"

"There is nowhere else I need to go," Morlac told him. "My business lies there and there alone."

"Forgive me for intruding—" The voice came from behind them, and upon turning abruptly to see its source, Morlac and the others saw two men who had apparently approached while they were speaking with the port master.

The first of the two men was tall and slender, dressed in fine silks and velvets of black and gray, with yellow and spun-gold trim. His angular features were handsome in a clean-scrubbed, aristocratic way, and his manner had the kind of polite arrogance that can be either charming or infuriating.

Clearly, he was a noble of the Phaedrocian Empire. And just as clearly, it was he who spoke.

The port master came sharply alert. "A thousand pardons, Baron. I did not see you. How may I serve Your Eminence?"

The first man handed a small coin sack to him. "There is enough there to cover all fees, and something extra for your troubles, my friend. I came to tell you that we are ready to sail."

"Very good, sir. Many thanks, sir. I shall hold the other ships till you are clear."

"Excellent." He turned to take in Morlac, Broct, and Glendauna, giving them a polite nod as he noticed their fine garments. "Forgive me, but I could not help overhearing . . . you seek passage to Neuphendurem?"

Morlac hesitated a moment before answering. "Yes, that is true. But it seems there is none."

"No commercial vessels, perhaps," said the first man. "But I myself am sailing in that direction. My ship is that one over there. There is much room aboard her, and if you would accept my hospitality I would be pleased to have you join me."

Morlac looked to see the vessel. Anchored in the harbor was a sizable galley with two lateen sails and twenty oars visible on the side that faced them.

"A most impressive ship, and a most generous offer," Morlac replied. He glanced to Glendauna and Broct, seeking their reaction to the unexpected proposal.

"Indeed," said Broct with an appreciative smile, "we could not ask for better transport."

Glendauna hesitated, an uncertain expression upon her lovely features as she sized up the ship and the Baron and the second man as well. A silent man he was, muscular and grim, who looked to be a bodyguard or servant. At last she said, "I . . . I suppose it would be rude of us to turn down this noble gentleman's kind offer. He has given us a way to reach Neuphendurem much sooner."

Morlac weighed the alternatives. Surely he would have to be a fool to pass up such an opportunity. "Very well, sir. We gratefully accept your offer. Is there . . . some way we may repay your kindness?"

The man gave a shrugging gesture. "Your company is repayment enough. Sea voyages are so tedious without others along to share them. Do you need time to gather your belongings?"

Morlac shook his head. "No, we are carrying all that we need to take with us."

"Come, then—let us board at once, for I must leave as soon as possible."

The five took leave of the port master and walked around to an area of the dock where waited a small vessel and two dockmen to row it. In a matter of a few minutes they reached the galley and climbed the ladder to its deck.

The ship looked even larger and more luxurious at close range than it had from the dock. The lower deck, from which the oars protruded, was enclosed. The upper deck had both forecastle and sterncastle, and several small deckhouses amidships between the masts. In its design and its finishing, one could hardly ask for a more seaworthy craft.

"I am Baron Kumil," their host introduced himself. "I live in Kadmudar, a nearby coastal town close to the Empire's western border. Have you journeyed far to K'Dral?"

"Yes," Morlac told him. "Lately from Kamuria, and from Goltos and Shola before that. I am called Morlac. These are my friends, Broct and Glendauna."

"A pleasure." The Baron directed them to the doorway of the ship's sterncastle. "Come, let us make ourselves comfortable while my crew gets under way."

Once inside, Baron Kumil showed them small but cozy cabins, then led them to a wide chamber at the ship's stern where several tables were being readied for a meal by another servant. He gave the servant orders to prepare servings for his guests as well. As the galley's sails were raised, the vessel began to leave the harbor. Through windows at the rear, the glories of K'Dral could be seen once more as its sultry splendor was left behind.

"I am not surprised you came from Kamuria," the Baron said. "For you see, I noticed the emblem of that renowned city upon your ring."

Morlac nodded. "A gift from a friend there."

"A well-placed friend, no doubt. And I see a certain proud

resolve in you two fine gentlemen. Have you done battle for the honor of some distant land?''

"Yes," Morlac replied cautiously. "In Shola."

"Ah, yes, I thought so. Such strong young bodies. Tell me, are you used to the sea?''

"Aye," said Broct with an impish smile. "You could even say we know it as well as the fish themselves.''

"Excellent," replied the Baron. "I do not expect a rough trip, but it is good to know my guests will not be discomforted by the waves.''

"No," said Morlac, gazing out one of the stern windows. "After our long overland trip it is good to be near the sea once more.''

Baron Kumil looked up as his servant appeared again. "Ah, good—the food is ready. Let us enjoy a pleasant meal and some conversation. We have nearly a two-day journey before us, with naught to do but relax. . . .''

"I have never been to Kadmudar," Glendauna was saying after their luncheon repast. "Will you tell us about it?''

The Baron brightened at the mention of his homeland. "Yes, of course. I would be pleased to. But in return you must tell me something of your home." He studied the young woman for a long moment, with a look of smiling appraisal. "I'll wager there is nobility in your own background. I have an eye for such things. Tell me, am I right? Yes—?''

Glendauna blushed a bit and gave an uneasy smile. "Well, yes . . . I . . . my father *was* a marquis in Goltos.''

"So I was right. Excellent! Very well, then. I shall tell you about Kadmudar, and you shall tell me about Goltos.''

They were sitting in comfortable seats away from the table, and Broct's attention drifted from the conversation. On the near horizon was a large island, mountainous and misty, which they were passing as they continued their southeasterly course. He recalled seeing it indicated on a map of the Phaedrocian Empire, but could not remember its name. He wondered what mysteries might be hidden within those mountains and those mists.

Out of the corner of his eye Broct now saw something move, something in the direction of the serving table. Cautiously turning his head, he was startled to see a hand reaching up from behind the table. A small hand, keeping low, probing for food upon the table's surface. The long tablecloth hid from view whoever, or whatever, was beneath it.

Moving with great stealth, Broct rose from his seat and silently stepped to the table. The conversation behind him continued, so he knew the others had not seen the hand and likely assumed nothing more than that he was still hungry.

He reached the table and hesitated a second, then as the hand closed around a choice fruit and started to withdraw, his own large hand darted with snakelike swiftness and grabbed that disembodied hand by the wrist.

"Quite a strange morsel we have here," Broct said loudly, attracting the others' attention. "Tell me, Baron—do all the fruits and vegetables in Kadmudar grow with stems so oddly shaped?"

There was a muffled whine of protest that became louder as Broct proceeded to haul the hand's owner out from beneath the table and into view. The Baron and the others were already on their feet and approaching.

"If this belongs to you, Baron," Broct told him, "then I apologize for the rough handling."

Baron Kumil stared with narrowing eyes at the young woman who struggled to be free of Broct's iron grip. An angry young woman, fair of face and form, with raven-dark hair hanging in curls past her shoulders. . . .

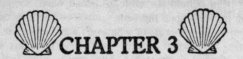

CHAPTER 3

The Baron's Secret

"No," said Baron Kumil in a hard, crisp tone. "She most definitely does *not* belong to me, in any sense of the word."

"Then a stowaway she must be." Broct studied the face and figure of the young woman he held. "And one with a familiar look about her. With one exception—"

The yellow-eyed giant reached up and tugged at her curly black hair. It came away in his hand, revealing a luxurious growth of red curls beneath.

"I thought as much." Broct gave a hard smile as she reacted, first as she lost her wig and next as she recognized him.

Surprise and anger flared upon her pretty face. "It is you again? What living curse are you that haunts me thus?" Her eyes next darted to his concealing cloak. "And just how many of you are in there, anyway—?"

The Baron faced Broct with a puzzled look. "You know this woman?"

"A less than perfect stranger she be, Your Eminence. Not more than three hours ago this sticky-fingered wench attempted to steal my coin purse and my ring."

"I see," said the Baron. "And so now she has stolen aboard my ship, for what purpose I can easily guess." He stepped closer and snatched a velvet pouch from her belt. Emptying its contents into his hand, he said, "The jewels from my cabin are here. We must have sailed before she had a chance to escape with them."

At that moment, the Baron's bodyguard, who had never

been farther than the doorway, approached the girl. "What shall I do with this thief, Your Eminence?"

"Do? Yes, Tyno, I wonder." Baron Kumil considered. "We cannot turn back, else we could hand her over to the authorities in K'Dral."

The bodyguard's expression had a cruel edge to it. "Perhaps we should test her swimming, sir."

"She be a strong lass, despite her looks," said Broct. "She might just make it to that island."

The pretty thief flashed a dangerous glance at Broct for his comment, then looked in feigned alarm at the waiting sea, and to those who considered her fate. "Oh, no . . . no, kind sirs! I would surely drown!"

"No," Baron Kumil said at last. "We shall not cast her into the sea. Despite her protests I suspect that would be entirely too much to her liking. Tyno—take her on deck and shackle her to the mast. I shall let the governor of Neuphendurem decide her punishment."

"Very well, sir," replied the bodyguard, with what seemed to Morlac like concealed disappointment. He took charge of the girl and roughly escorted her from the cabin.

"My apologies," Baron Kumil said to Morlac and the others once Tyno and the girl were gone. "It seems my crew have been lax on security. I shall have words with them." He smiled with casual charm. "Ah, well . . . at least we cannot say it has been a dull voyage thus far. Let us continue our pleasant chat for awhile, then I have a few matters I must attend to. Your cabins are ready, should you wish to use them, and you may go on deck if you wish. The weather seems quite mild."

"Our thanks, again," Morlac told him. "Your kindness and hospitality speak well of Kadmudar and the Phaedrocian Empire."

"It is my pleasure." Baron Kumil gave a slight nodding bow of his head. "You are my guests, after all. I only ask that you do not visit the lower deck of my galley. The oarsmen are a crude and vulgar lot. They cannot help it, being what they are. But I do not wish you to be exposed to them. . . ."

*   *   *

"I think I shall go mad!" Glendauna declared. She was snuggled against Morlac in their small cabin's bunk, still awake in the darkness even though it was well past midnight. Her slender shoulders twitched involuntarily with each rhythmic drumbeat.

"Try to ignore it," Morlac said in a soothing whisper. "Forget the sound, and try to sleep."

"How can I? How can *you?* It was bad enough before, during the day. Now it is insufferable."

"Perhaps if I got you some wine—"

"There is not enough on this ship nor all of K'Dral for that!"

It had begun in early afternoon, when the wind had strangely stilled and their magnificent vessel sat becalmed upon the Midnordian Sea. Baron Kumil ordered the sails lowered and sent word down for the oarsmen to begin rowing. Twenty oars on each side, forty in all, swung into position and began to dip into the gentle swells, straining against the water's plaint surface, propelling the vessel on. The oarsmen had to work in unison, lest their oars become tangled, and so they timed their movements to the slow, steady beat of a large drum somewhere on the deck below. And so the oars kept moving, rhythmically digging into the water, hour after hour, all afternoon and on into the night. Always to the slow, sepulchral, maddeningly steady drumbeat. *Tawmmmmm, tawmmmmm, tawmmmmm, tawmmmmm, tawmmmmm.* . . .

"How can they keep rowing?" Glendauna murmured against Morlac's shoulder. "Do they never rest?"

Morlac did not reply, for it was a question he had put to himself some time earlier and he still had no answer. He frowned, deep in thought. After a very long moment, he suddenly stirred and rose from the bunk.

Glendauna sat up, leaning forward with her hands on the polished wooden edge. "What are you doing—?"

"I am going to investigate," he told her as he quickly dressed. "Something is amiss here."

"You're not going below?"

"Below is where the mystery lies."

"But the Baron asked us not to. We should not disobey his wishes. He has been the perfect host—"

"Perhaps too perfect," said Morlac softly.

Glendauna fairly leaped from the bunk and grabbed her own garments. "Well, if you are going, then so am I!" She was silent a moment, dressing swiftly, then she looked up as she tugged on her boots. "You are not going to try to stop me?"

Morlac smiled and cradled her chin in the palm of his hand. "Stop *you?* I might as well try to hold back the sea. . . ."

Moments later, the two were at the door to Broct's cabin. Morlac gave two light, quick raps, paused, then rapped again. In an instant the door was open.

"I gather," whispered Broct, "that the serenade be unpleasant for you as well?"

The yellow-eyed giant slipped from his cabin and quietly closed the door behind him, joining his friends in the passageway. The door to Baron Kumil's large cabin was closed, and there was no sign of his bodyguard or any other servants.

The three left the sterncastle and emerged in the open. Moonlight painted the lowered sails and spray-moistened deck a pale blue. The masts and rigging were silhouettes against the starry sky. There was a man on watch, but his back was to them as he stood by the rail and stared out to sea. They slipped by him on the opposite side and made for the galley's forecastle, walking carefully upon the gently heaving deck.

As they passed the forward mast they saw a female figure slumped against it, her arms shackled behind her around the varnished wooden pole. The pretty thief raised her head with a glowering look as they moved past, but said nothing.

Morlac paused as they reached the forecastle and the stairs leading down to the lower deck. Between drumbeats he whispered, "Be careful . . . there may be guards."

The deeply throbbing boom of the drum grew in volume as they descended, step by step. The stairs were mostly in darkness, but as they reached the lower deck, lamplight cast its yellow glow upon the vessel's interior.

Morlac, Glendauna, and Broct crowded together in the entranceway, cautiously peering down the length of the galley. They frowned at the sight before them, and at first their minds refused to accept the truth of what their eyes told them. Then realization sank in, chilling them to their marrow.

Two men manned each oar, making eighty in all, sitting on rough wooden benches fastened to the deck in rows down both sides of the ship. Silent they were, with glazed eyes and cold, expressionless faces. Their arms moved in steady sweeping circles, all precisely in time to each stroke of the drum. There were men tall and short, fat and thin, young and old; warrior and merchant and beggar alike. They were similar in only one respect.

None of them were alive.

For these were not sailors nor even common slaves manning the oars. They were, each and every one, zombies. The reanimated dead, tirelessly rowing; ghastly slaves in the thrall of sorcery. Even the man at the drum had the same gray look, the same dead eyes, of a body stolen from its grave. And the same acrid smell.

"May the gods help us," Morlac uttered, his voice a dry whisper, full of horror. "The Baron is no mere noble on a pleasure cruise. He is yet another wizard, off to join the gathering armies at Neuphendurem . . . !"

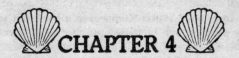 **CHAPTER 4**

Captives of Cauldos

"Yet another wizard?" said the Baron's aristocratic voice, directly behind them. "You insult me with such a commonplace description . . ."

Morlac straightened at the sound, and immediately found a dirk at his back. As he cautiously turned his head, he found the bodyguard, Tyno, at the corner of his vision, and just beyond him, the Baron. Another man stood behind Broct, also with a blade in hand.

" . . . and I assure you, my friends," continued Baron Kumil, "there is nothing commonplace about me. When my homeland of Kadmudar was encompassed by the spreading Phaedrocian Empire, it was no accident that I retained my barony." He paused a moment, then said archly, "Did I not ask you to avoid this deck?"

"We could not sleep for the drumming," Morlac said, his voice full of controlled anger. "How could you expect us not to be curious about oarsmen who never stop?"

"I should not have, I suppose. Still, I had hoped to delay their confrontation until we docked. It would have been so much more pleasant that way. Ah, well. I shall just have to forgo the pleasures of polite conversation for the remainder of the trip."

Morlac felt Shark tingling near his hand and briefly considered lunging away from Tyno's dirk long enough to draw the magicked blade. But in these close quarters, with Glendauna's life also at stake, he did not want to risk the consequences.

325

"So what now, Baron? Do you mean to add us to your galley slaves?"

"Oh my, no." Baron Kumil gave a hard thin smile. "I already have enough of those, and can obtain more easily. Oh, no, my friends. That is not the fate that awaits you. I have far better plans for two such fine warriors . . . and such a beautiful young noblewoman. . . ."

It was late afternoon of the following day when the galley at last reached the coast. Morlac, Glendauna, and Broct had each been locked into a separate cabin, without their weapons, and with nowhere to escape to should they somehow gain their freedom. The remaining hours of their voyage dragged by with excruciating slowness, and only in the last few did the wind spring up enough for the oarsmen to stop and the horrid drumming to end. And yet, arriving at Neuphendurem brought no sense of release, for their fates were still uncertain.

Even at this late hour of the day, the sun bore down with stark intensity as the three were brought out on deck for their first glimpse of Neuphendurem. The tropic clime was even more humid than K'Dral had been, and the air bore the scents of jungle foliage and the sound of strange birds.

"Such a barbaric land," Baron Kumil observed as his galley drew into port. " 'Twill take a century of work to make anything of it."

Morlac gazed across at Neuphendurem, and was struck by its strangeness. The Phaedrocian colony was a sprawling tangle of structures, a few of which were permanent but most of which were temporary and improvised. There was no real sense of order or design to any of it, and tents mingled with rough wooden buildings and odd stone structures that seemed nothing more than the ruins of some older civilization. A few structures combined all these disparate elements, and were a hodgepodge of stone walls, wooden walls, and tenting.

The crowd of people milling through the settlement had much the same look, rough and chaotic, and there was a disproportionately high number of soldiers and mercenaries among them. On the whole, the place had none of the sensual charm of K'Dral.

Morlac, Glendauna, and Broct were chained together by

shackles, which while not magical in nature were nevertheless effective. As the galley was nudged into place along the dock and the lines tied up, the Baron's men positioned the gangplank for them to disembark. The pretty thief who had spent most of the trip chained to the mast also was brought to the side of the vessel to join the others.

"The ship is secured, Your Eminence," Tyno said at last.

"Excellent," Baron Kumil replied, making minor adjustments to his expensive garments. "Let us be on our way. The governor awaits!"

As they were marched along the dirt pathways of Neuphendurem they passed enormous stacks of crates and crowded livestock pens. Supplies, no doubt, for the troops being readied for battle. But battle against whom?

Broct unobtrusively leaned toward Morlac as they walked, whispering, "Have you any ideas on how we might escape?"

"Not yet," Morlac told him with steely calm. "Let us see what happens. This may be a way of reaching Sordros."

"Half the trick is reaching him alive," muttered Glendauna. "The other half 'twill be staying that way."

They now approached a very large structure, and apparently an important one, judging from the number of guards posted outside. A semicircle of stone rose high into the air and was capped with a great canopy of striped cloth that sloped down to complete the circle. The forward edges were held aloft by spearlike shafts of wood, so that airflow could cool the interior.

Baron Kumil spoke with the guards at one edge of the tent, and after a moment they stood aside for the Baron and his party to enter. Inside the spacious area, the ground was covered with tiles of hard gray stone, weatherworn and pitted but still showing signs of having once been finely fitted flooring.

At the far end of the structure, sitting on a well-cushioned ornamental divan, was a large man wearing fine silken robes and expensive sandals, and enough gold jewelry to more than justify the guards standing on either side of him. Round-faced he was, with intense black eyes and a small thin mouth. He had about him a look of indolence and polished cruelty that was almost catlike.

Behind him on a decorative stand was a massive bronze plaque bearing the Phaedrocian crest with its two-headed bird of prey, clearly his symbol of authority. Attendants fanned him and held bowls of fresh fruit ready. And already a small crowd was gathering around the edges of the circular court; colony officials and hangers-on alerted by news of the galley's arrival.

A guard within escorted the Baron's party across the open court, stopping a short distance from the platform. Cauldos, governor of Neuphendurem, gave a formal smile.

"Baron—how delightful to see you once again. I thank you for responding to my call for aid."

Baron Kumil gave a courteous half-bow that did not surrender any of his own dignity. "Governor, it is my pleasure to serve you and your fine colony in any way that I can."

"It is not just the colony you are serving, but the Empire as well," Cauldos reminded. His eyes flickered with interest at sight of the four captives. "What new diversions have you brought me?"

"A plaguesome thief to face your judgment," replied Kumil with a gesture toward the red-haired wench. "And some guests of my own that may well serve our special needs, in a variety of ways."

"Splendid!" Cauldos drawled with wicked cordiality. "I shall see that all find the proper . . . accommodations."

"For now," said the Baron, "let us keep them here, for I wish to demonstrate something special I have brought you to aid your fight, and they will be helpful."

Cauldos brightened with anticipation. "A demonstration? When may I see it?"

"Now, if you wish. There are only a few minor preparations we need to make. And to perform this demonstration I must ask of you one thing. I need to have the body of a dead soldier."

Cauldos raised an eyebrow in interest as a surprised murmur went through the crowd. "I think that can be arranged, my dear Baron. . . ."

Dusk was rapidly approaching. Lanterns were being lighted beneath the tentlike canopy of Cauldos's colonial "palace," and all was ready for Baron Kumil's demonstration. The army generals had been summoned for the event, as had extra guards.

Morlac stood near the center of the court, at a goodly distance from Cauldos and the rest of the circle of watchers. He had been unshackled and given his sword and shield, but to assure his cooperation a half-dozen archers ringed the area with shafts ready, and Broct and Glendauna were still shackled and under guard at the edge of the circle. He was not certain what Baron Kumil had in mind, but his suspicions were enough to fill him with a sense of horror.

"It seems we are at last ready," said the Baron. "With your kind permission, Governor . . . ?"

"Yes, yes. Let us not delay further," Cauldos said with childlike impatience. He quickly gestured to two of his men beyond the edge of the crowd.

The watchers moved aside without any urging as the two guards came forward into the court. The burden they carried was enough to encourage a wide path. For outstretched on the litter between them was a corpse, stiff and ashen, yet recent enough a kill that it had not yet started to rot. The dead man still wore a soldier's garb, and the solitary wound visible was in the chest, where something had pierced his heart.

Stopping a short distance away from Morlac, the stretcher-bearers lowered their burden to the floor and hastily departed. Morlac stared at the lifeless form, wondering if it was some brave warrior slain in battle or a cowardly deserter executed by his own army. The ghastly thought even crossed his mind that neither was true . . . that this might be an unwilling "volunteer," some poor unfortunate sacrificed for the sake of Kumil's demonstration. But this latter thought he dismissed as unlikely, if only for the reason that Neuphendurem would surely need all available men.

Baron Kumil now approached the corpse. He faced Governor Cauldos and the assembled crowd with something resembling theatrical style. "You are about to witness a miracle . . . a power few of the Enlightened can yet boast. A power that I, Baron Kumil of Kadmudar, have mastered and now offer in the defense of Neuphendurem and the Empire's glorious progress—"

A hush fell over the crowd as the Baron reached inside his black-velvet tunic and produced a vial of amber liquid. Carefully uncapping it, he proceeded to pour a small amount of the fluid into the corpse's mouth, and a like amount into the open wound.

Now the Baron put the vial away and began tracing mystic symbols in the air above the dead man's chest. His brow furrowed with the intensity of his concentration, while softly from his lips came the words of a spell, dark and dangerous. Picking up a sword lying on the litter beside the corpse, he placed it on the floor near the dead man's hand.

"Now watch—" said Baron Kumil, stepping away toward the edge of the circle once more "—watch and you shall see how not even death can defeat the armies of Neuphendurem. . . ."

Morlac watched his retreat and saw the worried gaze of his friends. But his eyes immediately turned toward the corpse once more. Silence had fallen over the crowd, the silence of awestruck anticipation, and yet there was an impression of sound, a faint disturbance in the air, as dark forces rustled about the still figure.

And suddenly that figure was still no more.

Muscles that had been stiff and lifeless now began to twitch. The limbs awkwardly began to move and stretch, as if awakening from slumber. Perhaps worst of all, the eyes slowly opened, glazed and milky, staring with mindless rigidity.

A gasp went through the crowd. Cauldos leaned forward on his divan with eyes agleam.

The corpse's right hand groped to one side, then as it found the weapon its fingers closed about the sword hilt. Rising from the litter like some horrible nightmare vision, the dead man stood. He slowly turned to face Morlac.

"Defend yourself, valiant warrior," Baron Kumil cautioned Morlac. "If you can!"

With that, the reanimated corpse raised its sword and started forward. Morlac quickly grasped Shark's hilt and pulled the blade free. But even his magicked weapon seemed to sense the nature of his opponent, and its bloodlust wavered, uncertain and confused.

Its dead eyes ablaze, the corpse lunged forward, slashing

down at Morlac with surprising speed and strength. Morlac countered the blow with his shield, then deflected a second strike with his sword.

"The thing fights well for a dead man," whispered Broct at the edge of the circle. "Though it be reckless."

"Why should it not be reckless," was Glendauna's grim and worried reply. "For 'tis already dead."

Again the corpse lashed out, stepping to one side this time in an effort to get past Morlac's guard. And again, Morlac countered the blow. But this time he let his own blade flash out in a swift, hungry arc. Shark's tip severed cloth and leather, biting deep through ashen flesh as it sliced the dead man's chest. But no blood emerged and the nightmare warrior seemed oblivious to the damage.

On he pressed, still attacking Morlac with the same cold ferocity. His horid face, gray and drawn, flinched not as he struck or was struck. Never had Morlac faced an enemy such as this.

Morlac felt almost as overwhelmed and helpless as he had when first under Ardo's expert tutelage. And yet he was not fighting badly. Against any normal human adversary, every blow he'd struck thus far would have disabled or killed.

Again the nightmare creature struck, slashing at his legs this time. Morlac's reflexes were quick and he leaped above the blade's maiming sweep. In the same swift motion, before the corpse could fully rise once more, Morlac brought Shark down hard against the creature's shoulder.

The white blade crunched through bones and muscle, biting partway into the rib cage before withdrawing. The corpse shuddered back one step, two steps, three . . . then started forward again, still unfazed by the injury.

Avoiding the dead man's blade was becoming increasingly harder, and though he was able to deflect the blows for the most part, Morlac's arms started to bleed from numerous small cuts. The anger and the fear rose within him, and as he parried yet another thrust he abruptly swung Shark with one mighty grunt of effort.

The flashing white blade sliced through the dead man's sword arm just above the wrist and cut through his neck as well, sending sword and hand and head flying. The body itself dropped to its knees before him, sinking as if to bow.

Panting hard, Morlac breathed a sigh of relief. It was over. It was . . . wasn't it?

The toppled head upon the floor had fallen so that it still faced him, the horrid eyes still upon him. And now, to Morlac's horror. the body began to rise again, tremulously, inexorably.

Someone screamed within the court's circle of watchers and there were many gasps of astonishment. But they faded to stunned silence as the headless corpse now lunged straight for Morlac, imprisoning the white blade by impaling itself upon it, and toppling Morlac under its falling weight. The creature's one remaining hand shot up to Morlac's throat and tightened about it in a savage stranglehold.

Even as the blood began to throb and pound in Morlac's brain, he heard a strident outcry from the circle of watchers. He thought at first it was Glendauna, but he glimpsed her face and saw she was too horrified to speak. No, it was not she, for the sound came from the other side of the round court.

"Stop! Stop it, I say!" came the voice once more. Its owner appeared to be one of the nobles in attendance, not far from the area where Cauldos himself sat. And as the young woman who spoke threw back the hood of her shadowy cloak, a mane of black ringlets came into view, framing an oval face with sea-green eyes. Angry eyes.

The girl reached out her hand in a magical gesture and green fire crackled through the air. It struck the reanimated corpse with paralyzing force and made the creature's hand release its deadly grip.

Gasping for air, Morlac turned to gaze upon she who rescued him. As his vision cleared, there was no doubting who that person was.

Kadrana . . . !

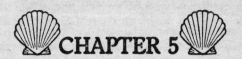

CHAPTER 5

Kadrana's Spell

Baron Kumil stepped forward, his angry gaze fixed upon the young woman who challenged him. Without even looking at the reanimated corpse he muttered a series of occult commands that caused it to cease its struggles and collapse beside Morlac. Then in a loud, clear voice he called out, "Who are you to make demands upon me?"

With regal self-confidence bordering on arrogance, she told him, "I am Kadrana, daughter of Sordros, the green magician. I do not wish to spoil your demonstration, Baron, but the man you have thus placed in mortal danger is Morlac, our captain of the guard in Shola. His fate is important to me."

The Baron was silent a moment, his eyes still narrowed in a dangerous look. Then some of his polished charm returned. "You have not spoiled my demonstration, my fine young lady. I have already proven the skills and powers I now offer in the service of Governor Cauldos. The fates of these prisoners lie in his capable hands, not mine."

"We, too, were called here to aid Neuphendurem," Kadrana said coolly, "and we, too, have proven our worth. Morlac and his friend—the other man you hold there—will be helpful to us and to our cause."

"Enough—!" Cauldos interceded firmly. "We are all allies here and I do not wish petty bickering to interfere with our plans. I will decide this matter in the morning. Until then, these people shall be held under my authority."

"As you wish, Governor," Baron Kumil said with cunning

politeness. "I will speak to you tomorrow about these men, and especially the young noblewoman. . . ."

A short while later, a banquet was being readied in the palace of Governor Cauldos; a banquet not to be shared by certain special guests in Neuphendurem. Far from the sounds of celebration, in a structure reclaimed from the ruins of a low stone building, these guests prepared for a long and uncomfortable night.

In one dark chamber lighted by a solitary candle and closed off by an added wooden wall with bolted door, two figures slouched against the still-warm stone. Their chains were long enough to permit then to sit upon the floor, but too short to allow any real movement within the cell.

Broct looked disdainfully at the shackles that bound his wrists . . . all *six* wrists, for his captors had been alerted by Baron Kumil to the yellow-eyed giant's extraordinary anatomy. He glanced over to his fellow prisoner with a look equally sour.

"K'Dral—" he said with contempt "—I wish I had never set eyes upon it . . . *or* you."

The pretty thief with scarlet hair whipped her head around to stare at him and spat out a reply. "That is a wish I most fervently share! You fool! If you had not exposed me aboard the ship I might have reached here undetected."

"My profound apologies," snarled Broct. "I be vexed with the delusion that thieves should be caught. And you *were* stealing from the Baron."

"Of course I was stealing, you great, excessive freak! I was hungry."

"I meant not the food, but the jewelry! You do not deny you boarded the Baron's galley to make off with his gems?"

The young woman's dark and lovely eyes sparked with indignation. "Deny that I do! The gems I took only for expense money. Boarding the ship I did to reach Neuphendurem, for it is well known there are riches to be had here. Almost enough money had I to buy my passage, and I would have done so, had I not failed to lift your coin purse."

"Sorry to disappoint you," Broct told her. "But you would not have been able to buy passage anyway. There were no ships sailing here, save the Baron's. He probably would have *let* you board, had you asked."

"What difference there is I do not see," she taunted. "He treats his guests as badly as a thief, for here we both are, chained to the same wall. Besides, I do not ask for what I want! I am Rila T'Faen, 'The Devil's Flame,' master thief, pickpocket, and thimblerigger. I have even taken a turn upon the stage as an actress, though I found there was little money in it."

"You seem to have taken a turn in the wrong direction, as well."

"And *you* seem an unlikely type to stand in judgment of others, my fine large sir," she said, each word dripping with venomous sarcasm.

Broct turned away, his eyes downcast. He had to admit, he had lived his own life with carefree abandon and little concern for laws. He was surprised by his own sudden moralistic tone. "I'm no perfect gentleman, that be true," he grumbled. "But still I do not see why one as beautiful as you must turn to thievery."

She blinked at his words and opened her mouth to speak, but hesitated. Then she found her tongue again and the angry words gushed forth. "What should I be, then? Some wealthy noble's mistress, trading on her looks, so long as they last? Or a whore perhaps you'd have me be, selling herself upon the streets of K'Dral?"

"No . . ." Broct replied softly. "No . . . I would not expect nor want that." He turned again to look at her, his steady gaze reproachful. "But even if you were such, at least it could be said you gave something in return for what you took, which is more than can be said now. . . ."

Not far from Broct's cell was another, also poorly furnished and sparse of light. This one, though, had but a single occupant chained to its stone wall.

Glendauna stood there, barely able to hear Broct's voice and that of the thief, and straining . . . hoping . . . to make out the sound of Morlac's voice, wherever he might be. But she knew not in which cell he had been placed, and had heard nothing thus far.

Still shaken she was by Morlac's close brush with death at the hands of Baron Kumil's zombie. And in the aftermath of that horror, their captivity, her first glimpse of the beautiful, powerful Kadrana, and her growing fatigue and hunger, a sense of confusion and despair was setting in, robbing her of her normal spirit. A tear crept down her cheek as she huddled in the near darkness.

Glendauna jerked suddenly to attention as the heavy door bolt clicked and the panel swung open. The silhouette of a muscular man appeared against the corridor's light, then entered. She saw at once that it was Cauldos's guardian of this strange prison. She backed closer to the hard stone wall, repulsed by everything about the man—his sight, his sound, his oily, unclean smell. And his touch . . . especially his touch.

"Just see what I've brought you," he rasped, carrying a tray with food and a goblet of wine upon it. "Quite a feast it is they're having tonight, the nobles and the rest. Plenty to go around, I say."

He put the tray down on a low, crudely made table near the wall opposite her. "Smells good, does it not? So close, and yet just out of reach." The horrible man came toward her now, stopping so near to her side that his stinking breath filled her nostrils. "That food can be yours, you know. *Can* be. So I want you to think about it while I'm gone. Think about how hungry you are. Think about it good and proper."

He reached up and let his rough hand stroke her face. She recoiled swiftly, shuddering at his touch, and turned her face away from his.

"Think you're too good for such as me?" he snapped. He grabbed her hair and jerked her head roughly around, bumping it against the hard stone wall. He kept his fingers tangled in her hair and continued to exert pressure upon it. "Let me tell you this—whatever you may have been somewhere else, you are *nothing* here, and as long as you are in my charge you had better worry about pleasing me. Understand—?" He gave her hair an extra tug for emphasis.

More tears ran down Glendauna's cheeks. "You're hurting me!"

"Hurting?" said he. "This is nothing, compared to what I

can do, will do, when I get back from my rounds. Oh, I'm looking forward to you, my prize lovely."

"Governor Cauldos will punish you—"

"Punish? Ha!" The guard gave a cold and wicked laugh. "Many's the time he has sat here and watched. He draws his pleasure from such things." Still holding her hair tightly, he let his free hand trace the gentle curves of the young noble-woman's body. Then he leaned closer to her face and whispered, "I shall be counting the minutes until my return. And you will be, too, won't you? *Won't* you—?"

At last he released his grip and stepped away from her. He took another long, hungry look at her and smiled with perverse pleasure. Then he turned and left the cell, closing and bolting the door behind him.

Glendauna slumped against the wall and wept, her shoulders sagging. But as the tears ran down her face an anger rose within her, surpassing the fear and the humiliation. An anger bordering on madness. An anger that brought a slow, grim smile to her lovely, tear-moistened features. A dangerous, murderous smile. . . .

Morlac strained with all his might against his bonds, but he had been shackled in place against the wall with double chains and even his considerable strength was not enough to budge them. He relaxed for a moment, then tensed anew as a sound from the doorway alerted him. Apparently the guard was returning.

He could hear the heavy bolt slide back, and the slight scrape of the door as it opened. But the figure that now entered the cell was definitely not that of the guard.

Kadrana stepped slowly inside and closed the door behind her. She stood there for a moment, silently studying Morlac with eyes that were compelling and unfathomable. When at last she spoke, her voice cut through the months since last he'd seen her as if they did not exist.

"So, my captain. Once more we meet."

The candlelight was flattering but she did not need its softening touch. If anything, she was more beautiful than ever. Morlac felt a familiar tug of emotion as memories and reality merged and reinforced each other. And he also felt a pang of guilt and anger, that he could still allow such feelings to exist.

"Yes, once more we meet," said Morlac. He rattled the chains that held him. "And it is the same as when first we met."

She stepped closer to him, reaching out a hand to caress his arm. "No, not quite the same, my proud warrior. Some things have changed. Here, I have not the power to release you as I did in Sordros's castle."

"You have the power to unlock my cell."

"A bribe to the guard bought me entrance, nothing more. Cauldos rules here—you should not doubt that. But I shall do what I can to see that you and Broct are released to me tomorrow. Cauldos needs our help, and will listen. For Sordros is readying a new band of sea-warriors to do battle, even now as we speak, and you could be their leader."

"Why would you wish *me* to lead them?" Morlac said bitterly. "I lost the battle for our village, as you should well recall."

She stepped closer and put her arms around him, resting her head against his chest. "That was not your fault! It was hopeless from the start. You did better against the invaders than any other man could have." Kadrana rolled her sea-green eyes up to meet his. "I have missed you, Morlac. Truly missed you. There has been no other for me since you."

Morlac made no reply, and she seemed to read in his eyes that he could not say the same. Kadrana looked away from his troubled gaze.

"It is good to hold you once more," she continued. "How well I remember each moment of our time together."

"I remember, too," Morlac replied softly. "And I remember how, when at last I allowed myself to love you, you abandoned me. How, at the very moment I faced Drygo and fought to protect you, you turned and fled, without a thought to my own safety."

"I was afraid! And I wanted to reach Sordros before L'Dron Kerr's army cut off all escape. Would you have wanted me to stay and be killed?"

"No. But if your feelings had been true and unselfish, I think you might have risked it."

She tensed as if the words had stung. "I am not brave, Morlac—that I admit. But do not deny what I feel for you. Did I not save your life this evening when the Baron's monster sought to slay you?"

Morlac nodded soberly. "Yes, and I am not ungrateful. I only wonder if you did it out of love, or out of necessity. What enemy does Cauldos fear so much that he brings warriors and wizards from the Phaedrocian Empire and beyond?"

Kadrana avoided answering his first question. "There is a kingdom south of here, native to this land. The people are primitive and treacherous. They would destroy Neuphendurem, and deny the Empire its destiny."

"And you and Sordros hope to win a place in such an empire?"

"Why should we not?" said she, some of her old imperiousness returning. "We have known power and positions of high authority. Do you think we could ever be content with less?"

"No, my princess," Morlac replied, with only a slight edge of sarcasm in his voice. "Tell me, why do you still maintain this deception about being Sordros's daughter?"

Kadrana shrugged. "It suits my purpose, and that of Sordros. Do not concern yourself with that. Just follow my lead when I speak to Cauldos tomorrow."

Morlac was silent a long moment. Now that he had finally found Kadrana and was within reach of Sordros himself, he was no longer certain of his goal. Certainly he did not wish to once again become a pawn in some despot's war; especially one in which the outcome meant nothing to him. Why had he not seen the wisdom in Broct's and Glendauna's advice, and turned away from his quest? Now, once more, he was at the mercy of others, others who only wished to use him. His fate and that of his friends stood as dark and forboding questions with few pleasant answers. The only thing that seemed certain was that his immediate fate lay in Kadrana's hands. Hers, and the Governor of Neuphendurem.

"Cauldos is one matter. Sordros is another. Will *he* want me back?"

"Leave that to me," said Kadrana. "I will convince him of your value. 'Twill not be hard. After all, you managed to find him here, despite his best efforts to avoid followers. He will respect your resourcefulness.''

"Perhaps," Morlac said. "More likely he will fear it."

"*I* do not fear it." Kadrana reached up and gently pulled his face toward hers. She gave him a long, lingering kiss that was at first tentative and uncertain. But her lips soon burned against his, her passion fairly exploding from her.

It was a kiss Morlac did not want, yet he found himself yielding to it. No, more than just yielding. But he should not . . . must not. He loved Glendauna now. He loved. . . . He. . . .

It was impossible not to feel the magic in Kadrana's kiss, a magic Morlac had done his best to forget. The sweet warmth of her body, close to his, was enough to arouse desire in a dead man. He found his arms straining against their shackles, eager to hold her, with escape only a secondary thought. What damnable magic be this, Morlac thought, that so overwhelms me? He sought to bring Glendauna's image to mind, to strengthen his resolve, and only partially succeeded.

Kadrana suddenly broke off the kiss, and Morlac at first thought she had once again read his mind. But then he realized there had been a click of sound, and that the door to his cell was opening.

Cauldos's guardian stepped halfway inside, an expression of wicked amusement upon his horrid face. "Time to say goodnight, my fair young miss. You'll be wanted, I'm sure, at the Governor's celebration, and I have my own matters to attend to here.''

Kadrana bristled with annoyance. "Yes . . . of course." She looked to Morlac as she stepped slowly toward the door. An odd mixture of emotions played across her young and beautiful face, and Morlac wondered if perhaps she had indeed read his thoughts about Glendauna. "You shall be free tomorrow," she told him, with what was perhaps reassurance. "Do not worry. . . . "

As the improvised prison grew quiet after Kadrana's departure, the sudden rasp of a key in the lock of Glendauna's cell seemed all the more harsh and startling. The door creaked open and the muscular guardian entered.

"Told you I'd be back, did I not, my prize? Are you eager to see m. . . ."

His words trailed off in puzzlement, for the chains that had held the girl now hung empty against the gray stone wall. The shackles were still locked but Glendauna had disappeared from them as surely as if she'd turned to smoke and vanished. But the door—surely the door would have held her, even if the chains had somehow failed.

The food on the table was gone as well, the platter and goblet overturned as if someone had eaten in great haste. The fact that the girl had succeeded in getting the food angered him almost as much as her escape. He did not want it to be that easy for her. No . . . not easy at all.

Something, he was not sure what, made him turn slightly, and then it was that he saw the girl. Or at least, he saw her lustrous, moon-haunted eyes peering at him from the darkly shadowed corner of the cell. A wicked smile spread across his ugly face.

"So there you are. Good. Very good. You little fool, did you really think you could hide from me? I don't know how you got loose from those chains, but you shall pay for it now. Pay for it dearly. I shall see to that."

The jailer walked slowly toward the corner where waited his captive, his cruel hands flexing in anticipation of what he would do to her, what special humiliation he would inflict upon this one. But all such thoughts ceased in the next moment, when, with startling clarity, he heard a low, dangerous sound, like a growl.

No, not *like* a growl. It *was* a growl.

The blood froze in his veins and he started to stagger back a step. But too late! For a large golden wolf now sprang out of the darkness and lunged directly at him, its eyes wide and wrathful, its sharp fangs reaching for his throat with deadly speed. . . .

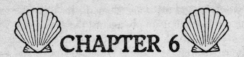

CHAPTER 6

The Outpost

Glendauna half-ran, half-stumbled along the silent prison corridor, her wild eyes brimming over with tears. The ring of keys she held tightly in her hand could unlock any of the doors she passed, if she could find the right key . . . and the right door.

She paused at the corner to catch her breath, wiping at her eyes with the back of her hand to clear her vision, and wiping also across her mouth to remove the unpleasant moisture at its corners. She spat twice with grim urgency to expel the horrid taste of the jailer's blood. A hand to her bosom to calm her racing heart, Glendauna listened for the sound of other guards. She heard none. So far, her luck was holding.

She rounded the corner and saw the door to the cell she had seen the yellow-eyed giant and the red-headed thief locked into earlier. She listened for a moment at the thick wooden panel, then leaned near to the crack to whisper.

"Broct—?"

There was a moment's hesitation, then a familiar voice within called forth, "Aye!"

Glendauna fumbled through the ring of keys, trying one after the other until at last one worked the lock. She drew back the bolt and opened the door.

A glance inside confirmed that she had the right cell, for there was her friend chained to the wall. She hurried to Broct's side and quickly searched once more through the keys to find one that would open his shackles.

"This be a pleasant surprise," said Broct. "How did you get loose?"

Glendauna's eyes met his briefly, then looked away as she began freeing his arms. "Never mind how. Let's just find Morlac and get out of here."

Broct frowned as he finally noticed her tear-streaked face and the state she was in. The fact that she had the guard's keys told him much, and he could guess the rest. But he remained silent. In a few moments that seemed to last an eternity, he was released.

Rila T'Faen was staring at them with an odd mixture of eagerness and reproach. Glendauna's attention was drawn to the pretty thief and she said to Broct, "What about her?"

Broct looked over at his unwilling companion. "She probably deserves whatever Cauldos has in mind for her," he growled. "But. . . ."

The yellow-eyed giant rubbed his many wrists for a moment, then he took the ring of keys and unlocked Rila's shackles, grumbling, "I have a feeling I shall regret this."

Though she seemed puzzled by this unexpected gift of freedom, she quickly stepped away from her chains and said, "To where do you plan to escape?"

"That I do not know yet. Why?"

"Because with you I will go," said she. "As distasteful to us both as that may be, it makes the most sense. Yes—?"

"Now I *know* I regret it," muttered Broct. He cautiously peered out the door to be sure the hall was clear, then motioned for Glendauna and Rila T'Faen to follow.

In the hall, Broct whispered, "Do you know where Morlac is being held?"

"No," replied Glendauna. "He was the last of us to be locked away. I only know that my cell was some distance back around the corner."

"Well," said Broct with a scratch of his head, "since it be clear the jailer wanted some space between us, and Morlac was the last, then he should be even farther along the hall than your cell. We must double back the way you came."

Glendauna winced at the thought of passing that way again, even though she had closed the door behind her in her flight, and would not have to see what lay within. "All right. We'd best find him quickly, before we're discovered."

The torchlit corridor seemed menacing and there were occasional groans and other horrid sounds of misery from some of the cells along the way. But most cells seemed empty, and for the moment at least the strange prison was deserted of guards. The three found their way down the long corridor Glendauna had so recently run, and at the end were faced with the decision of a cross corridor. Playing a hunch, Broct turned to the right and led them along another short row of cells. At the very end was a cell facing an open chamber that seemed a sort of guard post. But no guards were present. They approached the locked cell.

"Just the sort of place a special prisoner might be kept," said Broct.

Glendauna hurried past him with more eagerness than caution. "Morlac—?" she whispered urgently, close at the door.

"Glendauna?" came his cautious reply.

There was more frenzied work with the ring of keys, then at last the cell door was unlocked. Glendauna rushed in, going directly to Morlac and embracing him fiercely. Broct took the keys from her hand and set about releasing the shackles.

As soon as his hands were free, Morlac put his arms around the young woman, eagerly, comfortingly. He sensed that there was more to her distress than their separation and confinement. "Thank the gods you've escaped. But what troubles you, my lady?"

"I . . . I've . . ." she stammered. "Oh, Morlac . . . out of fear and anger I have broken the vow I made to myself." Her hand touched the ornamental neckpiece that was part of her Chalthax heritage. "The jailer. . . ."

Morlac nodded in understanding. He wiped away the tears that streamed forth anew and gently stroked her hair. She flinched as his hand touched the part of her head the jailer had struck against the wall, and Morlac frowned. He noticed the discoloration near her temple, just at the hairline, where her scalp had been jerked and blood lay beneath the skin. He kissed the spot with great tenderness, then his eyes turned toward the corridor with murderous anger.

"Shed no tears for the jailer, my lady. He deserves none. Should that degenerate still live, I swear I shall slay him myself."

"No—" said Glendauna, freeing herself from his embrace and pulling him toward the door. "No, there is no time for anything now but our escape. We must leave this place."

As they reached the doorway Morlac said, "Our weapons and things are over there in that chamber. We'll need them."

The hall was still clear, and the four crossed it with quiet haste. A large storage chest sat along one wall, secured with a small lock. Morlac took the lock in his hand and vented some of his anger upon it, twisting until it snapped from the hasp. Within the chest were their cloaks, packs, and weapons. Though still sheathed, Shark fairly throbbed in his hands as Morlac took it up and fastened its belt about him. It seemed to sense his killing mood and hungered for release from its own confinement. Morlac sought to calm himself, as much to quell his magicked blade as to still his own unreasoning rage.

Finding their way out of the prison was not difficult and the four managed to do so without encountering guards. The lack of manpower seemed strange until they realized there was little to guard here and much to guard at the palace this evening. The sounds of celebration echoed faintly across the way as Morlac and the others emerged into the darkness outside, but otherwise the colony seemed very much at peace.

Morlac paused as they traversed the dirt roadway, his finely tuned senses alert to all around him. "Strange," he said softly. "Kadrana told me of a kingdom to the south that wishes to destroy this colony. But Neuphendurem has not the look of a town in danger of attack."

"Aye," agreed Broct. "And what's more, though there be an abundance of soldiers and supplies, the place has poor defenses against invasion."

Glendauna gave Morlac an odd look. "When did you speak with Kadrana . . . ?"

"She visited my cell to tell me of her plans. They wish me to lead Sordros's new army of sea-warriors."

"What . . . what did you tell her?"

"I gave her no answer," Morlac said, and he knew that his

words did not truly answer Glendauna's unspoken question, either. "Come—I would yet find Sordros before we leave this place."

With their cloaks helping to conceal them, they headed away from both the prison and the bizarre palace of Governor Cauldos. Their caution and the crude dirt roads kept their footsteps silent.

"Morlac—" said Glendauna as they walked "—would not Sordros be with Kadrana at Cauldos's celebration?"

"No, she said he is at work readying his new army, and though I do not usually trust her words I think this time she speaks the truth. Besides, Sordros is not the type to enjoy such frivolities."

"That still leaves the rest of Neuphendurem," Broct observed, "and there be much of it to search in little time."

Morlac nodded with sober determination. "I know. That is why I seek first an easier place to find. A place we may be certain has men with knowledge *and* loose tongues. . . ."

Sounds of celebration not unlike those at the governor's palace emanated from the tents adjoining a small wooden building close to the docks. Golden lamplight spilled from beneath the tents' rolled flaps, and the smell of strong drink mingled with that of sweat and oiled blades. Serving girls wound through the jumble of crude tables and benches crowded with dockmen and soldiers and lower-class merchants, and there was such a vast sea of faces in this open-air tavern that it was a wonder any of the servers could recall who had asked for what.

Morlac stood silently a long moment outside the perimeter of lamplight, studying the groups of men within the tavern. Some it would not do well to approach. Others had the look of new arrivals, and would know little of the place. Finally, he selected a table near the edge of the tent that seemed to have a mixture of local workmen and a number of empty seats. He hoped none of them had seen him or his friends well enough when taken in chains from Baron Kumil's ship to recognize them now.

Glendauna stayed close to Morlac's side as they walked up to the group. Rila T'Faen squeezed past several wine-sotted soldiers leaving the tavern, then hurriedly joined Broct as they reached the table.

Morlac smiled when he caught the men's attention. "Evening, gentlemen. Do you mind if we join you?"

The man who had been talking studied the newcomers a moment, then shrugged. "If places there are to sit and your own drinks you buy, then who am I to stop you?"

"Thank you." Morlac took a seat at the edge of the empty row so that the two women were between him and Broct. He reached for his coin purse reflexively, before remembering that his money had been taken by the guards and was not among their belongings in the chest. He looked to Broct, whose expression showed a similar revelation. They were broke!

A serving girl hastened over and asked them for their order. There was an embarrassed silence while they tried to think of what to do next, then suddenly Rila T'Faen slapped a handful of coins upon the table.

"My turn it is to buy," said she brightly. "Ale is my choice. The rest of you order what you wish."

"Ah . . . ale will be fine," Broct replied, bewildered, and the others nodded in agreement. As the serving girl left, the yellow-eyed giant looked at Rila and said, "Where . . . ?"

Her only answer was a smile and a wry wink that made their heads turn in unison toward the group of soldiers staggering away into the darkness. Her brush past them had been profitable, it seemed.

The three exchanged glances with each other, then with Rila. Smiling oddly, Broct told the pretty thief, "I may just forgive you . . . this time."

Morlac mentally counted the coins on the table before Rila, then told the Phaedrocian man to whom he had already spoken, "Let us buy a round of drinks for you and your friends when the wench returns."

Already a bit in his cups, the man smiled and looked at his friends. "We'll not stop you. Will we, lads! Most generous you are, kind sir."

"Not at all," said Morlac. "It's good to be with real men. Too many high nobles and wizards around here to suit my taste. Right, Broct?"

"Aye," agreed the yellow-eyed giant with mock fervor, but he stole a quick glance around to be sure no one was watching them too closely.

There were nods and comradely mutters of agreement from the Phaedrocians gathered around the table, and Morlac knew he had struck a sympathetic chord. When the serving girl returned he ordered drinks for the others and paid for all at once. The girl was prompt in refilling the men's tankards.

"If it were up to me," said Morlac, half to himself, "I would have no traffic with wizards at all. But there is yet one I must find here, for I am transporting goods he wants."

"Goods?" said the man, with perhaps more than idle curiosity. "What sort of goods?"

Morlac wrinkled his nose. "Foul, stinking potions," said he, and was pleased to see the other man's loss of interest, "and other unspeakable things. 'Tis a job I like not at all, but a job nonetheless."

The Phaedrocian nodded glumly. "Yes, our work we must take where we find it. What wizard do you seek?"

Morlac shrugged with what he hoped was a convincing lack of enthusiasm. "I like one as little as the next, but this one is a strange one, name of Sordros. A green magician, he is."

The man opposite him mulled the name over a moment, then shook his head. "That one I do not know, though many of his kind have I seen here."

Morlac's hopes fell, but after another moment a workman near the end of the table brightened and said, "Sordros, you say?"

"Yes."

"A weaselly man with a single tuft of hair upon his head, high of voice and grim of manner?"

"Aye," said Broct. "The same."

"Him I remember," replied the workman. "A workshop of sorts has he not far from here, in a cove where the sea spills into rocky pools."

A perfect place, Morlac thought, for creating more sea-warriors. "Which direction?"

"East of here a mile or so," the workman answered. "But

you'll not find him there now. He has gone on with some of the rest to an inland outpost some miles south of here.''

"Be it difficult to find?" asked Broct.

"Not at all. Only one road there is leading inland, if a road it can be called. Follow it and you are there.''

"Thanks, my friend," Morlac told him, nodding with satisfaction. They would wait a few minutes more until their drinks were done and any lingering suspicions were dulled, then he and his friends would set out. Their escape from the small prison would not go unnoticed forever, and it would not do well to stay on the streets of Neuphendurem much longer. . . .

By noon of the next day Morlac and his companions were nearly a score of miles inland. They had traveled much of the night, resting only for a few hours in a cavelike pocket of rocky land that offered some shelter from the elements and beasts. The road that led them on was no more than a wide dirt path through dense foliage, but it was well-trod and deeply rutted from wagons heavy with supplies.

"This road," said Broct, "has seen much traffic for one that leads only to a mere outpost."

Morlac nodded grimly. "Whole armies have marched this way, and recently, from the look of it."

"This is not the sort of escape I had in mind," fumed Rila T'Faen. The oppressive heat and humidity had caused her scarlet tresses to droop. "Heading into more trouble we are. Stealing a boat and heading for K'Dral is what we should be—"

Morlac cut her off with a hasty *"Shhhh!"*, cocking an ear back down the road. A faint sound of hoofbeats approached. "Hurry—!" he told the others, motioning them off the road and into the foliage where they would not be seen.

They were well-hidden from view when the transport party reached the area. Four carts loaded with livestock and produce and two more burdened with wine kegs and sealed crates moved slowly along the uneven pathway. An escort of soldiers on horseback preceded and followed the carts, their alertness more routine than alarmed. Morlac and the others stayed motionless, barely drawing breath though there was more than enough noise to cover any sounds they might make.

At last the rumbling caravan moved past them and disappeared from sight. When even the sound of their progress faded, Morlac gathered the others together.

"It should not be much farther to the outpost," he told them. "Let us stay off the road, keeping it in sight so that we may follow it, but avoiding the gaze of any who may see our approach. Riders passed us in the night as well as now, and if they carried news of our escape then the outpost may be expecting us."

"Sound thinking," said Broct. "That be one place I have no desire to make a grand entrance."

Passage through the foliage was slower than along the road, but the four had not gone far when the outpost came into view ahead. It sat in a broad clearing at the end of the roadway, with guards visible around the perimeter. Morlac circled wide around the clearing, staying deep within the protective screen of foliage and leading the others to a high point of ground that afforded a good view of the compound.

On their stomachs they crept to the edge of a low cliff and peered cautiously down at the outpost before them. It appeared to be a small military base with a few wooden structures meant to house no more than thirty or forty men. But the place was bursting at the seams, with a profusion of tents stretching in all directions and at least a thousand or more soldiers already assembled. That number would be doubled when those in Neuphendurem reached the spot.

Morlac's keen eyes strained to make out details in the jumble of distant figures. "Do you see anything of Sordros—?"

Broct swept the scene below with his own sharp gaze. "No. But there be any number of places that be hidden from our view."

"I am sure he is down there somewhere," Morlac said softly. "I feel it, sense it. So does Shark."

Glendauna leaned close to him and said in a hushed and worried tone, "This shall be a terrible war, Morlac . . . so many soldiers . . . so many preparations. What enemy is so mighty that the colony must defend with all this?"

"One wonders," replied Morlac. "One wonders, indeed. But then, perhaps it is not merely a matter of defense."

Rila suddenly gave a small gasp of sound and Morlac started to look around at her to see the cause. But before he could begin to turn his head he abruptly felt the sharp point of a weapon pressed against his back. He felt Glendauna stiffen beside him and knew that she too had the same deadly threat poised against her back. Broct also let out a soft grunt of surprise and alarm.

Slowly and carefully, Morlac craned his head around to look behind them. There standing over them, with brass-tipped lances poised ready to impale them at the slightest wrong move, were five young warriors, sun-darkened and muscular, wearing little more than their bizarre ornaments and trappings of combat. Their expressions were utterly fierce, their intentions deadly serious. . . .

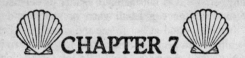

CHAPTER 7

The Warrior-King's Realm

The dark-skinned warriors did not take their eyes off Morlac and the others, but one of the young men turned his head slightly and made a series of brief whistling sounds like the call of some exotic bird. He followed this with soft clicking noises made with his teeth and tongue.

In less than a minute another party of men like the first suddenly appeared, melting out of the dense foliage with soundless grace. Leading them was a man who stood taller than the rest, well-muscled and lean, moving with a fluid and commanding ease. Like the others, he too had a knife, a bow, and a quiver of arrows, but he carried no lance. He looked at the four prisoners with an implacable expression, then exchanged words in a strange tongue with the man who had signaled him.

To Broct, Morlac said under his breath, "Seems we were not the only ones spying on the outpost."

The gaze of the dark warrior who appeared to be leading the group riveted instantly upon Morlac. He put his finger to his lips to signal silence, then gestured quickly to the lance-holders.

Almost as one, the warriors backed off the pressure of their weapons and motioned for Morlac and his friends to rise carefully. The sea-warriors and the two women did as they were ordered, moving away from the rise overlooking the outpost.

Quickly now, Morlac and the others were herded at lancepoint well around the clearing and ever deeper into the foliage, heading southeast on a course that would take them even farther inland. The tall warrior led the way, finding a path through the dense vegetation where none at first seemed visible.

"I grow tired of this, my sea-brother," Broct muttered to Morlac. "First prisoners of the Phaedrocians we be, and now of the Phaedrocians' enemies. There are but ten of these men, and they have not taken our weapons. If we must fight to escape them, then so be it."

The dark warrior halted in his tracks and turned to face them, a look of challenge on his noble features. Then his eyes seemed to shift, flashing a strange frown their way. In an abrupt blur of motion that caught even Morlac by surprise, the warrior plucked an arrow from his quiver, drew his bow, and fired directly at them.

The deadly shaft seemed to rush toward Glendauna, but it dove instead at the ground near her feet. She drew a sharp intake of breath as it hit, then did so again and reflexively jumped away from the spot.

This second reaction was prompted not by the arrow, but by what the arrow hit. For as she looked down she saw a large snake amid the foliage, scant inches from her foot. It was already coiled, its fangs ready to strike, for the warrior's arrow had pierced the open jaws and pinned the snake's head to the ground.

Morlac pulled Glendauna close to him, then turned to stare at the man who had very likely saved her life. The others also looked in stunned silence.

"We are not the Phaedrocians' enemies," said the dark-skinned warrior, and to everyone's great surprise he said it in the mother tongue of the northern lands. His voice was deep and resonant, his words clipped and precise. "*They* are *our* enemies. There is a difference. You were spying on them too, so I know you are not with them. But I still do not know who you are, why you are in this land, or if you can be trusted. *That* is why you are being guarded."

There was something about this strange man that Morlac admired. Perhaps it was his directness, his lack of guile and arrogance, totally unlike the pretentious and corrupt manner of the Phaedrocian nobles. There was a sense of honor to this man.

"I am Morlac, of Shola. These are my friends, Broct and Glendauna, and a . . . recent traveling companion, Rila T'Faen. I have journeyed here seeking a particular wizard. A wizard brought to this land by the Phaedrocians, in preparation for war."

"The Phaedrocians have brought many wizards here to aid them," said the man. "Why do you seek this one?"

"I served him, once, but I am not sure why I seek him now," said Morlac truthfully. "I only know that my fate is somehow linked with his, and that he may hold the answers to my future."

The dark warrior studied them all a long moment, mulling over Morlac's words. Finally, he said, "I believe you." He gestured to his men and they instantly withdrew the threat of their lances. "I am J'Bara, and I welcome you to this land. You say you were imprisoned by the Phaedrocians?"

"Aye," replied Broct. "And before we reached Neuphendurem, a Phaedrocian noble held us captive on his ship."

J'Bara nodded, looking away as his thoughts seemed to turn inward. "Neuphendurem is the Phaedrocians' name for it. They have defiled the Ghost City, and scattered the spirits of the Emui M'Bolo. That is bad. Very bad." He quickly looked back to Morlac and the others. "As prisoners I am sure you have had little to eat and little rest. Come with us as friends and we will offer you food and comfort. Or you may freely leave us here and now if you wish, and return to pursue your destiny. The choice is yours."

Morlac considered it. His primary goal had always been to find Sordros, and he was very near to doing that now. But J'Bara's words were true—they did need food and rest. Glendauna had already been through much . . . too much . . . because of his quest, and even Broct was looking fatigued. Perhaps these new strangers were no different from the other humans who had offered hospitality only to disguise their own deceit and treachery. Perhaps. But there could be no doubts about the intentions of the Phaedrocians, and at the moment, little chance of penetrating the outpost's defenses.

"What say you, my friends?" he asked the others. "Perhaps it is time we did rest, if you are of a mind to do so. I am not sure I trust my own judgment any longer."

Glendauna stayed close within the curve of Morlac's arm. "I follow your lead, my proud warrior."

"Aye," Broct agreed. "As do I."

Rila T'Faen studied them all with a perplexed pout. "Uncertain am I, myself. But little chance have I alone, in such a place as this, so it seems I am with you, too."

Morlac was troubled by the responsibility for their collective fates, and hoped he was making the right choice this time. "All right, then. Rest seems the more sensible path, for now."

J'Bara smiled and nodded approvingly. "Good. Let us hasten on. There is still much travel before us. . . ."

Two more hours passed as they continued to advance through the foliage, wending a path amid trees and vines, over the rocks of small streams and into the verdant tangle of jungle growth. The afternoon sun bore down through the leafy canopy, creating a lacy pattern of light and shadow and sending shafts of brilliance plunging through the steamy air. Only the passage of Morlac and his friends seemed to disturb the birds and other creatures of the area, and of them, Rila most of all. For Morlac and Broct, and also Glendauna, knew something of the ways of animals. But even they could not match the silent grace with which J'Bara and his men moved forward.

"The outpost grows strong," J'Bara said suddenly. "And I have learned they plan their attack to begin in two days. Not before. So for a time at least, you will be safe with us."

And after that, Morlac thought grimly to himself, where will safety be found? With a war erupting about them, where could they go? Even Rila's suggestion that they return to the coast and steal a boat seemed a plan fraught with difficulties.

Suddenly, as they pressed through yet another mass of green leafy growth, they emerged at the edge of a clearing. Stretching before them was a wide plain, and a vista so entrancing that it stopped them in their tracks, awestruck and gaping.

Cultivated fields spread wide before them, with fruits and

vegetables growing in abundance. On the far horizon rose a mountainous plateau, blue-gray and imposing against the sky, with verdant foliage rising halfway up the steep slopes. A great V-shaped rift in the plateau created a sheltered valley fanning toward them, and at the apex of that V a narrow waterfall cascaded hundreds of feet into a lake at the valley floor.

A river coursed out from that lake, heading due north for the coast. Mist from the falls wrapped all in a soft gray veil of mystery, and held aloft a shimmering rainbow that arced over the valley in many-hued splendor.

But most striking of all was the city nestled within that valley. Morlac had expected crude huts suitable for the "primitives" Kadrana described to him, and the manner of the dark warriors' dress had reinforced that notion. What he saw now was hardly crude.

J'Bara gave a sweep of his hand to encompass his wondrous realm. "Behold . . . N'Bikcumboro. . . ."

Elaborate buildings of two and three floors stood on both sides of the river, great rambling structures that skillfully blended the natural elements of the area with artful design. Covered porches and balconies followed the angles of the buildings, and lush gardens with flowering trees filled the spaces between them. Ingeniously constructed bridges curved over the river in several places, giving access to both sides.

On the eastern side of the valley, near the sheer face of the plateau, rose an even larger structure. White stone glistened in the afternoon sunlight, and running about its columns in concentric rings were wide bands of brilliant gold and emerald. And while the other buildings had roofs of timber and thatching, this marvel was covered by domes of sparkling gold.

So awestruck by the sight was Glendauna that the worries and torments of past days were erased from her delicate features. "It's . . . *beautiful*."

"It is home, for me and my people." J'Bara now faced the city, brought both hands up before his mouth, and trilled a sharp and resonant call loud enough to carry across the plain. An answering call came back like an echo, moments later.

J'Bara motioned for the others to follow. "Come—our journey is over. My people await us."

Though tired and footsore, Morlac and his friends scarcely noticed the remaining distance, for N'Bikcumboro stood before them, a glowing and magnificent gem in a verdant setting. As they drew near, hundreds upon hundreds of people became visible, emerging from the many buildings and gathering in the gardens and pathways of the city. All were smiling warmly, and most began to wave in greeting as the dark warriors and their guests approached.

The men and women were garbed in long wrappings of cloth that covered their torsos and hung to their knees, secured by broad waistbands. The fabric had been dyed in various colors and appeared to have beads and bits of metal woven into it.

As the warriors reached the edge of the city, women and children came forward to take their weapons and give them similar garments. But not for J'Bara. Two men approached him, both wearing elegant robes that set them apart as officials of the magnificent city. One was wizened, with gray hair and a slightly stooped posture. The other, as solemn as the first, was younger. It was he who approached J'Bara, received his weapons, and extended a robe.

"Thank you, Cashili," said J'Bara as he took the robe and slipped into it.

Different from the other garments, the robe was longer and of a solid-green hue. As J'Bara adjusted its folds, the man addressed as Cashili now produced a bundle of cloth and carefully opened it, extending it and its contents upon both spread palms. At the cloth's center were a number of heavy gold rings and bracelets, fitted with large emerald stones, and surrounding these lay a massive necklace of gold, formed in the shape of large seashells.

J'Bara put on each of the rings and bracelets with almost ritual precision, then solemnly picked up the heavy golden necklace and slowly placed it about his neck. When done, he stood transformed.

"Welcome back, J'Bara," intoned Cashili with warm formality. "Welcome back, O King of N'Bikcumboro."

Morlac and his friends gazed appreciatively at the man who

had escorted them here—no mere warrior, but the high ruler of this exotic realm.

Cashili now turned to face these visitors, and the other official approached them with a cautious look. The wizened man carried a short staff of ebony wood, the carved head of which encompassed a fist-sized emerald. Through this impressive stone, the man proceeded to peer at each of them in turn.

"These are my guests, and I vouch for them," J'Bara told the man, still speaking in the native tongue of the northern lands. Looking to Morlac, he added, "This is Madudu, our shaman. He is reading your souls."

The shaman moved past Morlac with a nod of approval, then studied Broct and Glendauna respectively. Each also received the same approving nod. But as he reached Rila T'Faen, who seemed more fascinated with the massive stone than the strange ritual, he frowned sourly and gave only a look of grudging acceptance.

J'Bara seemed amused by it all, but maintained his stately calm. "You have met our shaman. Now I introduce you to my chancellor, Cashili."

Cashili gave a slight, bowing nod. "We welcome J'Bara's new friends."

"Thank you," Morlac replied, but with a puzzled look added, "Do all your people speak the language of the north?"

"No," said J'Bara, "only some of us. I will explain. But first, let us bring you food and drink to refresh you after your journey. . . ."

As they finished their meal on a shaded terrace outside one of the large bamboo-and-timber buildings, J'Bara began his story. His manner was relaxed and friendly.

"My father was king before me," he told them. "And when I was younger, barely more than a child, he sent me on a journey throughout the northern lands. His friend, Cashili, was my guide, my guardian, my tutor. My father wished for me to learn the ways of men from other lands, so that I might be a better ruler when my own time to serve came. He was a very wise man, and so too has been Cashili."

"We are grateful to you," Morlac said, "for killing the snake, and for making us welcome here."

"It is our way to make visitors welcome here," J'Bara responded with an expansive gesture of his hands. "But that proved a mistake when the first Phaedrocian colonists journeyed inland far enough to reach our city. We treated them as guests, let them see all that we have here. They saw too much . . . wanted too much. When they returned to their colony, word spread of riches to be had here. Greed spread like fire. Soon, Cauldos himself plotted to steal our wealth and began sending thieves and soldiers. When he saw that we would fight to protect our city, he sent messages to his emperor, asking for help to fight invaders. But *he* is the invader."

"That makes far more sense than the story they tell," said Morlac. "But how did you learn of Cauldos's actions?"

"There are ways," the king said cryptically. "The Phaedrocians have not learned all the secrets of the Ghost City. Nor will they ever." He looked to be sure they all were through with their meal, then said, "Come—there is something I must show you."

J'Bara led them now across the nearest bridge and over to the magnificent building of white stone. As they drew near they saw that the gold and emerald bands about its columns were true gold, true emerald, and not mere painted decorations. And closer looks at the people of N'Bikcumboro revealed that their garments were adorned not with beads and bits of metal, but with real gems and golden decorations. Each man, each woman, each child, wore a small fortune.

The chancellor, Cashili, joined them at the entrance to the structure, and the several warriors who had stayed constantly in J'Bara's presence continued to do so. Inside, the building was cool and well-lighted by high-placed windows. Dazzling colors leaped from the walls where gemlike mosaics reached from floor to lofty ceiling, depicting historic scenes and cultural symbols.

"This is the palace of N'Bikcumboro," J'Bara told them. "But it is more than just a place for the king to sleep. It is where we revere our past, and celebrate our future. It has stood here since long before the birth of my father's father, and his father before him."

"Yes," said Cashili with a note of sadness. "But its future, and ours, is now in doubt."

"You must see this—" J'Bara said proudly, directing them to a pair of doors set in the center of the far wall. Two of his warriors quickly moved to open them for their king.

As Morlac and his friends entered after J'Bara, they found themselves in a great hall, simply furnished but more stunning than anything they had yet seen. Mirrored panels of unexpected fineness lined the walls, and the white flooring stones were laid with such precision the seams were barely visible. But what captured everyone's immediate attention were the seven life-size statues, cast in solid, purest gold, each one so heavy it would take a score of men to lift. They stood in two rows, facing the hall's center.

All of the figures were so impressive their sight prompted Glendauna to exclaim, "They look like gods!"

"We do not make images of our gods," J'Bara told her. "We do not think it fitting. These statues represent our previous kings. It is said that their wisdom and bravery lives on to be called upon by the living ruler. The statues have great meaning to us, but to the invaders they will only be booty to be melted down into coins for the coffers of the Phaedrocian Empire."

"Why make them of gold?" asked Broct. "It begs trouble."

"Because gold endures, and is beautiful," J'Bara replied matter-of-factly. "The mountains around us are rich with gold and gems. It is only natural we use them. Besides, the tradition began long before we learned of the treachery such things inspire."

J'Bara slowly approached the figure at the end of the shortest row of statues. His hand came to rest upon its golden shoulder. "This," he said with great solemnity, "was J'Koro. My father. How I wish he were here to advise me now. . . ."

There was a long moment of respectful silence in the great hall, then a sound from the doorway caught their attention. A young woman with large eyes and quiet, dusky beauty entered the hall. Her fine robe and the golden threads braided through her long hair were elegant without being lavish. She smiled as she faced J'Bara.

"Ah," said the king. "And here is my greatest treasure in all the realm. This is Liluvu, my wife and queen."

She nodded to the others, then quickly approached J'Bara

and took hold of his hand. They did not kiss, but their eyes sparkled with the warmth of an unspoken greeting.

The king of N'Bikcumboro now addressed them all. "There are still hours left before darkness. Let us all rest from our journey, then tonight we shall celebrate. It shall be our last chance for awhile. Tomorrow we must prepare for the invaders. . . ."

The night sky was a great dark canopy above N'Bikcumboro, sparkling with stars so bright it seemed great handfuls of diamonds had been thrown aloft and become imbedded there. The tall cascade of water at the rear of the valley could scarcely be seen in the darkness, but the rushing roar of its never-ending flow created a soothing sound behind the cries of beasts and jungle birds.

Night flowers blossomed among the trees and garden plants, spreading their perfume upon the mist-cooled breeze. Tame birds perched along the branches, their beautiful plumage rivaling the colors of the flowers. The torches and lanterns were lighted now in N'Bikcumboro. Their golden glow touched everything with magical charm.

"If this is not paradise," Glendauna told Morlac as they sat on a terrace near the palace, "it is as close as I hope to find." She had bathed and felt refreshed, and even put flowers in her hair.

"Yes, it is truly beautiful," Morlac agreed, and he gently kissed her. But he sensed a sadness and fear underlying her words, and knew it tempered the lovely spell of this place. There would be much on his mind this night.

Everyone in the city, it seemed, was gathered outdoors now. Meat was roasting over fires and mounds of corn and other vegetables steamed over smoldering pits. Drums and flutes and strange instruments created a wild, compelling rhythm that coursed through the night as if the land itself lived and breathed and pulsed blood through its veins.

Near Morlac and Glendauna, Broct and Rila T'Faen sat at another table, basking in the warmth and revelry that seemed unmindful of the dangers ahead. The yellow-eyed giant turned to the young woman beside him, studying her for a moment before speaking.

"You have been unusually quiet tonight," he told her.

She shook her head as if to clear her thoughts. "Stunned am I by this. I came to Neuphendurem to find riches, and here have I found more than ever I dreamed!"

"Riches!" grunted Broct. "Be that all you ever think of?"

"And why should I not? Too long have I been poor."

"Better to be poor," he snapped, "than rich at someone else's expense. Anyway, what are riches? Look around you. Be it only the baubles that you see? It be not the gold and emeralds that bring these folk happiness. They do not eat or drink them. They do not spend them."

"Spend them they could in other lands," Rila said wistfully. "As could we."

"Do not even think it!" Broct told her in a low and menacing tone. "Have you learned nothing these past few days? You be no better than Cauldos himself. You only lack his armies. Bah! I should have left you to rot in prison."

Rila T'Faen bristled at his stinging words. "*My* morals you curse? Last night you were not so pure and noble, when a soldier's stolen coins bought you and your friends drinks and information!"

Broct frowned and looked away. "That be true. Many times I have done what I had to, just to survive. A fact I be not proud of. But never out of greed. There be too many better things in life than wealth."

Rila was silent a long moment, a variety of strange emotions flickering across her troubled and pretty face. Then at last she said, "Why did you not?"

Broct gave her a puzzled look. "Why did I not what?"

"Leave me to rot in prison."

The yellow-eyed giant shrugged awkwardly. "Perhaps I did not think your crime deserved such punishment. Perhaps I did it to thwart Cauldos and Baron Kumil. Perhaps. . . ."

"Yes—?"

"Perhaps," continued Broct, "because I did not *want* to leave you behind. And because I still remembered the sweetness of your lips when first we met, that day in K'Dral."

The red-haired beauty gave him a look that was wry, almost mocking. But the look quickly softened. "And perhaps your first two answers do not matter so much as the last." She let her warm fingers gently stroke his face. "Of course, one thing there is you overlook, my fine large sir."

"And that would be . . . ?"

She slid her arms around him. "A stolen kiss, no matter how sweet, cannot compare with one freely given."

And then she set about to prove her point. . . .

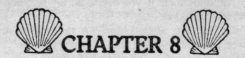

CHAPTER 8

Prayers and Plans

There was a sweetness to the morning, a gentleness and calm, that set N'Bikcumboro apart from the world beyond its boundaries. A perfect tranquillity that made it difficult to imagine the destruction preparing to sweep in upon the exotic realm. But that dreadful realization was beginning to show on the faces of its people as they went about their tasks.

Morlac and Glendauna crossed the bridge leading to J'Bara's palace, with Broct and Rila close behind them. All had slept later than they planned, for despite their worries it was their first restful sleep in days. Such was the spell of N'Bikcumboro.

Cashili greeted them at the entrance to the palace, giving them a nodding bow and a warm smile. "Good morning to our new friends."

"Good morning, Chancellor," Morlac replied. "Would it be possible for us to speak with the king?"

"Yes," Cashili answered. "In fact, J'Bara wished to call for you soon anyway. Come with me."

He led them inside and to the great hall, where he quietly opened one of the double doors. Morlac and the others could see past him. Inside the hall with his back to them was J'Bara, halfway between the two rows of golden statues. Morning sunlight streamed into the mirrored hall, bathing him in its glow. The king of N'Bikcumboro was down on one knee, his head bowed and his fingertips touching his forehead. He remained that way for another few moments, then he lowered his hands and raised his head. Whether he had completed his ritual or had merely sensed their presence and stopped, Morlac could not tell.

J'Bara arose and slowly turned to face the door. He gestured toward them.

"Come in, my friends. Come in. I have been praying for wisdom and strength. I will need both, if my people and our way of life are to survive." He strode toward them, greeting each in turn, taking their hands in his. "I am glad to see you looking rested."

"We owe you our thanks for that as well," Morlac told him.

"There is no need for thanks," J'Bara said. "Have you decided what you will do about this wizard you seek?"

"About the wizard, no."

"Before you do," replied the king, "let me tell you this. The time for battle grows near, and I cannot guarantee your safety here much longer. I have a boat, large enough for you and your friends. The river that flows from the waterfall will carry you to the sea and past danger."

"A generous offer," said Morlac. "But I do not wish to leave. I have decided to help you, if you will let me."

J'Bara looked at him strangely. "Why should you risk your life for us? This is not your fight."

"It was not before. But Baron Kumil and Governor Cauldos have made it so."

"Aye," added Broct. "Besides, you be our friend now. We can do no less."

J'Bara studied them all a long moment, a sad smile touching his lips. "I welcome your help, my friends. But I fear you are only asking to die with the rest of us. Make no mistake—we are brave fighters, fierce fighters. But my warriors barely number eight hundred, and I know Cauldos prepares over two thousand soldiers, with uncounted wizards and mercenaries. The odds do not favor us."

"Then," said Morlac, "we shall have to find ways to change the odds."

J'Bara shook his head solemnly. "I have been trying. But if our past kings know how, they have not yet spoken to me." He smiled wanly. "Sometimes you cannot trust legends."

Glendauna now spoke up. "Can you evacuate your people?"

"Yes . . . I *can* send them away from here. There is barely time for that. There are also many tunnels in the mountains in which we can take refuge, for awhile. But if we leave this beloved land, we are giving up our lives as surely as if we fight and die. Can you understand?"

Glendauna nodded. She knew the effect N'Bikcumboro had on her after only a day. These people had spent their lives here for generations.

Morlac was pacing about now, deep in thought. Still vivid in his mind was the memory of his village's battle against L'Dron Kerr's invading army, and the failure of he and his fellow sea-warriors to halt that invasion. It was a bitter memory, but there were lessons to be learned from it.

"You say," he asked suddenly of J'Bara, "that there are tunnels in the mountains?"

"Yes," the king told him. "Some are natural, some are from the mines."

"How many archers have you?"

"All my warriors are archers," J'Bara replied. "They are also good with knives and lances, but most know little about swordplay."

"Then they must fight the Phaedrocians in ways that fit their skills. We cannot beat Cauldos's armies with numbers. We cannot beat them with magic. But there may be other ways."

J'Bara's interest was aroused. "You have a battle plan?"

"No . . . not one plan," Morlac replied. "For one plan can fail. I think what you need are *many* plans, working together. What one does not do, the others shall. But still we need something more . . . something to give us an initial advantage."

Morlac stalked through the great hall, searching his mind for some trick of combat, some special defense, that could be brought to play against such overwhelming forces. He tried to imagine the form of attack the Phaedrocians would launch, and realized there was only one likely approach for such an army.

As his unseeing gaze drifted around the hall, his eyes abruptly focused upon the rows of golden statues. The past kings of N'Bikcumboro. So lifelike that they seemed ready to move or speak, the likenesses showed strong, proud men. They sparkled and glowed in the intensity of early-morning light. Could it be true that they had secrets to share . . . wisdom to impart? If they had not yet spoken to J'Bara, would they speak to him?

A frown twitched across Morlac's face, for almost in answer to the thought an idea sprang to life. A simple enough idea. Could it work?

"J'Bara," Morlac said carefully, tactfully, "troubled as you are by your great concerns, I think you may have overlooked something that could help us. The plans I would suggest will require much work and most of this day to prepare, and there is something I must yet do tonight."

The king's eyes twinkled with enthusiasm. "Then let us begin at once. Tell me your ideas."

Morlac proceeded to relate them, one by one, and with each passing moment J'Bara grew more enthusiastic, more hopeful. When at last he was done, Morlac added, "But these are only ideas, inspired by what I have seen here, and by what you have told me. You will know better than I if they have a chance of working."

J'Bara clasped his hand firmly. "I like your ideas. And they do have a chance. Perhaps our only chance. If all this works, my friend, you will have repaid our simple kindnesses a thousandfold. Perhaps legends may be trusted after all. And it does not matter to me into whose ear our kingly ghosts whisper, so long as we save N'Bikcumboro!"

Morlac was still troubled by one thing, though, and the thought of it made him turn to Glendauna. Taking her hands into his, he said, "I am making plans without asking you your wishes, and there is great danger in what I would do. Perhaps you and Rila should indeed use J'Bara's boat to reach the sea."

She stared at him with the same fiery spirit he had seen in her eyes when first they met and she had whirled, sword drawn and ready. "No," she told him firmly. "Not even if I could bear to leave you to such an uncertain fate would I go. J'Bara and his people are my friends too, now. They are not running away. Neither shall I! I am Glendauna, daughter of the House of Chalthax and Durkesh raised, and I do not desert my friends."

J'Bara added his hands to theirs. "I am proud to call you my friends, whatever happens."

"The choice be made then," Broct declared, placing his own large hand upon theirs. "To live or die, as best we can!"

"As best we can," Morlac and the others agreed.

Rila T'Faen gave a great sigh and shook her crimson curls. Then she too added her hand to theirs. "Growing softheaded I must be. . . ."

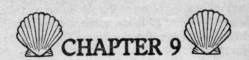

CHAPTER 9

Night Mission

The outpost loomed before them in the darkness, aglow with torches and ringed by sentry fires. Its forward boundaries had been extended since the day before to accommodate the swelling numbers of Phaedrocian soldiers crowding in.

"They are all here now," Morlac whispered to the others as they peered down at the camp from their vantage point. They had left N'Bikcumboro before dusk and it had taken several hours to reach the outpost.

"There be at least two thousand soldiers," Broct observed. "Cauldos must think it will ensure an easy victory."

J'Bara gazed at the massed troops through angry eyes. "Yes . . . no doubt he plans to overwhelm us quickly, so there will be enough of my people left alive to work the mines. He does not know that what they do as free men they will not do as slaves."

Glendauna crouched low beside Morlac. "You think Baron Kumil is the greatest threat among the wizards?"

"I do indeed," affirmed Morlac. "Sordros's skills are great, but even if he has created a dozen or more sea-warriors like Broct and myself it will not truly affect the battle's outcome. Besides, we are too far inland for some of his powers to work. Baron Kumil is another matter. He who commands the dead need fear no living army."

"Yes," agreed J'Bara. "What you have told me about his demonstration before Cauldos is truly frightening."

"That is why we must succeed tonight," Morlac replied, "if we are to have a chance tomorrow."

They watched a while longer to study the pattern of sentry posts and to look for points vulnerable to entry, then Morlac told them, "We must go to the northern side, where the road from Neuphendurem enters the camp. They seem to be less watchful there."

J'Bara nodded in agreement, moving silently back from their vantage point. He and the four warriors who accompanied him from N'Bikcumboro led the way through the foliage, staying well-hidden from the outpost. In minutes they were in place at a curve in the road, some little distance before the outpost's entrance and out of sight of the sentries.

Morlac told the others, "Broct and I shall try to get in as late-arriving mercenaries. Glendauna—you must keep watch on the outpost with J'Bara and his men. If there is trouble, we may need you to create a diversion so we can escape."

The young woman's clear blue eyes showed reluctance, but she knew what he suggested made sense. Besides, the three of them together would be more easily recognized than just the two. "All right," she said at last. "But guard your life well, Morlac!" She threw her arms around his neck and kissed him impulsively before letting him go.

Morlac and Broct had just stepped onto the road when a sound to the north alerted them to trouble. Faint at first, the dull rumble of wheels and the rhythm of horses' hooves grew steadily louder in the darkness. The two sea-warriors stepped back into the foliage.

"A wagon," said Morlac.

"Aye," Broct replied, listening intently. "But only two horses. No guards be riding with them."

"Does that suggest anything to you, my sea-brother?"

The yellow-eyed giant smiled in the darkness. "Aye . . . !"

The sentries guarding the outpost entrance snapped to attention at the wagon's approach. It came at a leisurely pace, drawing into the reach of the torches and becoming visible. The well-loaded wagon creaked and groaned under the weight of its cargo, but its wooden protests diminished as it came to a halt before the guards.

Two men rode its bench, a driver and his assistant, both clad in the garb of the Phaedrocian merchant class. Soft hats were pulled low over their brows against the night air.

"Taxes upon taxes do we pay," grumbled the driver to the other man, "but never do we get decent roads!" Then louder, to the guards, "Good evening, my fine young sirs. Your cargo have we brought."

"Cargo?" asked the guard nearest them.

The driver gestured at the barrels and kegs stacked high upon the wagon. "A fresh supply of wine and ale do we bring. Do you not want it?"

"About time," snapped the other guard. "Watered 'twill be by the time we get it, but 'tis still better than naught. I feared we'd go to battle with parched throats."

"Fear no more, my lad," said the driver. "Just show us where to deliver these. Weary we are from our long ride. Oh, and . . ." he reached behind him and produced two bottles of wine to hand the men on the sly ". . . here's a little something for you now, undiluted."

The guards glanced around as they quickly tucked the bottles away. Then the first man pointed within the compound. "Drive your wagon over there, just past the first building. There may you unload."

With a nod and a friendly wave, the driver urged his horses forward. The wagon creaked and shuddered, finally moving. As it rumbled into the compound the guards returned their attention to the road.

Morlac kept the horses going at a steady pace, threading his way between soldiers who moved restlessly about, and amid tents and refuse and empty supply crates. The camp was reasonably quiet, but tension hung over it like a cloud. Some men were sharpening wide blades to hack a path through the foliage, ahead of the marching troops. Archers restrung their bows and readied full quivers of shafts. Still other men prepared litters and drays, and Morlac suspected they were intended more for transporting treasure back to Neuphendurem than for carrying injured soldiers.

"I see no sign of Cauldos here," Morlac said softly.

"Not surprising," Broct murmured. "Most likely he be lounging about his palace, letting others do his evil work for him."

They brought the wagon to a halt by a row of crude tables set up to hold the kegs and barrels previously transported. A low-ranking officer hurried forward as Morlac and Broct swung down from their seats. They moved carefully, so that the swords concealed beneath their cloaks were not revealed.

"You're late!" said the officer.

"A wheel came off . . . nearly wrecked us. We had to fix it." Morlac had no idea why the wagon's original crew was behind schedule, but considering the road his story might just be true. As he and Broct started unloading the casks of wine Morlac told the officer, "We could use some help with these."

The man turned and called sharply to a dozen men standing nearby, then said to Morlac, "They'll unload the rest. Eager they all are for a drink. Just see that you take the empty barrels back with you. No room have we here for them!"

"Of course," Morlac replied. "Just let us stretch our legs a bit. Long and bumpy was that road."

Morlac and Broct set out, walking casually but with a definite objective. From their earlier vantage point they had seen a cluster of tents, off to one side of the troop tents, where several men in wizardly robes moved about. Baron Kumil was likely there. Fortunately, it was not far from the spot they left their borrowed wagon.

"Careful, now," said Morlac. "Even disguised as we are, there are those that could recognize us."

"Aye," agreed Broct with a woeful look at his own garments. "I'm sure these better fit the man we left trussed up. Lucky he be a large fellow."

Morlac put a finger to his lips for silence, as they were nearing one of the tents. The sides were down, but the entrance flap was tied up. As they passed by, Morlac caught a glimpse of a darkly clad figure within. A man whose black-velvet tunic and short gold-trimmed cloak were all too familiar. Baron Kumil! Morlac almost stopped in his tracks, but forced himself to continue on well past the entrance.

Keeping his voice low and his eyes still upon the tent, Morlac said, "There is the one we seek, my sea-brother."

"And there," said Broct, looking past him with narrowing eyes, "is the other."

Morlac's head whipped around, for he knew instantly what Broct meant. There, some distance ahead of them in the same row of large tents, was one painted with a familiar emblem . . . the horned staff of Tritus. And huge glass jugs of what could only be seawater stood in racks at each corner of the tent. Even as he gazed at it, Sordros's green-clad figure moved past the open flap, carrying something. Was Kadrana there, also? There was a glimpse of others inside, and though he could not see them clearly, Morlac knew instinctively they were sea-warriors, created much as he had been. He did not have to know them to feel a bond with them.

There in the night-shrouded tent before them was the green magician who had led them on a journey across much of the eastern hemisphere of Norda. The man who had tormented them, forced them to do his will, and then abandoned them to an uncertain fate. And now he was doing it all over again with a new group of transmutants . . . more sea creatures twisted by his spells into human form, their minds and memories merged with those of dead men.

Sordros . . . at last, there before them. And yet still unreachable.

"You know, don't you?" Broct murmured. "You know that we cannot confront him now. Not without jeopardizing all that we and J'Bara plan."

"Yes," Morlac said softly. "I know."

He stared at the tent a long moment more, his devil-brows set low above sea-green eyes ablaze with emotion, then he abruptly turned and cut between the tents, heading for the rear of the one occupied by Baron Kumil. Broct followed, keeping watch behind for any who might observe them.

There were a large number of supply crates and several empty barrels near the back of the tent that would shelter them from view. Morlac and Broct moved into this space, cautiously peering through small gaps in the tent's rear flap.

Inside, the Baron could be seen walking about a large table upon which an ornately decorated cloth had been spread. The table was covered with small amulets, almost to the point of overflowing, and Kumil was adding still more.

Baron Kumil looked up abruptly as someone entered the front of the tent. It was his bodyguard, Tyno.

"The wine has just arrived, Your Eminence."

"Excellent!" Baron Kumil replied. "I feared we would have to make other arrangements. The amulets themselves are almost ready. Only the final enchantment remains."

Tyno stepped closer to the table, his gaze upon the many amulets. "Do you really think it will work, sir?"

"Of course. Granted, I have not attempted this on such a large scale, but I have no doubt of its success." The Baron picked up one of the small amulets, suspending it from his hand by its slender loop of thong. "You must distribute these to as many of the soldiers as you can, Tyno. As many as you can. Especially among the first ranks."

"Yes, sir."

"Tell them the amulets are lucky charms, to give them strength in battle. Tell them anything . . . anything but the truth." Baron Kumil studied the amulet dangling from his hand and an evil smile spread across his aristocratic features. "Think of it, Tyno—once their wine is laced with my potion, and each man wears one of these, I need do no more. The reanimation enchantment will work on its own. Each man killed in battle shall rise up once more to continue fighting, an unbeatable warrior. There shall be no stopping them."

"Truly, sir, your wizardry surpasses all others'. Governor Cauldos and the Emperor will be most pleased with you."

The Baron gave a brief chuckle. "It is not their pleasure I work toward, my loyal friend, though for now it will suit my purpose well enough." He observed Tyno's puzzled frown. "Do you not yet see what we set in motion this night? To help win Cauldos's battle is all well and good, but when the battle's done, what shall be left? A great many soldiers will be killed by the other side, you may be sure. And when they rise again they shall be an army that answers not to Cauldos or even the Emperor himself, but to *me!* That is a power the Phaedrocian Empire shall have to reckon with. I tell you, my friend, we shall live to see the day when the capital shifts from Phendurem to Kadmudar."

Tyno shared the wicked smile of his master. "That I would welcome, Your Eminence."

"We must make haste, though," Baron Kumil added, reaching for an ornately fashioned bottle filled with dark amber fluid. He handed it to his bodyguard. "Here—it is the concentrated potion. You must see it is added before the wine is mixed and poured for the men, and you must be careful no one observes you. Go and tend to it at once, while I finish the enchantment. When you return you may distribute the amulets. And *I* must meet with the generals this night."

"Yes, sir," replied Tyno with a quick nod of a bow. He took the bottle of potion and turned to leave the tent.

Alone now, the Baron returned his attention to the amulets. Rolling back his sleeves, he closed his eyes and breathed deeply several times. With his hands extended palm down over the amulets, his fingers began to arch and stiffen with the intensity of his concentration.

His fingertips began to trace mystic patterns over the amulets, patterns echoed in the designs etched upon the charms' very surfaces. And words in a strange tongue began to cast a dark and deadly spell.

"Not this time, wizard!" Morlac said suddenly, directly behind him.

The Baron whirled in midsentence, his eyes bloodshot and wild, the pupils great pits of black. "What are you doing, you fool? The spell is not yet complete—!"

"And it never shall be!" Morlac shot out a fist as Kumil turned his head to call for help. The punch connected before any words could escape his lips and the Baron sagged to the ground.

"We'd best get him out of here," Morlac told Broct. "He said he has business elsewhere, so his man may not miss him for awhile. That will work to our advantage."

"Aye," agreed Broct. "And I think there be a way to remove him."

Quickly now, they dragged the unconcious wizard to the back of the tent and under the raised flap. Broct lifted his body and dumped it unceremoniously into one of the empty barrels littering the area behind the tent.

"There," said Broct, dusting his hands. "We were told to take back the empty wine barrels. Here be one!"

Morlac gave him a comradely slap on the back. "Excellent idea. Now let us leave while we can!"

Broct easily lifted the barrel even using only two of his arms. He carried it around the front of the tent with Morlac leading the way.

In a matter of minutes they reached the wagon. Broct slid the barrel with its wizardly burden into the back of the now-unloaded wagon and proceeded to help Morlac load the empty casks and barrels remaining in the area. They caught a glimpse of Tyno walking briskly by with an armload of amulets, but kept their faces turned from him and he did not take notice.

With a wave to the officer in charge, they boarded the wagon and drove it back through the encampment, stopping at the entrance. The same two sentries stepped aside to let them pass.

"So soon you are going back?" asked one of the men.

"For another load," replied Morlac, feigning weariness. "Need it you will, for the big victory celebration."

"Ah, yes," responded the guard with enthusiasm, obviously already warmed by some of his illicit wine. "Be on your way, then, and return quickly!"

"Good evening," Morlac uttered, then gave a snap of the reins to get the horses moving. The wagon did not protest so much with its lighter load.

They did not feel even reasonably safe until they were well out of sight of the outpost and around the curve in the road. Then it was that Morlac halted the wagon and they climbed down. From the underbrush emerged Glendauna, followed by J'Bara and his men.

"Were you successful?" Glendauna asked as she rushed to Morlac's side.

"Yes," he told her. "We have the Baron with us. Quickly now, let us bind and gag him like the others, before he awakens. A wizard who cannot utter spells or gesture magically should be nearly powerless."

"What about the merchants?" queried Broct.

"Put them in their wagon, still bound, and let the horses follow the road home. By the time they reach Neuphendurem it will be too late to alert anyone here."

"And then, my friends," said J'Bara, "we must return to N'Bikcumboro. There are things I must yet attend to, and we all need a few hours' rest before the battle begins."

"You're right," Morlac agreed. "For I'm sure Cauldos's troops will march at dawn. . . ."

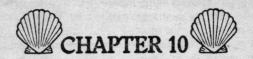

CHAPTER 10

Necromancer's War

The sun rose over N'Bikcumboro as it had done uncounted times before. But this day was different. This day, the air was not filled with birdsong or the awakening cries of jungle beasts. This day, an unsettling stillness hung over the land like a death-shroud.

A barrier stood just outside the exotic city, stretching wide across the valley entrance. A human barrier it was, made up of the people of N'Bikcumboro. A long row of dark warriors stood proudly resolute, their intent gaze fixed upon the far side of the clearing that stretched before them. Their metal-tipped lances standing ready beside them, the warriors were poised for battle. Green-dyed armor of bamboo and woven rattan covered their torsos, shins, and forearms, and knife belts, bows, and arrow quivers hung about them. All were so artfully designed that there was beauty in the warriors' strange aspect. But it was a purposeful and deadly beauty.

Another row of men stretched behind the first, with yet another behind them. A row of women knelt upon the ground in front of the warriors, as proud and intent as their men. Each woman held an odd shield upright before her, its green-fabric surface clean and unmarked by weapons.

At the center of the line was J'Bara and Cashili, garbed for war. Beside them stood Morlac, his shell-shield upon his arm and Shark ready at his side. Broct stood next to him, with Glendauna and Rila T'Faen just behind them, all with swords ready.

Rila T'Faen reached out and clutched at Broct's arm. "If

377

survive this we do not," she told him with a wry glance, "two great pleasures have I had, at least. One was finding you, my fine large sir. Helping tie up Baron Kumil in a fitting manner was the other."

The yellow-eyed giant gave a knowing smile and a wink. "Aye, my fair flame."

Behind him, Glendauna's soft voice reached Morlac's ears. "I could well say the same to you, my proud warrior."

Morlac gazed at her lovely and delicate face and was touched by the range of memories it evoked. "We have been through much, my lady, you and I. Never have I regretted that my path crossed Goltos. Never."

A faint breeze stirred about them, and behind them continued the rushing cascade of the waterfall. All else was still. But it was a stillness that could not last.

The first sounds came now from the far side of the clearing— the hack and slash of foliage being cut away, the sound of many feet marching. Cauldos's army was drawing near.

"There—" said J'Bara after another moment "—I see them!"

Morlac nodded soundlessly, his own sharp eyes watching as the first troops appeared at the edge of the clearing. The men who were cutting a path quickly moved aside as the marchers emerged.

"Good." Morlac observed. "It is as I thought. They have put their archers in the front ranks."

Onward came Cauldos's army of Phaedrocian troops and mercenaries. Most were on foot, some on horseback. They were men long used to victories, merciless men who had expanded their empire with bloody swords, ruthlessly crushing all opposition. Onward they came. Closer and closer with each step. They were halfway across the broad clearing separating the city from the jungle now, and drawing ever nearer.

"Morlac . . . ?" questioned J'Bara.

"Wait," said Morlac, watching closely the advancing troops. "A moment more."

Broct stood glaring forward, mindful of the past. "This be much like L'Dron Kerr's attack upon our village."

"Yes, much," Morlac replied with steely gaze. "But this time is different, my sea-brother. This time we shall win."

Still watching closely, Morlac saw an officer in the enemy ranks cry out an order. The sound did not reach his ears yet, but he saw the archers who advanced before the swordsmen drop to their knees and start to reach for shafts from their quivers. This was the moment he had waited for.

"Now, J'Bara! *Now!*"

The king of N'Bikcumboro bellowed a sharp command in his native tongue. Instantly, the women in the front rank reached around and grasped the cloth covering their shields. Quickly ripping it free they revealed the shields for what they truly were—mirrored panels removed from the palace hall. For these and not the golden statues were the source of Morlac's inspiration.

Angling the bright mirror surfaces to catch the morning sun, the women directed beams of intense light at the faces of the enemy. They saw with satisfaction that the Phaedrocian archers dropped their arrows and threw up arms to block the blinding light. The swordsmen, too, were caught off guard by the glare.

At another sharp command from their king, the warriors of N'Bikcumboro released their lances, which stood imbedded in the ground, and drew their bows. They handled the arrows carefully, then let fly a barrage of glistening shafts that filled the air.

Death rained down upon the Phaedrocian troops, still blinded by the mirrors. Two hundred fell dead in a matter of moments, hundreds more were badly wounded. And in the confusion that followed, yet another trap awaited those who came to pillage N'Bikcumboro.

"Look!" cried out a soldier, pointing to the fallen men near him. "The arrows—gold they are! Gold!"

The others looked in disbelief and saw that truly, the shafts did glisten with the color of gold. Throughout the first dozen ranks soldiers let their greed consume them as they sought to pluck the golden arrows from the dead and wounded, momentarily forgetting the battle. But their greed would cost them dearly. For man after man, the Phaedrocians released the shafts as quickly as they jerked them out, shaking their hands where the skin was torn by tiny barbs along the arrows' sides—barbs coated with swift-acting snake venom, so that each shaft might claim more than one victim.

Officers and sergeants began screaming orders at their men not to touch the arrows . . . shouting at them to advance and not be standing targets. And at last, their training took hold and once more they advanced across the clearing.

But as the army moved forward a new horror began. Many of the dead had about their necks the special amulets made by Baron Kumil. Within their veins was the potion that had been mixed with the wine. And now, their bodies not yet cold, the dreadful spell took hold upon the dead and one by one they rose. With lurching steps each dead warrior reclaimed his weapon and stood ready for battle once more.

But Kumil's spell was incomplete, interrupted as it was. Though primed for killing, the enchanted dead knew not *who* their swords were for. Friend or foe were all the same to Kumil's ghastly legion.

So even as the Phaedrocians advanced toward N'Bikcumboro's warriors, they suddenly found a new enemy springing up among their own ranks. The living fought the dead now, and as the size of the one army diminished, the size of the other grew.

A hideous, self-consuming war began to rage upon the clearing as the still-living Phaedrocians sought to remain so, and the reanimated dead fought tirelessly on to claim them. Behind them marched fresh troops from the rear, and while none of them wore the Baron's dreadful amulets their numbers were more than matched by those ahead that did. Seeing the nightmare vision that lay ahead, their officers quickly ordered these men to split and fan wide around the fighting. Breaking into a run, two large groups of soldiers now swept pincerlike toward N'Bikcumboro.

J'Bara gave a quick wave of his hand and the row of women kneeling before them grabbed up their mirror-shields and ran to one side, heading for the mountain caves. The king now commanded his warriors to fall back in the other direction, toward the city itself. Morlac and his friends moved with them.

The two groups of Phaedrocian soldiers remained divided, with those on the west side pursuing the retreating women toward the caves and gold mines. Those on the east ran after J'Bara's warriors, thinking they had them cornered.

But as both groups pressed forward into the valley rift's wide mouth, signaling cries rang out from above. On each front corner of the plateau that sheltered N'Bikcumboro, groups of J'Bara's men swiftly rose from concealment and drew their bows, sending a barrage of deadly shafts arcing down at the enemy. Few missed their targets. Scores of soldiers fell, but of these none were to rise under Baron Kumil's spell.

Though their numbers were thinning, the Phaedrocians still sought to conquer. Hundreds still ran after the fleeing women, following to the very mouths of caves and mine entrances, slowing only as they encountered the dark tunnels' interiors. Entering with caution, their swords probing the darkness before them as their eyes adjusted to the dim light, the Phaedrocians advanced after their unarmed prey.

The other group of men closed the gap with J'Bara's warriors just as they reached the center of the city, and it was here that the king of N'Bikcumboro ordered his men to turn and fight. Whirling about with fierce cries, the dark warriors hurled their lances at the Phaedrocians pursuing them, then picked up new lances awaiting them on the ground at this spot. The front ranks of Cauldos's men fell to this assault, but the rest continued forward. . . .

Off to one side, near the river that flowed through part of the city, a small building stood well away from all others. Within it were stored sacks of grain and stones for milling. Something else was stored here now as well.

Baron Kumil sat upon the hard floor, his arms and legs uncomfortably placed around the building's center post. His wrists and ankles all were tightly bound together, and a gag was well-secured across his mouth. The arrogant aristocrat who had imprisoned others now knew the taste of imprisonment himself.

But as the sounds of warfare raged outside, the Baron concentrated instead upon a small dark form that scurried near the wall. Attracted by the grain, a rat had entered the building. Though hungry, it was cautious in the presence of a human. As it paused in its darting walk, the rodent's beady eyes stared at Baron Kumil, looking for signs of danger.

The rat saw more than danger, though, for as it continued to stare it found itself transfixed by the wizard's gaze. It gave an alarmed squeak, then fell silent. The Baron's eyes seemed to be growing larger, commanding its total attention, and though the Baron's hands were bound securely there was enough freedom of movement in his fingers to create small patterns in the air. A small spell, a limited spell, but enough to capture the creature's tiny brain.

Slowly, maintaining its fixed stare, the rat crept forward. Nearer . . . nearer . . . until at last it reached the ropes binding the wizard's hands and feet. And then, under Baron Kumil's intense gaze, the rat began to gnaw. . . .

In the darkness of the mountain tunnels Phaedrocian soldiers stalked their prey. The women of N'Bikcumboro could not be seen, but the officer leading the troops thought he could hear their frightened breathing somewhere just ahead. Faint scraping sounds to his left alerted him to a passage cut through the stone, and he checked to be sure his men were close behind him. They advanced around the corner.

"Hiding will do you no good," the man announced, certain his words would carry to the women. "Your gold we seek. Lead us to it, and we may let you live." But he followed his words with a silent, evil sneer.

His expression did not last. For in the next instant the tiny scraping sounds became a great rasp of noise as barriers were pulled free. Tons of rock piled high within the tunnel section collapsed upon the men, burying them, trapping them, closing off the pathway leading deeper into the honeycomb of tunnels. Similar sounds came from the other nearby tunnels where Phaedrocians had unwisely entered. For many, it was too late to turn back.

In the city outside, fighting continued to rage. J'Bara's warriors defended themselves and their land with lances and knives and their own special fighting skills. Their supple bodies dodged sword thrusts with speed and grace, then dealt blows their enemy could not avoid. Their king was at the forefront, keeping the Phaedrocians at bay.

Cauldos's troops swarmed about Morlac and his friends,

seeking to destroy anyone in their way. In the midst of this maelstrom, Morlac stood his ground. His shell-shield blocked each lunging strike, each crashing blow. His magicked sword flashed through the air with hungry force, Shark's stark white blade turning red as it found its mark, again and again.

Near him, Broct fought with equal fervor, swords in his three right hands and his left hands wielding dirks. The yellow-eyed giant fended off two attackers at once while skewering a third. As yet another Phaedrocian charged toward him he whirled his flashing blades in a dizzying blur of motion that bedazzled the soldier, then delivered a strong kick to the man's chin that sent him flying backwards.

Glendauna used her Durkesh skills to full advantage, slashing with her dirksword and then letting its sharp side blades do damage on the return stroke. As the anger rose within her, a deep growl of sound escaped her throat . . . a sound more wolf than human.

Morlac risked a quick glance at Rila T'Faen, for he feared that she was ill-prepared for such fighting. But what met his eyes was a striking image. The red-haired young beauty was swinging her borrowed sword with great flourishes and lunges that kept the enemy soldiers well back. With each sweep of her blade words tumbled from her lips with dramatic eloquence, though their significance seemed to fit neither the clash nor the players upon this bloody stage.

Morlac arched a devil-brow in surprise. "*What* is she doing—?"

Broct shrugged. "I think she be acting. . . ."

Farther back from the fray, a Phaedrocian general directed his men toward the glistening palace just across the river. Several detachments ran for the two nearest bridges, their eyes upon the gold and emerald decorations glistening in the sunlight.

But a surprise lay in store for them, for as each group of soldiers started over a bridge, planks across the center abruptly fell beneath their weight, plunging scores of men into the swift-moving river below. Those that were not swept away became easy targets for the archers descending from the plateau above.

As Morlac watched, the general and a small group of

handpicked men now set out for the third bridge, mindful of the danger and likely to find a way past it. Morlac directed his friends to withdraw in that direction. "Let's head them off . . . quickly!"

It was a race for the base of the bridge, a race Morlac and the others won. They reached it barely before the Phaedrocian general and his men, and waited, swords ready.

From the corner of his eye, Morlac glimpsed a dark-clad figure well beyond the fray. Looking closer, he saw that Baron Kumil had emerged from the small storage building at the city's edge. The Kadmudarian wizard was throwing away pieces of rope from his bindings and glancing toward the battle within N'Bikcumboro.

"The Baron is free!" Morlac exclaimed, but could not long keep his eyes off the Phaedrocian soldiers advancing upon them.

"That bodes ill," said Broct as he threw a worried glance that way. And a glance was all he had time for.

A soldier lunged forward, and then another, and though Morlac and his friends defended against the blows struck at them, they allowed themselves to be driven back, slowly and inexorably, across the bridge. The clangor of their swords rang out with each blow, with each backward step above the river, echoing through the city. . . .

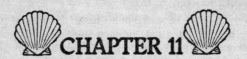# CHAPTER 11

Sordros Found

Forced across to the other bank, Morlac, Broct, Glendauna, and Rila regrouped on the royal terrace. A path led from it to the palace, a path they now sought to block. Guarding it at the rear edge of the terrace were two large statues of gold, shaped in the form of sitting panthers. Their emerald eyes glared down at all before them.

Morlac and the others moved between these statues as the Phaedrocians pressed forward. A soldier twirled his blade slowly before him, then brought it up to strike a crashing blow. Morlac parried the blade with Shark, then dodged behind the statue on the right to halt another soldier's attempt to go around on that side. From the corner of his eye he saw his friends defending themselves against the remaining soldiers.

As the first Phaedrocian started forward again, Morlac moved directly behind the tall statue and with a mighty surge of strength pushed it over. The statue toppled, crashing down against the terrace stones just as the soldier jumped clear.

But something strange happened then, something that caused the soldier to gaze down instead of continuing his fight. For the golden statue shattered upon impact into a dozen pieces, revealing an interior that was not glistening gold, but instead was dull and gritty white.

"Sir—!" called the man in bewilderment. "See this!"

The Phaedrocian general stared at the crumbled statue, grabbed up a broken piece, and examined it. He frowned mightily, then looked to where an emerald eye lay shattered on the ground. The rich green color showed only on the outer surface; the rest was clear.

Throwing down the piece in his hand, the general snapped, "Stone it is. Nothing but common stone, painted gold. And the emeralds are but colored glass!" With an angry swing of his blade he now struck the other statue which still stood near him. His sword broke free a chunk from the golden panther, revealing more gritty white beneath. "The same!"

Morlac and the others backed off slowly as the Phaedrocians ceased their assault. Their swords remained ready.

With disillusioned gaze, the general regarded the glistening palace beyond. "Lies! Lies the stories were! Fools we are, to have listened to men that cannot tell real gold from fake. There is no treasure here."

Stepping back a pace, seeming to forget Morlac and his friends even existed, the general looked around as the survivors of the tunnel traps staggered out, dirty and bleeding. The Phaedrocian officer surveyed the carnage in the city, and beyond in the clearing, as if truly seeing it for the first time. Of the thousands he had brought here, only three hundred or so still stood.

"Cauldos be damned!" snarled the general. "Much will he have to answer for, once I've spoken with the Emperor!" He gestured to his men to follow, snapping angrily, "Let us leave this accursed city! It is not worth our trouble or our lives."

With that, the Phaedrocians turned on their heels and ran back across the bridge. As they reached the other side they called sharply to the troops that still fought against J'Bara's men, and soon all were retreating from the city, taking their injured with them. J'Bara ordered his people to let them leave, and the warriors pursued them briefly with many fierce and threatening cries.

Morlac strained to see where Baron Kumil was, and at last he saw him begin to run also, away from N'Bikcumboro and also away from the retreating troops. But the wizard of Kadmudar chose his path unwisely, for his retreat carried him straight through the clearing where the worst carnage had occurred.

Morlac's keen eyes saw Baron Kumil halt in his tracks as

he suddenly realized where he was and who awaited him. Nine hundred dead faces swung about to greet him with their monstrous stares. The wizard's own army of the dead closed in upon their master, and as he was lost to view the Baron's scream of terror echoed through the valley.

The people of N'Bikcumboro were jubilant at the Phaedrocians' retreat. The women emerged from the caves, running to join their victorious warriors, and the wounded were quickly tended to. But as Morlac and his friends raced across the bridge to join them, concern still showed upon the seawarrior's face.

"J'Bara—" called Morlac "—it may not be safe yet! The Baron's living corpses still remain."

The king of N'Bikcumboro lost his joyous look and turned worried eyes upon the clearing. "How can we fight them? They cannot die again or be stopped by wounds, and they will not be fooled by false statues as the Phaedrocians were."

"Fire, perhaps," speculated Morlac. "Or—"

"Wait—" exclaimed Broct. "Look there—"

Their view was blocked at first by retreating soldiers so that they could not see what Broct had glimpsed, but then the Phaedrocian troops swung wide around the center of the clearing to avoid its nightmare legion. When once they passed, those in the city could again see what remained.

Oddly, the field was still now. The bodies that filled the clearing's center fought no more . . . stood no more . . . moved no more. The dead were as they should be, seemingly free from their spell-cast fate.

"It is over," said Morlac, his eyes grim despite his relief. "Perhaps the wizard's spell died with him."

"Aye," agreed Broct. "Or else he undid his magic just as he was struck down."

J'Bara surveyed his exotic realm, proud of it and of his people. "N'Bikcumboro has survived. *We* have survived. Some of our warriors are injured . . . some are dead, though not many. It could easily have been worse. Much worse." He looked to Morlac with sober gratitude. "We owe you a lot, my friend." His gaze took in the others. "All of you."

"I am glad we could help," Morlac told him sincerely. "This is a special land . . . a special people." His eyes turned toward the clearing, and what lay unseen, miles beyond. "But there is something yet undone, and little time to do it."

"Not Sordros—?" Glendauna protested in alarm.

Morlac turned to her and gripped her shoulders in his strong hands. "Let me do this, my lady. If not, I shall never know peace."

With that, he kissed her. It was a long, fierce kiss that frightened her, for it seemed to say that it might be their last. And then he tore himself away and started swiftly for the clearing.

"Morlac!" she called after him. "Wait—!" She began to follow, but with his longer stride he was already well ahead of her.

Morlac reached the spot where the nightmare legion lay, still now for eternity. The carnage sickened him. Gray bodies were collapsed atop other bodies, maimed and battered. Severed limbs and broken weapons were everywhere, and the ground was sodden with blood. Already the stink of it was overwhelming, and would soon grow worse.

His eyes searched quickly, compelled to find Baron Kumil's remains. But though the Baron's tattered cloak was visible, the man himself was not. His body should be here . . . must be here.

Morlac looked ahead to where the retreating Phaedrocian troops disappeared down the path they had hacked through the foliage. Swiftly returning to the outpost they were, and no doubt, from there to Neuphendurem. Something caught his eye, moving behind the troops, disappearing shortly after them. Though distant, Morlac was sure it was Tyno, the Baron's man, riding a horse and leading another with something thrown across it. A body, perhaps? Baron Kumil's? Could the wizard have survived? It seemed unlikely, or at least, so he hoped.

A sound attracted Morlac's attention, and he saw an abandoned horse near the edge of the clearing. He hurried toward it, snatching up a fallen mercenary's cloak and helm and disguising himself as best he could. He reached the animal, slowing so as not to frighten it, then took the reins in hand and mounted.

As he turned the horse toward the cleared path he looked

back at N'Bikcumboro again and saw Glendauna still running to catch up with him. The sight of her, and the fear etched upon her face, tore at his heart. But if he could finally confront the green magician, better that she not be there. The danger was too great. This he must do alone.

Morlac took one last look at her, and at Broct running close behind her. Then he cracked the free end of the long reins along the horse's flank and headed off. . . .

Traveling the cleared path was faster than the less direct route through the foliage, and though Morlac was careful not to join the retreating Phaedrocian troops, he still reached the outpost in little more than an hour. And now, as he drew near, he saw that there was more chaos than order in the encampment.

The surviving troops were spread thin in this place once crowded with men. Supplies and equipment were being thrown into wagons with great haste. The injured were being put upon the litters and drays originally intended for treasure, bandaged as best they could be. Grim-faced officers hurried about, shouting orders amid the confusion.

Morlac rode toward the side of the outpost where stood the wizards' tents. Some had already been taken down, and indeed, Morlac wondered if some of the magicians who answered Cauldos's call might not have been frauds who left before the battle's beginning.

Baron Kumil's tent still stood, but it was empty. Morlac saw nothing of Tyno or of Kumil's remains, and guessed the horses that carried them were galloping to Neuphendurem and the galley that lay anchored in its harbor. It mattered little now.

Sordros's tent came into view, the great glass jugs of seawater still standing at each corner, the horned staff of Tritus still emblazoned on its sides. A wagon awaited near the open flap, and as Morlac rode up he saw Kadrana emerge and quickly carry a small leather-covered chest to the conveyance, adding it to other belongings piled within.

She looked up with a start and a challenging glare as Morlac dismounted near her. But then her eyes widened as she truly saw him.

"Morlac . . . !"

"We meet again, dark princess." Morlac removed his borrowed cloak and helm. "Tell me . . . did any of the new sea-warriors return from battle?"

"I . . . I do not know, Morlac. I have not seen any." Her eyes darted toward the tent's interior and back again. "What are you doing here? When you escaped Cauldos's prison I thought you had surely fled Neuphendurem. Cauldos will have your head if he finds you."

"Cauldos had better worry about his own head," Morlac told her. "And you should know I could not leave. Not yet."

Morlac started for the tent opening and found Kadrana moving to block his path. Her sea-green eyes looked up into his imploringly. The black ringlets of her hair still held the rich scent of rare perfumes. Her alluring gown and the close warmth of her lush body still beckoned, to the man he had been . . . and the man he had become. It would be easy, so very easy, to yield to her wishes, whatever they might be.

Gently but firmly, Morlac moved Kadrana out of his way. He strode past the open flap and entered Sordros's tent.

The green magician stood inside, his back to Morlac, his concentration upon the magical implements he sought to pack away. As Morlac stepped closer he felt Shark tremble at his side. Was it an acknowledgment of the wizard's presence? Or an expression of Morlac's own pent-up hatred for the man? He did not know.

Sordros abruptly tensed, becoming aware of Morlac's presence. The green magician turned with slow precision, his eyes narrowing as they fell upon the grim sea-warrior standing there.

"So . . ." he said, in his strange and chilling voice unlike a normal human's ". . . it is you."

Morlac stared at this man who provoked both contempt and fear in him. "We have come full circle, Sordros. But you have made me travel many miles to find you."

"I did not ask you to find me," Sordros droned menacingly. "What has brought you here . . . misplaced loyalty, or murderous intent? I doubt that it is loyalty, for I sense you had a hand in our defeat this day."

"Questions brought me here," Morlac replied. "Questions

that have gone unanswered too long. And yes, I did help the people of N'Bikcumboro, for their cause was just."

Sordros seethed with anger. "You fool! You come here to ask questions and expect me to answer? You failed me in Shola, and you have thwarted my purpose here!"

"Failed you?" Morlac snapped. "You are still alive because of me. I slew your enemy, Drygo. I gave you time to escape."

"But you allowed L'Dron Kerr's men to conquer our village!"

"We fought under *your* battle plan, not mine. And we were hopelessly outnumbered by better-trained forces."

Kadrana spoke up from the tent entrance. "That is true, Sordros. And he did save my life."

"Shut up, girl," Sordros snarled. "I do not care to listen to his excuses, nor to your defense of him."

"Tell me *your* excuses, then," Morlac demanded. "Tell me why you abandoned me and the other sea-warriors in Shola. Have you done the same here with your new spell-cast slaves?"

"I owe you no explanation."

"Then let me offer one. You are a self-serving coward who used your own creations to save you, then you cast us aside without regard." Morlac was speaking slowly, angrily, emphasizing each word. "I truly think that the only thing you regret about the fall of our village is your own lost power and authority."

Sordros's glare became dangerous. "You risk much, coming here and taunting me."

Morlac stepped closer. "I did not come here to taunt you. That is only my anger speaking out, and rightfully so. I need assurances. I need to know if I have a future. I need some hope, however small, that your spell will not of its own unravel and destroy me."

"My spell is sound and strong—it cannot be broken unless I wish it. You need not fear that. What you *do* need to fear is my wrath, and you have well incurred that this day by destroying my chances to gain favor with the Phaedrocian emperor." Sordros drew himself up, his look becoming intense and imperious. "You are a strong-willed and clever creature, Morlac, as was Calrom before you. And that makes you far more dangerous to me than Drygo ever was, now, and in the future. A danger I shall most happily *destroy!*"

Green fire raged within Sordros's malevolent eyes and Morlac instinctively reached for Shark's hilt. But the magicked blade seemed frozen in its sheath.

The green magician sneered. "Do not think you can defend yourself with that, you fool! I learned my lesson with Drygo. Your sword can never be used against me."

"Sordros, no!" Kadrana cried out, rushing toward them. "Do not—"

The wizard's hand went up, ablaze with green fire, and Kadrana was hurled violently sideways through the tent. She crashed against a large traveling chest and sagged to the ground, limp and shaken.

"Kadrana—!" Morlac flinched at the sound of her impact and quickly turned his angry eyes upon Sordros. The magician's hands began to raise toward him, but Morlac grabbed his wrists in his own strong grip and immobilized them, twisting the palms away from him.

They struggled, the wizard and the warrior, supernatural force pitted against supernatural strength. A table was knocked over in their fight, scattering books and scrolls upon the ground. Then just as Morlac seemed to be winning, Sordros laughed an evil, blood-chilling laugh. His eyes turned into deep black pits, surrounded by tiny flashes that looked like green lightning . . . twin storms of fearsome force and deadly danger.

Sordros straightened, bending Morlac back and swinging him around toward the rear of the tent. His thin-lipped smile was cruelly victorious.

Sweat broke out on Morlac's face. His muscles began to quiver and weaken. Deeper and deeper he sank into the maelstrom in Sordros's eyes. He cursed himself silently, for he had indeed been a fool to underestimate the green magician's powers even this far inland. Things had come full circle all right, but this time he had won the war and was about to lose his life.

His hands began to shake uncontrollably, his fingers releasing from Sordros's wrists. His special resource, the great strength within his arms, was melting away. Morlac felt himself being backed closer to the rear of the tent, felt his knees buckling.

Morlac tore his gaze away from the magician but did not feel any release from the spell that gripped his mind and body. At the side of the tent he saw Kadrana still limp upon the ground, moaning and struggling to rise.

"Do not look for aid from her, Morlac," Sordros rasped, his voice strained by his efforts. "She can do nothing for you now. You have sealed your own doom, warrior."

Morlac staggered back, collapsing on one knee, struggling to keep his balance. Sordros's evil face loomed large before him. He saw the magician's clawlike hand reach toward him . . . toward the special amulet with the likeness of his original form. And he remembered only too well the fate of the sea-warrior, Xaja, reduced to a steaming, rotting corpse at Sordros's touch.

"You wanted to know if you have a future?" Sordros said tauntingly. "I give you now your answer. . . ."

Sordros's hand closed around the amulet and started to draw back. His lips opened to utter the words that would destroy him. In seconds it would be done.

But instead of words there came a crunch of sound and a gasp from Sordros's lips. His eyes lost their deadly numbing power and rolled up within their sockets. The fingers of his hand unbent, releasing the amulet from their dangerous grasp.

For a moment Sordros stood there, bent toward Morlac, quivering violently, the front of his robe pushed out and turning crimson. Then the green magician toppled and fell to the ground, to move no more.

Breathing hard, his strength returning, Morlac looked toward Kadrana, thinking she had somehow struck out at Sordros. But she had not. Still weak, she was just now rising from the ground.

Morlac now saw the sword protruding from Sordros's back, a dirksword with short side blades, sunk into the wizard nearly to its hilt. His gaze leaped to the open tent flap and he saw Glendauna standing there, wide-eyed and tremulous. It was she who had thrown the weapon.

Morlac got to his feet and moved quickly to her. She fell into his arms, tears bursting forth.

"Oh, Morlac—" she sobbed "—have I done something terrible? The Baron's spells were destroyed when he died. If I have doomed you—!"

"No, no, my lady. It is all right. Do not cry so. The spells were as different as the wizards who cast them. You have *saved* my life, not ended it."

He kissed her now, tenderly and consolingly, embracing her, crushing her to him with a fierce, possessive pride. He had almost lost her . . . almost lost everything. As he looked up, he saw a second horse next to his outside, and Broct just riding up on yet another. So they had found mounts of their own and followed him after all. Lucky he was that they had!

Morlac turned and saw Kadrana approaching slowly, looking at the two of them with a vacant and pained look. She glanced away as their eyes met, looking instead at Sordros's body and rubbing her own bruises.

"Are you all right?" Morlac asked her.

"Yes, of course," she replied, her sea-green eyes still staring at the magician's dead form. "Sordros was cruel and heartless. I am glad you still live, Morlac. I am glad someone saved you." Her moist gaze swung around to meet his. "I only wish I had been the one."

"You tried," Morlac said softly, "and for that I am grateful. I do care for you, Kadrana. Never doubt that. It is only that . . ."

"No words are needed," Kadrana said. "I have eyes. And I can see you have chosen well. Now, I . . . I must take care of Sordros's body, and finish packing. The last men are leaving this outpost, and I would journey back to Neuphendurem."

"We can help with Sordros and the packing," Morlac told her as Broct stepped into the tent behind them and surveyed the scene. "But why go back there, alone? I do not trust the Phaedrocians, and you could be in danger in Neuphendurem."

"They will not harm me. And even without Sordros's patronage I yet have powers."

Glendauna looked at this young woman she had long considered a rival, and softly said, "Come back with us to N'Bikcumboro, Kadrana."

"As what . . . ?" There was a flare of pain in her imperious eyes.

"As a friend."

Kadrana was silent a long moment. "No . . . I think not. I thank you for your offer, and I accept your help. But I must seek my future in other ways . . . other lands, even as you must seek yours." Her proud eyes found Morlac's and held them. "But our paths may cross again, my captain. Who knows what our destinies hold in store. . . ."

Days later, the peaceful beauty of N'Bikcumboro had been restored. The Phaedrocian dead had been consumed in funeral pyres, the thick column of smoke that arose serving as a final warning to those in Neuphendurem. All signs of battle were gone now. An air of celebration hung over all the exotic realm.

The broad stone terraces were set with tables and much food had been harvested in preparation for a feast. On the terrace before J'Bara's palace, Morlac and his friends, old and new, were gathered at a large table.

"This is to honor you, my friends," J'Bara told them. The proud warrior-king of N'Bikcumboro placed his hand upon Morlac's shoulder. "We have much to thank you for. You shall be our guests for as long as you wish, which I hope shall be a very long time indeed. Stay, and enjoy the pleasures of our land."

Morlac looked to Glendauna, as rested as he now, her gentle beauty more touching than ever. "Your wish is my command, my lady. Shall we stay?"

Her sky-blue eyes sparkled and smiled at him. "This *is* a lovely place. With you here by my side, there is no more I could wish."

Next to her, Broct turned to Rila T'Faen with a whimsical glare. "And you, my red-haired wench—what say you?"

Rila gazed at the heavy gold and emerald necklace given her, but looked next at Broct with even more admiration. "Who am I to refuse, my fine large sir!"

"Besides," said Morlac with newly found contentment.

"We cannot miss a celebration such as this, a celebration such as only scribes and storytellers dream of." With a look that encompassed them all he said, "There is after all much value in life, any life. And I, for one, wish to savor every moment of it!"

"Then it be settled. We stay!" announced Broct cheerfully. "At least," he added with a shrug, "until we grow bored with all this tranquillity and need some new adventure. . . ."

And so they did. . . .

Author's Afterword

The Acknowledgments section of this novel addresses thanks to a number of people, living and dead, but I sincerely feel a special word of thanks should go to you, the reader. Without readers, this humble spinner of tales is merely talking to himself. Without readers, the year spent in writing and the eleven years spent in back-burner developmental work would all be in vain.

So thank you, dear reader, for being my audience. I hope you have enjoyed Morlac's adventures, and I welcome your comments. Best wishes unto you—

Gary Alan Ruse

About the Author

Gary Alan Ruse served as an official correspondent with the U.S. Army Corps of Engineers in Vietnam and was Information Specialist of a Group Level P.I.O. office, editing a newspaper and writing for various military publications. While in Vietnam, he became interested in military research involving animals and in experiments in behavioral control through radio implants—an interest which gave birth to his first novel, HOUNDSTOOTH. He was born in Miami, Florida, in 1946 and attended the University of Miami, where he graduated with a B.A. in commercial art. While there, he also studied film, stage, television, and photojournalism.

His first sale was to *Analog Science Fiction Magazine* in 1972, and *Analog* has published a number of his other short stories. His novels include, A GAME OF TITANS, THE GODS OF CERUS MAJOR, and DEATH-HUNT ON A DYING PLANET.

New Worlds of Fantasy for You to Explore